ZODIAC ACADEMY

The Awakening

AS TOLD BY THE BOYS

CAROLINE
PECKHAM

SUSANNE
VALENTI

Place
Terra House
Hall
Mars Laboratory
King's Hollow
The Howling Meadow
The Wailing Wood
The Orb
Earth Observatory
Venus Library
Aer House
Fire Arena

The Awakening As told by the Boys
Zodiac Academy #8
Copyright © 2021 Caroline Peckham & Susanne Valenti

Interior Illustration by Sarah Goodman & Sloane Murphy
Formatting by Sloane Murphy

The Awakening - As told by the Boys/Caroline Peckham & Susanne Valenti – 1st ed.
ISBN-13 - 978-1-914425-04-2

This book is dedicated to fictional bullies.
If only real life bullies could be hot, brooding men with dark back stories
who worked through their inner demons for the sake of true love.
But no, they're a bunch of dickbags with Washer's greasy dildos for souls.
So screw you real life bullies! Go suck a mouldy Griffin turd while being
slapped repeatedly with a slippery salmon. And may the stars curse you with
the stench of a long-dead weasel, the grisly hair of an unwanted coconut,
and a face worthy of Mildred's hairy asscrack.

Note to all students: Vampire bites, loss of limbs or getting lost in The Wailing Wood will not count as a valid excuse for being late to class.

DARIUS

PROLOGUE

An explosion of wayward fire magic crashed into the wall above my head and I ducked down as Lance threw up an air shield to protect us.

The unearthly shriek that followed the attack was enough to make my limbs shiver with the force of the creature's power, the Nymph using its gifts to try and block our access to our magic.

"I'll take the right," I ground out the order and Lance nodded, holding his bright silver sword in his hand and preparing to dart out from behind the tree we were using for cover.

We were in the middle of nowhere up here in the far northern reaches of the kingdom and the cold air bit at my skin with a merciless savagery that I wasn't used to.

The Nymph shrieked again, its power washing over us in a wave and the beast beneath my flesh shifted uneasily, begging to come out and play. But I wasn't going to be freeing my Dragon unless I had to. It was too damn easy for some nosey fucker to recognise me in that form and we needed to stay unnoticed if we could.

I shoved away from the tree, racing to the right while Lance shot left with a burst of his Vampire speed, sword raised in hand and a snarl on his lips which revealed the sharp points of his fangs.

My boots crunched across hard packed snow, the frost threatening to make me slip and I pushed some of my fire magic into my flesh so the heat of it melted the snow around me and shored up my footing.

The Nymph shrieked again, rearing up to its full height of well over three meters and my heart pounded as I took in its gruesome silhouette which was painted against the backdrop of the full moon beyond it.

Its limbs were long and sinewy, coated in a hard, bark-like flesh which almost made it seem like a demon which had sprouted life within the depths of a tree. But despite its cumbersome-looking build, I knew full well that those things could be plenty fast enough when they needed to be.

The shockwaves of its power collided with me and I staggered as I lost my grip on my magic, the fire in my veins guttering out as it took my Element hostage.

I gritted my teeth and snatched the silver bladed hatchet from my belt made from purest sun steel, the weapon weighing heavily in my hand as my muscles bunched and I hefted it aloft. My pace faltered as I raced towards the creature, its power stealing the strength from my limbs and causing me to slip on the icy ground.

"Come at me then!" I roared at it, still charging towards the beast even as every instinct in my body urged me to run in the opposite direction.

The Nymph turned the full attention of its gleaming red eyes on me, an excited smile breaking across its twisted mouth as it swept its arms wide and that rattle sounded again.

The potency of it hit me full on that time and a Dragon's growl escaped me as I crashed to my knees in the snow from the force of it.

White, snowy powder exploded up around me as I hit the ground, the sting of the ice biting through my jeans as my racing heart seemed to slow and I found myself fully caught in the grasp of the creature's magic.

A juddering breath racked through my chest as my limbs lost even more of their strength, my bicep bulging as I fought to maintain my hold on the hatchet even as it slipped from my fingers and thumped down into the snow at my side.

A cloud of vapour spilled from my lips as the dull pounding of my heart banged in my chest and echoed on in my ears.

That was it. I was caught, held captive by my own flesh as the monster's power took hold of me completely and the enormous beast stepped up in front of me, one arm drawn back with sharpened probes for fingers aiming right at the centre of my chest.

My heart thumped in a dull, endlessly raging way as I looked up at the creature which would be my death and the cold bit at my cheeks.

Another breath fluttered past my lips, billowing before me as the freezing temperature seemed to dig its way beneath my bones and even the Dragon inside me seemed to fall away, leaving me here alone. Just me and my death, waiting beneath the moonlit sky to meet one another.

I tipped my head back, looking up at the creature as it reared over me with a look of glee in its blood red eyes.

How much easier my life would be if this really was just the end of me.

No more pressure to be the best. No more fighting day and night to appease a man who would never be appeased. No more living beneath the shadow of a monster so much more beastly than this creature could ever claim to be.

It was a shame I wasn't more accepting of that fate. Of the freedom death could provide me from the man who fought to make me the very worst version of myself by all means available to him.

But I hadn't been built to bow. And I had people who relied on me.

Which meant I wasn't going to be giving in to this fate.

The stars seemed to whisper similar thoughts in my ears as my gaze shifted beyond the Nymph to take in the clear, bright sky. Almost as if they were paying full attention to us here. And I swear they were saying not yet. Not now. *We have so much more in store for you, son of the Dragon Lord.*

A roar met my ears which was neither beastly nor terrifying - at least not for me, though for the creature before me I was willing to bet that sounded a whole lot like death on the wings of the wind.

A sword slammed through the chest of the Nymph, streaks of black blood coating the blade as its probes brushed against my flesh and the sharp prick of them cut into my skin just enough to break it.

"Die you motherfucker!" Lance roared, yanking the blade free again as a scream escaped the Nymph's lips which was caught by the wind and sent echoing away down the valley beyond us, even as its form fell apart and its body was turned back into the dark and festering shadows of the realm which it belonged to.

Lance fell to the ground as the Nymph disappeared beneath him and I slumped back onto my knees, sucking in a breath coated with ice as relief tangled with the adrenaline in my limbs and I choked out a laugh.

"Took your fucking time on that one," I grunted, my fingers swiping over the rips in my shirt as the warmth of my own blood met them, letting me know just how close a call that had been.

"There was a little one hiding over there," Lance grumbled, jerking his thumb towards a small copse of trees in the direction he'd come from. "Damn things had figured out our manoeuvre and tried to get the jump on me."

"Well fuck them," I said, a laugh falling from my lips as I located my hatchet in the snow and pushed myself back to my feet, letting my fire magic run loose down my limbs again as my grasp on it returned.

"Fuck them up the ass with one of their own probes," Lance agreed, shoving himself upright again before tugging me into a one-armed hug.

The ache in my chest which always bound me to him was appeased by the move, the brand on my arm which held the symbol of his star sign almost seeming to hum with satisfaction as he held me there for a moment and his hand slid up my chest.

"Fuck me, you're forward tonight, baby," I teased him as his fingers landed on the wounds on my chest and healing magic flared beneath his palm.

"Oh you know me, big boy, any excuse to cop a feel. But you might have to keep that Dragon dick tucked away for now because it doesn't look like this one had it."

I stepped away from him, ignoring the stupid bond which pined like a little bitch, wanting me to stay there in his arms like we were in some epic romance novel instead of a fucked up tragedy with a whole dollop of life threatening bullshit thrown in.

I moved to the spot where the Nymph had died, kicking at the trampled snow before lifting a hand and sweeping it across the ground to expel a wave of heat which melted the snow all around us and made it easier to search.

"Fuck," I cursed, having to agree with Lance's assessment as there was clearly nothing here. "Can you sense anything?" I asked him, turning to look at my best friend as he carved a hand through his dark hair and looked out over the snow filled valley.

"Watch my back," he muttered, sheathing his sword and taking the draining dagger from his belt instead.

I glanced around us, pulling the shadows closer as I made an effort to conceal us just in case. It was damn unlikely that anyone would have eyes on us out here in the middle of fucking nowhere on the edge of the kingdom, but it was always better to be safe than sorry. No one could find out what we were doing here. And more than that - no one could ever catch so much as a whiff of what Lance was about to do now.

I may have been a Celestial Heir, but even I wasn't above the laws regarding the use of dark magic and we couldn't risk getting caught casting it, no matter our reasons for it.

Lance lifted the blade and cut into his hand, his body going still as the shadows swirled around him and he tapped into them, bending them to his will and using them to try and trace the dark artifact we'd come here to retrieve.

I bit down on the inside of my cheek, my gaze shifting over the valley which spread out below us as I drew on the gifts of my Dragon and my eyes shifted into reptilian slits. My vision sharpened as I saw through my Dragon's eyes and I managed to pick out several trails across the snow which cut between patches of woodland like several sets of feet had run that way since the last snowfall.

Lance drew in a rattling breath at my side and I looked to him, already fairly certain of what he was going to say as he fought against the pull of the shadows and his eyes pooled with darkness for a moment. He pushed them back with well practiced moves, resisting the call of them and returning to me, his near black eyes meeting mine as his jaw set in a stern expression.

"In the valley," he said, jerking his bearded chin towards it. "Moving north."

"I guess it's time we fly then," I said, gripping the back of my shirt and yanking it off without waiting for his agreement.

I may have wanted to avoid unleashing my Dragon if I could, but we both knew it was more important for us to make sure that the Nymphs didn't manage to keep hold of that thing.

Lance raised a hand and tugged on the air around him with his magic, making the pack he'd brought with us hurtle through the air as he picked it up from wherever he'd abandoned it and carried it to our feet.

I kicked my boots off, taking no time to drop my pants and quickly stuff everything I was wearing inside the bag while Lance built on the concealment spells I'd started, drawing more magic to him as he created a cloud with his water magic to hang in the air around us too.

The moment I was butt naked with my tattooed flesh gilded silver by the light of the moon, I turned away from him and let the beast in me free. A snarl sounded from me as the ripping of my flesh and expansion of my bones gave way to the golden Dragon that tore from my Fae body and burst to life before him.

Lance shouldered the pack of my things and shot up onto my back with a spurt of his Vampire speed.

My scales tingled beneath his touch, my heart lightening with the childish thrill I got from denying my father like this and flouting his laws. No Dragon should ever be ridden like some common mule. His words echoed in my mind and if I could grin in this form then I would have been doing so. Ee-or asshole.

"Due north," Lance called and my wings snapped out either side of me a moment before I leapt into the air and I took off with a whoosh of power that had an exhilarated laugh escaping Lance's lips.

No matter how many times we did this, it never got old. There was a thrill here, a freedom and a joy which transcended the brutal reality of what we were doing and made me feel alive in a way I craved so fucking much. I needed this. This one thing that my father knew nothing about, which he couldn't taint or soil or force his hand into. This was mine. Ours. Our quiet defiance against the tyrannical rein he held over our fates and our way of saying fuck you to the things in our life which he controlled all too often.

With a few flaps of my powerful wings, we soared out over the frozen landscape below, the clouds of Lance's creation clinging to us and keeping us hidden from the possibility of prying eyes as we raced after our prey.

With my Dragon eyesight, it was so easy to pick out trails along the ground, see the tracks of the creatures which had fled while we fought their brethren. There were three of them, the trails only occasionally coming into view in a small clearing between the trees, but that was more than enough for me to keep up the hunt.

"Come on, Darius, move your ass. I know you can fly faster than this,"

Lance taunted from my back and I snarled as I beat my wings harder, rising to his challenge and tearing through the sky while he called out directions to keep me on track.

"I hear them!" Lance called, clearly using his gifts to track them too. "In that copse to the right."

My gaze zeroed in on the trees he'd pointed out and fire built in my chest with so much power that I could feel my scales almost rattling and my skin heating.

I circled once, dropping low and bellowing a roar which unleashed my fire on the trees and burned through them in a glorious blaze which ate through everything in its path in an instant.

The screams of the Nymphs hiding below us were like music to my ears as my fire consumed them and I roared again as I circled once more, waiting for the flames to die out.

We landed hard amid smouldering branches and falling ash, my claws tearing into the dirt at our feet as I came to a halt. We stayed like that for a moment, listening to the sounds of crackling branches and melting snow, but there was nothing remaining in the trees to jump out at us. The Nymphs had died beneath the power of my gifts and we were alone out here in the wastelands once again.

"Subtle, man." Orion leapt from my back, his boots sinking into the mud as he strode away from me and I shifted back into my Fae form in the centre of the burned ring within the trees.

My bare feet sank into the mud and I grimaced at the sensation, glancing up at the still burning embers which were trying to gain purchase in the trees that surrounded us as a mixture of ash and snow fell from the sky to taint my skin.

"You got it?" I asked as Lance ducked down, picking something up and looking at it before striding back to meet me.

"I got it," he affirmed, tossing me the pack so that I could get dressed once more.

"What is it?" I asked as I tugged my jeans on, shivering as the cold air caressed my heated flesh.

"An amulet of some kind," he said, turning the golden object over in his hands and holding it out for me to assess.

The Dragon in me raised its head at the prospect of treasure, but instead of the heady need to claim it which would have been my usual gut reaction to any shiny, valuable item like that, the beast in me recoiled instead.

"It's old," I grunted, forcing myself to take it and turning it over to reveal the faded glyphs etched into the back of it. "Seven or eight centuries at least." The gold was tarnished and smoothed by the touch of many hands over all those years, but there was something more to it. Something festering at its core which spoke of the darkness within it and the shadows which Lance had been able to sense clinging to it. "Any idea why they wanted it?"

"Maybe it helped them tap into more of the shadows?" Lance suggested though he didn't seem sure. "In any case, I imagine it would be best off destroyed."

"Agreed." I held it out before me and pushed away the desire to hurl the damn thing as far as I could throw it as the cloying darkness of its power washed over me. "Stand back."

Lance did as I commanded, backing up several paces and casting an air shield around himself in anticipation of my power.

When I was certain he was safe from it, I held the amulet out in my fist and began to pour Dragon fire from my palm in a concentrated ball of energy.

My fingers clenched around the gold as it heated in my hand, my teeth gritting against the foul feeling of the shadows as they fought and writhed against the might of my gifts. But I didn't let go, snarling as I funnelled more and more of my power into heating it, my teeth grinding with determination as it fought against my will like the thing had desires of its own.

A shrill scream sounded entirely within my own skull and the shadows began to bite at my arm, my flesh breaking and splitting beneath the ghosts of fangs as I continued to burn them with all I had.

I dropped to one knee as exhaustion tugged at me and I fought with all I had to keep pouring the Dragon fire into the cloying darkness that pooled in my hand.

With a snarl of effort, the gold finally melted, the molten liquid pooling in my hand as the fire battled to destroy it and all that had been contained within it.

The shadows screamed louder as they tried to escape my fire, but I had them in my grasp and there was nowhere for them to go.

Just as the last of them were about to be consumed, my fire burnt out and I cursed as the heat fell from my flesh and one, lone slither of darkness pushed its way into the cuts on my hand and dove beneath my skin.

A pained sound brushed past my lips a moment before a groan of pleasure tumbled after it and I was dragged into the dark where the shadows lingered and their realm seemed so much closer than it ever had before.

Pleasure washed down my spine, making my flesh spark and tingle as the darkness called to me like an old friend. I'd been down this path before, but only ever with Lance at my side and the draining dagger leading me here.

Whispers sounded in the dark as I struggled to find something to anchor me in the Fae realm, something to cling to and help me turn back.

More, the voices seemed to urge and I knew they wanted my blood, my all, my everything.

My heart pounded furiously as I tried to maintain the peace of mind to resist their pull, to fight against the pleasure they promised and keep myself out of the dark.

A voice was calling my name in the distance. A voice I knew and loved. But it wasn't enough. I was falling, drifting, succumbing to the pull of the dark.

But then there were more voices whispering in my ears, these filled with light and promises of fates untold, their caress gentle and probing as they pushed images into my mind of things that had yet to come to pass.

Green eyes peering into my soul and the brush of lips against mine so hot and powerful that I could taste that kiss right down to my core. A name in the dark which sounded like a plea or a promise and words which hung in my mind like they'd been spoken from the stars themselves.

Choose wisely, Dragon born. The greatest treasure is the hardest won.

A hand crashed against my face and I sucked in a sharp breath as the cold pierced right through me and I found myself lying in the mud beneath a taunting sky while Lance knelt over me and snarled a demand for me to come back to him.

I blinked groggily, the words and visions of the stars fading from my mind as I fought to hold onto them with a desperation that told me in no uncertain terms that only bad would come of it if I didn't.

But it was impossible. Harder than trying to hold back the tide, and as I looked into the concerned face of my best friend, they fell from my grasp and drifted away from me like the seeds of a dandelion caught on an ill wind.

"What happened?" I slurred, exhaustion biting into my limbs as I fought to summon my magic and found it floundering at the edges of my reach.

"You're tapped out," Lance grunted. "After the shadows drew you under you started convulsing, haemorrhaging magic until the whole forest was at risk of both burning to nothing and being flooded all at once. It was all I could do to contain it with my own power before you burned through it all, but I managed to tear the darkness from your veins once you did."

I glanced down at my forearm as I felt a slice of pain there and Lance's hand clamped down on the jagged wound that he'd cut into my flesh with the draining dagger. He had a matching wound of his own on his arm, but he healed me without paying it any attention.

"You pulled me out?" I asked groggily, managing to push myself to sit up and ignoring the way my head spun from the effort.

"Yeah," he grunted. "Don't ever fucking do that to me again."

He punched my bicep which only served to make my head rattle more and I groaned as I fought to try and piece what had happened back together.

"Did you *see* anything in the dark?" Lance asked, his hand moving to cup my cheek, his rough palm grazing against the stubble on my jaw as he drove more healing magic into me to banish the headache which was damn near blinding me.

I tried to think back on what I'd *seen* in the shadows, but it was nothing more than a blur of darkness and the promise of pleasure I knew they'd never truly offer me.

"Nothing," I sighed, wishing I'd at least gotten something from my trip into the dark beyond this pounding in my skull.

"Well at least you destroyed that thing," Lance said with a shrug, healing himself at last before standing and offering me a hand to pull me to my feet too.

I let him, my body sagging with fatigue the moment I was upright and he wound a hand around the back of my neck, pulling my head down so that my forehead pressed to his for a moment and we gave the bond that hung between us a little reprieve.

He tossed stardust over us without releasing me and we were yanked into the stars a moment later, travelling through the world in the blink of an eye before landing in the centre of my room at the academy. The warmer air pressed against us as I sighed in relief.

"Another good night hunting," I said, managing a grin as I stood upright again.

"I'd call it successful," Lance muttered. "I don't know about good."

I grunted an agreement to that on account of me feeling like utter shit right about now and dropped my jeans again as I headed straight for my bed, snagging a fresh set of boxers on the way.

I dropped down onto the golden bedspread without bothering to crawl beneath it and cursed the empty feeling in my bones which signalled my lack of magic. I hated feeling like this and I basically never let myself get tapped out the way I was now. It fucking sucked.

"Here," Lance muttered, moving to the chest at the foot of my bed and using his air magic to scoop a pile of treasure from it which he promptly dropped all over my chest.

I wheezed out a breath as the weight of it almost winded me and cursed him out as I shoved the coins and jewels out around me to get more comfortable. But I wasn't really mad because I could already feel the heat of the gold pressing against my skin, replenishing my magic and easing some of the tension in my exhausted limbs. By the time I woke, I'd be well on my way to restored again.

"So this is it," I murmured, letting my eyes fall shut as Lance dropped down on the bed beside me and threaded his fingers behind his head.

"Yep," he replied gravely, the reality of what he was set to do now pushing in on both of us. It was the last day of term and in the morning he was due to set off on a mission at my father's command which might just change everything.

Neither of us knew what was going to happen when he went to the Mortal Realm, but if he found what he was being sent to search for then our entire world was likely to fall into a tailspin.

"It'll all work out," Lance said as the seconds dragged on and I nodded.

"I know. I trust you," I said and it was true. I trusted him more than any other Fae I knew. Even the other Heirs, even my own brother. Because Lance knew all of me, every dark, damaged, fractured piece. The good and the bad. He knew the full extent of what my father was and what I had to endure daily to appease him. He knew the struggles I faced and he'd been by my side throughout them all.

"Just keep your eyes on the end goal," he said and I cracked my eyes open as I felt him setting something on my head, the weight of a golden crown from my treasure falling heavily on my brow.

"Always do," I assured him, straightening the crown as it began to slip.

We locked eyes, that unending bond hanging in the air between us, that one intrinsic goal laying there like it always did. I needed to keep working tirelessly to achieve it. I needed to continue to grow in strength in every way I possibly could. I needed to harness my power with everything I had so that I could rise up and challenge my father. It was all that mattered. All we worked for. The only chance either of us would ever get at any real semblance of freedom in our lives. I needed to take Lionel Acrux's place on the Celestial Council and there was nothing I wouldn't do to achieve that. *Nothing*.

Lance relaxed against the pillows as he saw that steely determination burning brightly within me. Because that was all that counted. All we aimed for. And no matter what it might take, we were going to achieve it.

We fell silent as sleep drew in on us and my eyes drifted shut once more. Tomorrow, term would end and he would leave for the Mortal Realm to seek out the Vega twins. Just another fucking speed bump placed between us and the man I needed to conquer. Just another thing we were going to need to push aside if we wanted any hope of reclaiming our own lives and building something for ourselves which wasn't overshadowed by the monster who'd made me.

So I'd do what it took to get them out of our way. Because nothing was going to stand between us and the freedom we were owed so bitterly. Nothing. Not even the daughters of the Savage King himself.

ORION

CHAPTER ONE

Three months in the Mortal Realm and I was finally getting close to my goal. The crystal in my hand hummed with the energy of a nearby Vega and I waited for her to appear with a prickling sensation rolling down my neck. This one was Gwendalina, or Darcy as she was named here. The crystal recognised each of them in turn and the differing vibrations in my palm told me which of them was approaching. I could practically hear her name whispered by the crystal, it was something intangible, on the edges of my consciousness. I could feel her. And it didn't feel like a heavy cloak of darkness wrapping around me the way I'd expected, it felt like sunshine in my palm.

A couple of Tarot readings and a little nudge from my friend Gabriel after he'd called me last night had led me here today, standing outside some guy's house as rain drizzled lightly around me and I kept it back from my skin with the most subtle air magic I could conjure. Though honestly mortals were sceptical enough of the world that if I stood here on a gust of air and did fifty backflips while conjuring a water horse, someone would find a way to discredit it. They'd write it off as some trick or illusion. Technically I wasn't allowed to cast in front of mortals, but also technically I'd never been one for following the rules.

It took a lot of skill to break the law multiple times a week alongside the son of the most ruthless Councillor in Solaria. But we managed it, partly as a fuck you to the grand old Dragon Lord, slightly because we wanted to hunt Nymphs – which was another layer of illegal in itself - but mostly because we had a score to settle with said Dragon Lord, and I was working to give Darius Acrux an edge against his father when the time came to unseat him from the Council.

Of course, Lionel Acrux had been trained in dark magic by my own mother and father so really I was just repaying the favour in kind to his son to make sure he could face whatever his asshole father threw at him. We were only playing as fair as Lionel was, so who gave a fuck if it was illegal? Breaking the law only mattered if you got caught. Which I didn't plan on doing. Because that would land my ass in Darkmore Penitentiary and screw ever going there. That place was a death sentence in itself, so if I had to die in my attempt to destroy Lionel Acrux, at least let it be outside in the free, star damned air.

My fingers buzzed as the energy in the crystal grew more frantic and my mind daggered back onto my task. And more specifically, my problem. Because ensuring Darius sat his ass on the Council had been my one purpose worth living for these past years, since I'd been bound to him as his Guardian and forced to give up my life in pursuit of Darius's future. And the only comfort in that was that I'd one day see Lionel fall at Darius's hands, and know that I'd been responsible for that in some way, helped hone his Elemental magic and taught him in the ways of dark magic so he became the most fearsome opponent Lionel had ever faced.

But now…fucking now, there was an issue with that plan. The kind of issue that no one could have predicted, apparently not even the greatest Seers in the land had *seen* it coming. At least not until the Vegas had turned eighteen and their magical signature had stirred into existence, then every Seer in the kingdom had felt it. The shift in fate. The huge fissure metaphorically ripping up the centre of our world and changing everything.

The Vega twins were alive, the two girls born of the old king and queen of Solaria and thought to have been lost in the fire that devoured their parents after they were murdered by Nymphs. I swear I'd felt it too, waking in the early hours of the morning on the eleventh of June as the stars seemed to whisper something in my mind which I couldn't understand, but I'd known without having to decipher the words that it was crucially important. I hadn't slept another wink that night, speaking with Darius who'd been roused too, plagued by nightmares of fire and death.

The next day it had been announced that their magical signatures had been detected in the Mortal Realm and the Councillors had called a meeting to decide how to proceed. But I'd known from the moment it was declared that this would happen. They'd be found and brought to Solaria to train because that was the law. And even if it hadn't been, the Councillors could hardly ignore the raving lunatic royalists who'd partied in the streets like wild animals when the news of the Vegas' continued existence had been announced. I swear to the fucking moon, if I had to watch one more news report of a royalist rejoicing by stripping their clothes off and shaking their tits or cock at the camera, I was gonna kill myself.

Anyway, Lionel had thought it would be a great idea to elect me to be the one to fetch the Vegas so I could 'suss them out' for him. And now it had been three star-damned months since I'd started hunting the Mortal Realm -specifically the entire state of Illinois – for the two changelings twins who were about to alter the history of my world. So that was my summer gone, and I'd be back to teaching little assholes at Zodiac Academy tomorrow.

Today was my last day to get my hands on the twins and I'd finally pinpointed their location, so I needed to get hold of them ASAP and drag them to their Awakening tonight.

"Come on, where are you, you little life-wrecker?" I muttered under my breath.

My gaze was fixed on the road, the heightened sight of my Vampire Order making my eyes twitch onto anything that moved, from the yawning cat across the street to the squirrel moving up in the tree above it and shaking its tail aggressively.

A flash of blue in my periphery made my head whip sideways and I frowned as I spotted the back of a girl with blue-tipped hair as she ran through a garden to my left. She made it to the open window of the house I'd been watching, reached up and started hauling herself inside. Her sneakers kicked against the wall and she growled angrily as she fought to get up, her head disappearing through the window as I sidestepped to get a better look at her.

Her ass wiggled left to right as her hips got stuck in the tight gap – an ass that was drawing way too much of my attention. My fangs prickled as they extended and I ran my tongue over them, fighting down that carnal urge in me. It was just a reaction to her power level, I was sure, so I wasn't gonna think much into that. Besides, why shouldn't I take a bite out of a Vega? They weren't going to be helpless for long, so why not make the most of it while it lasted?

Probably better get them to class before I went about savaging them though. I was supposed to be a professional after all.

A police siren droned in my ears and I worked to tune out the blare of it, my senses too sharp when it came to noises like that.

The girl all but fell inside the house and my eyebrows arched. *What the fuck is she up to?*

I walked alongside the house and used a concealment spell to drag the shadows closer around me as I slipped through the front gate and headed up to the window to peer inside. Was this Vega a little thief?

The police sirens drew closer and one glance sideways said they were about to pull up, so I put on a burst of speed and shot away to the garden, vaulting the fence and darting behind the cover of a tall tree. I wasn't supposed to use my Order gifts like that, but I also didn't have a single fuck to spare on the matter.

A cop ran up to the door and battered the thing down with a couple of his friends and I cursed. *The first day I catch up to one of the Vegas and she pulls some dodgy theft and gets arrested?*

Yeah…no. That wasn't gonna happen. I wasn't going to return to Solaria empty handed. Again.

My Atlas buzzed in my pocket and I took it out, finding a message from Gabriel. I'd asked him to keep an eye on my fate today and it looked like it had paid off. He was a good friend and one of the best Seers in the kingdom. We'd met several years ago while I'd been studying at Zodiac and he'd been sent here on a field trip from his own academy. I'd ended up being drugged with a lust potion by a fangirl and he'd looked after me – after the potion had made me try to suck his cock. Damn, me and him were unlucky with shit like that, but we'd weirdly bonded over it. I was still sworn to secrecy over the second time someone had tried to drug me and Gabriel had ended up as the victim. He said if I ever told anyone what had happened to his dick that day, he'd kill me. But he knew he could trust me. Still made me laugh whenever I thought about it though.

Noxy:

Vision unclear, but you need to take the cash, Orio.

What cash?

"Hey – stop!" a female cop called.

My head snapped up as the thump of footfalls sounded this way and I glanced out past the tree as the cop chased Darcy Vega across the grass. The girl was already on her knees by the fence with a wad of cash stuffed into the back of her belt as she started clambering through a hole beneath it that looked like it had been dug by an animal. The cop was gaining on her, powering her arms back and forth like a superhero.

"I need this money – it's not even his!" Darcy cried just before the cop grabbed her ankles and started trying to haul her back.

That's my Vega, bitch.

I shot out of my hiding place, cursing this day as the money tumbled free of Darcy's belt and fell everywhere.

"No!" Darcy shouted in anguish.

"Sarge!" the cop cried for backup as I came up behind her, her body falling into my large shadow.

"*Let go of her*," I commanded, using Coercion to make her listen.

The cop immediately released the girl and Darcy scrambled away under the fence before kicking it in fury.

I scooped up her cash before she could even think about trying to get hold of it again and I pushed it into my pocket.

I looked over the fence as shouts sounded behind me and I was forced to run away in a blur of speed, vaulting through gardens and trying to keep my eye on the blue tipped hair of the Vega running through the trees to my left. I finally made it to those trees and rushed into the shadows, casting a silencing bubble around me to keep my movements hidden.

But as I looked around, I couldn't see where the fuck she'd gone.

Fate's closing in on you, Darcy Vega. You can't outrun me.

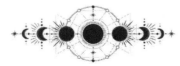

I'd followed the humming of my crystal to a rundown part of the city and now I was sitting in a bus shelter as I waited for one of the twins to appear again, twisting a Tarot card between my fingers as a sleeping drunk guy who stank of beer and piss sat beside me. The crystal was only good enough to get me into the general area they were in and as their power level was so strong, it couldn't help me lock down a location more specifically than this.

Fuck this day. Fuck this job for that matter. Even though my life had been stolen from me a long time ago, I had still never gotten used to being Lionel Acrux's skivvy. Some Fae were cut out for being subservient but I certainly wasn't one of them. I'd dreamed of ruling my own life since I was a kid. It had been bad enough when my mother had expected me to join the illegal family business of assisting the Acruxes with any and every dark magic need they could desire, but to now be forced into it and work as a professor of all the star damned things, just so I could keep an eye on Darius, it was soul destroying. Literally. Because my soul was in pieces since that magical bond had been forced upon me and the constant urge to protect Darius at my own detriment now lived in me like a foreign body. It was a succubus feeding on my life force, and sure I loved Darius as a friend, and sure, I wanted to protect him in a normal he's-my-best-friend kind of way. But I hadn't planned on giving up my free will for the guy, or tolerating a single second more of his father's bullshit than I had to.

I'd had a chance to play for the Solarian Pitball League. I had literally been on track to be a star and I'd given up so much during my time studying at Zodiac Academy because of that. I'd missed out on partying, on drinking with friends, on *having* friends. I mean, yeah, I was a Vampire and solitude was one of my favourite things anyway. But maybe I could have had...more. Now any chance of more had been well and truly flushed away by Lionel, and any sadness I'd felt about missing out on drinking was forgotten considering I was potentially a borderline alcoholic these days.

A punk of a Pegasus had broken into my office last term and stolen a bottle of bourbon from my desk. Suffice to say, the little asshole had triggered my magical alarms and I'd thrown his ass in detention, making him roll in Griffin shit in his boxers until he broke out in an unbearable rash. But he'd already managed to sink most of my bourbon before I got there. That was around about the time I'd realised I might have a drinking problem.

A sheet of rain had swept through the city and it was persistently damp now as I sat impatiently there in the shelter and darkness began to fall. The drunk jerked awake with a hiccup, then lifted an old beer can still clutched in his hand to his lips, shaking out the final drops of it into his gaping mouth. My gaze slid firmly back to the road as I rolled the crystal within my palm, the low, thrumming sensation of it telling me both twins were close. But where?

Together, their magical signatures felt like night and day, coinciding in perfect harmony with one another, like they couldn't exist apart. The sensation was warm and cool at once, and they didn't feel like Solaria's utter and catastrophic downfall – which was what I'd expected. These were the children of the Savage King, daughters of cruelty, oppression, murder. Their family name left a bitter taste in my mouth and I wasn't going to be fooled by the feel of them. The Savage King's magical signature could have felt like kitten kisses and cotton candy for all I knew. Didn't mean he wasn't a raging motherfucker who'd ruled with an iron fist and made the entire kingdom fear him.

"Saw a cat over there this morning," the drunk slurred as he pointed across the road and I offered him a hard glare which warned him that I was not in the mood for conversation. I enjoyed talking with very few people in this life as it was and I loathed small talk with strangers. Especially drunk ones who stank of piss. "It looked like you." He jerked his chin at me and my scowl deepened. "That's the look it gave me!" He gestured at my face and my fangs prickled with the urge to rip his throat out so I didn't have to listen to his rambling a second longer. "It had the most angry face I ever saw. And I thought, that cat's unhappy, he is. He's sad inside."

"Stop talking," I commanded, using Coercion to solve my problem and his next words died in his throat. Mortals were putty in my hands; it was far too easy to manipulate them. Which was why we had strict laws in place that forbid us from doing so. Last year, a mortal trafficking ring had been exposed in eastern Solaria. They'd been kidnapped from this realm and were being

Coerced into sexual slavery for Fae. Fucking twisted. Mortals couldn't even survive in our realm for that long, so that story had taken an even darker turn when the FIB had uncovered the first mass grave.

My kind had the capability to be evil. It lived in us all. Our entire society was built on gaining power and we were all easily swayed into claiming it over weaker Fae than ourselves. I guessed mortals were a tempting place to gain a power high when your magic wasn't strong and you were beat down by Fae with superior gifts daily. A lot of the assholes involved in the trafficking ring had been weaklings, half had ended up in Darkmore Penitentiary, half had died during the raids. I hope they'd been screaming when they went. There was nothing that sickened me more than a Fae who abused their power. I guessed that was because I knew what it was like to be crushed beneath the heel of someone I couldn't win against. And Lionel Acrux was the epitome of an abuser. He beat his son black and blue to try and forge him into the image of himself, but Darius wasn't like him, no matter how much he wanted him to be.

As darkness fell entirely and the drunk got on a bus at last, the door of the apartment block across the street opened and Roxanya, AKA Tory, stepped outside in an oversized leather jacket and what looked like men's jeans and biker boots. The energy shifted within the crystal in my palm as she crossed the street and I tugged my hood up, using magic to draw the shadows closer around me. Her magical signature invaded the crystal until all I could feel was what felt like the cool kiss of the moon against my palm. It was strange how two twins could feel so different, but I supposed all siblings were unique in their own ways. My sister had been the opposite of me. Optimistic, funny, playful – *fuck, I miss her.*

Tory jogged off down the street and I stood up, heading after her at a distance and running my thumb over the crystal like I was trying to urge something else out of it. I was partial to the night considering my Order was linked to the moon, but for some reason I missed the touch of sunshine in my palm and the warmth of her sister's presence. I ignored that odd feeling and followed Tory as she walked a few blocks. Her headphones were in and her head bobbed occasionally with whatever she was listening to and I internally rolled my eyes at her. Did this girl have a death wish? She was walking through a rough part of town at night and anyone could have come up behind her with a knife. Or sharp teeth.

She eventually turned into a multistorey carpark, pulling up her hood and ducking her head as she walked straight beneath a security camera. I flicked my fingers, using a gust of air to snap the camera clean off the wall and gently lowered it onto a grassy verge as I followed Tory inside. My vague plan was to corner her, explain she was a lost Fae princess who needed to come with me tonight to her Awakening then go pick up her sister along the way and get going. It was either that or kidnap them, but that was a plan B I'd only resort to if I had to. I had specific orders from the Councillors to 'be professional.' Which was bullshit, but whatever. I'd give it one good attempt, but either way they were coming with me tonight because I was done with the Mortal Realm. I couldn't feel the stars here in the way I could in Solaria, and with each passing day my magic felt harder to grasp. It was taking its toll on me and I needed to go home before I got ill. I'd probably spent more time here than I ever should in my lifetime.

I lost sight of Tory but there was only one place she could have headed so I started walking up the ramps to the higher levels, the crystal in my hand urging me toward her.

As I rounded onto the third level, a blonde woman in a tiny pink dress, high heels and fishnet stockings stumbled out of an elevator and her eyes landed on me. "Well hey there, cowboy, you looking for a ride on a wild pony?"

"No," I said simply, walking towards the next ramp, but she jogged after me, laughing raucously like I'd said something particularly funny. I wasn't sure what exactly was funny about my dismissive refusal, but each to their own.

"I guess a pretty boy like you has a wife waiting at home for him, huh?

But what are you doing out so late without her? Are you looking for trouble?" she asked, trying to take my arm but I just quickened my pace so she couldn't. As a Vampire, I could move faster than the wind if I wanted to, but I could also walk consistently at the pace of a late commuter without breaking a sweat.

"Come on, two hundred for the night," she offered, breaking into a jog to try and catch me.

The roar of an engine sounded and I cursed as I rounded the next ramp and shrank back into the shadows just before Tory came speeding past me on a motorcycle, tearing down the ramp at high speed.

The hooker came running up the ramp toward me and I growled in frustration. *"Shut your eyes,"* I commanded the girl and her eyes stamped closed immediately. I put on a burst of Vampire speed and tore back down through the parking lot, following the humming of the crystal in my palm as I raced after Tory Vega.

Fuck this night.

I raced through the city in a blur after her on that motorcycle, moving fast enough so as not to be seen, knowing this was breaking a bunch of rules but not giving a shit anymore. I needed to get hold of the Vega twins and take them to Solaria soon or I was gonna lose it.

I finally reached a bar where Tory's energy hummed louder within the crystal and I slowed to a halt in a dark alley across the street.

I crossed the road, walking past the row of motorcycles outside and shoving the door open. It was like one of those moments in the movies where everyone looks up and knows you're entirely out of place there. But did I give a fuck? Not one. Because I was the most deadly creature in the room, even if I was wearing a nice shirt.

My fangs pricked my tongue as huge biker dudes with tattoos on their tattoos glared at me over their beers. I walked straight up to the barman, ignoring them all and walking over to Tory Vega who was throwing back a tequila shot, her baggy outfit now changed out for something far more clingy and showing off a lot more skin.

Finally.

"Can I have a word with you?" I asked, fighting to keep my tone polite when all I wanted to do after this long ass three months was throw her over my shoulder and toss her into a cloud of stardust, sending her all the way to her new life. But I guessed I could spend my very last aura of patience on trying this the nice way.

"Are you lost?" she asked with a smirk. She looked me up and down, clearly thinking what everyone else in the bar was as I studied her pretty features and the suspicion in her green eyes. This was my enemy. She may have been small, but that meant nothing when you were Fae. The power residing within her veins made my throat burn with the need to drink from her, but I reckoned that was a surefire way to scare her off for good. And as I had a job to do…

"No. I've found exactly what I'm looking for," I replied, trying to tune out the droning heavy metal music which was playing havoc with my heightened senses.

"Good for you. I'll see you around." She started to walk away from me but that was gonna be a fuck no, so I grabbed her arm.

"What the hell do you think you're-" she started.

"*Take a seat with me,*" I Coerced her, done with asking nicely.

She instantly dropped into a chair by the bar and I sat down beside her, releasing her arm. She had absolutely zero mental shields, and though I'd expected that, it still took me by surprise. Even without magic, Fae were taught young to work on mental blocks that helped them fight against Coercion, but this girl seemed to have zero ability to resist me. That was gonna make their time at the academy hell until they could figure it out. Pity.

I felt the bartender looking between me and Tory and I resolutely ignored him as I gave this pain in my ass my full attention.

"You drinking tonight then, Tory?" the bartender asked as he filled another shot of tequila for her.

"I think I'll give it a miss after the events of last weekend," she said and I guessed that meant she was a regular here. This kind of looked like a place where dreams came to die – and I'd know all about places like that.

The bartender leaned closer like he was settling in for a chat. "Well one of these days I might-"

"*Leave,*" I commanded in irritation and the guy instantly headed to the far end of the bar.

Tory raised an eyebrow at me. "I think that's my cue too," she said, hopping down from her seat and slipping back between the crowd of leather-clad bodies just like that.

"Give me the fucking strength, stars," I muttered, rubbing my eyes and shoving out of my own seat. I pushed after her through the crowd, moving with a spurt of speed while no one was looking and snatching hold of her arm. I wasn't letting go this time. I had the Vegas in my sights at last and I'd be taking them back to Solaria kicking and screaming if I had to.

"We need to talk," I growled, but it didn't look like she heard me over the loud music.

"Back the fuck off," she snapped, twisting her arm out of my grip and disappearing into the throng of bodies again. A few assholes overheard her and stepped into my path, cracking their knuckles like goons as if they really thought they were about to give me a beat down. It was laughable really.

"*Get out of my way,*" I snarled, my voice ringing with magic and they all scarpered like cowering mice. I strode through the gap that had opened up for me, hunting for Tory as my fangs sharpened in fury. *That's it. I'm done.*

I strode through the bar to the exit, throwing the door open as my upper lip twitched with the urge to peel back on a snarl. But showing a bunch of mortals my fangs probably wasn't the best idea, so I kept my inner Fae in check as I headed onto the street and my gaze locked on Tory on the back of some dude's bike.

"*Stop!*" I roared, trying to Coerce the guy driving, but he loosed the throttle at the same time so my voice was lost to the roar of the engine. A snarl really did escape me then and I marched across the street into the shadows before sprinting after her with my Vampire speed, tearing along the roads in a blur that I just had to hope no one could see.

The guy dropped her off a block away from her home and I followed her all the way back to her apartment. I waited in the darkness of someone's porch while she unlocked the door then shot up behind her, figuring I finally had her cornered and I wasn't gonna fuck it up this time. They were both gonna hear me out and if they didn't like what I had to say, well tough shit. That wasn't my problem.

"We didn't finish our chat," I called to Tory, knowing I was gonna freak her out but at this point I didn't give a damn. She looked back, her eyes widening with fear at finding me right there behind her and the pounding of her heart reached my ears.

Proving she didn't actually have a death wish in this city, she turned and fled up the stairs.

I walked calmly after her, kicking the door closed and carving my fingers through my hair. I was tired and pissed off, and I didn't wanna be here in the first place. So now this was gonna be done in asshole mode. Which happened to be my default setting.

I shot up the stairs, my mouth watering as she continued to run and the urge to hunt her burrowed into my core. It was damn tempting, but entirely against the Vampire Code and I'd probably be thrown in prison for it considering who these girls were.

"*Stop!*" I called, Coercing her to do so and she did. For all of two seconds anyway, then she fought it off and kept running.

I arched a brow, kinda impressed by that considering she had zero training but then my mood sharpened to rage again because for fuck's sake, I was getting tired of this game.

I put on a burst of speed and shot up behind her, slapping my hand over her mouth to stifle her scream. In that moment, the urge to feed reared up in me like a beast. I'd caught my prey. I got to eat. That was only fair.

I gritted my jaw, fighting hard against that instinct and taking a slow breath.

Don't bite her. Keep your shit together.

I swallowed down the jagged lump in my throat and fought away the thirst, but the strength of her power tugged on the instinctual needs of my Order and begged me to devour every drop of her blood.

No. I'm not doing it. I'm not a slave to my thirst.

"I'm Professor Orion. I'm not going to hurt you and *you're not going to scream. You want to let me in.*" I released her and stepped back as she stared up at me, fear bright in her eyes, but she was caught in my snare now, the power of the Coercion I used leaving no room for her to wriggle out of it this time.

She opened her mouth as if she was going to refuse my command, then shoved her key in the lock and turned it.

"Come in," she said sweetly. *Better.*

I stepped close to her in case she somehow got it into her head to run off again, knowing these Vegas must have been immensely powerful even if they didn't know it yet. I offered her a flat smile as I followed her inside and pushed the door closed behind me, casting ice within the lock for good measure to keep it shut tight. While Tory wasn't looking, I took the rock from my pocket which was concealing my satchel with my notes in it and removed the magical cast keeping it hidden, slinging the satchel over my shoulder.

I took in the tiny, rundown apartment with a sweeping look then my gaze moved almost involuntarily to the girl curled up on the couch watching TV. Her head whipped around and her eyes fell on me and her sister, making my heart bunch up into my throat. The prickling in my fangs grew immediately more demanding and the urge to feed from her was almost impossible to fight off. Facially, she was the same as her sister in every way, the only difference between them the blue tipped ends of her hair, and yet…

My gaze roamed over the crease between her eyes as she frowned at us, then my attention shifted to her lips as she wet them. Full. Pink. Appetising – *fuck, stop it.*

This girl was beautiful in a way that ran somehow deeper than her skin, in a way I could *feel.* She took me in with equal scrutiny and for a moment it felt like we were two animals about to rip into each other's flesh. No, it was something other than that. It wasn't a fight I wanted, my cock was stirring in my pants and a possessive growl was building in my throat. Both Vegas were attractive, but something about this one was mesmerising. I couldn't for the life of me tear my eyes away from her.

"Hell no." Darcy stood up, giving me the opportunity to study the pyjamas she was wearing which were covered with fluffy bunnies. My lips twitched as my fangs tingled harder. She looked like one of those rabbits, innocent, wide-eyed, just like my prey. Yet something told me what lived in her was purely feral and not easily tamed. "Go to his place, Tor, are you crazy? Are you really expecting me to clear out so you can defile our only bed?"

Great. She thinks I'm here to fuck her sister.

Not that it matters what she thinks. She's going to be my student as of tomorrow.

Tory shook her head. "Obviously not. This guy just...well he wanted to come in alright?"

"And that's acceptable why?" Darcy asked in utter confusion and amusement ran through me. This was quite fun actually. She was too fucking cute getting all angry while wearing those ridiculous pyjamas.

"What are you staring at?" Darcy demanded, addressing me for the first time and my eyebrows arched. *The bunny girl bites.*

"I thought I was coming here to collect a couple of eighteen-year-olds. Must have gotten the wrong apartment, little bunny." I chuckled, enjoying the way her cheeks pinked and she started getting flustered. I could hear her rampant heartbeat from here. And it was making me hungry.

Her eyes fell to the pyjamas she was wearing and her cheeks blazed with more blood. Blood I wanted to know the taste of. No, I *needed* to know the taste of it. Did it taste like her magical signature felt? Was her blood liquid sunshine? Warm and so fucking inviting that keeping myself from it right now was the biggest chore I'd ever faced. Feeding from this girl would be the eighth deadly sin, but fuck if I wanted to commit it.

"Who the hell are you? And why are you in my home insulting me?" Darcy looked to her sister again and Tory gave her an apologetic shrug before turning to face me.

Darcy moved to join her, slipping off the couch and standing shoulder to shoulder with her twin, giving me a chance to compare them up close. I gazed down at the two little thorns in my side and wondered if I was standing in front of the biggest threat to ever face Solaria. I was caught off guard by how much I didn't instantly hate them. And I hated everyone, so that was saying something,

"*You were getting me a drink*," I shot at Tory and she promptly walked into the kitchen and poured me a glass of water, giving me an opportunity to study Darcy up close. What was it about this one that was so alluring? My instincts were going haywire and my throat was burning with the thirst. I hadn't fed in too long, that's what it was.

Darcy stared at me with equal ferocity then her brow pinched as realisation crossed her features. "You're a cop. You were there today."

"Where exactly?" I asked innocently, liking the way my mere presence seemed to rile her up into a storm.

"Don't play dumb with me." She pointed at me as her heart rate picked up even further and I liked that I was affecting her like this. Though I definitely shouldn't have been thinking the thoughts crossing my mind about her. *That blue hair would look so fucking good wrapped around my fist.*

By the stars, she's gonna be your damn student, idiot.

Tory returned, thrusting the water into my hand with a strained expression as she tried to fight off my Coercion and Darcy frowned at her, clearly sensing her unusual behaviour.

I offered her a word of thanks then tipped the water into my mouth, hoping it might do something to shift the ache for blood from my throat. I drained every last drop, each time I swallowed hoping it would weaken the bloodlust a little, but as I finished it and placed the glass down on the kitchen counter, I found myself even more bloodthirsty than before.

Maybe I just need some space.

"I've been chasing around after you two all day." I strode to the couch, throwing myself down onto the spot Darcy had vacated and stacking my hands on my stomach.

"Just leave Tory out of this. I was the one who took the cash," Darcy said, worry lining her voice and I thought it was pretty funny she believed I was a cop when I was a lawbreaker through and through. *You have no idea what I'm capable of, princess.*

"Except you didn't get the cash, you dropped it," Tory pointed out and I smirked.

"You mean *this* cash?" I lifted my ass and tugged the wad of money out of my back pocket, waving it above my head.

Tory strode over and snatched it out of my hand, perching on the coffee table before me as she counted every last note.

When she was satisfied it was all there, she looked up at me with an icy glare and I saw a glint of Fae in her. Nothing that would give me nightmares though. On the whole, the Savage King's daughters seemed pretty un-savage if I was being honest. And as I looked around their crappy apartment, I started to feel uncomfortable. This place was a shithole and they were royalty. If they'd been raised by their parents, they would have been richer than every Fae in Solaria. They would have known wealth unlike anything they could even imagine. They wouldn't have been counting out that cash like it was the thing that provided them life itself.

I'd been building a file on them while I was here, going through their hospital records, their foster homes, building up a picture in my mind of the life they'd led. And honestly, it was a shitty one that I wouldn't have wished on any kid. I didn't wanna feel sorry for them, because they were about to be on the other side of a war I'd be firmly their enemy in. But witnessing the hell they'd been enduring was unsettling.

"So what do you want?" Tory demanded. "People don't just hand cash over unless they want something for it, Mr Orion."

"Professor," I corrected, figuring it was best to set the boundaries now. Especially as I was still thinking about little miss bunny pyjamas in my periphery and what her body might look like beneath all that baggy material.

"How old are you?" Darcy asked.

"Old enough to be a professor." My eyes whipped back onto her and I was instantly snared in her trap again. Maybe she was a Siren, her Order about to emerge, and she was somehow wielding her powers over me already, drawing me in and becoming a dark desire I couldn't ignore. *Sure, I'm gonna go with that.*

Darcy moved to stand before the couch, folding her arms as she waited for an explanation.

She looked stern, but she was exuding fear too, uncertainty, and she kept looking at me in a way I couldn't quite understand. But I had a feeling it was the exact same way I kept looking at her.

"*You're going to listen to me and remain calm and collected,*" I said in a powerful tone to Coerce them and make sure this went off without a hitch now I had them cornered.

Darcy nodded easily and fuck, I liked that. I liked it too much, having her obey me. She was a princess, daughter to a man I despised, my mortal enemy right here in the flesh. And I owned her in that moment.

She dropped down beside Tory on the coffee table and they both gave me their full attention. *At last.*

I beamed at them satisfactorily, preparing to pop their sad little poor life bubble and thrust them into a world of unimaginable riches, fame, and more enemies than they could shake a stick at. One of which was me, because I was firmly team Heirs – despite how some of them irritated me – and even more firmly team Darius Acrux.

"Since your eighteenth birthday, you have both been giving off a signature that my kind can sense from a world away. Literally." I paused, letting those odd words sink in. Darcy opened her mouth to ask a question but I held up a hand to stop her, continuing on before they could start freaking out. "I will explain, just *keep calm*."

Darcy nodded and I took one torturously long moment studying her mouth. By the moon, that *mouth*.

"Go on," Tory encouraged. *Right yeah, the stuff and things I have to say.*

I leaned back in my seat, rubbing a hand across the back of my neck. "I'm not a beat-around-the-bush kinda guy, so here it is: you're not human. You're Fae. Which means you have an unawakened power in you defined by the stars themselves. You belong in Solaria: a mirror world of earth where Fae rule. Are we keeping up?" Amusement simmered through me at dropping the bomb just like that. Maybe I was enjoying rattling the Savage King's twins just a little.

They both shared a look that confirmed they thought I belonged in an insane asylum so I just continued on, figuring they'd either believe me or they wouldn't but when I dropped their asses off at Zodiac Academy, they'd likely get the message.

"You're both Gemini," I stated. "Hot-headed, hence the Coercion I've used on you to keep this all running smoothly. Especially as we're already running late," I muttered, lifting my wrist to check my watch. I really was pushing the limits now. Their Awakening was due to start any minute.

"Gemini...as in the star sign?" Tory asked.

"Precisely," I said. *Ah good, they're not absolute morons.* "Gemini is an air sign so once your powers are Awakened you'll-"

"Hang on," Darcy spoke over me and my fingers itched with the urge to punish her for that. If she'd done so in my classroom, I would have made her pay severely for it. As it was, I supposed I could be lenient this once. She'd soon learn I was not to be fucked with anyway. Of course, then my treacherous mind ran to the dangerous place where my punishments involved me pushing her down on my desk and spanking her ass raw, and I cursed myself internally.

What the fuck's the matter with me?

"Do you really expect us to believe we have powers? Like *magic*?" Darcy scoffed.

"Honestly? I don't care what you believe. But I have a job to do and part of that job is explaining this to you. Frankly, I'd rather not waste my breath as you're going to find out soon enough anyway," I said, my tone sharp enough to cut through glass and her eyes narrowed on me like she wanted to rise to the challenge in my voice. *Come at me, little Fae, I'll show you what real power looks like.*

"What does that mean?" Tory asked with a frown.

"It means I've been trying to speak with you all day, but apparently breaking and entering and stealing motorbikes was on your agendas so I've been running around after you like a dog. And I really don't like chasing people about so let's just say I'm not in the best of moods right now."

Darcy pursed her lips and that bratty expression got my fangs prickling again.

My mouth tightened in irritation and I checked my watch again, finding we were out of time. "Right, we're going." I stood, tugging out some stardust from my pocket and they both stared up at me in utter confusion. *Oh it's about to get a whole lot more confusing, Vega girls.*

"Wait a minute." Darcy stood too and I gazed down at her with a bland expression that gave nothing away of the voracious hunger I was feeling over her. "You said we're Fae? What does that even mean?"

"We're a different race. A better one." I shrugged and she scowled in a way that sent a hot flash up my spine. By the stars, this *girl*. "Careful Miss Vega, expressions like that are punishable in my classroom."

"Vega?" Her nose wrinkled and I remembered they literally had no idea about anything. "That's not my name. Wait, please tell me you've got the wrong twins?"

I shook my head in frustration. "That is your true surname in Solaria. No one will call you anything else once you get there, mark my words."

"Er- excuse me?" Tory cut in. Her jaw was gritted as if she wished she could have shouted those words, but thanks to my Coercion she was just an angry dog on a leash. "We're not going anywhere with some creep from the lobby. What drug are you on exactly? Judging by the fancy attire I'm gonna guess coke?"

I gave her a predator's smile at those words, the fire in both of their eyes making the monster in me rear its head. "Look, I have far better things to be doing with my time than standing here in a dingy apartment with a couple of girls who think I'm an addict with a screw loose. But I didn't get a choice in the matter. So just humour me, will you?"

"You haven't explained anything." Darcy shook her head in refusal. "And why should we believe anything you say anyway?"

I snatched up my satchel, flipping it over and pouring the contents out onto their coffee table. A waterfall of papers fell everywhere, pages and pages of every piece of information I'd collected on them during my time in the Mortal Realm falling onto the surface.

I sifted through it all, extracting a photograph of their adopted mortal parents on their wedding day. Darcy snatched it from my hand, hugging it to her chest as tears gleamed in her eyes like she thought I'd been about to burn it.

"What are you doing with a photo of our parents?" Tory hissed.

"They're not your parents," I said coolly. "You're Changelings. Fae born. Elementals with natural magic flowing in your veins. Your real parents swapped you for the twins born to that couple." I pointed at the photo in

Darcy's hand and her brows tugged together.

Those people were just mortals, and these girls were not grasping the magnitude of who they really were.

"That's not true. You're insane. Why would they do that?" Darcy demanded.

"My guess? You were in danger," I said with a shrug. The queen must have foreseen their deaths, but if she'd known it was coming, how come she hadn't been able to change her and her husband's fate? "Or maybe you just annoyed them as much as you're annoying me right now and they decided to swap you for less irritating twins."

Tory looked like she was about to punch me and I would have laughed my head off if she'd have tried.

"Get out," Tory said in a measured tone like I'd actually listen.

"Fine, I tried." I took the small silk black bag from my pocket and untied the strings. "Shame to lose out on your inheritance though. Your real parents were the wealthiest family in Solaria."

"Right," Darcy muttered, but I'd dangled the carrot and it looked like Tory was gonna bite.

"Wait...wealthy?" Tory asked, stepping closer, her anger clearly lessened. The way she'd snatched that cash from me had shown exactly how desperate they were for money, so if that was what it took to entice them, then there was plenty of it to do that with. But it looked like Tory was more lured by it than Darcy.

"It can't be true, Tor," Darcy said under her breath.

Tory shrugged one shoulder. "Let's hear him out." She gave her sister a look I couldn't see and I fought a smirk.

"Yes. *Hear me out,*" I insisted and suddenly Darcy nodded, influenced by me again and giving me another little power trip. I tugged the photo from Darcy's grip, eyeing it for a moment with a frown. "Look, I'm not trying to shatter your little daydreams about this couple but they're just two random humans who got caught up in something much bigger. You don't know them from Adam. And neither do I for that matter. The fact that they're dead is a tragedy but they aren't your blood. And blood's all that matters in my opinion." *Especially when your blood is the Savage King's blood.* I shrugged, glancing between them. "You two would do anything for each other, I hope? Because this shitty life can go away like *that*." I snapped my fingers. "All you have to do is agree to enrol at Zodiac Academy. You'll get full board, have your own beds-" I gave the couch a pointed look, "-and your inheritance will cover the cost of your stay plus you'll receive a monthly stipend from it. Once you graduate, it's all yours. But only when you graduate. That's the law."

"So you want us to go to some school?" Tory asked.

"Yes. But not just any school. The best school." It really was the fucking best. "So what do you say?"

"I say you're crazy," Darcy said and I had a vision of showing her just how crazy I could be. Not an appropriate one though. The kind where she was pinned beneath me gasping my name.

Focus.

"Yeah... but I do want the money." Tory elbowed Darcy in the ribs and she frowned.

"It's full board?" Darcy looked to me again, pulling on a lock of blue-tipped hair. It was very distracting.

"Every meal," I swore. "So?" I tapped my foot impatiently.

Neither of them answered.

"*Just say yes and come with me,*" I growled, over this conversation.

"Yes," they both said in unison without a moment's hesitation.

I grinned from ear to ear, my job finally complete. "Should've done that in the first place." I jerked my chin at Darcy. "*Go get dressed*, if you show up like that at Zodiac you'll be eaten alive by the other students." *And me.*

She headed out of the room and I was left with Tory as she remained under my spell.

"So there's…a lot of money?" she confirmed.

"Heaps," I confirmed and her eyes glittered.

A beat later, Darcy returned from the bathroom in tight jeans which clung to her round ass and a black tank top that hugged the hourglass curves of her body. Ah, great. Why couldn't she have been covered in Heptian Toad skin?

For some reason, her twin of the exact same figure hadn't stirred anything in me, but this one had my cock throbbing and my mind spinning with filthy fantasies I could never, ever act on. *You fucking idiot.*

"You mentioned magic…" Darcy said probingly.

"Yes," I said, attempting to look elsewhere only to find myself staring at her again. "Water, air, fire, earth. You will both possess one Element, perhaps two. Your parents were very powerful, so I expect you will be immeasurably gifted." *And if you are, the Heirs are going to lose their shit. But of course you are, of course you'll make this difficult.*

I prised open the silk bag, pinching some stardust between my fingers and sprinkled it in my palm.

"What's that?" Tory whispered as Darcy inched closer to get a look at it.

"The rarest substance in Solaria and the quickest way to travel: stardust." *This will be fun*. I lifted my head with a demonic smile. "Welcome to your Awakening."

I blew the stuff right into their faces and they gasped in time with one another. The stardust cascaded over us and their shitty apartment faded away as we were yanked into the ether between worlds, carrying us to Solaria, taking me home at last.

My feet hit the ground and Darcy stumbled into me, her forehead bumping against my chest. Her hand pressed to my stomach and the point of contact sent a burning, almost unbearable need in me to take hold of her. Bite her, claim her - *get a fucking grip.*

I grabbed her shoulders, jerking her around to face the circle of new students in The Howling Meadow ready for their Awakening as my heart thrashed and rioted in my chest.

Darcy stepped away from me and my fingers balled and unballed as I stared after her, a growl rolling low through my throat as I worked to fight against the thirst, and the other, hungry part of me which had awoken.

Darcy glanced back at me in alarm. "What's going on?" she asked, her green eyes dancing with panic. I guessed this really was a mindfuck.

"Did you just drug us?" Tory rounded on me.

"What is it with you and drugs?" I muttered. *"Remember to keep calm,"* I commanded, needing them to get through this without making a complete scene.

I had to know what Elements they possessed. Lionel would be waiting for me to call and give him a play by play of everything that had happened tonight, everything I'd learned about the Vegas. But there was one thing for sure I wouldn't tell even Darius about this night. That I felt a pull to one of them that defied all logic and made my hatred for them deepen. Because of all the concerns I'd had about the Vega twins returning to Solaria, none of my imaginings had conjured up this.

Maybe it was the power of their blood that called to me, but as it was only Darcy who had made me fucking burn with unwanted need, I doubted I could put it down to that. One thing was for sure, I'd be cutting these twisted urges out of me just as soon as I could. And they were not going to affect anything about what came next. Because the Vega twins would not be ascending to the throne. It was my duty to make sure of that. And no girl with blue-tipped hair in bunny pyjamas was going to fuck with my plans.

DARIUS

CHAPTER TWO

Laughter filled the room around us as we sat in our usual spot, lounging together on the red couch in the centre of The Orb while making sure everyone around us could see just how relaxed and unconcerned we all were.

The other Celestial Heirs were putting on a show, laughing and joking, complaining loudly about how long The Awakening was taking this year and suggesting that maybe the Vegas had turned mortal during their time away from Solaria and didn't have any magic in them anymore.

I didn't need to put on a show the way the others did. Not that there was anything out of the ordinary about Seth mouthing off while Caleb laughed his ass off and Max bolstered the emotions which were running high all around us. But I knew there was an edge to their behaviour tonight. Because this was when everything we'd spent our entire lives preparing for could change. Not that I had any intention of letting that happen.

Seth started telling a loud and in-depth story about some pack gang bang he'd been taking part in last night and I tuned him out while every Wolf in the room panted over the details. A lot of them started batting their eyelashes, flexing their muscles or biting their lips in hopes of getting an invite to the next session, but all of that sharing shit wasn't for me. If I was going to take a girl to bed with me, then I was going to be her one and only focus and she sure as fuck wouldn't have time to be thinking about someone else.

I reclined in my seat, my mind wandering as I went over the conversation I'd had with my father this morning about the return of the Vega twins today. He had hoped that Lance would have been able to locate them months ago, return them to the fold. Then he'd wanted them to spend those few months in Solaria staying with the Celestial Families so that they could figure out for themselves early on that their place was beneath us now. And to make certain that they had no insane ideas of reclaiming their father's throne.

I knew what my father had intended to do with that time. He'd been planning on filling the twins' heads with all the worst deeds the Savage King had ever committed and making absolutely certain that they believed in his plans for the future of Solaria.

He'd even mentioned the use of Cyclops manipulation to me if it came down to it and I knew that he had more extreme plans than that in mind too. Not that he even deigned to share much of his plotting with me. But he had wanted those girls beaten before they ever came to this academy. Though of course the stars had chosen another route.

I already hated the twin girls who were currently standing beneath the stars and calling for their power to be Awakened. They'd made this last summer hell for me and my brother. Their mere existence and the fact that Lance had been struggling to track them down for so long meant that Father had been in a perpetually bad mood.

The Celestial Councillors had been having meeting after meeting about the return of the Vega twins and what it meant for the entire kingdom. The royalists were a serious pain in our asses. They'd been fairly harmless in the years since the Savage King had died, because without an heir to the Vega bloodline, there was no one for them to rally behind. The worst we'd had to contend with was them insisting upon my father and the other Councillors fighting for dominance to see if a new king or queen would emerge between them.

But the four families had always been evenly matched and when the tournament had taken place, that had only been proven for the whole of Solaria to see. And it had only cemented the bond between me and the three men sharing this couch with me today.

The entire kingdom had been happy with the plans for us to rule after our parents. They'd wanted it. There hadn't been any alternative. Until now.

All of those long and clearly aggravating meetings with the Celestial Council had ended with my father in a raging temper and his return to the manor inevitably ended in a violent outburst of some kind.

I'd taken the brunt of it during the summer, shielding Xavier and our mother from his wrath whenever I could. But now that I was back at Zodiac Academy, my gut felt knotted with concern for them, left in that house with him.

I had one shining beacon of hope for their safety though. One single purpose which my father had snarled in my face while pinning me against his office wall this morning. I needed to get rid of the Vega problem for him. He wanted them broken, unable to even raise their gaze to meet ours, let alone consider standing against us. And I was more than happy to take on that task if it meant keeping him happy, keeping my family safe from his rage.

I rubbed a hand over my jaw, imagining I could still feel an ache in the bone where he'd broken it before I'd left to return to the academy. I knew that I'd done a perfect job of healing the injury, but sometimes the echoes of the pain he inflicted upon me lingered all the same.

"Here we go," Seth hissed excitedly, dropping down onto the seat beside mine and practically bouncing up and down as the first of the newly Awakened students began to file into the room.

An excited shriek drew my attention to my right and I spotted Geraldine Grus clutching what looked like a handmade welcome home card in her fist while her whole body vibrated with excitement, making me wonder if she was about to lose control of her Order form.

"Hey, Grus!" Max called, drawing her attention for a moment, though she looked less than pleased about that. "Have you been flicking the bean over this moment all week? Because you look about ready to come from excitement alone."

"I very much doubt you have the skills required to know when a lady is about to orgasm, you vulgar ruffian. So kindly take your eyes off of my visage and return to your lollygagging with the other mutts on the reject pile," she replied with a dismissive wave of her arm.

Max's scowl darkened and he flicked a hand out, using his air magic to whip the card from Geraldine's grasp and directed it over to us. He snatched it out of the air with a wicked smirk and I glanced at the watercolour painting of two girls sitting on a throne together while a very Geraldine like figure prostrated herself on the floor at their feet.

"Give that back you clam handed cretin!" Geraldine cried, taking a step towards us before pausing and looking back towards the door where the new students were continuing to file in.

There was no sign of Lance, or any twins yet but my pulse was picking up and I exchanged a dark look with Caleb. This was it. Any minute now we'd look upon the faces of the girls set to throw our world into chaos.

"Look at this shit," Max growled, thrusting the now open card in front of the rest of us and I glanced down to read the note written within it.

Oh glorious queens who were lost for so long,

Where have you been all this time you were gone?

I wished on a star for a miracle to come,

And now you've returned, I know I got one.

I missed you more than words can say,

And I pledge my devotion to you on this day.

I threw a glare Geraldine's way, but she'd lost all interest in us, her wide eyes now fixed firmly on the door where the new students were entering The Orb as she looked fit to burst with excitement all over again.

"Fuck that," Caleb muttered, flicking a flame at the card so that it was reduced to ash in less than a heartbeat and Max laughed loudly.

My lips parted to say something, but I forgot what it had been as my gaze fell on the girl who had just stepped into the room.

My thumping pulse picked up speed for a wholly different reason as I drank her in. Long, black hair tumbled down her spine, her green eyes turned up towards the curving roof as she drank in the sight of the building she was in. Her lips were full and primed for tasting, but the set of her mouth said she was more used to frowning than smiling. She was without a doubt, the most stunning creature I'd ever laid my eyes upon and I couldn't help but stare at her as she moved deeper into the room with the other students.

I felt a silencing bubble closing around me as one of the others tossed it up to allow us to speak freely, but I didn't look away from her. My gaze was riveted to her as I drank in every small movement of her body and each expression crossing her face. I didn't give a fuck about the Vegas showing up tonight anymore. I just wanted to know that girl a whole lot better than I did.

"Holy fuck," Caleb murmured beside me and a deep growl rolled through my chest as I got the impression his gaze was fixed where mine was.

"Mine," I snarled, the beast in me waking up and my eyes shifting into reptilian slits as if my Dragon was aching for a look at her too.

Every muscle in my body tensed and I was filled with the insane urge to get out of my seat and stride straight up to that girl and claim her in front of every fucker here. I didn't even know her name. I didn't know what Order she was or how powerful she was or any of the things like that which should have mattered to me. But I didn't care. Because the only thing about her that mattered in that moment was that I was laying my claim.

The Dragon in me demanded it.

"Well shit, I didn't consider the fact that they might be hot," Seth cursed and I frowned a little at his words, trying to piece them together.

"That'll make things more interesting," Max agreed.

"I wanna know how good they taste," Caleb said with a barely stifled groan.

I didn't want to listen to any of them, but their words kept pushing in on me while I continued to stare at my mystery girl.

"Oh great, Nova is straight in for an ass licking," Seth groaned just as our Principal made it to my girl and caught her arm.

I frowned, my brain finally catching up to the words of my brothers as I tore my gaze from the temptation of that beautiful creature to the students closest to her.

My heart lurched as I spotted the girl right beside her, wondering how the fuck I could have missed the fact that there were two of them while I'd been so caught up in staring at her.

The second girl looked strikingly like her sister, though for some reason I felt like I'd know which was which in the dark. I wasn't sure what it was. But despite their equally attractive looks, my attention was pulled back towards the first girl like the stars wanted it to be on her.

Nova kept prattling on to the twins while my brothers all hissed plans back and forth between each other. Our parents had been more than clear on this. The Vega twins needed to go. We were expected to make sure that happened. That was all that mattered. My dick's interest in getting to know one of them a whole lot more intimately had no bearing on anything.

Movement in the crowd drew my attention and I looked around on instinct, tearing my gaze from the girl I couldn't want and spotting Lance as he slipped between the students.

The brand on my arm itched like it wanted me to run to him, hold him tight and sniff his hair just a little. Fuck, I'd missed him. Though at least the bond hadn't been driving me towards him while he'd been away in the Mortal Realm. In fact, the bond had been so deadened by the split between realms that I'd been able to keep up a perfectly normal routine while he was gone.

Of course, I'd still missed him. He was the one person in this world who I could be entirely honest with. I loved the other Heirs, but there were things my father made certain I didn't share with them, plus things I chose not to because I didn't want them trying to step in. Not to mention the hobbies me and Lance took part in.

If they had a clue just how bad my father was, I was certain they'd try and do something about it or get their parents to, but I knew that would only make things worse. Lionel Acrux was my cross to bear, and I wasn't going to be burdening them with him too.

Lance arched a brow at me, trying to convey some message while looking like someone had just taken a shit in his bourbon. He took his Atlas from his pocket and shot me a message as he headed towards the other professors at the side of the room.

I pulled my Atlas from my pocket, glancing down at the message and feeling something inside my chest crumpling away to nothing but dust as I drank in the information he'd just given me and let the others read it too.

Lance:

Both Vega twins just unlocked ALL FOUR elements. Shit is about to get interesting.

"That can't be true," Seth scoffed, looking between my Atlas and the twins who were still talking to Nova, looking like a pair of lost lambs.

None of us bothered to answer him because we could hear the rumour spreading across The Orb now as the students who had been there to see it with their own eyes all whispered excitedly about the Vega twins gaining all of the Elements.

My pulse was thundering now, my mind skipping over the reaction I knew my father was going to have to this news. I needed to go to him, be the one to tell him about this and take the brunt of his fury over it otherwise Xavier and my mom would be the ones to suffer. But as I glanced about at the gossiping students who surrounded me, I knew that wasn't going to happen. The rumour was spreading, it would be in the hands of the press before I even managed to leave this fucking room and his wrath would only be worse if I walked out on my responsibilities here.

I quickly sent my brother a message to warn him, hoping he would have enough notice to get himself and Mother out of the house for the evening. Or even just to fucking hide until Father was forced to leave them for another meeting with the Celestial Council. Which would definitely happen once this information got to them. Because this was bad. People already knew that the Vegas were bound to be more powerful than us and now they were the first Fae to claim all four elements in fuck knew how long too. The royalists were going to have a fucking field day over this.

Darius:

The Vega girls got all four Elements.

I didn't need to say more than that to my younger brother. He'd know exactly why I was telling him that.

Xavier:

Two steps ahead of you, dude. I already arranged for mom to take me to visit with one of her boring friends tonight. I knew them coming back wouldn't go well, no matter what way it worked out.

I breathed a sigh of relief at knowing he was safe for now and shoved my Atlas away again.

Geraldine Grus was sobbing happy tears while murmuring, "All praise the heavens and their divine intervention! Today two stars were returned to walk among us and lead us all into prosperity!"

"Fuck. This is bad," Max said in a low tone while making an effort to keep looking like he gave no shits.

"Bad?" Cal scoffed. "This is a fucking disaster. Every fucker in the kingdom is gonna think this is some sort of sign from fate-"

"No they're not," I said firmly, refusing to even consider these girls as a threat. Because if they were stronger than we'd allowed ourselves to believe, if they were more capable and fiercer, then we just needed to up our game. It didn't matter in the end. "We have a goal and we stick to that. We go as hard as we have to."

My muscles tensed as I tried to figure out just how hard that might be. I'd lost a lot of my limitations a long time ago. Father had seen to that. I knew how to take all kinds of pain and I'd learned exactly how best to inflict it first hand too. The point was, that when it came down to it if I had to pick between some girls I didn't know and my own family's safety then there was no question of how far I was willing to go.

Besides, I did believe in this decision myself. The other Heirs and I had spent our entire lives training for our positions. Ignoring our strength and power, we were still the best candidates for the role of ruling this kingdom. We knew its people, its laws, the needs and requirements there were to provide everything that Solaria had to have to prosper. The Vegas had grown up as mortals. They knew nothing of our people, let alone how to run a kingdom and I refused to allow them to get strong enough to threaten the safety of Solaria as a whole by challenging us for our rule over it.

"Can I have everyone's attention?" Nova called and everyone in the room fell quiet, wanting to hear what she had to say about the Vega twins.

Seth shifted beside me, his arm brushing mine in his Wolfy way and I allowed it, knowing he needed the solidarity. He leaned forward eagerly, tilting his head to one side as he surveyed them, balancing his chin on his fist as a low, warning growl escaped him, soft enough that only we would have been able to hear it even without the silencing bubble.

"This year's attendees have been joined by two particularly important girls," Principal Nova said, with a big smile as every fucker in the room stared, on tenterhooks. "I am delighted to announce that we have recovered the missing Vega Heirs and brought them back under the protection of our great nation. For seventeen years the Vega twins were lost to us, believed to be dead. But to our great surprise, with the surfacing of their powers on their eighteenth birthday we were able to track them down in the Mortal Realm and return them to their rightful place amongst us."

A long, tense beat of silence fell as eyes turned our way, gauging our reaction while we held ourselves in check. Then Geraldine lost her shit and leapt to her feet, screaming and clapping and generally looking like a fucking idiot. Others joined in and some asshole got in my way, blocking my view of the twin with the black hair.

I moved before I could stop myself, leaning forward and resting my forearms on my knees as I drank in the sight of her. I knew I needed to stop, to pull my gaze from the bare skin of her waist and the tanned flesh there which ached for the touch of my tongue. I shouldn't have been staring at the curves of her body or thinking any of the things which were currently circling through my mind, but fuck. She looked like the most perfect kind of seduction.

I dragged my eyes up and over every inch of her body, lingering on her mouth for a beat too long before finding her eyes. My fist clenched as I met her green gaze and it felt like a shot of power snapped from her soul right into mine. I was held captive there, wanting her and hating her for it. Hating her for all the reasons I knew I had to hate her, but just fucking wanting her all the same. *Fuck*.

There was a challenge in her gaze which needed stamping out and as she raised her chin a fraction, still maintaining eye contact with me, I couldn't help but think up all of the best ways that I'd like to bring her under my control. The Dragon in me was shifting beneath my skin at the challenge she presented, hungering for the chance to put her in her place beneath me. And ideally if I could get her there willingly, then I could show her how good it could feel to be beneath me anyway.

People were still clapping and cheering and she moved her gaze away from mine. Not like she'd been forced to back down, but more like she was just done looking at me. And another growl rumbled in my chest at the thought of that. People didn't do that shit to me.

"They're coming over," Seth hissed excitedly. "Be cool, be cool."

"We're all cool, dude. You're the one bouncing," Cal teased as the silencing bubble surrounding us was withdrawn.

My jaw ticked at the audacity of our fucking principal, but I was willing to let it slide, mostly because I wanted this confrontation. I wanted a chance to look at these girls up close and in the flesh and see what they were made of for myself.

"Gentlemen," Principal Nova purred as she gave the twins a nudge towards us and they eyed us cautiously. The one with the blue tips to her hair looked like she wanted to be anywhere other than here while the darker one looked inclined to punch one of us if we pushed her the wrong way. *Bring it on, baby.* "These are the Celestial Heirs," Nova went on, naming us from left to right. "Max Rigel, Caleb Altair, Darius Acrux and Seth Capella." If our names meant anything to them they didn't let it show, their gazes skimming over us like we were of very little interest to them and not at all relevant in their lives. But that was all about to change. "This is Gwendalina and Roxanya Vega-"

"Those aren't our names," the object of my attention interrupted in a hard voice which made me both pay attention and want to make her submit to me even more than I had before she opened that pretty mouth of hers. "I'm

Tory and that's Darcy."

"I'm aware that your Changeling family gave you the names of their birth children," Nova said, sounding amused and Caleb grinned widely as he watched the twins with interest. "But now that you're home you don't have to keep using-"

"I like my name," the blue tipped one interjected.

"I'm sure as shit not going to start going by Roxanya," my girl agreed in a tone that closed the subject for further discussion.

I rolled the idea of her preferred name around in my mind, finding I both liked the idea of that and didn't at once. If I called her Tory, then I could let myself forget who she was. *What* she was. I could play pretend with these fantasies I was having and maybe let myself get a little carried away with them too. But that would be a problem. If I let the idea of her being a Tory creep into my mind then I might start to forget that she was so much more than that. So no, I wouldn't be using that name, I'd be sticking with Roxanya. Or maybe Roxy, because that had a ring to it which I knew would roll right off of my tongue with a Dragon's growl whenever I deigned to speak it. And the fact that she didn't want to be called that only encouraged me further. I was starting to think that there would be worse things I could spend my time doing than making this girl all hot and irritable for me.

Principal Nova pursed her lips like she was planning to argue against the use of their mortal names, but the twins glared at her in a way that made it pretty clear their decision was made on this. She sighed like that irritated her then turned to look at the four of us again. "Well whatever names you go by, you're still Vegas. The last in your line and rightful holders of the Solarian throne once you come of age. So long as you pass your assessments here and go on to graduate from Zodiac you will reclaim the throne from the Celestial Heirs." She waved a hand at the four of us and my upper lip pulled back a touch as I fought against the urge to snap at her for that little suggestion. As our principal, she was in a position that demanded respect, but I'd gladly inform the

Celestial Council of where our principal's loyalties lay in regards to the throne. As Nova looked to us again, her eyes sparkled with amusement. "I do hope you hadn't gotten too comfortable with the idea of holding the throne together. I'm sure you'll want to be the first to offer the girls the hand of friendship as they embark upon this journey of education."

The four of us outwardly bristled at that suggestion, my brothers' postures shifting just as my own was and the amusement falling from us as we formed a united front without even needing to look between each other. The Vega twins were nothing more than an inconvenience to us. One which we had been tasked to deal with promptly. And we'd be getting that job done before the week was out if all went to plan.

I raised my chin, letting my eyes drag over Roxy's figure again as I gave the two of them my most charming bullshit smile, the one the cameras loved and let me get away with saying whatever the fuck I liked.

"Did you say they've been hiding in the Mortal Realm?" I asked Nova curiously, like I didn't know that already. Like I hadn't been getting updates from Lance during his hunt for them with every little drop of information he found on them included. "Without an ounce of training at all?"

Roxy's eyes were on me and I flicked my gaze up to meet hers, drinking in the suspicion in those big green eyes of hers as the corner of my mouth lifted in amusement. She saw right through me. I could see it. I could see *her*. And the monster in her was all hungry fire and determination.

"Well I'm sure you boys will be more than willing to bring them up to speed." Nova patted the twins on their shoulders affectionately then strode off and abandoned them to us.

The four of us perked up instantly, each of us leaning a little closer to the two girls who still stood awkwardly in front of us, looking like they wanted nothing more than to be anywhere else.

Seth nudged me subtly and I could feel his excitement. This was a game to him. He was a dog with a tasty snack in his sights and I knew he was looking forward to chewing it up and spitting it out. I didn't miss how his eyes followed the one with the blue-tipped hair either, which was fine by me as my interest was locked on the other.

"Can you feel that power?" Caleb asked, leaning towards the girls with a smile playing around his lips and I knew in that moment what he was planning. I could practically feel the hunger in him and I had to force back a growl which rose in my throat at the thought of him biting them. Biting her. I wasn't sure what it was about Roxy which kept making me focus on her. Maybe it was the fire in her eyes or the way she didn't even seem to give a fuck about being thrown at our mercy. Or maybe I just really, really wanted in her panties. But either way, I was filled with the desire to tell Caleb and the others to back the fuck off and leave her to me.

But I didn't. That wasn't how the four of us worked. So despite my instincts craving that, I held my tongue, biting down on any commands I might have been aching to bark at my friends as I waited to see how this would play out.

Gwendalina stepped back, seeming to be done with us as Roxy frowned at Cal. The rest of us just watched, waiting, knowing he was on the edge of breaking that leash of control he held over his base instincts. He hadn't fed from anyone today and now I was starting to realise why. He'd decided to get a taste of Vega.

"I guess we'll see you around," Roxy said dismissively, turning her back on us and making the four of us straighten in anger instantly.

We shoved to our feet and the room fell quiet as we moved to box the twins in, testosterone and anger rippling through the air as we closed in on them. No. Fuck no. They weren't going to be turning their fucking backs on us.

"That was a little rude," Seth growled in a low tone as he looked down at Roxy, his hair spilling forward as he pushed into her personal space.

"Cut them some slack, Seth," I said as I stepped closer too, making sure they had nowhere to run to. Roxy bristled and I swear the flash of rage in her eyes shot a jolt of excitement right to my cock. *Fuck she'd look good being bent to my will.* "They don't know how it works here yet. I'm guessing you didn't realise that turning your back on your superiors is considered an insult?" I asked her kindly, though I could tell she knew there was nothing kind in my question. It was a warning. Plain and simple. They needed to figure out how this was going to work and fast or they'd be regretting it.

Roxy turned her gaze on me, tilting her head back to look up at me. She didn't even flinch. Not a flicker of fear or concern on her face, just disdain and irritation as she sneered at me openly. I wasn't sure anyone had ever dared to look at me like that before and it sent a little spike of adrenaline racing through my limbs. This girl was going to pose a challenge. I could see it already. And I couldn't even pretend that the idea of that didn't excite me a little.

"Superiors?" she asked, arching an eyebrow at me and making a good show of seeming wholly unimpressed. "I don't see anyone superior to me around here."

"Well maybe you should look a little closer, *Roxy*," I taunted, baiting her, waiting to see how she liked the sound of that and wondering how long it would take before I'd have her begging me to call her it while I pinned her beneath me.

She looked around at the four of us like she was far less than impressed, her sister doing the same at her side before she shrugged. "I can't see anyone better than us here. How about you, Darcy?"

"Nope," Gwen replied dismissively.

I opened my mouth to continue that discussion, but before I could get so much as a word out, Roxy very purposefully turned her fucking back on me again. The two of them shoving Max and Cal aside as they started to walk away like they seriously thought we'd let them get away with that shit.

A snarl ripped up the back of my throat, my skin heating as my fire magic flared in outrage and begged me to put them in their places beneath my heel.

"I think they could do with a lesson in how things work around here," Max growled as they just kept fucking walking like they didn't have a care in the world.

"On it," Cal said with a wide grin, shooting forward before I could say a word against it and making my blood boil even hotter as he slammed right into my girl and threw her back against the nearest wall.

"Cal," I snarled in warning, knowing he could hear me despite me keeping my voice low, but the asshole just grinned wider like he knew I'd been planning on staking a claim on her and didn't give a single shit about it.

"Wanna beg for forgiveness?" Caleb purred, eyeing her throat hungrily.

"What the hell are you doing?" Gwen yelled, trying to get to them to pull Caleb away from her sister, but Max got to her first, laughing darkly as he yanked her into his arms and held her back.

Roxy still didn't give up, trying to pull her wrists out of Caleb's grasp while I forced myself to remain statue still and watch them, folding my arms over my chest in an attempt to hide the tension in my body.

The Dragon in me was a possessive motherfucker and all I could think of while I watched her in his arms was that I would really enjoy tearing him away from her and beating the ever living shit out of his pretty boy face. Fucking asshole. I might have loved him, but right now I would have happily torn his head from his shoulders for touching what was mine.

Only the fact that I knew that made no fucking sense and that we had an audience of Fae who would happily sell us out to the press held me in place. It wasn't like I had a reason against putting her into her place. I just wanted to be the one doing it.

A breath of laughter escaped me as Roxy tried to knee him in the balls and Seth grinned at me excitedly as he nuzzled into my side for a moment. Sadly, Cal avoided the ball shot and managed to firm up his hold on her.

"Last chance," he offered, toying with his food. We all knew he wouldn't be letting her go without taking a bite now no matter what she said.

"Fuck you," Roxy snapped and that really only made me like her more. Yeah, I could admit I liked her. She had fight in her, the kind of spirit that couldn't be broken easily. And I could see it was going to take more than I'd expected to fulfil the promise I'd made to my father to get rid of her and her sister. But I relished the challenge in her eyes, the beast in me more than ready to go up against her and win.

"I hoped you'd say that," Caleb replied, dropping his mouth to her neck and biting her before she could voice any more complaints.

Roxy yelled in alarm, bucking against him and trying to fight him off despite the fact that she had no chance now that his venom was in her blood.

A crowd had gathered to watch, plenty of them keen to see the first showdown between the Heirs and the lost princesses and I was pleased to say that we were clearly coming out on top even if I was planning on kicking Caleb's ass as soon as I got the chance.

Max kept hold of Gwen despite her thrashing and cursing him out and I could tell he was having a feast on her rage while she lost her shit.

Roxy's gaze fell to me while Caleb continued to drink from her and for a moment the look in her eyes sent a spike of guilt tearing through my chest. She had no fucking idea what she'd just walked into by coming back here and if she thought this was bad then she was in for one hell of a ride.

I hardened my gaze, smirking at her to make sure she could see all the worst pieces of me. I could practically see the hatred forming within those big green eyes of hers. And despite the fact that that should have been exactly what I wanted from her, I couldn't help but feel like I'd just fucked up somehow. Like I'd failed at something without even knowing what it was. But if the defiance in her eyes was anything to go by then I knew that this wouldn't be our only showdown. So I was going to have to tighten up my hold on my feelings over this shit because it had to be done. These girls could put the whole of Solaria at risk and it was my job to make sure that didn't happen.

So game on, Vegas. This was only going to be the beginning.

My gaze fell to the point where Caleb's hand was pressed against her waist and a growl rumbled in my chest as I forced myself to remain still. She'd gotten the fucking point already, so why the hell was he still holding onto her like that?

My muscles locked as the desire to rip him off of her mixed with the need to see her put in her place within me and I gritted my jaw against the desire to move towards them. I didn't know why, but I wanted this girl to be my problem. Not his. And the desire to lay that claim down was making the Dragon beneath my skin writhe with need.

But before I could make any stupid decisions like striding over there and tearing my best friend off of her, a furious snarl tore from the lips of the other Vega who Max still held in his grasp.

"Let me go!" Gwendalina commanded and I almost laughed at her before an explosion of energy tore from her body and damn near knocked me off my feet.

Max was hurled clean across The Orb with a surprised cry before slamming into the wall on the far side of the space and tumbling out of sight amongst the students there. I was pretty sure I heard Geraldine Grus whoop and call him a pestersome plankton.

My lips parted in surprise as Caleb jerked away from Roxy to see what the fuck had happened and Seth practically started vibrating with the desire to fight.

I caught his wrist in my grasp, squeezing once to warn him to back off as I schooled my own features. Every fucker in this room was looking at us and no doubt there were more than a few Atlases recording the whole thing too. There was no fucking way we were going to let anyone see that the half terrified looking girl standing before us had just taken us off guard.

My gaze skimmed over the twin with the blue tips to her hair as she gaped in the direction she'd hurled Max, her hands still held up before her and the look of shock on her face making it clear she hadn't been expecting that any more than the rest of us had.

I kept my expression flat, my mind spinning as I took in this turn of events. She may have been new to her powers, but there had been no mistaking the raw brutality of that energy she'd just used. I wasn't going to let her know that it had been anything unusual or noteworthy though.

"You're gonna regret that," I said simply, my muscles bunching as I forced myself to remain still.

Seth grinned wickedly at my side, clearly hearing the threat in my voice and more than ready to make a start on our plans against these girls.

Roxy shoved Caleb away from her, clutching her neck as he licked his lips to taste the last drops of her blood and my gaze was instantly riveted on her once more.

"What the hell is wrong with you, you psycho!?" she snarled at him.

Caleb started laughing, several of his little fan club joining in while I painted a smirk on my face at her outrage too. It looked like the poor little Vegas really didn't know what they were getting themselves into by coming here.

Gwen moved towards her sister, closing the distance between them with concern filling her eyes.

"Are you alright?" she asked as Roxy looked down at her blood-stained fingers and she just nodded, looking more pissed off than upset about her little bite.

The urge to step forward and heal it away to remove the evidence of Caleb's touch from her flesh filled me and the Dragon in me huffed with annoyance as I resisted it. No matter how much the sight of those puncture marks on her neck pissed me off, I knew it was better to leave her with them. Healing might make it seem like I cared about her wellbeing, but that couldn't have been further from the truth.

Max shoved his way through the crowd as he stalked back into the fight, shoving his sleeves up as the crowd of onlookers parted for him quickly, not wanting to fall prey to his rage.

"Back off," Roxy spat at him, moving closer to her sister as if she planned on saving her from the wrath of the oncoming Fae. I ignored the tug I felt in reaction to that - I knew full well what it was like to put myself between my sibling and danger and it looked a lot like she and I held that trait in common.

"Or what?" I asked, wanting her attention back on me while Seth laughed like a hyena, no doubt having trouble controlling his excitement over the drama unfolding around us.

Geraldine Grus shoved through the crowd looking furious and my upper lip peeled back at this show of her support for the fucking royals. It was exactly what we'd feared - the royalists would all start emerging from the corners they'd been hiding in since the Savage King had died and the political stability of the kingdom was going to be unbalanced. And with the Nymphs closing in around the edges of Solaria, we couldn't afford that kind of distraction. My father and the other Councillors had good reason to need the Vega problem dealt with quickly, and my brothers and I were more than up for the task.

"Or we'll fight for our queens!" Geraldine cried, planting herself between the twins and Max who raised his hand anyway, looking more than happy to fight her first if he needed to.

"Multiple Element freshmen, it's time to choose your houses!" Principal Nova called loudly and I took the opportunity to intervene.

There wasn't a lot to be gained by us advancing on the Vegas now. They had no training - hell, they'd probably struggle to summon any more magic at all right now, so it wasn't exactly going to be a hot look for us to force them beneath us with brute force tonight. It would only stoke the flames of the royalists' bullshit. I could see the headlines now 'Heirs attack untrained Vega Princesses on their first night in Solaria.' Fuck that. We could play a much smarter game.

Seth and Cal seemed to be thinking along the same lines as me and we shoved past Grus and her little gang of followers to intercept Max.

"Not now," I growled at him, laying a hand on his shoulder and urging him to turn away. He gave in with a grunt of frustration and we moved away from the Vega twins to discuss our next move.

Nova was gathering all the freshmen together in preparation for them choosing their Houses.

"I'm gonna take great pleasure in destroying those two," Max snarled, his embarrassment over being caught off guard like that clear, but hell, none of us would have expected an untrained Fae to be able to pack a punch like that, let alone call on their magic without the first bit of understanding on how to do so.

"We've got plenty of time," Caleb said. "I'm personally hoping to get that blood on tap in Terra House because she tasted like fucking ecstasy."

I growled at him and he arched an eyebrow at me, a smirk tugging at the corner of his lips like he could sense the challenge in the air between us without me needing to say a damn word on the subject. The asshole always did love to push my fucking buttons.

"I say we give them hell at the hazings tonight," Seth said excitedly. "Give them a real taste of what it takes to be Fae. They'll run from here so fast we won't even remember the name Vega by this time next week."

"I hope they choose Aqua then," Max said in a low growl as he narrowed his eyes at the twins across the room. "Because I want some payback before they leave this place."

"House Captains!" Nova beckoned us over as the rest of the students took their seats again. We strode forward to stand before the assembled freshmen and I had to fight a smirk at the look of horrified understanding as it dawned across the twins' faces. My gaze zeroed in on Roxy as she scowled at me and I had to fight an actual smirk. *Yeah baby girl, we rule this place. Better start getting used to that.* "State the name of your house and why the freshmen should pledge to join you. And for a little suspense, we›ll leave the newest Heirs 'til last," she said excitedly.

I fought the eye roll I wanted to offer Nova for her theatrics over the return of the Vegas. She was fucking loving this. No doubt every Fae in the room was too. There hadn't been any chance of anyone challenging us and our power in all the time we'd been here. Hell, the day we arrived at Zodiac Academy, we'd already had years of magical training and we challenged the four House Captains for their places and moved ourselves straight into the best rooms in each of our respective Houses. No one had doubted our power then and I'd be fucked if they were going to start doubting it because of a pair of girls who had been raised by mortals. My father called Nova a power slut. She'd follow whoever held the most sway in the room and up until now that had been us. And I intended to keep it that way.

Max stepped forward first, scraping a hand over his mohawk with a challenging grin which I knew meant he was out for blood. "Water focus, House Aqua. My house is for those who have what it takes to face the deadly sea of life in Zodiac without flinching."

"Thank you for that poetic description," Nova said, clearing her throat before indicating for Cal to speak next.

Caleb dutifully stepped up, smiling his pretty boy smile in that way that got girls panties to combust and pissing me off even more as he dragged his eyes over my girl. "Earth focus, House Terra. And terror is exactly what you'll get if you don't fit in."

Roxy muttered something to her sister as she shot a venomous look Caleb's way, and I was pleased to see that she at least didn't seem to be inclined to turn all blood whore for him. If she'd started panting over the idea of him biting her again, I had to admit I'd probably have thrown down with him here and now. I didn't know why it was pissing me off so much, but it was. I'd claimed her the moment I saw her, and I knew that with his Vampire hearing he'd been damn well aware of it. Which meant this was a challenge to my command. And of course, I should have expected that because there wasn't a single one of my brothers who would bow to the others, but it still got me all kinds of pissed at him.

Seth pranced forwards, looking all cute and puppy like though I knew that only meant he was even closer to going for the kill. He had his heart set on playing with the Vegas tonight and this little show was all dirty tactics. "Air focus, House Aer. Life with us is a breeze." He even gave the twins a welcoming smile and by the looks they were giving him in return, they'd just fallen for it too. More fool them.

I took my turn next, not minding the way Roxy's gaze fixed on me the moment I stepped forward. She was drinking me in, assessing me just like I was her and if I wasn't mistaken, the two of us were headed for one hell of a showdown pretty damn soon. I just hoped she enjoyed the taste of defeat.

"Fire focus, House Ignis. We aren't for the faint of heart. And frankly I don't see anyone in this line-up who's good enough to join us," I taunted, offering up a challenge which I was sure they'd be too afraid to take up while kinda hoping they tried anyway.

Nova started moving through the freshmen who headed towards the four of us as they picked their houses, waiting to see what we had in store for them, but I didn't pay them any attention. None of them mattered. Not one. There was only a single focus for me in this room and I just waited on the two of them to take their turn picking at the end.

When it was just the twins standing there, my pulse began to quicken. They wouldn't pick Ignis. I knew it. I'd made it clear they wouldn't be in for an easy ride with me and the way Gwen was whispering in her sister's ear and giving Seth a hopeful look, I could tell they'd fallen for his trap. But before they could get the words out, Principal Nova interrupted them, making the game a whole lot more interesting.

"You will have to pick differently girls, I'm afraid. Each House is very competitive and we encourage everyone to take part in the healthy rivalry. As you have so much power, it wouldn't be fair for one House to be at such an advantage."

I watched as Gwen's face dropped, her lips parting and panic darting within her eyes. Roxy just looked pissed. So fucking pissed. And I couldn't help but take pleasure in the sight of her jaw grinding and the way she gave absolutely no shits about letting us and the whole world know that she hated us. I wasn't sure why I found it so hot, but getting under her skin was quickly becoming my favourite new hobby.

"Well that's just perfect," she muttered, glaring over at us like we were a thorn in her side sent to ruin her day.

"We'll be housed separately?" Gwen confirmed with Nova.

"Ohh are you gonna cry?" Max taunted, his amusement thickening the air so that I had to fight off the desire to laugh with him.

"I choose fire," Roxy announced loudly, taking me by surprise and making my heart jerk in my chest. Had I heard that right? Was she seriously choosing me over the others? Why? Did she have a death wish or was she just proving how fucking stupid she was right now?

Or was it something eternally more interesting than that? Was she rising to the challenge I was laying down? Because I didn't want that - I just wanted her to turn tail and run from here like she was supposed to. And yet...the idea of going to bat against this girl was making my pulse hammer and the beast in me stir with excitement. Was it possible that she might actually be looking to make a stand here?

Roxy stalked towards me, her gaze defiant and holding mine like she didn't feel the least bit intimidated by me. She didn't even move to stand behind me like the rest of the freshmen, instead taking a spot right at my side and tilting her head just the smallest fraction as if daring me to do my worst.

I looked right back, drinking her in, taking in the fire that burned in her soul and the heat which seemed to simmer between us. This girl was going to be trouble. I could tell already. The best kind of trouble there was.

"Air," Gwen announced, but I hardly noticed, all of my attention taken up by the girl at my side.

Roxy rolled her eyes and looked away from me, folding her arms and turning to give me her profile as she glanced around the room. Dismissing me just like that. But that wasn't going to work for me.

"So what is it? A death wish or stupidity?" I asked as the other Heirs began leading their Houses away to start their initiations. I'd get to that, but for the moment, Roxy Vega had all of my attention.

She turned to look at me with bored eyes, her gaze dropping to my boots before crawling all the way up my body in a languid, lazy inspection that made my fucking dick jerk in my pants.

"I've known a lot of men who talk a big game in my lifetime, but most of them are just posturing assholes who don't have the balls to back it up. And I get the feeling that just might be you all over," she said, her voice this rich, seductive purr which had me hanging on every word.

I took a step closer to her, inhaling her air and forcing her to tilt her head back as she looked up at me.

"Nah," I replied in a low voice just for her. "I don't buy that for a second, Roxy. You didn't pick me because you thought I was full of shit."

"No?" she asked, holding my gaze and not looking the least bit inclined to back up which said a lot for her backbone. Or her idiocy. I still hadn't figured that out yet. "Why don't you enlighten me then?"

I licked my lips as I gave her the exact same kind of assessment she'd just offered me, spending more time than was necessary appreciating her curves before landing right back on that defiant flare in her big green eyes.

"I think you're looking for something to wake you up," I said slowly. "Something to rattle your cage and get your heart pumping. You aren't hoping I'm less than I make out - you're hoping I'm all of that and more. Because that fire in you is looking for something to make it burn hotter."

"I can promise you, you don't make me any kind of hot," she deadpanned, folding her arms over her chest.

"Good," I growled, moving in closer, wanting her to break, to back up, push me back a step or even just flinch. But she didn't. And somehow that only drew me in more. "You made a mistake picking my House. You won't be able to escape me now."

Roxy snorted, shaking her head at me like I was so fucking dumb. "I don't need to escape you, asshole. I don't need to do anything at all so far as you're concerned because beyond this moment, you won't even feature in my thoughts, let alone my fears. So how about you just keep out of my way and I'll keep out of yours? Because I seriously don't have space on my calendar for any of your drama."

She brushed past me before I got a moment to say another word, her arm knocking against mine just enough to show me the level of disrespect I was dealing with when it came to her.

A growl sounded in the back of my throat as I watched her walk away from me and my mind raced with all the ways I'd like to make her bend to my will.

Father had told me I was going to have to break the Vegas when they arrived here, but I had to say, I'd never expected to hunger for the challenge as much as I was right now. Roxy Vega had just laid out the gauntlet and I'd be certain not to disappoint her now that the game was on.

SETH

CHAPTER THREE

I had a little bluebird in my grasp and I was excited to see how well it could fly when I clipped its wings. *Damn the moon, this bluebird is pretty though.*

I led the Aer freshman across campus towards my House and my pack grouped around me, brushing their fingers over me as I picked up the pace and offered them a few smirks, Darcy was among the new pledges, my prey. Everyone here tonight was at my mercy and it was giving me a power high that had my head spinning.

We passed through The Wailing Wood and adrenaline coursed through my limbs as moonlight spilled through the branches, kissing my flesh. The moon winked at me through the branches and I winked back at her, sharing our little secret. She knew the deal, I'd be Alpha dogging tonight and she had my back like always.

We emerged from the trees and headed onto the sprawling clifftop where the huge tower stood, stretching up high above us, the dark grey bricks ancient and weathered. Vertical windows were built into the walls and at the very top was an enormous rotating wooden turbine which moved in a magical breeze cast there by the Fae who'd built it hundreds of years ago. Supposedly my great, great, great, great Uncle Felps had helped build those turbines and his power still resided within the eternal magical wind that turned them.

As we reached the entrance, I turned to face my victims beneath the arching doorway and they stared at me with excitement and nerves warring in their eyes. I raised a palm and cast air at the triangular symbol above the door, making it glow before the iron door unlocked.

"Freshmen, get your asses in front of me because I'm only gonna say this once," I called, my pack mates looking to me with a keen energy burning in their expressions.

I took in the new power at my academy as my pack surrounded me, their hands sweeping over me and their heads bowed in respect to their king. I could feel the stars watching this interaction and I knew it was important, especially as my gaze settled on the girl who'd just blasted one of my best friends across The Orb. A growl built in the back of my throat, but I didn't let it show on my face. No one hurt my friends and got away with it. Especially not a girl fresh from the Mortal Realm with big innocent Bambi eyes. She looked like prey in every way, and I'd be sure to make a slow and torturous meal of her.

"You don't get into Aer unless you use your power on that symbol." I pointed to the triangle above the door which was the sign of my dominant Element. "As it's your first day, I've already opened it but as of tomorrow if you can't conjure air, you don't get a bed in my House."

A flicker of determination crossed Darcy's features as she rubbed her fingers together to feel the magic within them, then she shared a smile with a beanie-hat-wearing boy beside her.

"Now." I smiled wide, showing rows of shiny teeth that could eat them all up if they ever crossed me. "Let's get on with it." I looked to Darcy, curling my finger to beckon her closer, needing to assess my enemy. Maybe I could make her submit to me, force her into the bottom feeders of my House and make her serve me like an Omega. Yeah, I liked the sound of that. A pet Vega.

She frowned, hesitating for one second before walking up to me and I slung an arm over her shoulders, tugging her hard against me. I breathed in the scent of her, finding I liked the sweetness around this girl as I stroked my fingers along the bare skin of her arm. She tried to pull away, but she was in my trap now and I held her tighter, reaching my fingers up into her hair instead. All of this goodness wasn't what I'd expected from a Vega. I'd pictured sharp teeth, claws and her father's angry face. But she was a red and juicy apple on a tree where all the others had grown black. Perhaps her darkness lived on the inside...

"Initiation!" I called and the swarm of older students behind the freshmen descended on them, shoving black linen bags over all of their heads.

I continued to paw at my new pet before leaning in and inhaling the sugary sweetness of her hair. *Submit, little pup. I'm your Alpha. And you're all mine.*

She shuddered, trying to push me back again but there was no magic in her attempt and I almost laughed as I kept hold of her. I ran my tongue up her cheek, tasting my enemy and finding her far more appetising than I wanted her to be. *I really could eat this one up. Bite by delicious bite.*

"Ergh!" She brought her hand up to slap me, but I caught it with ease, grinning at the defiance in her eyes. Yep, this girl was blackened on the inside just like her Daddy. And that darkness was going to spill out once she learned how to control her power. But if she was my little bitch at that point, then it wouldn't really matter.

I laughed at her furious expression. "Chill out, babe. This is how I say hello."

I cocked my head, showing her I meant no harm, when I really meant the exact opposite. She frowned, seeming to buy my puppy dog act and my heart jumped faster in excitement.

"Right," she said uneasily. "I'm just still trying to figure this all out."

I laughed then turned back to the crowd, my arm still locked tightly around her. *You'll figure it out soon enough.*

"What's your Order, babe?" I nuzzled against her ear and she stiffened from the contact. This Vega needed a long, hot bath and a chill pill. But I supposed she'd have to settle for a dip in utter humiliation. The other freshmen were getting nervous as they waited for something to happen, the bags over their heads blotting out all the light. But I was cool with them waiting. Waiting would only make them more afraid.

"Err.. what?" Darcy asked. *Holy shit, she doesn't even know about Orders?*

"You know...Siren, Vampire...Werewolf?" I asked curiously as Ashanti moved up behind her and started braiding her hair. It looked quite good in a braid actually. But this wasn't a besties hair styling party, this was a dominance move, and Ashanti was styling it just how she liked it to look, not how the pretty little Vega wanted it.

"I don't know what you're talking about," Darcy said as I pressed my nose to her neck and breathed in deeply. She was appetising. Like strawberries and the gilded blood of a princess. Maybe I'd dom her down and mark her with my own scent.

I chuckled, pulling away. "You really are from the mortal world. Don't worry, babe, those powers will surface soon." I nodded to Ashanti, and she stuffed a linen bag over Darcy's head, making me grin like the Wolf I was. She steadied herself against me and I loved that she thought I was the person to place her faith in right now. My friendly act had paid off. But she was about to meet the monster beneath my flesh.

I let go of her so she was left with nothing to hold onto and my pack grouped around me with excited smiles, waiting for my next move. Kylie was among them, supressing a giggle as she watched the games play out and I knocked my knuckles against her cheek with a smirk.

"If you don't pass my initiation you don't stay in Aer, got it?" I barked and half the freshmen flinched. Not my Vega though.

A murmur of ascent went up that made me scowl. I was an Alpha. Their House Captain. And they would show me more fucking respect than that.

"You will reply with 'yes Alpha'. Let's try again," I commanded. "Have you got that?"

"Yes Alpha!" the freshmen called but my eyes were on Darcy who remained resolutely silent. I ground my jaw, my instincts blazing, telling me to put her in her place.

I yanked her against me once more and felt her muscles go rigid in my arms. "Answer me, pledge."

"Yes Alpha," she said, but it sounded forced. It wasn't nearly as satisfying as I would have liked, but it was a start.

I released her and she stumbled backwards, almost knocking into Frank who stepped casually out of her way with a mocking grin.

"MOVE!" I bellowed like a drill sergeant and my pack and any older students here surrounded the freshmen, dragging them after me as I led the way inside. Kylie jogged to keep pace with me and I slung my arm around her shoulders as she gave me a mischievous smile, batting her lashes at me. I silently slid a pair of scissors from my pocket, passing them to her with a wink.

"Gimme those when I ask for them, kay babe?" I whispered and she nodded eagerly, pocketing them for me.

A few of my pack mates kept close to me, brushing my arms and pushing their fingers into my hair, causing Kylie to pout. I definitely needed to have a chat with her now she was at Zodiac. I didn't really do girlfriends or boyfriends because exclusivity was dumb to me when I was used to nightly orgies with my pack. Why go monogamous with one Fae when I could have three taking turns sucking my cock? Kylie had been a great distraction over the summer, but she was less distracting now I was back here. Like, not really distracting at all actually. I'd forgotten that she was gonna be Awakened tonight. Anyways, maybe she was down for pack life. Maybe she'd enjoy being bent over while Frank pounded her from behind and I watched her across the room while fucking Alice. Guessed we'd find out.

I increased my pace up the winding white stairway that circled higher and higher into the tower, adrenaline buzzing through my body and making me want to start yipping like a pup. But I kept that shit in check. I was in cool mode now. And I didn't let anyone see that mask slip except the Heirs.

Eventually, we reached the top where the common room was located and all the freshmen were panting, not used to the daily climb yet. This tower was home to the best asses on campus because there was nothing better for your glutes than stair climbing. Fact.

"Forward," I commanded as I guided them into the common room and we had to weave through the grey stone lounge filled with woollen rugs and cream armchairs. I flicked my fingers, sending a cold wind through the room that gusted around the bag-headed freshmen, making them believe we were outside. A few murmurs of fear reached me from the pledges and Kylie supressed a laugh while a vicious grin curled up my lips. I didn't make her participate in the initiation 'cause I was nice like that. Her tits looked top dollar tonight too which helped. And I considered this my apology for the rampant sex party I'd had the moment I got back to the academy.

"You're now at the top of Aer Tower," I announced and some whimpers left the freshmen. "Line them up on the edge." *Let's see if I can make the Vega squeal.*

I moved to stand before the step where the freshmen were all forced to line up and a bunch of the older students had to cast silencing bubbles around themselves to stop their laughter from being heard. I folded my arms as I fixed my gaze on the one who had the blue tips of hair hanging from her hood, ready to see her grit. A few of the freshmen called out pleas and I gave them dry looks. Darcy's feet were the first to reach the edge of the step while others were wrestled into place beside her.

I ran my tongue over my teeth, my gaze not wavering from her as she lurched backwards in fright and Alice shoved her back into place.

When the struggling stopped, I circled around them all, moving to stand at the back of the line as I assessed their quaking little knees.

"You are air born, pledges!" I shouted. "The wind is your ally. If you can't harness it, you don't deserve to live here. Or at all for that matter."

Darcy shook her head and a murmur of fear escaped her that sent a ripple of satisfaction through me. I had a Vega princess frightened and at my mercy. And all I'd done was shove a bag on her head and place her on a step. Getting her to bow to me was gonna be as easy as finding the moon in the sky. I bounced on the balls of my feet as that thought washed through me. I couldn't wait to tell the other Heirs how snappable Darcy Vega was. She was gonna be my new chew toy. My little Aer House servant. Yes! This was gonna be so much fun.

I nodded to my pack mates who knew my plan and they hurriedly cast silencing bubbles around all the freshmen except Darcy, dragging them off to one side of the room and leaving her alone.

Kylie sniggered as she appeared beside me, following me like she was on a leash and I ignored her as I raised my hands at Darcy's back, air magic still blasting around her and making goosebumps rise on the exposed skin of her arms. Her hand reached out to find someone beside her, but there was no one there. She was a lonely duck and I was going to make her quack for help.

I let the silence ring for a second as people fought to contain their laughter at her standing there, teetering on the edge of the step.

"Wait," Darcy choked out. "I don't know what I'm doing."

"You'll figure it out, girl," Kylie called in encouragement.

Darcy started trembling and a vicious smile pulled at my mouth as I fell into the darkness within me, enjoying every second of this. Vega Princess? More like Vega mouse. It was going to be far too easy to break them, and I was kind of disappointed they weren't going to be more of a challenge.

"On the count of three you'll jump and if you don't stop yourself from hitting the ground, then you're gonna go splat. And if you don't jump, you'll be pushed," I explained in a bright tone.

"What the fuck?" she snapped, finally losing all politeness.

"One!" I called, ignoring her as I waited for her to back out of the jump and start pleading. "Two!"

She stopped shaking and I frowned. "Three!" I cried.

She jumped, making my eyebrows shoot up in surprise.

Her feet hit the floor and Ashanti ripped her hood off, everyone dropping their silencing bubbles as raucous laughter filled the air. I didn't laugh, caught off guard by her jumping from that edge. She'd believed that was the top of the tower...

"So funny, Sethy," Kylie said, nudging me and I finally let out a low laugh, enjoying Darcy's embarrassment as even the freshmen joined in laughing at her. But they were wrong to laugh because she hadn't failed here, she'd won. And that just wasn't gonna work for me.

I walked around her, assessing her as I slapped on a grin, not liking the writhing feeling in my chest that told me she wasn't a complete mouse after all.

"That's not funny," Darcy blew out, her hair all fucked up from the hood and looking sexy as hell. She smiled, fucking smiled like she found the joke amusing and that wasn't gonna do. She was meant to be the butt of it, not part of it.

I caught her wrist, dragging her forward as I assessed her, my hands skimming along her chin then into her hair as I hunted her eyes for what I knew was lurking in her. And there it was, hidden deep, but I could see it. Her Fae, burning in the depths of those dark green eyes. And it wasn't even close to innocent. *Hello, Savage Princess.*

"What's really not funny is you and your sister showing up here to steal *our* throne. We've worked our asses off to earn that right. Our four families have ruled for nearly twenty years since the fall of King Vega and Solaria has been much better off for it. Our parents divide the power between themselves and as the sons of the Celestial Council, we will soon take that responsibility from them. So we don't intend to just sit back and let you take the throne from us and return Solaria to the shitheap it was when your father ruled," I snarled, holding on tighter to her as my Alpha told me to force this girl beneath me before she got any ideas about trying to do the same to me.

Her face twisted in anger. "I don't want your throne." She tried to wrench her wrist free from my grip but I wouldn't let go. *Bullshit.*

I needed to push her further. Needed to break her before that animal in her eyes sprouted wings and realised how high it could soar.

I turned her to face the crowd in front of me. "Who says we really throw her off the tower this time?" My heart beat to a powerful, hungry tune. I loved raising the stakes of this power play and she was the one who'd jumped in the first place, so it wouldn't be that hard to do it again now, would it?

"What?" she gasped as the whole of House Aer roared their ascent. "Get off of me!" She threw her shoulder back at me but I didn't let go, hauling her toward the huge set of glass doors that led onto the balcony. I hesitated for a second, wondering if I was going too far. But then I remembered my mother's words to me. *Don't ever let your enemies see you have a heart.*

I'd always been the cruellest of my pack, it was what made me such a powerful Alpha. She'd encouraged my ruthlessness, showered me with gifts every time I showed no mercy to Fae who tried to challenge me. It was what I was best at, what I was honed to do. And yet some small part of me occasionally rose its head and told me to stop. But I couldn't listen to it. When I'd told my Mom about it, she'd said that voice was weakness and that I should never let it affect my decisions. If I was going to rule the kingdom one day, I needed to be cold, detached, make choices for the greater good without latching any emotion to them. But as a shiver ran through Darcy's flesh into mine, that little voice grew louder and told me to stop. So I did what I always did when that voice got too loud, I shut it out, let myself drift into the calm, dark waters of my inner Fae and let it take over every part of me. I was numb here, draped in cruelty, and that was where I belonged.

I dragged Darcy up to the stone wall at the edge of the roof and the students crowed excitedly behind me, while others murmured in concern.

"Are you crazy?!" she yelled desperately as she fought to get my hands off of her. But the wheel was in motion and there was no going back. I had to do this. To show her who was boss, to keep that Fae lurking in her crushed down.

My pack started howling as the light of the moon washed over us and I tilted my chin up to it, bathing in its silvery light. Then I shoved Darcy firmly up onto the wall and she looked back over her shoulder, finding the whole House watching her through the glass windows.

I glared coolly up at my enemy, ready to break her in front of everyone. They'd see her crumble and beg and plead. And only when she was on her knees for me would I let her off this wall.

"Please, just let me down," she whispered, her voice quavering with fear.

I smirked, enjoying having this so-called powerful princess begging me for mercy already. Kylie pushed through the crowd, appearing beside me again and taking my hand in hers. Her clinginess was starting to get to me which was odd considering how clingy I could be sometimes with my pack and the Heirs.

"Jump," Kylie said and a growl built in my throat. *This is my circus, babe, don't start talking for the ringmaster or I'll crush you too.*

Darcy searched for a friendly face among the crowd, but came up short, looking back at me.

"Let me down," she demanded, almost forcefully enough to have a ring of Coercion to it.

I released Kylie and moved right up to the wall, gripping Darcy's ankles to show her I could launch her off this tower at any second.

"Alright," I said after a long pause, ready to immortalise this night as the one where Seth Capella broke a Vega. "But you can only get down when you've cut off all of your hair."

Kylie passed me the scissors I'd given her and I took them, brandishing them for the crowd to see.

"What?" Darcy gasped in horror. *Yup.* They'd call her Darcy Egga after this on account of her bald head. Or maybe Baldy Vega, or…something better, I didn't have time to decide that right now anyway.

"It's that or jump." I shrugged and laughter rang out from every direction.

I held out the scissors to Darcy and she clenched her jaw, determination roaring in her eyes. *No, no, back down, babe. Show the world you're not fit for the throne.*

Give me your dignity, hand it over and prove who the real Heir here is. Prove you're just a mouse who couldn't even rule a kingdom of fleas.

Her fingers flexed and the wind picked up under her power. Was she going to fight me?

I quite liked the idea of that. I could force her to her knees and beat her as easily as breathing. She wasn't even trained. It would be idiotic, but I'd be happy to rise to any challenge she threw at me.

She glanced over her shoulder at the drop from the tower and a frown pinched my brow as I realised she wasn't about to fight me, she was thinking of doing something far more dangerous.

She turned and I stepped forward, my lips parting as I was about to shout out and tell her to stop, but she was already jumping, diving off the fucking tower in a move I hadn't thought she'd ever even consider.

I leapt up onto the stone wall as screams and gasps of shock swallowed up the curses leaving my lips. She fell at a furious pace, falling through the air with her hair streaming upwards behind her.

She was gonna hit the ground, she couldn't cast air magic on command like that, she'd only just been Awakened. *Fuck – holy shit on the moon – fuck!*

My fingers twitched as I prepared to catch her with my own air magic, my heart drumming furiously against my ribcage.

"She's gonna die!" Ashanti gasped.

"Oh my stars," Kylie said as she recorded the whole thing on her Atlas, her eyes alight.

I was about to stop Darcy from impacting with the ground when she caught herself on a gust of air and came to a sudden halt.

My shoulders sagged and I carved a hand over my face, my relief dying a fast death as a bunch of students around me started whooping and cheering her on. My teeth locked as she won the favour of so many people at once and I turned and shoved my way back through the crowd, pissed as all hell. I needed to talk to the other Heirs, but first I needed a friendly blowjob and a head massage. So as I howled for my pack to follow and Kylie was nearly knocked down beneath them as they ran after me, I led them away to my bedroom and fell onto my bed with a huff.

"It's okay, Alpha," Ashanti purred, straddling my lap and I grabbed her hands, putting them in my hair.

"Stroke me." I pouted and she nodded, getting to work teasing her fingers through my hair.

Frank started kissing my neck and I let out a breath as they worked to tease the tension from my body. But the blue haired Vega was firmly on my mind when Ashanti started riding my cock and when I shut my eyes, all I saw was Darcy in her place, working to please her superior. I got the feeling that was a fantasy that wouldn't be as easy to make into reality as I'd first thought. But maybe it wasn't all bad. It definitely made things interesting anyway. And if I had to destroy her bite by bite, then I'd at least get time to enjoy the meal I made of her.

DARIUS

CHAPTER FOUR

I took my place before the entrance to Ignis House with the rest of my inner circle drawing close around me as the terrified looking freshmen all waited to find out how this was gonna go down.

The challenges were laid out pretty simply, but I'd made certain to put a few additional extras and more difficult challenges in place for when the new Vega tried her luck. In fact, I wasn't planning on letting her make it through the gauntlet at all. The tasks I had designed for her would be difficult for a Fae with several months of training, especially for some practically mortal girl with no idea how to control any of her Elements, let alone the volatile power of fire. If she wanted a bed tonight, then she'd have to beg me to let her in despite her failure.

Although as I considered giving her a bed, I couldn't help but think about offering her a spot in mine. Father had told me to make sure she and her sister dropped out of the academy so that they forfeited their right to challenge for the throne - he'd never said anything about me not being allowed to enjoy her company before she left.

The students fell silent as all eyes turned to me without me having to do so much as lift a finger and I reined in the smug smirk which was biting at my lips as they all fell under my power just as simply as that. I stepped forward so that I was blocking the hulking entrance into the glass monstrosity which was Ignis House, and I twisted my fingers subtly as I took control of the flames which filled the fire above my head, moulding them to follow my command.

A Dragon emerged from the belly of the flames; its body was deep red with glimmering gold outlining each of its scales. I filled its mouth with flaming teeth then unfurled its huge wings until they spread out wide on either side of it.

The freshmen gasped in awe as they watched the Dragon prepare to take flight, its jaws opening wide as I built a roar in its chest from the crackling rumble of burning embers.

My gaze fixed on Roxy Vega like an arrow on a target as she stood there, her eyes wide with awe at the beast I'd created and that sense of satisfaction growing in me as I breathed in her reaction to my power. With a flick of my wrist, the Dragon blasted fire over the heads of the freshmen, low enough to make them scream and leap out of the way. All of them but her.

Roxanya tipped her head back to watch the fire as it tore past her, the light warming her cheeks as she drank in the display without so much as a flicker of fear and my interest in her only heightened. Who the hell was this girl who'd just been plucked right out of the Mortal Realm and yet could stand in the face of powerful magic without flinching? She was a mystery I needed to unlock, a question I ached to answer and a problem who I was starting to think may just be a whole lot harder to deal with than we'd first expected.

"Fire is the most potent Element of all," I called, drawing the attention of the freshmen back to me as the fire Dragon burned out and I released my hold on the magic that had constructed it. "It brings light to the dark, warmth in the cold and can destroy everything placed in its way. Only those born with veins filled with the heat of the sun and hearts blazing with the true power of the flames can enter our House and claim their place amongst us."

My gaze was fixed on Roxy Vega, but she seemed more interested in muttering to some little blonde chick who stood beside her. My jaw ticked as I realised I wasn't holding her attention the way she'd captured mine and I went on with my speech.

"So who wants to be the first to try and gain access to the greatest House in Zodiac Academy?" I challenged, holding my arms wide as I waited to see if any of them would be brave enough to volunteer to go first.

They glanced between me and each other warily and I wasn't all that surprised to find them hesitant to step up. There weren't many Fae like me and the other Heirs who always rose to a challenge no matter how difficult it may have seemed. Though all Fae were born and bred with the desire to claim their own power, the sad fact was that there just wasn't all that much room at the top of the pecking order and most of them weren't born with what it took to rule.

Even the lost Vega princess hadn't stepped out of the crowd, though as my gaze moved to her again, she looked my way, seeming to be a little confused about what was expected of her here. Her eyes met mine and it was as if none of the rest of the people surrounding us were even present anymore. It was just me and her and I was calling her out. *Come on, baby girl, why don't you come show me what you're made of?*

As if she'd heard me, she suddenly stepped forward, an unimpressed look falling over her features as the crowd moved aside for her without her even having to tell them to get out of her way. They could feel it - that well of power inside her which demanded their respect and warned them to back off. She was exuding the same kind of power that I did and she wasn't even trying.

My spine straightened as she kept on walking, making her way towards me while looking decidedly unimpressed and not the least bit afraid. Fuck I wanted to know what made her tick. I wanted to pull her apart and find out what went on beneath her skin. Because if her blood ran as cold as the aura she was giving off then I was going to have trouble with this little ice queen. But that description just didn't seem right to me, because more than once I'd seen a flash of heat in her, the kind of fire that I just couldn't resist getting closer to, needing to find out what it felt like to burn in it.

"First one in always gets the toughest run of it," I warned her, hunting for some flicker in that ice cold facade, some evidence that she was rattled, some crack in her armour. But there was nothing. "Feel free to back down if your mortal upbringing has left you unprepared to face the gauntlet."

"We're all going in one way or another. I'd sooner get this over with quickly," she replied dismissively, seeming to be looking for cracks in my mask too. The problem was, I wasn't wearing a mask, I really was an uncaring asshole and she'd do well to figure that out fast.

Irritation prickled through me as she failed to show the slightest signs of fear and I couldn't help but take a step closer to her as the Dragon in me bristled beneath my skin. I just wanted to breathe in her air, figure out her angle, understand who she really was and why she seemed so determined to stand against me.

"Maybe you should have picked an easier House to join," I warned in a low tone, pushing her a little more. "I don't get the feeling you're cut out for the trials of this one."

"Well you made it in," she said with a shrug, her gaze flicking over me dismissively and making my blood heat. "So it can't be that hard."

A growl rumbled in the back of my throat, but she didn't even wait long enough to allow me to finish our conversation and I watched in a mixture of shock and anger as she turned her fucking back on me again, striding into the gauntlet without so much as a backwards glance my way. What the fuck was that about?

I watched her walk away from me, my gaze staying glued to her ass which was hugged oh so perfectly by those skintight jeans she wore, and I pushed my tongue into my cheek as I just stared after her. Was that it? No backwards glance, no hesitation, no sign at all that she was even a little afraid?

One of the seniors used his earth magic to seal the way closed behind her and I had to grit my teeth against the desire to tell him to stop so I could keep watching her walk away. Damn this girl. Damn this fucking girl. She was clawing her way under my skin and I was almost certain she wasn't even trying to do it.

"I'll see the rest of you on the inside - if you can make it through the gauntlet," I said loudly, flicking my fingers so that an explosion of fire magic tore over the heads of the freshmen and made them all shriek with a mixture of fear and excitement before I turned and headed inside.

The earth magic shifted before I had to ask and I was given access to the stairs which led up to the common room.

"Don't go easy on her," I said as a few of my closest friends within the House banded around me. "In fact, I think it might be a good idea if we make her challenges difficult for even a senior to pass. A Savage Princess should be able to cope with more than the rest of the masses after all, don't you think?"

The excited guffaws of the group surrounded me as a few of them darted off to do just that, one of them excitedly calling out that she was going to shift into her Nemean Lion form and scare the shit out of the Vega while she was trying to figure out how to cross the burning coals.

I left them to figure out how else to make the gauntlet more challenging then smirked to myself as I considered what I'd make pretty little Roxy Vega do to earn her way into my House when she failed.

Maybe I'd keep it simple and just make her beg in front of everyone. That would be a pretty powerful visual after all, the Vega Princess on her knees at my feet begging me to do her a favour.

I licked my bottom lip as the mental picture of her on her knees for me gave me all kinds of other, even better ideas for what she might like to do while she was down there and I was so lost to that fantasy that I almost flinched as Marguerite suddenly appeared in front of me.

"Hey sweetie," she purred, sucking on her bright red bottom lip as she looked me up and down like a feast she was hoping to devour and I paused on the threshold to the common room, trying to give her the attention she was looking for.

"Hey," I muttered.

"You looked so hot out there, scaring all the freshmen and making them quake in their boots," she went on, taking my arm as I moved into the huge common room where fires roared in every hearth and most of the existing students had already gathered to welcome the freshmen into our ranks.

The space was decorated with dark wood and deep red walls, the coloured glass of the orange and yellow windows breaking up the space and allowing some moonlight to shine through them.

My crew were already huddled around my favourite spot in the room, all of them full of excited energy over the games taking place tonight and they cheered as they saw me approaching.

The keys to the rooms for the new freshmen were laid out on the table between them and I scooped one up, the metal warming in my palm as I turned it over between my fingers and wondered whether she'd be earning this the hard way or if she'd just give up once she realised how hard I could make her life here.

I dropped into my favourite chair, turning it so that I had a better view of the stairs where the freshmen who completed the gauntlet would appear if they made it through. Where *she* would appear.

As I leaned back in the wingback and spread my legs wide, I couldn't deny the little thrill I was feeling at this game. I'd been waiting for the Vegas to arrive. Hell, it had been months since we'd first learned of their existence and been expecting Lance to bring them back here, but up until now it had never really been on me to deal with them. At least not initially. I knew my father had been hoping to have a few months or even weeks to 'welcome them home' and get his claws well and truly lodged into their spines before they ever set foot in this academy. But fate hadn't guided them to him. He'd landed them with me. One of them specifically. And I couldn't help but feel like that was no accident on the part of the stars. Roxy Vega had been brought here, gifted to me so that I could be the one to bring her to heel. And the thought of doing just that was a thrill too tempting to resist.

Marguerite dropped down on the arm of my chair, folding her legs in my direction and flashing me the expanse of long legs in a clear attempt to tempt me in. She made it so fucking easy. And there in lay the problem. Firstly, in that it wasn't exactly exciting to fuck her because there was no effort required on my part, but secondly in that I hadn't gotten rid of her yet either. I mean, she was hot and eager enough, but she wasn't exactly a whole lot of thrilling in the sack. Though as Seth had put it, a willing body was better than jerking off and at least she wasn't a stuttering fan girl like half the Fae I met. She could offer me full sentences even if the contents of them tended to bore me to tears. It probably made me an asshole but I hadn't promised her shit and she knew I was engaged anyway, so it wasn't like she was under any delusions about the point of our time together.

"Those Vega chicks are seriously hot though, you have to give them that," Milton crowed and a bunch of the other guys all agreed vehemently, commenting on the twins' looks and making jokes about fucking the two of them at once. He was one of those loudmouth types who always loved to shout every errant thought that crossed his mind, but as a lot of it was pretty amusing I didn't mind it so much. His dark hair fell into his eyes, resting on his monobrow and I couldn't help but stare at it a little as he high fived a couple of the other guys.

"They didn't seem like anything special to me." Marguerite sneered and the girls closest agreed in the way that jealous bitches always banded together.

I snorted in amusement at the clear threat they all felt and Marguerite turned her gaze on me.

"I thought they looked totally plain," she drawled, her hand moving to my chest and slipping down. "Don't you think so, sweety?"

"I think you should look again," I said, knocking her hand aside and jerking my chin at a chair across from me. "Gimme some space, I need to concentrate on the initiation."

Marguerite looked caught between arguing back and ignoring me, but as I arched an eyebrow at her and let the Dragon show in my eyes for a moment, she quickly hopped up and scrambled away from me.

A prickle tracked down my spine and I glanced up at the archway which led into the common room, my entire body falling still as I spotted a bare footed, soot stained Vega Princess striding towards it with victory flaring in her eyes.

My heart leapt in surprise and I glanced at the time, frowning as I took it in. That was fast. As in faster than any of the freshmen should have been able to make it through the gauntlet even without my followers making it more difficult for them. *Fuck.*

Who the hell was this girl?

Some of the others looked up too, spotting her and gasping, muttering about her time and gasping in awe over how quickly she'd made it through my fucking challenges.

That wouldn't do. Not at all.

I could practically hear my father's sneering voice now, feel the smack of his fist against my flesh as he took out his fury over my failure at this one simple task on my body.

I shoved to my feet in a fluid motion, conjuring fire to fill the doorway before she could step through and bringing the entire room into a hush of total silence as they all stared at me in surprise. But no, I wasn't going to let her do this. I was going to set an impossible challenge and even if she dared complete it, I'd make sure she didn't manage to come out on top of this.

"Final challenge," I called, loudly enough for her and everyone else in the vicinity to hear me clearly. "If you really want to be one of us, you're going to have to leave everything from your time with the mortals behind."

I moved my fingers at my side, bringing the flames under my command, urging them to follow my instructions and burn just for me. This would take a lot of concentration, but if she was brave enough to try and complete the task I was setting her then I'd make sure her victory was coloured with enough embarrassment to douse any admiration she might have gained from it. Once I was certain I held the flames beneath my will and was confident they'd do no more than singe her flesh if she touched them, I went on.

"You can step through the flames once you're ready to leave your mortal trappings behind. The fire will burn them all away, but your flesh will remain unscathed," I said with a grin, wondering if she'd really do this or not. It took balls to step straight through a wall of fire even if it was your Element, but she'd already more than proved that she had balls bigger than most Fae I knew. If she completed this challenge then she wasn't going to like the consequences much because I may not have been going to let the flames burn her flesh, but the rest of her possessions were fair game. And she had been warned after all.

I expected the seconds to drag, to tick by while she considered the challenge and turned my words over in her mind. But that didn't happen. Yet again the girl with the burning eyes surprised me with her gall and with her chin high and steps sure, she strode right on through the fire.

My jaw clenched as I concentrated on keeping the flames from hurting her, but I could feel every flick of flame and tendril of fire as it worked its way through her clothes like water washing away a line of sand.

The scent of burning fabric filled the air and Roxy's eyes widened in alarm as she clutched her long, ebony hair, but that wasn't the price I'd claimed from her.

My heart thrashed and my throat bobbed as the last of her clothes were burned from her flesh and I found the result of my hasty plan coming together right before me as the Vega princess I'd sought to humiliate stood there utterly naked.

The cocky remark I'd been meaning to toss her way lodged in my throat and the flames at her back fell away as I just drank in the sight of her, stealing a look at her body even though I knew I wasn't owed it.

I was an asshole. A total fucking asshole. And yet I couldn't not look. She was all firm muscle and perfect curves, her tits full and heavy with peaked nipples that made the Dragon in me growl with the desire to step closer to her. Her skin was tanned and satin smooth, making my fingers twitch with the urge to touch her and see if she felt as soft as I was guessing she did. And shit, my dick really liked the idea of that.

Laughter broke out all around me and I smirked along with them as I just stared at her, unable to move a single inch, utterly captivated by the beauty of her even as I watched the realisation dawning in her eyes and the utter fury filling their green depths.

Fuck, she was even hotter when she was furious. I seriously wouldn't have minded her taking that anger out on my body all night long. I'd be more than happy to angry fuck her until her body bent and bowed and finally gave in to the power play between us. I'd force her beneath me physically as well as with my power and maybe she'd find she liked it there just fine.

Or maybe she'd stab me to death and cut my cock off for good measure because the look she was aiming my way said that was a whole lot more likely than me getting to spend the night ruining her. But it was a damn nice fantasy to indulge in for a few moments.

I waited for her to crumple, to throw her hands around her body and maybe even to start crying. My gut twisted at the thought, but I steeled myself against that moment of weakness and held my head high. Because this was better. Better she fell apart now and realised where her place was here in this academy and in Solaria as a whole. She needed to fall at my feet and beg me to stop. To make it clear to everyone here and in the entire kingdom that she couldn't stand against me. And once she'd done that, I wouldn't have to be her villain anymore. I'd get this done now and that would be it. My father would be sated and I would be able to focus on my plans to overthrow him once more.

But she didn't do any of that.

"Motherfucker!" Roxy snarled, starting towards me with her hand curled into a fist like she wanted to strike me. She jerked to a halt again just as fast, though not because she was afraid. She glanced down at her naked body and seemed to be using that as the reason to restrain herself. "I had nearly three grand in my pocket! Do you know how hard my sister and I worked for that money?"

I almost laughed at her outburst. She was standing there naked in front of the entire House and her anger at me was more to do with some money? What was she, a fucking pauper?

My grin widened as I took in her words. Was she serious? She cared about a few grand more than the embarrassment of her nudity? Although I guessed it wasn't all that strange for Fae not to care much about revealing their bodies as most of us had to strip in order to shift unless we were happy destroying our clothes all the time. But I had thought she might be a little more aggravated over it given the audience and her lack of choice in the matter.

But as the laughter continued to titter out around the room, I guessed I'd achieved what I'd meant to and I couldn't even say I was entirely disappointed with her continued fire. It awoke something in me. Something I hadn't even realised I'd been missing but damn, she was making me think about it now because I'd just realised how fucking bored I'd been recently.

I was so stuck in this endless rotation of classes and training to be a Councillor one day, mixed in with the constant threat of my father's shadow looming over me and my brother that the only times I ever felt truly awake these days were when Lance and I went hunting Nymphs. And we hadn't even been able to do that for months while he'd been hunting Vegas in the Mortal Realm instead.

I loved the other Heirs and I found relief in their company and a challenge in training with them as we were so easily matched, but I hadn't felt this in a long damn time. I hadn't had another Fae look me in the eye and let me know outright that they didn't give a fuck about who I was or what I was in...ever. Shit. If I didn't watch out, I had a feeling I might just get addicted to that fire in this girl's eyes. The honesty of her dislike of me and the refreshing taste of her open hostility on the air.

"Your room is on the third floor, end of the corridor," I said, unable to come up with another challenge for her that wouldn't just make it look like I was floundering. I wanted her brought to heel but I'd take this much for tonight, twist the hurt of this embarrassment a little and see if she'd crack. "If you wanna go and find something to wear?"

She gave me a look of utter contempt and it made my cock throb as her nearness just compounded the desire I was already feeling for her and made me get all kinds of insane ideas about what I'd like to do with this little princess if I got her to myself for long enough.

She made no attempt to cover herself, no sign of shame in her frosty features as she stalked forward to claim her key, a sneer touching those edible lips of hers.

Her jaw was tight with rage which she was doing nothing to hide and as she reached out to snatch the key from my hand, I couldn't help but ache to bring her closer, draw her nearer, see just how far she'd go in this denial of my power over her.

Her fingers curled around the brass key, but I didn't release it, instead using my hold on it to tug her a step closer so that only a breath of space divided our bodies. I looked down at her from my imposing height, dominating her space with the bulk of my body and making sure she took in every last inch of height I had over her.

"Of course, if you'd rather just come on up to my room, I can give you a *real* welcome to the House of Fire," I suggested my gaze dropping down to her body, the noticeable bulge in my pants making it clear enough how much I meant that offer. I probably shouldn't have been making it at all, but the beast in me couldn't help myself. Dragons saw something they wanted and they took it. And I hadn't seen something I wanted as much as this girl in as long as I could remember.

Our gazes collided and the heat there was almost strong enough to burn, the tension between us crackling so loudly I was surprised the whole room couldn't hear it. But then her gaze shuttered and her lips pursed, her eyes dropping down to take me in, my skin buzzing everywhere they landed as I could feel the want in her while she assessed me.

But as those deep green eyes met mine again and I gave her a knowing smirk, I couldn't tell what she was thinking. I didn't know if she was going to bow to this heat between us or just stoke the flames, and the fact that I didn't know had my heart thumping in anticipation deep in my chest.

She shifted an inch closer to me, tilting her mouth towards my ear and making my flesh spark with the need to take her, own her, destroy her in all the best ways. But just as my cock began to get overexcited at the prospect of all the ways I could make her scream for me given enough time, she spoke and it wasn't in the sultry purr I'd been expecting, her voice coming out loud enough for everyone to hear instead.

"I wouldn't come near you even if someone held a knife to my heart and told me that the world would end if I didn't," she snarled, snatching the key out of my hand as my surprise at her words made me forget to keep my grip tight enough to keep it. "So why don't you take a long, hard look while you can. Because I can promise you, you won't be seeing this again."

The laughter died out around the room as everyone in attendance seemed to take a collective breath, each of them waiting for my retaliation.

But I wasn't entirely sure what that should be. I was taken aback by her behaviour, her brazen disregard and unbridled distaste for me so clear that my lips parted on a reply which failed to come. I had her here, standing naked amongst a group of her peers and shamed in front of all of them, yet she'd somehow just flipped the table on me. Rejected me, loudly and clearly in front of the entire room. I wasn't sure I'd ever had a woman reject me at all, let alone so blatantly.

Before I could come up with the best response to her barb, she slammed her shoulder against my arm and stalked away from me like I was no one and nothing at all.

I turned to watch her go, my traitorous gaze falling to the perfect curve of her tanned ass as she fucking strutted out of the room towards the stairs that led up to the dorms like she didn't have a care in the fucking world.

Whispers broke out around the common room, but she just kept walking like she couldn't even hear them. My skin prickled as I heard a few sniggers aimed my way and my muscles bunched with frustration as I realised she was going to walk out of here with the last word.

"You should be more careful about the kinds of enemies you make around here, *Roxy*," I called after her, needing to end this interaction on my terms even if she had taken me by surprise yet again.

She didn't so much as glance back at me, just continuing on at her unhurried pace up the stairs and out of sight.

I forced a laugh which was quickly echoed by the sycophants surrounding me and dropped back into my chair, falling silent as I let them all joke and laugh about the Vega princess. But there was more than mocking jeers filling the room. There were enough of the guys discussing how hot she was to set my temper boiling and more than a few awed murmurs about the way she'd handled me too.

My gaze narrowed on the fire as the rest of the freshmen began to appear after their trial, but I had no interest in any of them.

I was caught up on the princess who had just gone to bat with me and damn near come out on top. Maybe I'd been hasty in assuming I could squash her easily. She was the Savage King's daughter after all.

I was going to have to rethink my tactics because it seemed clear to me now that this girl wouldn't be forced to bow as easily as we'd all hoped, and I was guessing that meant her sister wouldn't either.

But while I sat there, feigning interest in the freshmen being initiated into Ignis House, my mind wasn't occupied with thoughts of how I could get rid of the Vegas. It was stuck on one of them in particular. And I wasn't even fantasising about how I would enjoy taking command of her body with mine. No. I was caught on that look in her eyes. The fire, the challenge, the hatred. And no matter how much I tried to convince myself that I hated that look, I knew in my gut that I was lying.

I stuck it out for another hour, pretending to give a damn about the freshmen coming in after surviving their trials while Milton and some of the others made a leader board for the Fae who had completed it in the shortest time.

Roxy Vega's name sat at the top unmoving no matter how many of them came through. No matter the fact that all of their tasks were easier than hers had been. I ran my tongue over my teeth as I waited to see if any of them might challenge her, but none came close.

Marguerite dropped into my lap after a while, her mouth moving up my neck while she pushed her fingers beneath my belt, tugging a little like she intended to start caressing my cock right there in the middle of the room.

"Shall we sneak off for a bit, sweety?" she breathed, her lips skimming my ear and doing nothing at all for me. "You can have me any way you want me."

I sighed because I didn't want her any fucking way I wanted tonight. I didn't need her laying there beneath me, gasping and moaning while I fucked her and doing nothing at all to make it more interesting.

She didn't burn for me like Roxy Vega did. She didn't offer up any kind of challenge. And all of a sudden that was a whole lot more boring than it had seemed before.

"I've got somewhere to be tonight," I said abruptly, pushing to my feet and damn near dropping her on her ass.

She scrambled to right herself, calling out to tell me to send her a text if I wanted her to come up to my room later and I didn't bother to reply as I stalked away towards the dorms. I never invited her to my room and she knew it. If I wanted her, I went to her dorm and I had her there. It was sex, not a relationship and I didn't want her in my private space any more than I wanted to hang around for a sleepover after we were done. She knew that, but she kept pushing for more recently which probably meant it was time I moved on because I wasn't the kind of man who could offer her more. I was never going to be that kind of man for anyone. My father had seen to that with my arranged marriage even if my own personality didn't make it clear enough regardless.

I headed up the stairs, ignoring the calls from various people for me to stay and party with them because I just wasn't in the mood anymore.

I pulled my Atlas from my pocket and sent a quick message to the other Heirs, asking them to meet me at the Hollow and the responses came back fast enough as they agreed.

I jogged up the stairs within Ignis House, the mixture of black and red decoration making the place feel warm even without the added burning sconces everywhere which lit the open space.

As I reached the third floor, I paused, my gaze tracking to the room where I knew Roxy Vega now resided, wondering what she was doing in there, feeling the strangest urge to just walk over and knock on her door.

But I had no other plans for how to deal with her tonight and it was blindingly obvious that I wouldn't be a welcome visitor at her door, so I decided to just leave her be. For now.

I made it up to my room and rolled my shoulders back as I strode inside, tossing the door closed behind me and tugging my shirt off as I prepared to shift. The Dragon in me was restless tonight, like it had caught the scent of a prey it wanted to hunt but had found itself shackled instead.

A growl slipped through my lips as I thought of the defiant curve of Roxy's mouth as she'd shot me down. The urge to head back downstairs and continue this game of cat and mouse with her tugged at me.

I ignored the impulse, kicking off my shoes and unbuckling my belt as I continued to strip off.

I rotated my shoulders again, my back itching at the point where my wings would burst free when I gave in to the call of my Dragon. The new ink I'd gotten there this summer flexed across my shoulder blades and I looked at it over my shoulder to the full length mirror beside my closet.

I'd woken up on the eleventh of June with the image seared right into the backs of my eyelids and the urge to mark my skin with it itching at me so insistently that I'd headed out that day to get it done. The Dragon and the Phoenix curved around each other like they were playing out a scene from legends long since dead but something about the way the two of them almost seemed to actually move across my skin always set me at peace when I looked at them.

I moved to the full length window at the side of my room and pushed it open, feeling the breeze of the night air against my face as I looked down at the terrifying drop below me.

I opened my arms wide as I looked down then I slowly began to pitch forward until the push of the wind wrapped its fingers all around me and suddenly I was falling.

I counted as I fell, adrenaline spiking through my veins as I waited and waited, the ground rushing nearer with every passing second, my death hurtling towards me inevitably until the very last moment when I released the beast which lived inside my soul.

The enormous golden Dragon sprung free of my limbs, wings spreading wide and catching the breeze a moment before I could hit the ground.

My claws tore into the soft grass as I beat my wings hard then I was speeding up towards the stars, a roar echoing from my lips and making the glass structure of Ignis House shudder.

I flew fast, aiming for the heavens and powering up higher and higher until the air cooled all around me and nothing but silence could find me.

I closed my eyes as the starlight gilded my scales, bathing in the feeling of the celestial beings watching over me for a long moment before snapping my wings shut and diving back down towards the ground once more.

I shot down like a speeding bullet, my gaze zeroed in on a dense patch of trees at the centre of The Wailing Wood where King's Hollow lay waiting for my arrival.

I opened my wings again, banking hard and falling into a smooth glide as I closed in on my destination and by the time I landed I was practically gentle, my bulk only making the treehouse groan for a few seconds before the violent swaying ceased.

I shifted back into my Fae form and moved to open the hatch in the roof before dropping down inside the cosy space.

Caleb was already there, lounging in a chair beside the fire and flicking through something on his Atlas, his hand coming up in greeting while his gaze stayed fixed on the screen.

I crossed the space and tugged out some sweatpants, pulling them on before moving to join him, snagging the two of us some beers on the way.

"So?" Caleb asked, tossing his Atlas down and grinning at me as he opened his beer.

I considered playing dumb, but I couldn't see what purpose that would serve so I just shrugged, taking a swig of my drink and holding his eye as I spoke.

"She's impressive," I said honestly. "For a girl who grew up in the Mortal Realm and had no idea about magic or Fae or anything important before tonight, I'm surprised how fast she managed to adapt."

"Not to mention how fucking hot she is," Caleb replied, his dark blue eyes twinkling with a challenge that the beast in me instantly rose to.

"Obviously," I muttered in agreement.

"So I take it from that assessment that you didn't manage to break her yet?" he went on.

I shrugged. "I pissed her off pretty good, but no, I wouldn't say this is over that easily."

"Does it make me an ass if I admit I'm kind of pleased about that?" he asked with a grin. "I mean, don't get me wrong, I want the two of them to bow just as much as anyone else does. But we've been waiting for them to arrive all summer. It would be pretty dull if they just went down without a fight after so much suspense."

I thought of the furious gleam in Roxy's eyes as she refused to back down to me and I couldn't help but agree on some level.

"They still have to bow," I pointed out. "It would be better if they did it sooner rather than later."

"Where's the fun in that?" Cal asked with a shrug. "I'm personally more than happy to keep biting them and riling them up as often as possible. Angry blood is always so much hotter on the way down."

"Is that so?" I eyed him with irritation in my gaze and the smirk he offered said he fucking knew it.

"You still trying to lay a claim on her?" he taunted and I cursed myself for uttering such a claim in the first place, but the challenge in his eyes said it was far too late for that now.

"It's already done, brother. She's in Ignis now. That means she's mine," I said plainly though I was sure he would be able to detect the undercurrent of a command in my tone.

"We'll see."

The sound of the door banging open halted our conversation and we looked around as Max and Seth moved into the room. Max strode away to grab some more beers and Seth came bounding right over to us like an excitable puppy.

"She fucking jumped, you guys! For a moment I was like woah, did I just kill a Vega? But then it was like pow, she fucking flew! I mean, she didn't fly, she just kinda hung there in the air a bit above the ground instead of going splat and then she fell on her face. But everyone was going crazy for it. It was seriously cool...you know aside from the fact that she should have come out of this whole thing looking bad and ended up looking kinda good...I was mad at first but then my pack gave me multiple orgasms and now I'm thinking this challenge is just what I've been missing. We can have so much fun with smashing them!"

I groaned at his summary of how the other twin had faired in her initiation and swiped a hand down my face. Seth nuzzled against my side before dropping down on Caleb's lap and swiping a tongue up his cheek in greeting.

"Get off, mutt," Cal grumbled, shoving Seth so that he fell on his ass.

He bounded upright just as fast, jumping back into the spot beside me on the couch before flopping down on his back and dropping his head in my lap.

"Stroke my hair," he begged, giving me the big eyes. "I have a tension headache."

"Yeah? Well I have a case of blue balls, so unless you wanna help me out with that, I'm not gonna be stroking your fucking hair," I joked, shoving his face aside though not hard enough to actually knock him off of me.

"I mean...is that a serious suggestion or..."

"Not serious," Max replied for me, his Siren gifts brushing against me as he took his seat opposite Cal. "But you had a little shot of lust over the idea, Seth."

"Oh I'm sorry, am I not allowed to appreciate the hotness of my friends? You know I'd always consider some camaraderie BJs to help ease our stress, though I feel like Darius might choke me with his Dragon dick so I might have to take it slow if I-"

Caleb swatted Seth's forehead with a vine he conjured for the job and Seth cursed as he forgot about the likelihood of me ever agreeing to best friend blowjobs in favour of whimpering over the minor head wound.

"So what does this mean for them?" Max asked, shifting the topic back to the Vegas and pressing a serious mood into the room with his gifts in an attempt to get Seth to focus.

"The Councillors made it clear what we need to do," Caleb replied with a shrug. "And you know how our parents can get over anything that might tarnish our reputations. If word gets out about them passing their initiations with impressive results, they'll only demand we work faster to put the twins in their places beneath us.

"Well I don't care how impressive they were at some pointless school initiation," Max said. "They're still just a couple of untrained girls. We can take them out fast enough."

I nodded my agreement as Seth started barking out ideas for how to break down the girls' resolve like he was more than excited to get started. Some of his plans were dumb, others funny and a few might just have been brilliant.

I wondered how far we were really going to need to go with all of this though. It seemed to me like a pair of untrained girls were never really going to be able to pose a threat to us anyway. We had years of training over them as well as lifetimes of being groomed to take the power we'd been born to. I didn't care what power ran in their veins because when it came down to it, I just couldn't believe they'd be a match for us.

So as I sank a few more beers and Seth finally convinced me to half heartedly play with his damn hair for him by giving me the puppy dog eyes for ten minutes straight, I began to relax.

Roxanya Vega might have been more than I was bargaining for, but that didn't matter in the long run. Because she may have been the daughter of the Savage King, but I'd been reared in the image of a monster just as brutal and I didn't know the meaning of losing. So if we had to up our game plans against the two of them then so be it. I wasn't going to let a pretty face and fiery soul stand in the way of my rise to power and the demolition of my own personal demon. So the best thing she could do would be to get the hell out of my way.

ORION

CHAPTER FIVE

I woke with my arms wrapped around Darius and a headache pounding at the base of my skull. I was disorientated for a second before I remembered last night. Swerving Francesca staying over because I wanted to cuddle Darius – I mean, talk to him about the Vegas - then bourbon. Lots of bourbon.

Darius's forehead was against mine and his muscles tightened on me in his sleep as he mumbled something about someone stealing his gold. I released a slow breath as I reached a hand up to heal my headache away and take the edge off my hangover as I remained in his embrace and let the Guardian Bond have its feed. I definitely wasn't this Dragon's gold hoard, but damn if I'd be telling him while the magic binding us urged me to enjoy every second in his arms.

When my eyes flickered open, I found myself looking at him too intently and a fresh wave of anger crashed against my chest because of his father. Fucking Uncle Lionel with his grand ideas and his disregard for anyone else and their wants. I was here because of him, wrapped around his son like

I'd die if I wasn't this close to him, and sometimes it did feel like that when we spent too long apart.

I didn't resent Darius for any of it. He'd been there on that cliff and watched my sister die right beside me, bound and forced to kneel. He was just another one of his father's victims, though sometimes I feared how hard his heart was becoming because of that. I was pretty sure I was one of the very few people he showed his softer side to, and the only one he talked to about Lionel. I could say the same of him though. I'd always been a loner, my nature inclined that way due to my Order, but I'd used it as an excuse to avoid people too, to keep Francesca at a distance, to have alone time from my colleagues, to sit and drink and drink and drink...

I had no idea where it was all going to end up for me, but this path probably led nowhere good. The further I walked along it, the more withdrawn and bitter I became. My smiles were growing rarer and my light had dulled a long time ago. This hollow life was probably going to kill me one day, and maybe that would be for the best.

"Is that your cock digging into my hip?" Darius murmured as he stirred.

I reached between us, grunting as I tugged out the empty bottle of bourbon. "You wish, baby."

He chuckled as he opened his eyes, holding onto me for a few more moments before rolling onto his back and swiping a hand down his face. I immediately missed the contact and curled my hands into fists as I forced myself to roll away. When I'd first been bonded to him by Lionel, I'd struggled to keep any distance at all, and it had been a seriously fucked up adjustment for us both to get used to needing each other so much. Him sleeping here was risky as hell and it wasn't something I allowed very often, but last night the bond had been flaring so fiercely that getting him in my bed had been necessary for my sanity. And from the way he'd held me too, I had a feeling he had felt the same way.

Darius swiped his Atlas off my nightstand and yawned, letting out a stream of smoke from his lungs and wafting it away with his hand as he looked at the screen.

"Shit." He sat upright. "It's nine o'clock. I'm late for class."

He shoved out of bed and I cursed as I got out too, shooting away with the speed of my Order and showering in a minute flat before tearing back to my room and drying off with my air magic along the way. Darius was already halfway out the window and he paused as I dragged my clothes on.

"You're teaching the Vegas first period, right?" he asked and my gut clenched at their name. The name which could change the entire fate of Solaria. The name we'd sat discussing for hours last night before we'd passed out.

I'd taken some information out of the file I'd built on them so Lionel wouldn't get hold of it, hiding the real file in my desk while passing on the copy to him. It wasn't much, but withholding a few details meant Lionel wouldn't be able to build complete numerology charts on them which could help him make predictions on their capabilities. If anyone was going to beat them, it was Darius, not his father. So he was the one I was ensuring had the edge on them, but if Lionel found out he'd be furious.

I ground my teeth and grit out, "Yes."

"Assess everything about them. Strengths and weaknesses. I want a list."

"Yeah, yeah." I shoved my fingers through my messed up hair. "Meet me at Jupiter Hall tonight. Eight o'clock. I wanna start teaching you a new spell down at the beach."

He grinned, nodding as fire flared in his eyes then he ran off out of sight and I flicked my fingers, casting some concealment spells around him as he went in an attempt to hide him from any teachers looking this way.

"Coo-ee! Are you there, Lance?" Brian Washer called from outside my front door and I buckled up my pants with a groan, my shirt still hanging open as I shot to the door, figuring it was best to distract him while Darius was still sneaking out of Asteroid Place.

I unlocked the door, tugging it open and squinting out at him as the morning sunlight streamed into my face. He was wearing a gleaming blue spandex onesie which outlined his dick and balls so perfectly that I had to fight the urge to scoop my eyes clean out of my face.

I levelled him with a look that said I was not in the mood for being chatty – though when was I ever? - but as usual, he didn't seem to get the message.

"Just thought I'd check you were up. You know it's after nine, don't you Lance?"

"I'm aware," I said flatly.

"You have your first freshman class today, don't you?" he asked, his eyes moving down to roam over my bare chest.

"Oh, do I?" I asked sarcastically. "Damn, I'll have to cancel my morning synchronised swimming lesson."

He chuckled, swatting my right pec and a low growl of warning rose in my throat.

Man, I need coffee. It's too early for this.

"Don't go taking up morning lessons without including me, silly. I'm still yet to get you to join me for my yoga routines." He started squatting, his muscular, tanned thighs bending right out either side of him as he went up and down a few times before staying down and starting to pulse.

His face was on a level with my crotch and I quickly did my fly up as I realised it was riding low and took a step back. If this asshole wasn't fucking my boss, I'd have put him in his place a long time ago. As it was, I was under strict instructions from Uncle Lionel to behave within my role here as a professor, and pissing Elaine Nova off was one of my no-gos.

I'd had to make a star vow about that after my first few weeks teaching here, when I'd figured I'd just get myself fired as a fuck you to Lionel. I'd rarely turned up to teach my classes and had been obnoxious to anyone who'd tried to call me out on it, including Elaine. I'd even snuck up on Professor Astrum once and bitten him which kinda went against the code of professional behaviour between the faculty. That guy was a royalist and fucking hated me as it was, but now he was the ringleader of the I Hate Lance Orion Club.

Lionel had had to show up to smooth things over. He'd dragged me to Elaine's office and scolded me like a naughty kid whilst sweet talking the principal. She was a sucker for strong Fae, always kissing ass to whoever held the most power in the room, hence why she was currently asslicking the Vegas. I guessed she'd made some new bets on who was gonna win the throne. Anyway, she'd let me stay and Lionel had forced me to play professor to the best of my abilities. It meant the worst of my anger lived on the inside of me these days more than the out. But no one ever said I had to teach with a smile on my face, so every little asshole in this place fell at the receiving end of my rage whenever I needed an outlet. It was actually kind of therapeutic to put mouthy students in line. I'd earned my title as a hardass teacher here fair and square and as I now had no other goals in life, I focused on raising the bar of how much I could make the students despise me. You could say it gave me some sort of job satisfaction.

"You could be as flexible as me if you worked at it, Lancey." Washer bent right over so his ass was in the air and he started swaying it left to right.

"As tempting as that is, I think I'll pass, Brian," I said dryly. "Spandex wouldn't suit me."

He stood upright, his hands on his hips as he started lunging instead and I swear to the moon, his junk looked at me through that material. And it was twitching. "You could always do it naked. I often bathe my buttocks in the sun's rays. You could join me for some long, hard lunges like these and feel your low hanging fruit warm in our mother sun's eye."

"I'm good," I said, fighting a grimace. "I'd better get to class." *Anywhere is better than here.*

"Of course! Enjoy your lesson. I hope those Vegas don't get you all worked up over their wet spots."

"What?" I balked.

"Oh sorry, that's the old Water Elemental lingo in me coming out," he waved a hand at me. "I call my students' strengths their wet spots. If they're doing poorly, I mark them down as dry, then damp, moist, wet, right up to gushing like a waterfall. It's a cute little sliding scale strictly for my notes. I'm looking forward to seeing how wet the Vega girls are."

"I really think you should use some different terminology," I said, my nose wrinkling.

Was he fucking kidding me with this shit? I'd seen a professor get fired from here because he fed air to a drowning girl in the lake by breathing it directly into her mouth with his air magic. I mean yeah, he could have used his hand, because what the fuck? But it still seemed extreme. The rules on no student-teacher relationships were very clear though, and even saying something suggestive could get you in serious trouble. But I swear Washer got away with it sheerly because he was making Nova come at night. He may have been gross, but he was a pretty powerful guy and I guessed his Siren powers helped her to not be repulsed by him.

"Whyever would I do that?" he laughed. "My wetness scale is wonderful. I even have symbols to go with each wet spot, would you like to see?"

I'd literally rather crack my own skull open and let a crow feast on my brains.

"I've gotta go to class." I was seriously fucking late at this point. Not that I was ever really on time seeing as I liked to push Lionel's little boundaries which he'd set for me at this school. I was the absolute minimum of a decent teacher, always sitting right at the boundaries of what I could get away with as a way to remain defiant without breaking any rules. I doubted he gave a shit though, so the defiance didn't really serve any purpose except stopping me from going completely insane over being under his heel. That, coupled with the fact that I was teaching his son dark magic right under his nose, and I was able to keep my mood levels just above the suicidal line. And if that wasn't a reason to celebrate then I didn't know what was.

"Alright, have a good day. Oh and I'll send you some photos of my yoga routine so you can try out a few moves," he said, but I'd already shot away back into the house, a shudder running down my spine as I prayed he wouldn't send me any such thing.

I did up my shirt, threw a tie haphazardly around my neck and tugged on a blazer before tearing out of the house and using air magic to leap over Washer as he started bending and flexing again.

I shot all the way to Jupiter Hall, then figured fuck it and turned back to The Orb, speeding inside and slowing to a halt by the morning buffet as I made myself a coffee.

I took my time, elbowing a jittery looking boy out the way as I poured sugar and milk into the cup in copious amounts before taking a sip to make sure it was right.

"Can I just grab the-"

I bared my fangs at the boy I'd knocked aside who was trying to get to the sugar bowl and he ran away with a scream of fright. I shook my head at the weak display and shot away again, careful not to spill any of my coffee by casting an air seal over the cup and racing into Jupiter Hall. I slowed to a walk as I reached the corridor leading up to my classroom, sweeping my hair back and taking another long drink of my coffee.

Ah, caffeine. One of my few friends.

I shoved the door to my classroom open, mentally preparing myself for the first freshman class of the new term and ready to start assessing the Vegas' strengths. I kicked the door shut behind me and sipped on my cup of coffee as I fought to banish the heaviness left on me from last night. Darius and I had talked late into the night about the Vegas, but our attention had eventually turned back to our even bigger problem. The Nymphs were growing more volatile, popping up way more often than they used to, and I didn't like the sense of dread in the air. One simple Tarot reading was enough to tell me something big was coming, I just couldn't *see* what. Even Gabriel couldn't give me any straight answers and his fortune telling skills were unrivalled.

Though I suspected he knew more than he could say. And I supposed he had to in case he changed the coming fate, though his advice just left me in a daze of confusion.

Follow your heart, it won't lead you astray, he kept saying. Like some sort of fortune cookie on blast. What the hell did that even mean? My heart led me to guzzling bourbon and watching old recordings of the Pitball games I'd won back in my glory days. Ergh, I was old before my time. A withered man with withered dreams. I should have been living it up in the Solarian Pitball League right now and these should have been my glory days.

I sighed, my gaze firmly forward as I strode up to my desk and tried to drown out the whispers filling the room from my new students. The curse of the Vampire ears. Gossip.

"Oh my stars, he's even hotter up close."

"How old is he? How can he be a professor here?"

"My mom said he almost made it as a Pitball player for the league once, but he threw it all away."

I ground my teeth at that last statement, cursing Lionel Acrux once again for stealing my life from me. But it was all down the drain now, a long gone memory which I'd had to let go of.

Fine, okay, maybe I chewed on that memory like a dog with an old bone sometimes, but mostly it was in the past now. I wasn't the hopeful, foolish boy I'd been when I'd been studying here. Five years had hardened me into a man who had a short fuse and zero tolerance for bullshit. And I swear all the students in this academy ever seemed to do was spew bullshit.

I listened for the Vegas, not looking their way, though the urge to do so was burning at me. And in particular, *her*. The one with blue-tipped hair who wore bunny pyjamas and smiled at her sister like not a single dark thing lived in her soul. Not that I'd been paying attention.

I placed my coffee cup down on my desk and picked up my digital marker, turning to the board and writing across it in bold lettering.

Time to show the little shits that they're not in high school anymore.

Zodiac was an elite school designed for elite Fae. Only the best of the best got to attend academies to receive their magical education while the vast majority stayed on in high school for a further four years when they turned eighteen to learn how to wield their powers. And Zodiac Academy was the best academy of all, so they needed to prove they deserved their place here. As being a dick came naturally to me, I was more than happy to start driving the point home that I would seriously enjoy getting them expelled if they didn't impress me. And I was one impossible asshole to impress.

YOU DO NOT HAVE A PLACE AT ZODIAC ACADEMY.

I swung around to assess their reaction to that, realising I hadn't even done up my tie yet and taking a moment to fix it. I was a professional after all, thanks to old Lionel.

"Do you always get dressed on your way to work, sir?" asked a boy in the front row in a taunting voice. He had blonde tipped hair and a dudebro vibe about him that instantly rubbed me the wrong way. That coupled with what he'd said made the hunter in me raise its head and I finished tightening the knot at my throat as I fixed my gaze on my first victim.

"Name?" I demanded of him.

"Tyler Corbin."

"Well Corbin, you're not here to cast judgment on a single thing I do. In fact, it's entirely the other way around. So if I want to show up naked five minutes before the lesson ends, I will."

A few of the girls giggled and my gaze immediately flicked to Darcy Vega for the first time to see if she was one of them. Her gaze bored into me and my heart shoved its way into my throat. But there was no hint of a giggle on her lips. Good, fuck the gigglers. They drove me insane.

I pointed at a blonde girl who was out of her seat, her lashes all fluttery and her face full of way too much confidence for my liking. "Sit in your seat or you can stand on your desk for the rest of the lesson, Miss...?"

"Kylie Major," she sighed then fell into her chair, tossing her hair over one shoulder.

"Read this out, Major," I directed, pointing at the board.

She cleared her throat a few times and the dark-haired girl beside her suppressed another giggle that made me bristle with irritation. "You do not have a place at Zodiac Academy."

Chatter broke out again and I folded my arms, sick of all this noise as I gave everyone a look that told them to hush the fuck up. They obeyed which was something, but I didn't feel like they were quite getting the message yet.

I let the silence ring out for a moment until all of their attention was firmly fixed on me. "You all have a mid-term assessment which will decide whether or not you continue here at Zodiac. We call it The Reckoning because it will decide the fate of your entire lives. Zodiac Academy is the most prestigious school in Solaria and we won't waste time on anyone who can't prove their worth. If you fail it, you're out. Back to whatever crevice of this world – or any other world -" I gave the Vegas a hard look and Darcy's throat bobbed, making my fangs prickle demandingly, "-you came from. Is that clear?"

"Yes," they all said in unison, but that wasn't good enough.

"Yes what?" I pressed, needing them to understand that I was to be respected, because frankly I held their fates in my palms and I didn't take kindly to insolence.

"Yes, sir," everyone corrected, but I only watched Darcy Vega saying those words, her full lips moving around them perfectly. I liked that more than I cared to admit and snapped my attention away from her once more.

She's a student and your mortal enemy. Not a good combination to be distracted by, idiot.

I pressed a button at the base of the board and the words were erased. "This is Cardinal Magic where I will attempt to give you a basic understanding of all practical magic, simple divination and astrology. Today, I'll be introducing you to the Orders of Fae. None of you will be casting a single spell in my classroom until you have a basic foundation of knowledge to work from, so pay attention."

A groan sounded from several of the students in response and I tutted under my breath. They wouldn't last here if they weren't up for hard work. It was a Fae eat Fae world and as boring as the basics may have been to them, they were crucial to harnessing their magic. But if I had to throw a few whiners in detention and watch them shovel Griffin shit, then so be it.

"Everyone will need to be at the same level of understanding by the end of term. Whatever you think you know, you will soon learn there is much more that you do not." I took my blazer off, getting too fucking hot in here as my mind kept darting to the blue-haired Vega girl and the thought of her blood in my mouth.

I should have fed from Darius before he left this morning. Fucking stupid.

Obviously I was thinking about drinking from a Vega now, their power was like a magnet to my Order. That was what I wanted. My fist in her hair, her head wrenched back, her neck exposed while I drove my fangs into her and stole magic from one of the most powerful creatures ever born.

My cock twitched at the thought of that and I decided I was hot for power. Wouldn't have been the first time. Definitely wouldn't be the last. And why shouldn't I drink from her? No Vampire had claimed her as their Source yet, and the only one who could take me on was Caleb Altair.

If you're hot for power, why aren't you looking at Tory Vega too?

Shut up.

I tapped the board and a diagram appeared with a small selection of Orders listed on it.

ORDERS OF FAE

TAENIA

(Parasitic Orders)

Vampire

Siren

MUTATIO

(Mutating Orders)

Dragon

Manticore

Griffin

Cerberus

Pegasus

Werewolf

Nemean Lion

Hydra

Caucasian Eagle

Chimera

DIVISUS

(Spliced Orders)

Minotaur

Medusa

Centaur

Cyclops

Sphinx

Harpy

I faced everyone again, finding Darcy's eyes glittering like jade or emerald or – *who gives a fuck what gemstone they resemble?* "You each have an Order, most of which will have been apparent since childhood. Let me have a show of hands who does not yet know their Order."

Tory and Darcy slowly raised their hands and a boy in a hat did the same beside them along with a bunch more students around the class.

I nodded stiffly, only caring about the Orders of two Fae in this room. Because whatever they Emerged as would play a massive factor into their power level.

"Email me after class." I turned back to the board and continued with the lesson. "The Taenia have just two divisions whereas if I were to write every Mutatio on this board we would be here until next week." I pointed to the middle column. "The easiest way to distinguish a Mutatio Order is that they will shift fully into a creature without humanoid characteristics. The Divisus Order can get confused with the Mutatio, but the easiest way to distinguish them is that the Divisus Orders maintain human-like characteristics when they have mutated into their magical form. The Taenia differ from the other two Orders in that they maintain human form at all times, except for one feature. Can anyone name the feature of a Siren which changes when they embrace their powers?" I looked to the class, finding several students with their hands raised.

I picked a girl at the back with long braided hair. "Sirens get scales." She twisted her hand and a shimmer of blue and gold rippled across her skin. "They're tough as hell and perfect for swimming."

"Correct," I said. This class may have been simple for some, but it was vital I brought the students all up to the same level of knowledge. And between the Vegas and Fae who came from isolated areas or had shitty parents who'd never taught them jack about their own world, this was an important lesson. "And what feature changes for Vampires?"

"Teeth," Tory offered in a sharp tone, a crease on her brow that told me exactly what she thought of my kind. Anyone who hadn't witnessed Caleb Altair driving his fangs into her last night had likely seen it on FaeBook this morning. He'd staked a claim on her, but nothing was official. Although as my gaze flicked to her sister, I was pretty sure I had a deal in mind for how we could work out our competition over them.

Some of the students snickered and I let them mock the Vega girl, because that was all part of this world. If she wanted their respect, she'd have to earn it, and I sure as hell wouldn't be helping either of them attain that.

"Correct, Miss Vega." I rested my hands flat on my desk and peeled my upper lip back, my fangs extending as I exposed them for the whole class to see. Fuck, I was hungry. My throat was burning with a need my coffee couldn't do anything to satisfy.

Darcy's face paled and I grinned darkly at the glint of fear in her eyes, running my tongue across my fangs before letting them retract. *Are you scared of me, princess? How terrified would you be with my fangs in you then? Maybe I'll find out soon enough.* Though that thought came with another jerk of my cock and I smothered that idea. If she tasted too good, I could get hard in front of the whole class and then I really would be in trouble.

Darcy's nose wrinkled at me and I realised she was disgusted with me. I tried to ignore the flash of heat that burned in my chest over that and ploughed on.

"And what is the purpose of Vampire fangs?" I asked.

"To suck magic out of other Orders!" Miss Major called out, seeming excited, but fuck knew why.

"Correct," I said, deciding I wanted to feed. Maybe if I drank from someone, I could get my mind off of the one I really wanted to drink from. "Any volunteers?"

Nervous laughter rang out and my dark smile grew. Freshmen were so deliciously vulnerable, I was like a wolf standing in a room full of rabbits.

"No?" I pressed, strolling casually into the aisles between the desks as I started my hunt. "Because in Solaria, Fae don't tend to ask for what they want, do they?"

I paused beside the desk of the boy wearing a beanie hat just beside Darcy's desk and the boy's eyes widened. *I'll give her a show up close which will frighten the living hell out of her. Then maybe she'll start getting the message to go back to the Mortal Realm and stay well away from the throne of Solaria.*

"Name?" I demanded of the boy.

"Diego Polaris," he said. "And as a teacher, sir, don't you have to ask for blood?"

Didn't realise the kid was a comedian. I snatched his arm and dug my fangs into it, drinking deeply from the vein. The boy released a yell of pain and - *holy mother of fuck, what the hell is that? He tastes like a foot.*

"Stop!" Darcy demanded and I extracted my fangs, wiping the blood from the corner of my mouth and fighting a heave as I looked up to find her on her feet with rage in her eyes. My revulsion gave way to surprise at her little display and my brows arched.

The Fae in me reared up and a growl built in my throat at the challenge in her eyes. *Alright, here it is. The Vega backbone on display. So now the crushing has to begin.*

"Problem, Miss Vega?" I asked. *How far will you take this little challenge, trouble?*

She glanced over her shoulder at her sister who shook her head to warn her off. *Clever girl.*

Darcy sank back into her seat and satisfaction rippled through me at hearing her heart beat wildly out of rhythm. Her upper lip curled a little as she turned her head away so she didn't have to look at me anymore. I lingered there for a couple of seconds, fighting the urge to rip her out her seat and get the vile taste of Polaris's blood out of my mouth with the sweet nectar of hers. I just knew she'd taste like a dream. I had to know for sure though. I fucking had to.

No. I've gotten a semi from drinking from Darius before, what could happen if this girl tastes even better?

I marched back to my desk and dropped onto the wide leather chair behind it. "You have ten minutes to describe the shifted forms of each Mutatio in the table. Go." I plucked up my coffee cup, drained the last of it then sat back in my chair, picking up my Atlas.

I found Gabriel had sent me a video and I clicked on it, fighting a snort at the tiny snake in it who was wearing an equally tiny cowboy hat.

"Great, we'll just sit here for ten minutes then," Tory said under her breath, folding her arms and I ignored her complaints, but kept my attention trained on them in case they said anything worth listening to. So far, I didn't have much to report back to Darius, except that they were clueless and maybe that was good. Because their naivety to the Fae world meant they were about as much a threat to the throne as that foul tasting hat kid. *He must be a Heptian Toad.*

"Are you okay?" Darcy whispered to Polaris and I fought the urge to look up as I listened for his response, but none came. *Of course he's not okay. He's not gonna last a week here. Might as well start saying your goodbyes, Miss Vega.*

I shot a message to Gabriel in response to the video.

Lance:

That cowsnake doesn't look like he'd be good for much wrangling.

A photo came in of a plastic cow now sitting beside the snake and I bit down on a laugh.

Lance:

Clearly I was mistaken.

Noxy:

Clearly.

Aren't you in class right now?

Lance:

Yeah. First freshman CM of the year.

Feel free to come put me out of my misery.

Noxy:

Haha, it can't be that bad.

How's the Vega watch going?

I stole a glance at Darcy then forced my eyes back down at my Atlas as the pinkness of her lips taunted me.

Lance:

I don't think they'll be any trouble.

Noxy:

Are you sure about that?

Lance:

They're clueless. How much shit could they really stir up?

Noxy:

Just don't underestimate them too much, Orio…

Lance:

What have you seen??

Noxy:

Nothing.

Lance:

Liar.

Noxy:

Just follow your heart.

Lance:

Eat a dick.

Noxy:

Is that an offer?

Lance:

You wish.

Noxy:

I do. Every night on every star in the sky.

I swallowed another laugh and my hearing picked up a whisper towards the back of the room that made my amusement die in a wave.

"Orion is so hot," Kylie whispered.

"Yeah and he knows it." The girl beside her smothered a laugh.

"He does know it, because he has Vampire hearing." I looked up from my desk, pinning them in my gaze. "So if you don't want detention for the next week, I suggest you keep your petty thoughts to yourselves about me and any other member of faculty for that matter."

The girls' mouths dropped open and Darcy supressed a laugh. Apparently she didn't like the blonde girl. Which was the only thing we had in common. Though I didn't really like any student except Darius, so there was that.

"Oh come on, Professor, as if you don't love having a bunch of girls drooling over you," Tyler called out from the front row, shoving a hand into his blonde-tipped hair to mess it up.

Well you just made my day, you frosted-tip prick.

I rose from my seat, wandering casually toward the boy with a smile that told him I was thoroughly amused. Of course, that was just a trap and the guy fell for it as he grinned from ear to ear at me. *Stupid little freshman.*

In a surge of movement, I cracked Tyler's head against his desk and the entire class inhaled sharply as my smile died a quick death.

I pointed a finger and swept it across everyone in the room in warning. "To me, each and every one of you is just a pair of ears. Ears that are going to listen to me speak and no one else in this classroom. If you want to talk to your little *BFF* in the seat next to you, go ahead. But you'll join Frosted Tips here in detention tonight. And trust me when I say, detention with me is not a fun experience."

"Detention?" Tyler gasped as he rubbed his forehead.

My eyes narrowed on him as I gave him a fierce look that dared him to say another word. He backed down like a good boy, nodding quickly.

"This place is crazy," Darcy whispered to Tory.

"Batshit," she agreed and I wondered if I could pull them up on that to show them a lesson too.

Darcy's Atlas pinged loudly and just like that, the stars answered my plea. My gaze narrowed on her and she waved a hand in apology as she scrambled to find the mute button. But instead of finding it, her gaze fixed on the screen as she read the notification.

I watched in deadly silence as she tapped on it, continuing about her merry life as she moved to read the message. Then, I had to assume audacity was her middle name as she offered her Atlas to her sister to read it too while they shared eyebrow raises and Darcy even stifled a laugh. Darcy then took her time tapping on the screen and at this point everyone in the class was staring while I slowly crept closer to both of them, as silent as death on wings.

Darcy's Atlas pinged once more and she winced, her eyes snapping up and locking with mine.

"Miss Vega, are you entirely dense?" I snarled, my pulse thumping to a heady tune in my ears, telling me to bite her, begging me to.

"No," she said fiercely and I started to think Gabriel was right. These two were trouble. The obnoxious kind.

"Then why are your Atlas notifications switched on in my classroom after I gave you a clear warning to turn them off?" I snapped.

"I didn't realise-" she started but I cut off her bullshit excuse, my mouth twisting into a demonic smile as I prepared to put her in her place.

"Don't ever lie to me," I growled and a little of the colour in her cheeks drained away. "Let's hear it then. What does this message say that is obviously important enough to interrupt my class?"

Panic. The beautiful kind, crossed her features as she glanced down at the message on the screen. She was in my snare, baited and caught and now I'd be having her for dinner.

"Out loud. Now," I demanded and Tory started shaking her head, her own concern clear at what her sister was about to reveal to the class. My mind went on overdrive for a second as I wondered if she was about to read out some filthy message from a guy. But she'd been in Solaria one day, she could hardly have hooked up with anyone yet. Not that it mattered.

Of course, it wasn't unheard of. I'd had to break up an orgy in The Orb the first fucking day Seth Capella had joined Zodiac. He'd been at this school an hour. An *hour*.

But Darcy didn't seem like the type of girl to have been tearing her clothes off and diving into a pack orgy on day one at a new school in an entirely different world to the one she'd lived in her whole life. You never could really tell though.

Darcy cleared her throat as a few giggles sounded from her classmates. Diego shot her a sympathetic look as she began to read it, every syllable enunciated.

"The lump of muscle who teaches your Cardinal Magic class. Just to be clear, you'll recognise Orion by the scent of bourbon on his breath-" a big inhale sounded from the whole class, "-the permanent scowl stamped on his face and the general air of failed dreams about him since he lost his chance at playing for the Solarian Pitball League."

My teeth slammed together in a vice and blood pumped furiously through my body. Who the fuck was sending her messages like that about me?

Darcy's eyes lifted to meet mine and I glared at her with the intensity of the sun as laughter built in the classroom. I needed a culprit, and then I'd find said culprit and slam their head through a wall.

"And which of your many, *many* friends sent you that colourful message?" I asked, deadly calm, a lion in the grass. *I will find you, and I will fucking kill you.*

"I don't know. It's sort of... anonymous," Darcy said weakly, offering up her Atlas.

Anonymous? That wasn't good. And I could see the truth in her eyes so she probably wasn't lying. But why would someone bad mouth me to her? What was the purpose of it?

"Everyone return to their work," I barked, striding back to my chair and sitting down as I whipped up my Atlas again.

As I was about to send a message to Gabriel, Tory whispered something which caught my attention.

"Do you think we can trust this Falling Star person?"

"I don't know," Darcy replied thoughtfully. "It's hard to know who to trust in this place."

Are you really going to trust a message from some anonymous loser with a vendetta against me?

They clearly weren't getting the message about chatter in my classroom so I waved my hand, deciding I wanted Darcy squirming for me again. It was rather thrilling actually. I wondered how much blood I could drain from her face this time.

She frowned, glancing around like she wasn't sure what I wanted and that made this all the more fun.

"Miss Vega if you're not standing up in the next three seconds, you're going to regret it," I barked.

"Which Vega?" Tory asked, barely concealing her jibing tone.

My eyes snapped to her. "The one who has tried to individualise herself by dyeing the ends of her hair blue. It has failed by the way." *The only thing it's ensured is that I can't stop thinking about what it would look like spilled across my pillow while my hand is braced against the wall above her.*

Stop.

The temperature in my body was rising too high and I needed an outlet right now. So she was going to take the brunt of it because it was her fault those thoughts were in my head in the first place.

Wait a minute, maybe she's a Siren. Maybe her gifts are starting to Emerge and she's so strong than she's capturing me in the trap of her allure. That would make a lot of sense.

Darcy pressed her lips together at the insult, deciding not to do as I'd asked. Which was a very bad choice, because I didn't like being disobeyed. Not one bit. Especially in my classroom, and especially when I was already worked up.

"Stand up," I commanded.

"If I say no are you going to smash my head into the table?" she asked through gritted teeth. *I'd rather my headboard.*

Shit.

"I'll do it." Tory rose from her seat but I raised a hand, my gaze fixed on her sister.

"I didn't ask you," I snarled.

Tory pouted then dropped back into her chair, rolling her eyes.

Darcy obeyed at last, standing up and raising her brows with a mock bored expression as she waited for what I was about to say. I could hear her heartbeat though, my senses were entirely focused on it, so I could tell exactly how unnerved she was. And the beast in me liked that a whole lot.

My mouth hooked up at the corner as I finally got her where I wanted her. At my mercy.

"Tell me the qualities and abilities of a Nemean Lion." I smiled like a psycho, wanting to get under her skin and make her fear me. I was the hunter in the room and she was the prey. And that was how things were going to stay too. But I needed to get a rise out of these girls to see what they were capable of. And there was no time like the present.

She shrugged. "I don't know."

"I thought not," I said quietly. "But while everyone else was working you thought it was a good time to speak with your equally useless sister?"

Tory rose abruptly from her seat. "Who are you calling useless?"

"Am I not speaking clearly enough?" I asked coolly.

She pursed her lips and didn't answer.

I surveyed them for a moment, then a delicious idea for a punishment coiled through me like a viper. *"Both of you climb onto your desks."*

I Coerced them and the two twins scrambled onto their desks as everyone in the room started chattering excitedly. I was too Fae not to enjoy having that power over the Savage King's daughters. It was a high like nothing I'd known before.

I moved to lean back against my desk, pushing my hands into my pockets and nodding to Diego. "Polaris, please explain loud and clear to the ignorant twins on your left what Coercion is."

Diego got up, his chair legs scraping across the floor with a screech. He adjusted his beanie hat, throwing them an apologetic glance before answering. "Coercion is one of the Cardinal magics gifted to all Fae without exception. It's the ability to control those of weak mind and is particularly effective on mortals."

"Tell them why," I pressed, my amusement increasing as I continued to watch the girls.

Diego cleared his throat. "Because most Fae learn how to perform a simple shield on their minds to block basic Coercion from a young age."

"Thank you, sit down," I told Diego and both girls looked positively fuming.

"We've never been taught any-" Tory started but I cut over her.

"*Quiet,*" I commanded then looked to the rest of the class. "The Vega twins need to learn how to perform a simple shield. To encourage them to do so, you are all assigned the task of Coercing them at any given opportunity from here on out."

Kylie squealed her delight and several more of the class laughed. If they made it through the next couple of weeks with the whole school targeting them, I'd be very surprised. This was the perfect time to strike at them and I'd promised Darius I'd help remove the problem they presented him. So I'd happily stoop to these levels to get the job done.

"What?" Darcy gasped. "How are we supposed to learn to do something we've never even heard of before now?"

Your problem, not mine.

Tory was still struggling to open her lips after I'd ordered her to stay quiet, but she was working really damn hard at it.

I ignored her question, pointing at Tyler in the front row, ready to get the show started. "Stand up, turn around, one command."

"Are you kidding me right now?" Darcy blurted, trying to force herself to get off the table, but she couldn't do it. *You're in my trap now, Siren girl. And you're not going to fuck with my head anymore.*

Tyler grinned in excitement and I was kind of annoyed by giving the guy a reason to be happy. *"Jump up and down and flap your arms like a chicken."*

The twins did just that and I watched with a smug grin as they made complete idiots of themselves and the whole class roared with laughter.

"Who's next?" I asked and Kylie's arm flew into the air faster.

"Go ahead." I nodded at her.

She stood up with a malicious expression on her face and I wondered how far she was going to take this.

"Screw this," Tory snapped, kicking her Atlas off the desk and my arm shot out as I cast air magic to catch it, sending it right back to where it had come from.

I opened my mouth to berate her but the classroom door opened and Elaine Nova strode in. She surveyed the scene with a look of interest then smiled at me. "How is everyone's first lesson going?"

"Terrible," Darcy muttered and my eyes flashed her way. My gut tugged slightly at her miserable expression, but I immediately smothered that reaction. *She's a Siren, don't fall for it.*

I released them from my Coercion and Darcy dropped off her desk, folding her arms as she glared at me. *Don't hate the player, hate the game, princess.*

"The twins are behind," I told Elaine bluntly. "They don't know a thing about the Orders. Beyond that, they don't have even a basic shield against Coercion and I doubt against any other magic either. So they'll most likely be dead before the end of term."

"Hmm." Nova glanced their way. "Well that won't do." She tapped her lower lip and I wondered if she might just expel them now to save on the funeral expenses, but I guessed that was a bit too much to hope for. "They'll have to have Liaisons for tuition once a week."

I nodded. "That's the least they need."

"They'll need the best for the job," she said thoughtfully.

"Right." I scratched my short beard, losing interest in this conversation. If she wanted them mentored, then that was her problem.

"So you'll have to tutor one of them and I'll elect another professor for the other."

My fury went from ten to a hundred and a snarl built in my throat. "I coach Pitball most evenings, I don't have time for that." *No fucking way am I being a tutor to one of my enemies.*

"Yes but you only coach for an hour, then you have the whole evening at your disposal," Nova said brightly.

"You're right, I'd *love* to give my private time up for this," I said dryly and Nova beamed as if she hadn't registered my sarcasm.

The principal looked to Darcy and pointed. "Tory, you'll be taught by Professor Orion and-"

No. And no with a slice of fuck no.

"I'm Darcy," she corrected.

"I – er – of course you are," Nova backtracked. "So you'll be with Orion and Darcy I'll let you know-"

"I'm Tory," her sister huffed and I saw my fate closing in, the doors slamming in my face and offering me no way out. I quickly ran over my options in my mind and figured this was going to happen anyway, so I needed to take advantage of it. At least I'd be in a position to learn more about them, find their weaknesses like Darius needed. That was a good thing. Even if the idea of it was making heat crawl up my neck.

"Right er-" Nova started but I stepped in.

"Blue, you're with me." I pointed at Darcy and she scowled at the nickname. *Well it looks like you just bought yourself an eternity of being called that then, didn't you Blue?*

If I had to do this, then I'd at least be getting my kicks out of it. I'd get so deep under her skin, she'd lose her mind trying to claw me out. But I was still pissed I had to give up my free time for this. My life was already owned in so many ways by other people, now a Vega was taking a piece of it too.

"Right," Nova said. "You should start tonight; they need to get on track as soon as possible."

"Great," I bit out. There goes my down time laying on the couch getting wasted.

"I'll leave you to it then." Nova turned on her stilettos and headed out of the room, snapping the door shut behind her.

I sighed heavily, marching back to the board as I thought about having Darcy all to myself in my office. That didn't seem like a very safe place to be. For her or me. How was I going to stop myself from biting her? *Well maybe I don't have to... I'll just angle my boner away if I get turned on by her power and shoot away to hide behind my desk before she sees. Simple.*

By the stars, am I really making a boner escape plan?

"*Sir?*" Kylie moaned and I decided I hated her there and then for her whiny voice alone. "Are we not doing Coercion anymore?"

"No," I growled. "Sit down and shut up. That goes for all of you."

I turned back to the board and pushed away all thoughts of having Darcy alone in my office with her blood as fair game and focused on the lesson I needed to teach. But as my fangs pricked my tongue, I felt my inner monster make a decision that would be impossible to go back on. Because tonight, when she came to my office with her blue hair and defiant eyes, I was going to get a taste of that girl and show her what true power looked like.

CALEB

CHAPTER SIX

I shot across the locker room for our Fire Elemental class and pushed a hand into my blonde curls as I stood before the mirror, taming out the tangles that had formed in it from racing across campus to get here today.

"Who are you trying to impress?" Darius asked dryly from behind me where he sat on one of the benches, lacing his white sneakers for the class.

My gaze shifted to him in the mirror and I gave him a taunting grin. "Who do you think?"

Darius huffed out a breath which was laced with smoke from his Dragon and he leaned back in his seat, arching a brow at me with his shirt still fisted in his hand and his inked chest bare. He flicked a silencing bubble up around the two of us before continuing.

"Seriously? You're planning on flirting with the girls our parents have specifically tasked us to get rid of?" he asked.

"Yeah, man," I confirmed, my gaze shifting from him back to my own appearance as I continued to tussle my curls until they fell into the perfect kind of haphazard mess to soak panties for miles around. "The Vegas are seriously hot and seriously powerful. Tory tasted like a fucking drug and I plan on getting high on her over and over and over again. I know we've gotta get rid of them and all that, but I see no reason to miss out on the good times while we can grab them."

"So go after the other one," Darius muttered. "Roxy is in my House and I want her under *my* heel."

There was a ring of command to his tone which just wasn't gonna fucking fly with me and I straightened my spine, turning to look at him with an eyebrow raised.

"Under your heel, yeah?" I teased. "Because I'm getting the feeling you want her under you in a much more interesting way than that."

"You know what our parents want us to do," Darius replied, not answering my taunt as he got to his feet and tugged on the shirt which was provided for this class, the dark red material clinging to his flesh like a second skin and outlining all of his muscles just like mine was for me.

"Yeah, yeah," I agreed flippantly because I knew what the official Council line was on the matter. The Vegas were a threat we couldn't tolerate and they needed to go. I heard it loud and clear. But my mom wasn't always as cut and dry as the rest of them and she'd given me further instructions than just blindly trying to force the Vegas out. She wanted me to figure them out, work out what made them tick and decide whether or not they really could pose a threat to us. After all, we'd all been intended to serve beneath the Savage King's daughters one day if fate had played out differently and they'd grown up here with their parents alive, so she wasn't willing to just blindly ignore the threat their level of power could cause us. Which meant she wasn't opposed to me getting a little more friendly with the girls if I wanted to. And sure, she hadn't at any point told me to try my luck with one of them, but she also hadn't banned me from it either. And ever since I'd sunk my fangs into Tory Vega's throat, I'd been hooked on the idea of her as thoroughly as a drunk was hooked on booze, so I wasn't going to be backing off just because Darius didn't like it. "No one said I couldn't have any fun along the way though, did they?"

Darius's eyes flared with irritation but if he wanted to tell me to back off then he was going to have to flat out say it. Besides, I had no intention of agreeing to that even if he did.

"Those girls are going to be trouble," he said, glancing in the mirror and sweeping his own dark hair back away from his face with much less care than I'd just given to mine.

"Oh I'm counting on it," I replied with a dark laugh.

We strode out of the locker rooms and Darius let the silencing bubble fall away as we strode out into the colosseum like structure where our lesson would be held. I called on my fire magic, letting the heat of it roll through my veins as I prepared for our class and one look at Darius said this one was going to get messy.

Yeah, he was all kinds of pissed at me over the Vegas, but I was willing to bet it had a lot more to do with wanting one for himself than it did with following our orders like good little Heirs.

Professor Pyro was chatting to a couple of freshmen who had already arrived for the class and I moved to stand against the wall next to the girls' locker room with one goal in mind.

Darius came to stand at my side, an irritated noise escaping him which he clearly had no plans on expanding on, so I just offered him a grin which revealed my sharpening fangs.

"Let me guess, you have a taste for Vega?" he deadpanned.

"Yeah. And seeing as our latest little problem fucking hates it when I bite her, you should be egging me on. Because all you care about is hounding them out of here, right?"

"Right," he agreed but that demonic look in his eyes said he was holding his tongue against more he wanted to say.

"She got under your skin last night then, huh?" I pushed and he shrugged.

147

"I guess. She has a way of taking me by surprise, but I'll have her in hand soon enough."

"I bet."

Just then, Tory Vega strode out of the locker room with another little freshman girl at her side and my gaze fell to the curves of her body in the skin tight outfit required for this class. The blood red material hugged her round ass so perfectly that I wanted to sink my teeth right into it like it was a damn apple.

I cut a glance at Darius and the heat in his eyes had practically turned volcanic as he watched her, that dark anger in him stirring with a primal kind of desire which had my hackles raising. I'd heard him when he'd tried to claim her the moment she'd arrived here and one glance at the rigid muscles and fierce hunger in his eyes made it more than clear that he still wanted that. But there lay the problem, because I wanted to lay my claim on her too and I wasn't a creature who would easily back down.

I stepped out of the shadows, stalking after her as she walked away and my gaze stayed firmly locked on that ass of hers as I drew on my earth magic and a smirk tugged at the corner of my lips.

A twist of my fingers had the ground bucking at her feet and she almost fell, arms wheeling to steady herself while her friend scrambled aside. I gave her a moment to believe she'd survived that, then bucked the ground hard enough to take her out.

She fell backwards and I shot forwards, catching her before she could hit the ground and sweeping her down in my arms like a lover dipping a girl for a kiss.

"Thanks, I-" she began, but as her dark gaze focused on me and my cocky smile, she cut her words off flat, anger brimming where gratitude met a swift death.

"You wanna watch out for that. The ground around here can be mighty unpredictable," I purred, tugging her upright but keeping hold of her arms like I was still steadying her - but I wasn't going to be letting go any time soon.

The little blonde freshman backed up, her eyes wild and searching for any signs of a teacher to intervene, but they wouldn't. This was a Fae eat Fae world, and I was hungry for a taste of this one.

"Right. I'll be sure to do that." Tory snatched her arms out of my grip took a step back like she thought it would be so simple to escape me. With little more than a twitch of my fingers, the earth beneath her feet bucked again and my heart leapt as she fell on her ass at my feet, an offering at the altar of a deity.

Barely smothered laughter rang out around us as the other students moved closer to watch the show and Tory made a move to get up, but I wouldn't be allowing that.

I pounced before she could do more than scramble backwards a few inches, my knees landing either side of her hips and a grin on my face which revealed my sharpening fangs as they tingled for a taste of her blood. I could practically smell it from this distance, the power in her veins humming like the intoxicating scent of addiction which I was more than happy to succumb to.

"Oh for the love of god," she snarled, slamming her palms into my chest and I couldn't say I hated the way her hands felt against my body. "You'd better not be about to-"

I caught her wrists as she tried to shove me again, a low snarl escaping me as I forced her down beneath me, my body pressing to her curves and my cock liking that a whole hell of a lot as I brought this powerful creature to heel and drove her into the ground beneath me.

My fangs found her throat without me even making the conscious decision to bite her and the gasp that escaped her lips as they pierced her flesh was enough to make a groan of pleasure build in my chest.

I drank deeply, the heavenly taste of her singing over my tongue and washing down my throat as her rich power spilled inside me and filled me to the brim.

Instead of just giving in like I expected her to, Tory started cursing me as loudly and colourfully as she could imagine, her hips bucking between my thighs in an attempt to force me off of her despite the way my venom had weakened her.

I growled in reply to her struggles, driving her down beneath me and losing myself to the bloodlust as the taste of her power totally overwhelmed me. She was like the best kind of sin, my body and the beast in me falling prey to the allure of her and my cock was definitely more than a little interested in her too. Luckily for her, the way I had her pinned meant I wasn't actually dry humping her while taking her blood so she probably wasn't aware of that little fact but the more I got of her, the more I wanted and I knew I wasn't going to be giving her up after this. Darius may have wanted to lay a claim too, but I was willing to pick up the gauntlet of his challenge because this girl was all the right kinds of obsession which I was aching to dive into.

"That's more than enough, Altair," Professor Pyro sighed from somewhere nearby and I was forced to remember the class surrounding us. "She needs *some* energy left if she's going to be able to perform in my class today."

I forced myself back with some difficulty, withdrawing my fangs and licking the last drop of blood from Tory's soft skin before pushing myself back and peering down at her.

She looked seriously good pinned beneath me like that, black hair fanning out across the ground and dark eyes flaring with a furious kind of hatred that just got me even hotter for her somehow.

"You have no idea how good you taste," I commented, licking my lips to chase the last of her taste from them while she scrunched her nose up at me.

"You've got what you wanted from me so why don't you just get the hell off of me?" she demanded, yanking at her wrists again while I kept them pinned in the sand above her head. I probably should have been letting go, but she was so unlike any other Fae I'd ever met that I found myself lingering, drinking her in and trying to figure her out.

I tilted my head as I regarded her and a slow smile spread across my face which I knew would only serve to incite her further. "You know, I'm not sure I've ever fed from anyone who hates it quite as much as you do," I commented. "The other Fae have grown up knowing about my kind and they just accept this as part of the chain of power but you..."

"Yeah, I hate it," she snapped. "So why don't you get your kicks feeding off of someone who enjoys your twisted brand of creep and leave me alone?"

Did she just try to give me a command? Oh no, that shit wasn't going to fly with me. If she thought she hated me before then things were about to get really interesting. I released her suddenly and leapt to my feet, my hard on thankfully sinking enough that the tight outfit I was wearing probably didn't reveal it to everyone in attendance.

"This girl is my personal Source," I declared, my gaze trailing across all of the Fae in our class and making sure there wasn't so much as a flicker of dissension from that claim. "If any other Vampire wants to feed from her then they can take it up with me, spread the word."

Tory shoved herself to her feet, looking like she'd dearly enjoy punching me as her fists closed at her sides and her eyes flared with rage. "I'm not your personal anything," she said.

"Feel free to try and stop me, sweetheart," I teased, knowing she had zero chance of that. "But until you manage it, you can consider yourself my own personal juice box."

Tory looked ready to spit, but her attention was snared by Darius as he laughed loudly from the front of the crowd to our left. She looked even more pissed to find him watching our little interaction and I could tell that she hadn't picked up on the tension in his posture as he stood with his arms folded across his broad chest. His poker face was damn good and I was sure everyone around us believed he was thoroughly amused by seeing me grind the Vega princess into the dirt and bite her against her will. But I could see the demon in his eyes as his gaze moved from her to me and I knew he was pissed.

I cocked an eyebrow at him in a challenge and he lifted his chin in reply.

Yeah, we were going to be working through some of our Alpha bullshit really fucking soon because the tension between us was tight enough to snap. We still loved each other, but sometimes the other Heirs and me had to go head to head just to relieve the tension of all the testosterone which hung in the air around us. And it wasn't like any of us were afraid of a good fight - in fact, I knew for certain that we all relished it, and with Tory Vega's power flooding my veins, my own blood was humming with the desire to give him what he wanted.

"Well if all of the Vampires are fully replenished, I'd like to get on with my lesson," Professor Pyro announced loudly and Tory abruptly turned her back on the two of us in a clear dismissal.

A deep growl rumbled from Darius's chest at the insult and I barely suppressed a hiss, my muscles tightening with the desire to put her in her place once more. No one turned their fucking backs on us and got away with it and now this little thing had done it twice.

I took a step towards her, but Darius caught my arm, the barely restrained anger in him clear as a single word fell from his lips, so low that I only caught it with my Vampire hearing.

"Later."

I tensed, not liking him telling me what to do, but I could see the sense in it. Our Vega problem was clearly going to take a while to fix and she'd literally just been pinned at my mercy in front of the whole class. We didn't need to prove our dominance over her again just yet.

"As it's the first class for the freshmen, I want the rest of you to pair off and take some time reacquainting yourselves with the techniques you learned at the end of last year. You should have been practicing over the summer and I'll be coming around to look for improvements once I've got these guys going." Professor Pyro shooed the older students away but me and Darius stayed where we were, our gazes fixed on the defiant little Vega.

"What are you still doing here boys? The last I checked, you were sophomores," Pyro said as she fixed us with a penetrating gaze.

"We just wanted to see how powerful the new Heir really is," Darius said, his lips twitching in amusement as Tory shifted uncomfortably in front of us though she still refused to turn and face us again, like having two monsters at her back was no concern to her at all.

"Well unfortunately for you, ogling the new girl isn't part of the syllabus," Pyro replied haughtily, shooing us again and we were forced to leave unless we wanted to try and pull rank with a teacher.

Tory turned to watch us go and my hackles raised as I saw her eyes sweeping over Darius's body in a clear eye fuck. Nah, that wasn't going to work for me. I elbowed my Dragon friend as he eye fucked her right back and he turned away to stalk across the arena with me with a grunt of frustration.

"So, am I going to be beating your ass now or are we saving all of that pent up aggression for later?" I taunted.

Darius cut me a look, his eyes flashing with the golden slits of his Dragon for a moment as smoke coiled from his nostrils and I grinned in anticipation of our fight.

"Now it is then," I agreed, flexing my muscles as we kept walking, heading for a wide open area on the far side of the arena where we could really show off our power without having to worry about any powerless idiots getting in our way.

"Maybe you should consider getting another Source," Darius growled as he flicked his fingers, flames writhing over his hands like scurrying ants.

"Give me one good reason why you would want me to do that and maybe I'll consider it," I tossed back though I absolutely wouldn't be considering it. Tory Vega's power was an indulgence I had no intention of ever giving up unless she grew powerful enough to stop me from claiming it. And as there was no chance of that happening any time soon, I fully intended to have my mouth all over her as often as Faely possible. And as I tossed a glance back at her again, I was happy to admit to myself that I was hoping I could do that with or without my fangs being involved. That girl was hot and she didn't just take our shit. I liked the bite in her almost as much as I liked biting her and I wanted to get closer to her for more reasons than just claiming her blood.

Before I could get too lost in that daydream, a ball of fire slammed into my chest and I was hurled across the arena before crashing into the wall so hard that the air was driven from my lungs.

Darius laughed loudly, his dark eyes flaring with excitement as I shoved myself to my knees and I snarled at him for the cheap shot while sparing a moment to heal the pain of my injuries from my flesh.

Then it was on.

I leapt to my feet and hurled a fireball directly at him, using it to blind him as I raced around to his left with my Vampire speed and fired my real shot at his side instead. Of course the asshole had been expecting that and he dropped to his knee, his fist crashing into the sand and sending a ring of potent flames out around him in every direction before he even locked on to my new location.

I threw my own power back at him, forcing the flames to part around me and firing a series of missiles his way.

Darius stood and took the blow, his jaw gritting as he dug his heels into the ground and just let the magic crash into his chest like a psychopath, ignoring the pain of the fire and relying on his suit to stop it from burning him.

He took the time to craft his magic into a more refined shape and I rolled my eyes as a huge Dragon built entirely of flames lunged to life at his back.

"So predictable, man!" I taunted, shooting aside as the fire Dragon roared and more flames spilled from its mouth in my direction.

The other students were starting to pay more attention to us now, some of them racing away to safety on the far side of the arena, others surging closer to watch the show. But I couldn't spare any attention for them, my eyes staying glued on my opponent as I raced around him and conjured my own fire creations into existence at my back.

Snakes built of flame sprung from the ground in the wake of my footsteps, my intention to take down his Dragon with the might of many instead of just going at him head on with another huge creature.

Darius laughed as his Dragon took flight, the beast crashing into my snakes which spat flames of their own and lunged at it in response.

I tried to keep hold of them, but as the Dragon crashed into them, their flames began to merge with the beast as Darius stole control of the magic and latched it to his own.

I created more and more of the serpents, aiming them after the Dragon as it took off and began firing down on them from above while a smile bit into my cheeks at the strain of welding so much power at once.

It was burning from my flesh, making my whole body sing with the buzz of flexing my magical muscles and one look over at Darius gave away just how much he was enjoying this fight too. But this was more than just a game of war, we were fighting for the win and neither of us would be giving in easily.

My snakes began to overwhelm his Dragon and a laugh of victory tumbled from my lips as I saw it coming, but of course the bastard wasn't done. With a snarl of effort, Darius raised his hands and conjured a second Dragon out of the water fountain to our left to rival the size of the first, his brow beading with perspiration at the effort of commanding so much power all at once. But it was worth it. And though I scrambled to reinforce the fire magic of my snakes, they didn't stand a chance against so much water and as the glimmering Dragon dove into the swarm of my creatures, he doused them out of existence and my magic shattered.

Darius gave a cocky whoop of victory and I scowled at him as I panted through my exertion and the two Dragons did a victory lap of the arena.

"Always the cheat," I called, folding my arms as I glared his way because the asshole knew we'd been playing with fire and bringing water into it was a bullshit move.

Darius started laughing and I shot towards him with a snarl, ready to finish this fight and come out on top after all.

I slammed into him before he even realised I was coming, my fist colliding with his solid jaw as I took him to the ground.

Darius snarled at me as he quickly fell into the fight, the animosity and anger that had been brewing between us finally finding an outlet as we gave in to the brutality of our punches and the satisfaction of trying to beat the ever loving shit out of each other.

His fist cracked against the side of my skull like a stars damned anvil striking a blow at my brain with the force of his fucking Dragon muscles. He was a huge bastard and his physical strength was damn near impossible to match no matter how big I was myself.

"Fucking - Dragon - asshole," I hissed between blows and he laughed as he managed to roll us so that he was on top of me, his fists crashing against my chest in punches powerful enough to crack my fucking ribs.

I snarled ferociously as I lunged at him, my forehead connecting with his nose and making a loud crack ring out which was swiftly followed by a curse of pain and a spill of blood.

I managed to get the upper hand for a moment, landing on top of him and using my speed to strike his ribs, chest and stomach over and over again before Darius roared and threw his weight up to flip us over once more.

His hands locked tight around my throat and I hissed between my teeth as he began to choke me out, a savage grin on his face beneath the blood which now stained his teeth.

"Mother-fucker," I ground out and his grip increased, his knee driving down on my chest as weight pressed me down.

I tried to buck him off but the pain from his weight crushing my cracked ribs was damn near blinding and despite my thrashing, it soon became clear that I'd lost this fucking fight.

Darius's eyes flashed with deadly intent as he continued to choke me out and I was pretty sure the asshole would actually wait for me to black out unless I admitted defeat.

But I didn't want to do that. Even as spots danced before my eyes and my lungs burned with a desperate, hungry energy, I still didn't want to give in. But my ears were ringing and my limbs were growing weak and with a furious sense of frustration, I forced my hand out and smacked it against the ground beside us three times to let him know I gave up.

Darius grinned widely as he released me in an instant, straightening up and healing his own face before swiping the blood away with his water magic.

I sucked in a few huge breaths then started laughing as the tension finally fell away between us and I looked up at the big bastard of a Dragon who I loved with all the ferocity of the sun.

Darius offered me his hand and I took it, letting him pull my to my feet as I pressed my other hand to my ribs and healed the damage to them so that I could take a deeper breath.

"I'll get you next time," I warned him, slapping his back.

"You said that last time," Darius mocked, elbowing me and I had to suppress a groan. Power wise we were all definitely evenly matched but with Darius's Order influencing his build he was now over six and a half foot tall and his muscles had muscles on them so even my six foot two couldn't compare. *Asshole.*

I opened my mouth to respond, but a prickle along my skin made me look around instead and I found we had an audience I hadn't been expecting.

Tory Vega stood there with her arms folded and a look of resignation on her face which almost overshadowed the clear dislike she was giving off. Professor Pyro was at her side and it was clear they'd been waiting for us to finish for some time.

I pushed a hand into my hair as I gave Tory my attention, eying her neck as I ran my tongue over my fangs. I'd just used a good chunk of the magic I'd stolen from her and I couldn't help but wonder if she might have a little more going spare...

"I have a new assignment for you, Mr Acrux," Professor Pyro said, her gaze on Darius and my attention peaked.

"Yes, Professor?" Darius asked, giving her his polite teacher voice which did very little to hide the brute in him in my humble opinion.

"I'd like you to give Tory here some one on one tutoring to help her learn to harness that tempest of power within her. I tried to guide her myself but she needs someone more powerful than me and as the most accomplished fire weaver in the academy, you were the obvious choice."

Darius's attention flicked onto Tory, his spine straightening as he regarded her the way a wolf might eye a lamb and I had to suppress a chuckle because I knew for a fact that he would have absolutely zero intention of helping a Vega do a damn thing.

"Of course, Professor Pyro," Darius agreed, though I knew it was bullshit. "Only, I do have a full timetable at the moment so it may be better for her to choose someone else."

"Okay," Tory agreed with a bright smile, making it clear she absolutely didn't want his help anyway and I had to fight a laugh as Darius bristled at the insult. "Never mind." She began to turn away from us but Professor Pyro stopped her.

"That's not a problem," Pyro said firmly, giving Darius a pointed look. "You can train her on Thursday evenings after dinner and we can add Mondays if necessary."

Darius's gaze darkened and I could practically taste smoke on my tongue from the fire which I knew was burning in him at that command. No fucking way he'd be doing any such thing and for the look on Tory's face it was pretty clear she didn't want him to anyway.

"Yes Professor," Darius agreed and Pyro nodded before leading Tory away again.

We watched her go and I leaned a little closer to my friend as my eyes stayed glued to that perfectly round ass of hers.

"How are you going to get out of that then, brother?" I teased.

"Simple," Darius replied, his gaze still very much locked on the Vega princess too. "I won't. But if she actually expects me to show up then she's going to have to make me. It's what a real Fae would do after all."

I sniggered at that, knowing full well that Tory wouldn't be able to do any such thing. And as she tossed a glance back over her shoulder at us, it was pretty damn clear she wasn't in any way happy about this either.

DARIUS

CHAPTER SEVEN

I tore down the Pitball pitch with Orion's voice ringing in my ears as he roared his encouragement from behind me while I kept the heavy earthball tucked tight beneath my arm.

"Take them down!" he bellowed, all signs of the miserable Cardinal Magic Professor banished while he gave in to his love of the game. I only wished he could have been living his dream of playing in the League rather than having to throw his passion for it into training us. It wasn't even like he'd be coaching any of us into the League ourselves - at least not any of the Heirs, because our fates were written for us even more firmly than his had been.

The rest of the team ran at me from the other end of the pitch, all of them set against me as I charged and tried to get a pit against the odds. I relished the challenge of it. The swell of my muscles, the rampant thumping of my heart, the pounding of my feet across the mud and thrum of my magic at the surface of my skin.

Seth howled as he raced to intercept me, the ground trembling beneath the might of his earth magic as he willed it to take my feet out from under me.

I threw my free hand out, casting a bridge of ice above the ground too and making my boots stick to it just enough to stop me from slipping as I raced across it at full speed.

Seth tried to leap up onto the bridge to stop me, but I melted it everywhere he tried to land, laughing as he cursed me and circling away from the main force of the team ahead before trying to cut back towards the looming pit in the centre of the pitch.

Caleb came for me next, throwing out flames to melt my bridge but instead of fighting them, I encouraged them, letting my bridge fall apart as the flames engulfed me and hid me within them.

I changed direction sharply, quickly casting an illusion which looked like me and sending it sprinting out of the flames in the opposite direction to the one I was planning on taking.

"Come at me you rascal of a reptile!" Geraldine boomed from beyond the fire and the ground trembled as she sent earth magic chasing after the fake me.

I sent the flames up in an explosion as I dove out of them, closing my eyes just before a blinding flash erupted from them and the rest of the team cried out in shock, cursing me.

"I'm blind!" Seth wailed. "I'll never see a hot rack or a rocking cock again!"

I laughed as I opened my eyes again and I sprinted on, racing back the way I'd come and finding my tricks had worked on almost every member of the team. But as I turned my head to look for Max, my stomach plummeted. Of course the Siren had been able to sense the lack of emotions in my decoy, but where in the stars was he-

A body crashed into me from above and I swore as I was crushed beneath Max as he plummeted from the sky with a booming laugh, using his fucking air magic to get the drop on me.

The pitball fell from my hands and rolled aside as I was forced to fight him off, coating my fists in ice and fire as I began to pummel him.

Max laughed as I punched and swore at him, trying his hardest to keep me locked beneath him while the others raced closer.

But with a surge of effort, I managed to get my knees up between us and threw him off of me.

With a Dragon's roar, I threw my hands up in the direction of the rest of the team as they raced towards me and fire bloomed from my palms in a wave of power that sucked me dry as I expelled it to hold them back.

I grabbed the ball and started sprinting practically before my feet were even back under me again.

A clamour of noise sounded from behind me as the rest of the team all fought to get through the wall of fire and I grinned in triumph as the pit loomed ahead of me.

I felt the moment my magic shattered, my power burning through and leaving me tapped out and the roar of a challenge which sounded at my back only urged me on as the team took chase.

The earth bucked beneath me, air blasted into me, fires bloomed around me and a torrent of water crashed into my spine but just as I felt someone's hands on my back, I launched the pitball with all of my strength.

I slammed into the ground, my shirt tearing down the back as someone tried to yank me backwards by it a second before a heap of bodies landed on top of me and I was crushed beneath them.

But despite my face being pressed into the mud and the weight of all of them crushing me down, Orion's bellow of celebration still found me as my ball landed in the pit.

"That's how you fucking play Pitball!" he roared and a mixture of curses and cheers sounded from my teammate as they all scrambled off of me.

I shoved myself upright, a laugh on my lips as I scraped the dirt from my face and the other heirs all leapt on me, thumping my back and congratulating me on a brilliant play while promising to do even better themselves the next time we practiced.

The flash of a camera caught my eye and I glanced up at the empty stands in time to see the camera go off again, a middle-aged looking Fae snapping away furiously.

"No paparazzi are allowed on academy grounds!" Orion shouted, shooting past us in his own mud stained pitball uniform as the trespassing Fae squeaked in alarm and took off as fast as he could.

He raced out of sight a moment before Lance caught up to him but the scream that followed said he hadn't gotten away.

"The stars only know why they'd be snapping pictures of you four lugamuffins anyway," Geraldine said, drawing my attention to her as she bent in half at the waist and started stretching, touching her toes and pointed her ass at us. "No doubt they were hoping to catch a glimpse of the beauty of the true queens and the camera went off by accident."

"Nah, Grus," Max replied, his gaze moving over her ass unashamedly as he pushed his fingers through his mohawk. "They wanted to get a snapshot of the four of us looking like a housewives' wet dream. And clearly they got it."

"Pish posh," Geraldine replied, straightening. "I can admit that the Dragon boy is one devilish specimen if you discount his entire personality, but the mutt needs a haircut more than I need my lawn watered twice a day, and the biter can only pull off the pretty boy polished ensemble - mud and muck does not become you."

"Hey," Caleb snapped. "I look plenty good all rough and ready."

"I've never known a rough and ready man to sport a manicure, you puffed up pompom," she laughed. "And don't get me started on the solemn salamander." She waved a hand in Max's vague direction dismissively then strode away with her little royalist buddy, ending the conversation without so much as a warning.

"And what about me?" Max called after her, striding along to catch up.

"You didn't mention me!"

"You are the fish, you bothersome barracuda, the salty seabass, the dangling dogfish, the puffed up pufferfish, need I go on?"

"Is that because I'm a Siren?" Max asked, stalking after her while the rest of us trailed behind. He always let her drag him in to her nonsense, but it seemed like way too much work for me.

"People say my hair is nice," Seth muttered, running his fingers through his long, dark locks while he scowled at Geraldine's back.

"It's shit hot, man, ignore her," Cal replied and Seth instantly perked up, sidling closer to him.

"You think? Because I think you look totally fuckable right now all covered in mud. In fact, I'd definitely suck your dick if you wanna go get drunk in the shimmering springs again like the last time when we-"

"Speaking of fuckable, you should have seen how hot Tory Vega looked pinned beneath me while I bit her in Fire Elemental earlier," Caleb interrupted him, shooting a smirk at me. "Don't you think so, Darius?"

"Girl looks fuckable every time I lay my eyes on her," I replied sardonically, refusing to rise to his bait.

"Hell yeah she does," Seth agreed. "I mean who would have expected the Vega twins to be so fucking banging?" He bit down on his fist with a groan. "What do you think the chances are of us convincing the two of them to join us in an Heir/Princess orgy before we have to kick them the hell out of here?"

"Well seeing as there would be four dicks and a pair of siblings in that fantasy, I'm going to be saying no thanks," I interrupted him. Besides, one Vega was more than enough for me and I had my focus firmly fixed on her. I didn't know why because the two of them looked identical and yet...they just weren't. Not to me. Roxy Vega had captured my attention and she wasn't letting it go any time soon.

"Boo," Seth complained. "You're so fucking vanilla, Darius. I swear if I wasn't convinced you fuck like a hellion with all the anger of the Devil at your back, I'd be convinced you were a boring lay. I bet you've never even sucked a cock, have you?"

"Dude, you're the only one of us who likes a side of dick with your pussy, that doesn't make him vanilla," Caleb said with a shake of his head and I snorted my amusement.

"Don't knock it 'til you've tried it," Seth replied instantly, giving Caleb a nudge. "I'd be gentle with you...or rough? When you fantasise about it, how would I be? Do you wanna top me or would you be down for me topping you because I promise that when you-"

Caleb cast a gag of leaves to cover Seth's mouth and I laughed as he glowered at him over it.

Just as we made it to the door of the locker rooms, Orion called out to stop me and I turned back to look at him as he shot across the pitch to meet us.

"Uncle Lionel has been trying to get hold of you," Lance said with a bitter tone to his voice which spoke of our shared hatred for my father. "He kept calling while I was trying to shove that photographer's camera up his ass, so I had to just smash it and tell him to fuck off instead."

I gave him a tight smile at the joke which was probably pretty close to the truth and nodded my head.

"Alright I'll call him now," I agreed, looking forward to the idea of that about as much as I would have been to an enema.

"I'm gonna run a few laps of the pitch before I call it a night, then I've got my liaison with the blue twin."

"Make sure you find out all you can for us," I urged and he nodded.

"I'm on it, you know you can count on me."

I headed away from him as he started to run his laps and made it into the locker rooms as the rest of the team were heading out to get back to their evenings.

"You coming, man?" Seth asked, bouncing on his toes excitedly. "The moon is high tonight and I'm feeling frisky."

"I gotta check in with Father," I said and the three of them groaned sympathetically for me. "Just go on ahead and I'll catch up when I'm done."

I waved them out of the room and they left me to it, none of them bothering to change out of their Pitball uniforms as they headed off covered in mud. It was our tradition to get dinner while still wearing our trashed, muddy Pitball training gear after practice so none of them bothered hitting the showers.

I sighed as the door swung closed behind them and tugged my Atlas from my bag before dialling my father's number and sitting down on one of the benches. I slipped a hand into the side pocket of my bag and tugged out a handful of golden rings and a couple of thick gold chains which I tossed over my neck and dropped beneath my shirt. I pushed the rings onto my fingers and released a slow breath as the heat of the gold against my skin soothed a little of the tension in my chest and I slowly began to draw some power back out of the precious metal to replenish myself. I'd have to sleep surrounded in the stuff to fully top up, but this at least would take the edge off and give me something to work with for now.

I cast a silencing bubble around me as I waited through the rings and leaned my head back against the wall, closing my eyes while I waited for him to answer. The asshole was expecting my call, so this was all just some power play bullshit while he no doubt sat in his fucking office and just watched the phone ring.

"Darius," he answered finally just as the call was about to cut out.

"Father," I replied in the same dry, flat tone he used with me.

"I take it your training went well."

"Very," I agreed. "We should destroy the opposition in our first game of the season."

"Well if you didn't that would be highly embarrassing," Father agreed in a curt tone. "Let's cut the pleasantries though, boy, you know why I'm calling."

Pleasantries? The only pleasant interaction I could recall having with him was when I'd bid him farewell when I'd moved into the academy. Fuck him.

"The girls are tougher than we expected," I said, knowing he was pissed about the fact that they were still here despite us only having had a few days to work on getting them out.

"Or perhaps you and the other Heirs aren't cut out for the task?" he suggested. "Because it seems to me that the attentions of the four boys destined to rule over this kingdom should be more than enough to intimidate a few practically mortal girls."

I swallowed the lump in my throat at the coldness of his tone, my entire body locking up at the underlying threat in his voice.

"You wouldn't want to fail me on such a simple task, would you, boy?"

"No, Father," I replied, my voice just as cool and unwavering as before. I knew well enough not to ever let him see he had me rattled.

"Good. I'll expect you home for dinner this weekend with your brother and I. Hopefully you will be able to show him a good example of how well you managed to deal with this threat to your rule. Because if you don't get rid of them then their continued attendance to your academy is going to end up with undesirable consequences. And neither you nor Xavier should really need any more lessons in undesirable consequences, should you?"

"No Father," I ground out, my hatred for this beast of a man eating me alive from the inside out almost as much as I hated myself for the knot of tension which filled my gut at his words.

It wasn't even the threat to me which had that fear building inside me, though I could gladly admit I was no fan of his fists laying claim to my body, but it was the implication that he would include Xavier in this. That he would punish my brother if I failed to get rid of the Vegas as if he could be held in any way accountable for it. But that wasn't what this was about. Father knew I was able to take my own punishments now no matter if I hated them. I'd learned how to take my beatings and hold my tongue. I'd grown accustomed to seeing the colour of my own blood. I could break a bone without screaming. I knew the rhythms of that well by now. But Xavier wasn't like me. He couldn't help but flinch when my father raised his fist, and I couldn't bear to allow him to meet the end of it because of my failures.

Father liked to tell me often enough that love was weakness, and I knew he was aiming to prove that to me every time he hurt me by hurting my brother. But I'd do all I could and all I had to to stand between him and the monster who had raised us.

"They'll be long gone by then," I swore, pushing my hand into my hair and gripping it by the roots.

"They'd better be." Father cut the call and I had to fight against the urge to hurl my fucking Atlas away from me and allow it to smash into a million pieces against the far wall.

I breathed in and out deeply through my nose as I fought to contain my rage and then I let myself channel it in the direction it needed to be aimed. At the Vegas. The two lost girls who had had the misfortune to be found again. It didn't really matter what I thought of my father's orders - it never did. All that mattered was getting them out of this academy and out of the running for the throne as soon as possible. So I guessed I was just going to have to up the ante.

I pushed to my feet, tugging a spare Pitball shirt out of my bag and pulling it on to replace the one that had been torn off of me before looking back out to the pitch. Orion was still running laps and I called out in goodbye before leaving him to it and heading back out of the Pitball stadium and started to walk towards The Orb.

I chose a path that led through The Wailing Wood and tried not to let my feet drag as I thought about my father's threats and my brother's predicament stuck in that fucking house with him. I couldn't wait until this time next year when he'd be at the academy too, at least offered safety with distance from the man who had sired us for a lot of the time if not all of it.

I strode down the familiar paths with my head full of my father's words and my mind on meeting up with the other Heirs again so that we could come up with some new strategies to rid ourselves of this Vega infestation.

But even as I tried to consider how best to make their lives unbearable, I couldn't help but think about the defiant glint in Roxy's eyes as she'd stared me down after her initiation. I wanted to capture that look and bottle it to keep with me at all times. That look had made me feel more alive than anything had in a long damn time and the thought of having to run her out of here before I'd even gotten the chance to taste it again made my jaw clench with irritation. But this wasn't about me or my insignificant desires. When had anything I'd desired ever mattered anyway? I was just a pawn in my father's plans and he'd given his instructions clearly enough.

A flash of blue light out in the woods caught my attention as some student cast it out there and the animalistic growl of someone in their Order form carried to me on the wind. I ignored it, not interested in anything any of the other students were up to tonight and knowing they wouldn't dare disturb me anyway. I may not have been at full strength by any stretch of the imagination, but the gold I was wearing had given me enough magic to toy with if I needed it and I continued to draw energy from it with every passing moment that it remained in contact with my skin.

But as I strode down the path, I spotted someone up ahead of me who had frozen at the sight of the light and my brows arched as I managed to pick out the outline of her profile in the moonlight which crept through the trees. The stars must have been favouring me tonight.

I wet my lips as I took in the sight of Roxy Vega standing there, the predator in me sensing her fear like I could scent it on the wind and my father's threats ringing in my ears.

I hated the person he forced me to be sometimes. But nothing mattered more than protecting Xavier from him. So with that in mind, I pushed aside the rioting thump of my pulse as I took in the sight of the girl who had claimed all of my attention since the moment she'd arrived here and flicked my fingers, sending a wave of heated energy slamming into her and knocking her off of her feet.

That knot in my gut tightened as she screamed in fright but I ignored it, finding that place in my soul where I retreated whenever my father raised his fist and blocking out anything I may have felt aside from the need to get this done.

I strode forward as she rolled over, throwing a hand up defensively as she yelled, "Get away!" while squinting up at me in the dark as I came to stand over her.

Fire flared in my palm as I surveyed her and disappointment filled me as I realised this wasn't my Vega at all. It was the sister. Gwendalina. The one with the blue tips in her hair. I hadn't really had much to do with this one yet, so I wasn't entirely sure how to expect her to react.

I slapped a wide smirk on my face as I looked down at her and decided to test her grit for myself.

"Whoops didn't see you there, Vega." I held out a hand with a deep chuckle, knowing she'd see through that bullshit and expecting her to rip into me for it like her sister would, but this one didn't take the bait like I'd expected.

Gwendalina reached up and took my hand, her gaze wary and untrusting as she let me heave her to her feet while I felt her trembling a little from the fright I'd given her.

"Was that you out there trying to scare me?" she demanded, raising her chin and jerking it towards the darkness of the trees to our right.

"Out where?" I asked in a bored tone, dampening my disappointment over not finding her sister here and wondering why I even gave a fuck which one of them it was. I released her hand and pushed my fingers through my dark hair, feeling mud in it from the practice and scruffing it up to cover it a little.

"Over there." She pointed into the trees, shifting closer to me and making me wonder if it had been me who had frightened her at all. Was she seriously looking to me like I might be safer to be around than whatever she thought was out there?

"Dunno what you're talking about," I said, glancing into the trees and seeing nothing there. It would have just been a student in their Order form or something anyway, she was only afraid because she was practically a human, not used to things going bump in the night.

I suppressed a sigh, my disappointment over finding the wrong twin mixing with the dark feeling in my chest as she looked to me for comfort when I knew I was the thing she should have been fearing. I needed her gone, but scaring her in the woods didn't seem like much of a way to achieve that and suddenly I just wanted to get away from here. To find the other Heirs and form a solid plan to drive the Vegas out without having to look into her eyes as she sought out something in me which wasn't there. I wasn't good. I wasn't her rescuer. I was just my father reborn, exactly how he wanted me to be. No matter what thoughts I may have had on the subject. At least not while he still ruled over me. I made a snap decision and made a move to leave, not wanting to have anything more to do with that fearful look in her eyes.

"See ya." I went to walk away from her but she caught my arm, her fingers digging into my bicep as she halted me and I looked down at her in surprise, unsure if I should have been bracing for an attack or not.

"Would you mind maybe...just walking me out of the woods?" Gwen gave me an imploring look and for a moment I wasn't the monster in her eyes. I stilled as I took that in, wondering why the hell she'd look to me of all people for help.

I quickly covered my surprise by snorting in amusement. "You scared, Vega?"

"*No,*" she insisted but that was absolute bullshit and we both knew it. She cleared her throat as she went on. "I just don't want to get lost in here. I've got a meeting with Professor Orion in five minutes."

Last I'd seen, Orion was still running laps of the Pitball pitch and I was willing to bet he'd be stopping for a shower before heading to their little Liaison so there was no chance of him being on time for that. "Pfft, he'll be late anyways, you're not in any hurry." I tried to shake her off but to my confusion, she held on tight.

I opened my mouth to tell her to get off of me, but she beat me to it with a single word which somehow pierced through the asshole in me and made me pause. "Please."

Fuck how many times had I said that word to my father in hopes of making his punishments stop? How many times had I heard it spill from Xavier's lips with the same wish?

I didn't give a damn about some terrified little Vega Princess all scared and alone out in the woods, but that fucking word. That one plea which rang in my ears with the taste of my own blood coating my tongue.

Fuck it.

I sighed heavily then turned around and yanked her along with me, walking fast and forcing her to keep up whether she liked it or not. I wasn't going to give too much thought to what I was doing or why I was helping the girl I'd just promised to get rid of. It had nothing to do with her anyway. This was just me trying to prove a point to myself. I just wanted to know that no matter how monstrous I became while being forced to walk in my father's shadow, I still held a little light of my own which he couldn't smother. I could still be my own man when I wanted to be. And I wouldn't be a callous creature who ignored a plea for help when I heard it.

Gwen stumbled along at my side, and we both stayed quiet as I led her through the woods, heading straight for the closest exit and wanting this strange interaction to end as quickly as it had begun.

But of course the stars had decided to spurn me for not taking the opportunity I'd been gifted and a voice called out to me before I could complete this simple task.

"Bro!" Seth howled a moment before he burst out of the darkness still wearing his mud stained Pitball uniform despite the fact that the material was half torn off of him. "Who's your date?" he asked excitedly as he reached us then scowled as he recognised her. "Don't tell me you're hanging out with a

Vega?" he mocked and I released an internal sigh. So much for me attempting to not be an asshole for once.

Seth tossed a Faelight up over his head to help us all see each other better and the predatory glint in his eyes told me exactly how this was going to go from here as he looked at the girl clinging to my arm.

"She's scared," I explained in a dry tone without bothering to explain what that meant from my point of view.

"I'm not scared," Gwen insisted but she definitely sounded scared, so she wasn't convincing anyone.

Seth's eyes lit up with excitement and I almost said something, almost told him to just leave it and let her get to her Liaison...but I didn't. Because the moment my lips parted, I remembered my father's threat and I knew that there wasn't ever going to be any kind of choice that I would make which would sacrifice my brother's safety for the sake of some frightened girl I didn't even know. So I bit my tongue and hardened my resolve and ignored the piece of me which spat words in my mind accusing me of being just like him. The man I hated above all others. But maybe I had to be like him to defeat him. And if that was the case then so be it.

Seth moved closer, running his hand over my arm then moving to nuzzle Gwen's hair like he was greeting a member of his pack. Except the move was all Alpha and domineering, meant to show her her place, though she lurched back and scowled at him rather than accepting it.

"I'll walk you out, babe." He took her free arm, trying to tug her away from me and I was almost relieved at that. To just let him do what he was planning and have nothing more to do with it. Then again, that probably made me worse than I already was because I knew that look in his eye and he was out for blood tonight.

Gwen looked to me for help and my gut twisted sharply. Why the fuck did she have to keep looking at me like I might have been something I wasn't? Why was she trying to have faith in me when I had none in myself? I wasn't her saviour. I wasn't even my own saviour yet. And the sooner she realised that the better, so I just gave her a cold stare in reply. But as Seth went to drag her away to do fuck knew what, a word spilled from my lips which made him pause.

"Wait," I said, my lips tilting into a cruel smile as I offered her the only thing I could - two monsters instead of one. Though she would be better off for it whether she knew that or not. "She needs to give me a proper goodbye first."

Seth shoved her back towards me with an excited laugh, because I hardly ever joined him in this kind of game. But I knew him, knew how he got and he would be satisfied by me playing along which would curb his darker intentions.

"*Kneel*," I commanded, lacing my voice with Coercion and Gwen dropped to her knees, glaring at me with a look of betrayal in her eyes which only pissed me off. Because why the fuck was she laying any kind of faith in me in the first place? I didn't need her looking at me like that. I needed her to see what I was and if this was what it took to do it and to make sure she never made the mistake of expecting something better from me again then so be it.

"*Kiss my foot.*"

I barked a laugh as she instantly did what I'd commanded, letting the feeling of the power I held over her stamp out any other feelings as I gave myself to this game and refused to back down.

Seth laughed raucously. "Let's make her dance for us," he suggested. "Max and Caleb should be here any second, they'll lose it when they see her doing the cha-cha-cha."

"Don't you dare," Gwen snapped, her hateful gaze on me as she finally banished any silly thoughts of me being a shining knight in favour of seeing me for what I really was. And that was good. Because it was all I was ever going to be to her.

I took her arm, dragging her to her feet with a vicious smile as I gave in to that dark in me and let it swallow me up.

"I have a better idea," I purred, watching the panic flare in her eyes and knowing I should relish that. This was what I had to do, what it would take to shield my brother.

"Get off of me," she snapped, trying to pull away as I gave in to the beast in me and allowed the challenge in her eyes to stoke the flames inside me.

I released her and she backed up a few steps, glancing between me and Seth as he moved closer to me, his arm brushing against mine and his smile darkening as he urged me to give in to his pack instincts and I indulged him.

Yeah, this was going to be fun.

"*Run*," I barked and she turned and fled without a second thought, falling to the command of my Coercion as I slapped a hand against Seth's chest to hold him back.

"Wait for it," I said in a low tone as he practically hopped up and down with excitement and a dark laugh escaped me too. This was just a game. The kind all Fae learned to play one way or another and we were just giving her an education in what it took to be one of us.

Seth cupped his hands around his mouth and howled in anticipation of the hunt and the moment she rounded the corner ahead of us, we took chase.

Our feet pounded against the dirt track beneath us, laughter spilling between us as we pushed ourselves as fast as we could go and I relished the feeling of uniting with my brother and running at his side.

We were gaining on her, rounding the corner and closing in with each step as she ran for her star damned life and the lights of The Orb and the other campus buildings up ahead appeared through the trees.

With every step we got closer and Seth reached out, ready to pounce a moment before she threw her hands out and cast a gust of wind at her back which sent her hurtling forward and out of reach.

I released a surprised laugh and Seth howled again, the call of an Alpha Wolf to his pack as she tore away from us, so close to escaping that I almost felt bad for her when Max and Caleb stepped into her path a moment before she could escape the trees.

She crashed straight into them, almost knocking Max on his ass as Caleb wrapped his arms around her, using his strength to keep the two of them on their feet.

"Woah there, horsey," he said pushing her hair back as he gave her a hungry look.

She tried to back up but bumped into Max as he closed in on her from behind and he chuckled in amusement as she looked up at him fearfully.

"Out for a moonlit stroll?" he asked, his power humming in the air as he worked to get a read on her emotions.

Seth and I reached them, falling still as we panted through the rush of our run and closed the net around her.

"Let me past," Gwen demanded, not sounding so scared anymore as she raised her chin and stepped toward Cal purposefully.

He pushed her back with a grin and Seth caught her, his arms curling around her shoulders as he nuzzled against her again, trying to dominate that fiery temper we'd awoken.

"I need to go," she growled. "I have a meeting with Professor Orion."

"Orion?" Caleb asked angrily, tugging her out of Seth's arms and into his again. "Is he getting blood from you already? Private meetings just for you and his teeth, huh?" He bared his fangs at her and she gasped, shoving him back and fuelling the push with a punch of air magic that forced him to let her go.

"Lucky for you I filled up on your sister earlier," Cal taunted but she wasn't listening, instead focusing on darting for the gap that had opened up between Caleb and Max.

We all closed in on her, moving as a unit as easily as we drew breath and stopping her attempt at escape.

"Power of four?" Max suggested with a grin, leaning closer to our prey as he named the game we'd come up with when our magic had first been

Awakened and we'd played pranks with it on any unsuspecting Fae we could sneak up on.

"Brilliant idea. That'll stop Orion feeding from her tonight," Caleb said with a laugh.

"What the hell are you-" Gwen began, but before she could finish her sentence Max raised his hands and water crashed over her, soaking her from head to toe.

Gwen wrapped her arms around her chest to try and cover the transparency of her white shirt which was now revealing her black bra beneath it but none of us were interested in that. We were playing one of our favourite games and she was about to be the punchline.

Caleb wielded his earth magic next and mud circled up around her, caking her in the brown sludge and making a laugh tumble from my lips as she wiped the back of her hand over her eyes and blinked out at us.

Seth and I moved to stand before her, his arm butting against mine as we both wielded our power together to finish the look.

I used what little power I still held in my limbs to cast a fire burning in my palms and Seth blasted air magic over the top of it, drying the mud to her body and making her look like some kind of troll that had been living beneath a bridge for the last ten years.

"Argh!" she shouted furiously. "Get this off of me!"

Seth snapped a photo and we all fell about laughing, her utter indignation only making the whole thing funnier as she glared at us beneath the caked-on mud. Some lightness found its way back into my soul as my brothers all clustered around me, laughing and slinging their arms around my neck as the joke broke through the darkness which always lived in me these days.

I jerked my chin towards the trees and we ran off, leaving her there while we continued to howl with laughter. We'd go eat dinner, bask in the success of our prank and leave the discussions over what we could seriously do to get the Vegas out of the academy later. But for now, I was just happy to be enjoying the company of my friends.

Besides, she'd asked me to get her out of the woods and I'd done it. She'd never requested I didn't have a little fun with her along the way.

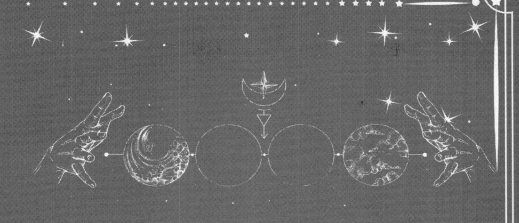

ORION

CHAPTER EIGHT

I stood in the shower in the locker room of the Pitball stadium, scrubbing the mud from my hair after the training session. The team had left and I should have been leaving too, heading to my office for the Liaison with Darcy Vega. But I still hadn't fed and my plan to drink from her tonight had meant I'd been distracted all through training.

Max Rigel had looked at me like he couldn't work out what my emotions were doing and I'd had to focus so hard on mentally shielding myself from his probing gifts that I now felt frayed and on the edge of losing control. The Vegas had only been at this academy one day and I was already in this much turmoil, what was going on with me?

I just needed to feed. To sink my fangs into Darcy's throat and drink away as much of that power I could grasp.

A hungry growl left my throat at that thought and my cock hardened, betraying me. *It's all about the power. It's not about her.*

I fisted my hard length, figuring it was best to take the edge off rather than turn up to my office feeling like this. Maybe I should have seen Francesca last night and I wouldn't be this pent up. Or maybe it had something to do with coming home from the Mortal Realm, my Order desperate to be sated and leaving me with more hunger than I was used to. Yeah, that was it. The Mortal Realm had fucked with me and once I'd fed tonight, everything would go back to normal.

Fuck the Vegas. This was their fault. They were ruining everything and they hadn't even done anything yet.

I groaned as I leaned my forearm against the wall and the hot wash of water ran down my back as I stroked my length in furious pumps of my fist. I was gonna be late. Not that that was unusual for me. She deserved to stand there waiting with a pout on her lips – *fuck, those lips*. My hand moved faster and I screwed up my eyes as I worked to force her out of my head. She wasn't what was getting me hot. It was her blood. I pictured swallowing it, drowning in the heady feel of the royal's power and the way she'd be weakened in my arms, unable to use any of her magic as I stole it away. It'd be a just punishment for this headfuck she was giving me. She'd gasp and her eyes would widen with fear as I took control and crushed her to the wall of my office. I'd hear her begging me, but I wouldn't stop until I'd drunk away the well of her power and taken it for my own.

Her body would mould to mine as she submitted, and I'd become the centre of her world for a short snapshot in time. I'd be close enough to feel her heart pounding against my flesh, her breaths against my skin. And maybe she'd like it, being at my mercy. Maybe she'd draw me closer, maybe her defiant mouth would find mine once I was done with her blood and maybe I'd find out how high those tanned legs went beneath her little skirt – *no. By the fucking moon, no.*

I came, pleasure sweeping through me followed by a healthy dose of guilt for where my mind had just wandered. The heated water of the shower swept over me, stealing away any evidence of the sinful thing I'd done over a girl who was so off limits, she might as well have been a massive red flag with a warning siren on it.

I finished washing and shot out of the shower, drying my body off with air magic and tugging on some jeans and a white shirt stashed in my locker. Then I scrubbed a hand over my face and took a breath to sharpen my thoughts. Despite that shameful fantasy I'd just indulged in, I felt better, more in control. And I was sure once I'd fed that would be the end of this madness.

I grabbed my Atlas and sprinted out of the locker room with a burst of my speed, tearing out of the Pitball Stadium and across campus in the direction of Jupiter Hall.

I slowed to a casual stride as I made it into the building, taking out my Atlas and sweeping a hand through my still damp hair. I had a message from Gabriel waiting for me and I frowned at the weirdness of it. I was pretty used to this kind of thing seeing as he was a Seer, but he never usually had much insight into what was going on in my life. He must have been turning his attention towards me for whatever reason lately, but that gave me the uncomfortable feeling again that something life changing was coming. And since the Vegas were now here, I had to assume it was to do with them.

You're not getting Darius's throne though, girls, mark my fucking words. I've worked too long and too hard to get revenge on his father with him, and he star damn deserves it after all the shit he's been through.

Noxy:

Your new path is gilded in sunlight and surrounded by shadow. Don't step off of it.

Lance:

In plainer terms?

Noxy:

The darkness is your closest friend, but it's time to let it go.

Lance:

Wait...has the Lion got your Atlas again? It's not funny, asshole. Don't you start drunk-texting me fake predictions like last time. I got stuck up that mountain for sixteen hours.

Noxy:

It's me, Orio. And you need to listen to what I'm telling you. And not telling you. The answers lay in between my words.

Lance:

Can't you lay it out for me straight, just this once?

I knew he couldn't though. A Seer's curse was seeing the future but being unable to always speak it because then the future would shift. So I was doomed to try and solve this riddle on my own.

Alright...darkness...path...sunlight. I'm too tired for this shit. I need a drink.

Noxy:

Call me later.

Lance:

Will do.

I tucked my Atlas away and my heart did something strange as I rounded the corner into the corridor that led to my office. Then my eyes fell on a girl standing there coated in dried mud from head to toe with a glint of blue hair peeking from her smothered form which told me exactly who it was. What in the actual fuck had happened to her?

"I hope that's not a fashion choice, Miss Vega," I said coolly, my gaze dragging from the top of her right down to her mud caked shoes, amusement rippling through me and my mouth hitching up into a taunting grin.

"Oh yes, I just *love* rolling in mud in the evenings," she deadpanned, clearly pissed and most likely embarrassed as hell. I had a feeling I knew exactly who had done this and I hoped it meant she was getting the message about staying here. She didn't seem particularly broken by it though, just angry. Though it was hard to tell with all that mud on her face. *Maybe I should leave her like that so she's less easy on the eyes.*

I moved close to her, pushing my key into the lock and heading inside, leaving the door open for her to follow and sensing her trailing after me. The air seemed to charge with an energy so fierce that I felt it right down to my soul and I fought the urge to look back at her to try and figure out if she felt it too. Though it was impossible to tell through the layer of mud slicked to her skin.

I moved to sit in my chair behind the crescent-moon desk built from cherry wood. It had belonged to my father and I'd had it moved here from his old office at my family home. My mother Stella had bawled for days afterwards, saying I was disrespecting it by moving it. But as I gave exactly zero fucks about her opinion, I hadn't lost much sleep over it.

Students' laughter carried in through the open window and every other person was talking about Darcy Vega being covered in shit, so I guessed her new look was now doing the rounds on FaeBook. I bit down on a grin. *How unfortunate.*

My gaze flicked to her and her hands balled into fists as she clearly heard some of the mockery too. Her heart was thumping to an uneasy beat that made me momentarily want to soothe it. But instead of indulging in that insane thought, I snagged out the bottle of bourbon stashed in the cupboard in my desk along with a crystal glass and poured myself a measure. The scent reminded me of him too. My father's favourite brand of bourbon, The Silver Circle.

He only ever drank as a celebration of his new discoveries. He was always creating dark spells, or finding ways to wield dark objects that had long been forgotten in our world. All illegal of course, but that didn't take away the skill he'd possessed. I'd been too young to understand all of it and that was hard to bear sometimes, because I hadn't appreciated him enough, hadn't realised how precious and fleeting our time was together.

If I could have that time back, I'd spend every spare minute I had with him, learning all that he knew, asking every question I never got to ask. But that was the way of death, sometimes it crept out of the shadows and stole away loved ones without warning. Other times, it descended like a dark cloud, a storm rolling towards shore from a distant horizon, the warning there, but the arrival just as inevitable. I hoped when I died, I had time to say goodbye to those who mattered. Luckily for me, there wasn't a long list of those.

I drained the glass of bourbon and let it burn hotly in my chest, remembering Gabriel's words to me. I was definitely leaning into the dark, so I supposed I'd better try and steer myself into the light. *Just one more drink first though.*

I smacked my lips, placing the glass down and moving to refill it.

"Excuse me?" Darcy said sharply and my eyes flicked up to where she was still standing, rooted in place like a mud statue.

"Yes?" I asked, my mind moving from that morbid place onto her. This dangerous little creature who had no idea yet of the threat she posed.

"Well, it's just that apparently I'm standing in your office looking like a swamp monster and watching you get drunk," she said sharply.

"That does appear to be happening, yes. Very observant, Blue. Or perhaps I should call you Brown now?" I started laughing, the bourbon taking effect, or perhaps it was the ludicrousness of her right now. She was so damn mouthy for someone who looked like a bog monster and was currently the butt of every joke in the school.

She placed her hands on her hips and I made a vague attempt to rein in my laughter, but it wouldn't stop coming. She just looked so ridiculously adorable. *No*, scrap that last word.

"Right, screw this." She marched toward the door, and my smile dropped flat in an instant.

Oh no you don't, I haven't had my feed yet.

I waved my hand, casting heated air over her to scrape off the mud before using my water magic to wash it away, then I sent it all flying straight out the window – hopefully into the path of some little shitbag student. Her hair fluttered around her shoulders, the blue tips bright and falling smoothly down her spine. *What's with the blue anyway? And why is it so aggravatingly enticing to me?*

She turned to face me and I cast a harsh wind in her direction, forcing her back against the door and deciding I was done waiting for the power I wanted to take. It was my right as a Vampire to go after the strongest blood source I could seize, and her blood had been running through my mind all day. I'd pre-jerked off to save myself a power boner in front of her, dammit. So this was happening and if I liked it, it would keep happening until she was able to stop me.

I shot over to her, her eyes closed against the onslaught of my conjured storm and her lips twisted in a snarl. I dropped the air magic, standing close to keep her from escaping as my heart pounded over how near I was to claiming my prize.

"Thank you," she forced out and I found my gaze wandering over her face, unable to ignore the beauty of her petite features, or the way those eyes seemed to swallow up my entire soul. *Siren. Definitely a Siren.*

"Your gratitude isn't what I want." I snatched her arm, ready to finally live out this fantasy in my head and find out what she tasted like. But before my fangs made it to her flesh, her palm smashed into my cheek with a loud clap that rang out in the space and left me utterly speechless as I tried to figure out if she'd really just slapped me.

I stared at her in surprise and she stared right back, my cheek stinging as I reached up to touch the place her palm had impacted. My pulse was thrashing and I couldn't stop drinking in the rebellion in those endlessly green eyes. And the worst thing was, I liked it. I liked the way my skin was burning, the feel of it so keen it was like waking up from sleepwalking, mid dream. I hadn't felt so much of anything in such a long time. I'd been living on autopilot, wandering this world like a zombie since Lionel had taken everything from me. But somehow, she'd cut through the dark fog that had been in my head for years.

"Don't bite me," she breathed, her pupils dilating, her throat bobbing in a way that told me she was nervous, on edge, desperate for me not to drive my fangs into her. But it was too late for that, I was too far gone down the rabbit hole, and that slap had solidified this need. I had to drink from her, it was instinct. And a depraved part of me wanted her punished more than ever now. Because a Vega did not get to come into my life and make demands of me. She was the Savage King's daughter, and no matter how small and innocent she looked with those soul-eating eyes, I knew better. Because I knew about the blood that ran in her veins, I knew the cruelty that the King had delivered on our kingdom. And I knew that once this creature found her footing in this world, that evil could awaken once more.

I leaned down, nose to nose with her, so all I could see was those two deep eyes and the reflection of a hunter in them.

"How are you going to stop me?" I asked, wondering if she might try, if she'd use her inner Fae against me and I'd see how powerful she really was, how savage she could be. This close, I could smell her, and the scent was an intoxicating combination of strawberries and purest sunshine.

She took a slow breath, contempt pulling at her features. "I know how to wield air. I can push you back."

"Are you sure about that?" I shifted even closer, opening my mouth to reveal the sharp points of my fangs.

She shook her head as a V formed between her eyes. "Honestly? No. But I'm asking you not to and I'm telling you I'll try to fight you if you do."

She's asking me not to?

I wasn't sure I'd ever been asked not to bite someone. People had screamed and begged, but most shut up once they realised I had them in my grasp. It was the way of our kind. Vampires had to bite to gain their magic. But the plea in her expression said she didn't understand that, that she simply didn't want my fangs in her plain and simple.

I found myself taking a step back, but then the beast in me rose up and demanded I take what I wanted. I'd been fantasising about her taste since I'd first laid eyes on her. And this wasn't the human world anymore. This was the kingdom of Solaria, and if she thought she could ask nicely and get what she wanted, then she needed to learn a lesson fast.

She tried to move past me and I snatched her arm and sliced my fangs into her skin, letting go of my more urgent want to bite her neck, and knowing that I may have been doing this as a way to ease her into it. Because if I enjoyed her blood, I'd damn well be taking more of it.

Her blood hit my tongue and I lost all sense of everything as pristine light seemed to roll over my tastebuds. There was fire and so much power brimming in her that I could barely contain a groan as I drank my first mouthful. She gasped in horror at what I'd done, bringing her hand up like she was going to hit me once more and I snatched hold of it, slamming it against the door behind her, making my heart leap with adrenaline. In the next second, I pressed forward, crushing her to the wood with my chest and pinning her there as my bite deepened. I couldn't help but notice how good her body felt against mine, how her hot breath fanned against my neck and how her wriggling made her breasts grind over me. This was a thousand times better than any fantasy I'd conjured. This was like taking a throne among the stars themselves.

Her heartbeat filled my head and I drank another mouthful of the sweetest, most appetising blood I'd ever drunk. Her power flowed into me in furious waves that spoke of the depths to which her magic ran. I wanted more and more, all of it, taking and taking as I fell into a feeding frenzy and my mind sparked with the immensity of her strength.

The Vampire in me had taken full control, but it was a hungry monster and I could feel it going too far, taking too much. But I couldn't stop. I kept drinking beyond the point I should have as I devoured her magic and sank into the provocative taste of her.

Let her go.

Stop.

You have to stop.

With a surge of willpower, I yanked my fangs free and my head spun from the taste of her on my tongue and the power overflowing in my chest. She leaned back against the door and clutched the two bloody pinpricks on her wrist as she glared at me with venom in her eyes. But she could hate me to the ends of the earth if she liked, I'd still be coming back for more of her. I was hooked. And Darius would approve seeing as my bite had left her looking horrified.

Maybe she'd run back to the Mortal Realm to escape my bites. And maybe I'd follow her there, kidnap her and lock her up somewhere only I could get access.

Or maybe you're on a blood high and you'll actually do something rational like forgetting all about her once she's gone.

I gave her an even stare, figuring she needed the life lesson over this to banish some of that haunted look in her eyes. "Everything in Solaria is about power, Miss Vega. Don't forget that. Everyone takes what they want. It's our way. And if you don't start taking it yourself, you're going to fail at this Academy before you've even attempted to pass The Reckoning."

Her throat rose and fell, and she continued to glare at me like I was the Devil, and that was fine by me.

I headed back to my desk, dropping into my chair and releasing a satisfied sigh. *I don't think my thirst has ever felt so sated.*

I realised my cock was throbbing and I was growing one hundred percent hard over her – *not her, her blood.* My jaw locked as heat ran up the back of my neck. *Fuck.*

"Sit down." I gestured to the seat opposite me and her lips twitched in frustration before she obeyed. I forced my attention away from my raging hard on and poured myself another glass of bourbon, thankful of the desk to hide it.

"Isn't this supposed to be a lesson?" she bit at me.

"Nope. I'm supposed to be providing guidance for you. But I'm doing so on my time. And on my time, I like to have a drink. So here we are."

"Right," she said through tight lips. *You really do despise me, don't you Blue? Well you'd better suck it up, because I'm not going anywhere.*

"So what exactly am I going to learn here while you're enjoying yourself?" she asked in a clipped tone.

"Trust me, I'm not enjoying myself." I planted my glass down, giving her a hard stare. *You're the thorn in Solaria's side and I intend to find a way to remove you.* "Hand," I commanded and both of her hands curled up in refusal.

Does she have to make everything so damn difficult?

"Don't make me Coerce you. It's rather draining and I just added a nice chunk to my own power," I said.

"You mean you sucked out my magic like a mosquito."

"Sure." I shrugged. "Whatever colourful analogy soothes you." I grinned, sipping my drink, but immediately regretting it as I lost the taste of her on my tongue. "Hand, come on, we've only got forty more minutes of my life to waste."

She pressed her lips together, thrusting her right hand at me. It was time to start working out her strengths and weaknesses, then Darius and I could figure out how best to handle her and her sister. And I needed to get my mind off of biting her, of feeling her crushed to my door, owned by me.

"Flat on the desk, palm up," I instructed and she did so. "Is this your dominant hand?"

She nodded.

"Good, I'm going to do an assessment."

"What kind of assessment?" she asked suspiciously.

"Of your power."

"Okay..."

"Don't move. And don't giggle – for the love of the sun I hate the gigglers." I took her hand and brushed my fingertips over her palm, energy seeming to crackle from her skin into mine.

I glanced up at her, assessing if she was about to giggle, but she quickly flattened the laugh I saw building in her eyes and glared at me again.

I traced my thumb across the line at the centre of her palm and a filthy idea entered my head of yanking her across this desk by it and – *she's a student. And a Vega. And if those two things aren't reason enough, she's also not going to be staying here for any amount of time because we are going to figure out how to get rid of her and her sister. So for now, act like the fucking teacher you're supposed to be and work out her weak spots.*

"In palmistry mortals usually have four lines on their palms." I pointed them out from top to bottom. "Heart, head, life and fate. Fae, however, have a fifth line. A power line." I pressed my thumb to the middle of her palm again and she shifted in her seat as she leaned in closer to look. Her scent reached me and I stopped myself from inhaling, grinding my teeth for a second before I went on.

"Most Fae have shorter lines here." I turned my own hand over, showing her my palm and her gaze flicked to the triangular symbol of air tattooed on my wrist. "Mine extends two thirds of the way. Yours, however, is a complete line." I gave her an assessing glare. That power line of hers was the strongest I'd ever seen. Even the Heirs didn't have a complete line. And it made my stomach knot because if she and Tory learned how to harness this power residing in their veins, they'd be unstoppable.

"The strength of each particular Element is defined by these intersecting lines." I plucked a small palmistry ruler off my desk and laid it on her palm.

I worked through each line, knowing she had no idea what I was learning from these marks, and deciding I wouldn't be telling her about most of it. It wasn't all about power. There were indications to her fate written into her flesh here and I took note of it all, trying to pull apart the secrets hidden there. I examined a line along her thumb, grazing my fingertip across it and finding it fully intact. It was an indicator of willpower, which unfortunately she had a lot of.

Then I examined the marking termed the Girdle of Venus which curved under her middle finger and ring finger and gave me an insight into her temperament. Not everyone had one, but those who did were more compassionate, and I supposed that was worth noting. Though I doubted she'd be compassionate enough to give up her birth right to the Heirs once she embraced her inner Fae. I hoped she was long gone before she even had the chance to claim the throne anyway.

I found she was also gifted with a line called the Ring of Solomon which curved beneath her index finger. I frowned as I examined the rare line, the marking indicating a Fae who was self-sacrificing and good at heart.

It didn't add up. This was the Savage King's daughter. I'd expected to find some of his cruelty and selfishness written here, but if these lines were a good judgement of her character – and they were usually pretty fucking accurate – then I was missing something. Because she couldn't be compassionate and kind. Those weren't traits I'd been preparing for. But the truth was, I needed to crush this girl and her sister regardless of whether their hearts were in the right place or not.

My thumb glided onto the line that indicated her love life and a shiver darted down my spine that I swear she felt too as she shifted in her seat. I kept my gaze on her palm, the air in the room becoming thinner and a faint whisper seemed to carry to me that held no words I understood.

I glanced up at Darcy again, finding her looking elsewhere, though she was chewing on her lower lip like she was struggling with some internal war. I forced my gaze back to her palm as I drew in a breath and figured the stars were playing tricks on me. Maybe they were leaning closer now because this girl was more dangerous than her palm let on and I needed to be vigilant.

The markings spoke of a significant love in her life that would be wrought with hardship and emotional turmoil. It was split in places which indicated the worst of those hardships and the end of it was muddled with so many intersecting lines that it was hard to tell whether the love continued beyond them or if the relationship ended abruptly within those trials. I found myself feeling oddly possessive of her as I considered this coming relationship. She was mine. I mean, her blood was mine. And I wasn't going to allow some asshole to show up and claim her for himself.

I knew it was irrational, but I couldn't shift the feeling. This girl was not to be taken from me.

I finally started working on her power rankings, seeking out her Elements on her palm. Every Fae had markings for all the Elements, but they only became relevant once their magic was Awakened and their true power was known. I jotted down each tiny line which ran along her power line and did a couple of calculations to work out her power rankings for each Element, the numbers staring back at me making my throat thicken. *Holy fucking shit. They're going to be unstoppable.*

We need to deal with this fast.

I released her hand, finding my fingers slightly reluctant to let go and I flexed them as I pushed the numbers in front of her.

"These are your power rankings," I explained. "Ten is the strongest you can be in any Element. To put it in perspective, Miss Vega, even a seven is considered high."

She stared at the numbers with her eyes widening and for a moment I just watched as she came to terms with what she was seeing. I thought of this girl back in her shitty apartment in desperate need for money and a few decent meals, and for a heartbeat I wished things didn't have to be the way they were. But then I snuffed out that traitorous thought and grounded myself with the fury I felt towards her father. She was the enemy. *And a Siren. Definitely a fucking Siren.*

"Your weakest Element is fire, although I use the word *weak* very loosely. You're an eight in earth, a nine in water and a ten in air."

She glanced up at me with a thousand questions in her eyes and I had the hungry, undeniable urge to answer them all. "And we're this powerful because...our parents were royal? The king and queen?" She sounded like she didn't believe the words leaving her lips and I supposed it was a headfuck to find out you were a long lost princess.

"Yes. Your father was the most powerful Fae in Solaria. He held three Elements: fire, water and air. Your mother had just one Element: air. She was a Gemini like you and was named the most beautiful woman in Solaria." *Though I'd hazard a guess her daughters have her beat. This one to me is like a fucking magnet.* "That was after he returned with her from a faraway land his army had invaded. King Vega married her, disregarding tradition. The powerful families tend to breed with their own kind; it keeps bloodlines pure and usually produces offspring of the same Orders. The purer the line, the more powerful their magic."

"And not doing that is...bad?" she asked, leaning closer with curiosity burning in her eyes.

"No, just foolish. Their children are more likely to be weaker but...that is clearly not the case with you and your sister. Your mother and father have produced two of the most powerful Fae to ever walk in our world." I leaned back in my chair, needing more space between us as I swilled the whiskey in my glass.

"What were they?" she breathed and my gaze roamed over her mouth for a second. "What were their Orders?"

Damn, she looked so fucking sweet. She was hungry for answers and I liked holding them in my grasp. I was quietly glad I got to be the one to tell her all of this, and so long as she kept looking at me like I was the key to everything she'd searched for her whole life, I wanted to keep talking.

"Your mother was a Harpy and your father was a Hydra," I revealed.

"Hydra?" she whispered, a grimace crossing her features. "Like the monster with multiple heads?"

"Yes," I said quietly. "They are one of the rarest Orders in the world."

She took a slow breath as she tried to process it all. "So what do you think me and Tory are, sir?"

I'd never once been tempted by a student, or remotely interested in the fantasy of the forbidden. But she was so star damned alluring, and so fucking powerful, her talking to me like I commanded her respect was a sin in itself which my cock liked way too much.

I drummed my fingers on the desk then swallowed the last of my drink to try and drown some of the errant thoughts in my head.

"Trouble," I muttered.

"That's not fair. It's not like we asked for this."

My anger rose, because fuck her for making me feel like this. Fuck her for making this harder than it needed to be. I wasn't going to be distracted by her deer-in-the-headlights eyes or her naive little mortal looks. She was Gwendalina Vega. And if she'd been raised in this world, she'd no doubt be prepping to carry on in her father's footsteps right now. She may have seemed innocent, but give it a month or two and she'd find her feet. She'd start wielding her magic to her own benefit, and when she realised the throne could be hers, she'd fight for it. She'd fight ruthlessly and she might just win. And who knew what she'd become in the meantime? Monsters didn't grow out of the ground, they fed on power and became addicted to its company. Our kind strived for it, and she would too. She'd be just like every other power hungry Fae in this school in no time, and she might just be worse.

"What's not fair, Miss Vega, is that you and your sister now have a stronger claim to the throne of Solaria than the four Celestial Heirs who have been training their entire lives to rule." I slammed my empty glass down on the table and heard her heart rate jump sharply. "When your parents died, the Celestial Council claimed the right to rule together. But now you have returned, it is our law that you be placed upon the throne if you can prove yourselves strong enough to claim it. Which is just our damn luck." I glared at her, glad her heart was pattering and glad that I'd unnerved her. I wasn't her friend. I was the one fighting to keep Darius on track to take his father's place on the Celestial Council. And I'd worked tirelessly for years to do it. So I would not be fucking gentle with how I dealt with this. The world was in trouble. The Nymphs were on the rise and this girl and her twin were not capable of protecting our kingdom from them. "Do you have any idea of the dangerous times we're living in, *Blue*?" I demanded and my upper lip curled as I stared at her hair. The royal colour already branded on her like a flag hung there to mock me.

"No, but maybe if you'd tell me-"

"Tell you what? Even if I relayed the entire history of Solaria to you, do you really think that would be enough?" I released a dry laugh. "The world has already fallen out of balance and now you and your sister have shown up to tip the scales even further into chaos. Whole families are turning up dead. Powerful ones too. Your parents were the first but not the last and it's only a matter of time before-" I cut myself off, cursing myself internally. She had no right to know any of this. My theories, suspicions. They were for mine and Darius's ears, not this girl's. I didn't need her running off to gossip with her little friends and let the whole school know the dangerous accusations that I held within me.

"Are you saying my birth parents were murdered?" she asked in horror. *Fuck. Backtrack the hell out of here.*

"I'm not saying anything." I cleared my throat, pouring myself another glass of bourbon, knowing I'd be sinking the whole lot of this tonight.

"Anyway," I grunted, wanting to force the conversation elsewhere. "Your Order will emerge sooner or later. Your power source will give you a clue as to what you are so pay attention. Different Orders' magic is replenished in specific ways. A Werewolf draws their power from the moon, a Medusa draws from mirrors, and if you hadn't guessed it yet, a Vampire draws powers from others through their blood." I flashed my fangs at her and she shuddered. *You can hate me all you like, I'm not going to stop biting you.*

"Well I'm definitely not like you," she said coldly and the disdain in her voice cut into something within my chest. This was what I wanted though. We were enemies. The lines were drawn in the sand, and she was clearly starting to understand that now.

I glanced down at my Atlas, my lips tight as I started signing her and Tory up to all the Order classes. "If your magic swells, try to focus on what is in your immediate vicinity that you could be drawing power from. It could be the sun, the shade, a star damned rainbow for all you know, just keep your mind sharp. In the meantime, I'll sign you up to all of the Order Enhancement classes. Those who develop late tend to evolve under the influence of their kind."

A notification pinged on her Atlas and she took it out, scrolling through all the extra lessons. She looked up, clearly about to ask more questions, but I was done answering them tonight.

"You and your sister won't pass The Reckoning," I said, sure of it because I'd make it so. "The world doesn't need two ignorant girls in power right now. And as much as most of the Celestial Heirs piss me off to no end, they at least know how to deal with the Nymph population."

"Nymphs?" she questioned, latching onto the one thing I'd said which I shouldn't have. *Stop drinking, you idiot.*

I cursed, pushing the glass of bourbon away from me. "They're another race, don't worry about it. You'll be long gone before they become relevant to your life."

She folded her arms, that insolent look on her face again which made my fingers twitch with the compulsion to punish her. "Professor, I know you think I'm useless because I don't know anything about magic or Fae, but I'm not stupid. I can learn. Isn't that what these classes are supposed to be for? Guiding me? Catching me up on everything I've missed out on? So at least give me the chance to prove myself."

Oh you'll prove yourself alright, Blue. You'll prove you're unable to take charge over a single Fae in this academy, let alone the whole kingdom.

My brows arched and a smile brushed over my mouth. "I suppose that's only fair, Miss Vega. And as a Libra, I'm a sucker for fairness," I said and her lips parted in surprise.

I glanced at the large brass clock on the wall. "We're almost out of time and I have somewhere to be." I rose from my seat. "I'll send reading materials on Coercion to your Atlas. You will have a lesson with me every Monday evening. I expect you to have a basic grasp on shields by our next one. There *will* be a test." I smirked. Fuck, I loved a pop quiz. Making students panic was my forte.

Darcy got to her feet, raising her chin as she gazed coolly at me. "I plan on getting an A."

She headed to the door, but before she could get out of the room and have the last word, I whipped across the space in double the speed.

I wrenched the door open, looking down at her. "I don't do grades. With me, it's always pass or fail." I snatched her Atlas from her hand, signing off this lesson with my digital pen. Then I passed it back and held the door wider, taunting her as she moved to step through it.

I'm no gentleman, Blue.

I surged past her in a burst of Vampire speed and let the door swing closed in her face. It was childish, but it made me feel like I'd won something.

And it definitely made up for the mental slips I'd had during that fucking Liaison. Or at least, that was what I was going to tell myself.

I needed to get my shit together if I was going to continue tutoring her. Which I had to, so I really had to lock this down. Fast.

Outside Jupiter Hall, I found Darius waiting for me around the side of the building, leaning against the wall as he twirled a golden coin between his fingers. He kicked off of the wall, his eyebrows arching with the question I knew he was about to ask and I flicked a silencing bubble up around us, speaking before he could.

"She's a seven in fire, an eight in earth, a nine in water and a ten in air," I dropped the bomb and his jaw dropped in time with it.

"Fuck," he snapped.

"Yeah," I muttered. "I'll get Tory's rankings off Prestos, but it's not gonna be much different. If they become fully trained, you're fucked Darius, do you understand that?"

"Yeah, I fucking understand," he growled, looking like he wanted to punch me, or the wall, or anyone who got too close in that second.

"Professor Orion?" a male voice clipped and I immediately dropped my silencing bubble, glancing over my shoulder and spotting Professor Astrum approaching me, his eyes narrowed on us like two gun barrels.

"Evening, Ling," I said curtly, knowing the old guy hated me and the feeling was mutual.

He shot a narrowed eyed look at Darius before folding his arms. "Can I have a word with you? In private."

"Sure," I muttered, looking to Darius and nodding to him in dismissal like we'd been having a perfectly normal teacher-student interaction.

He glared at Astrum for a second before heading off down the path and I was sure he'd be waiting for me at the beach for our dark magic lesson when I was done here.

Astrum glanced around then stepped closer to me. "Listen here, Lance," he said, his upper lip peeling back as he looked at me like I was less than dirt to him. "You have a duty as a professor at this academy to teach all students to the best of your ability."

"Thanks for the reminder," I said dryly.

"I mean it," he hissed, pointing a gnarled finger at me. "The Vegas deserve a chance in this world just like every other Fae deserves a chance. I put my political views aside when I teach the Heirs and I expect the same of you when you teach the Vegas. We are conduits of knowledge and we must-"

"That sounds awfully like a threat, Ling," I cut over him in a drawl.

"Perhaps it is." He raised his chin and his fingers moved like he was about to cast.

I scoffed, running my tongue across my teeth as my fangs extended. "I'd relish a fight, I really would. But I'm not sure me breaking an old man's bones and making him scream will make your point any better. So maybe we'll skip the drama, yeah?" I suggested, wondering if he really was going to push me for a fight. I didn't wanna do it, but I would cut him down to size if I had to. The guy might have been powerful, but he wasn't as powerful as me and he certainly wasn't as fast.

He sneered at me, hatred clear in his gaze. "Your father would be ashamed of what you've become," he hissed.

"What did you say?" I snarled and he shook his head like he regretted those words leaving his lips.

"Nothing," he muttered, but I stepped forward to grab hold of him, intending to punish him for those words. But Nova appeared with Washer on her arm, smiling at us brightly as she approached and I was forced to back up a step.

"Good evening," Nova said brightly and Astrum nodded to her before turning and scurrying off down the path, avoiding the beating he must have seen in my eyes. Or maybe he'd already read it coming in his precious tarot cards.

Fucking royalist. I didn't even know what he meant about my father. If he'd been here, he'd hardly have been a fucking Vega supporter. He'd worked for the damn Acruxes. So I had to assume Astrum was losing his mind.

I was forced to make small talk with Nova and Washer for a minute before I made my escape and headed down the path in the direction of Air Cove. When I was sure no one was watching, I shot that way with a burst of speed that made my head spin and excitement war in my veins. Because I'd had a headfuck of a day and there was nothing better than focusing on secretly training Lionel Acrux's son how to wield dark magic, putting him on an even playing field with his tyrant of a father. Nothing could lure me from that path. It was my calling, the last chance I had of achieving some semblance of satisfaction in my life. And maybe the day Lionel fell at his son's hand, I'd finally find some peace.

DARIUS

CHAPTER NINE

I sat in my favourite chair in the common room, feigning interest in the conversation from the group surrounding me as I enjoyed the heat of the fire beside me and thought over my plans for getting the Vegas out of this academy once and for all. My stomach was rumbling for breakfast, but I was putting it off, waiting on something I probably shouldn't have been wasting my time on.

My gaze flicked to the stairs which led up to the dorms and my jaw ticked as I found some random girl hurrying down them instead of the one I'd been watching for since I'd arrived here half an hour ago.

The FaeBook post Milton had circulated was the talk of the room and every time some asshole mentioned how much he'd enjoy fucking a princess, my patience grew thinner. Not that I'd said anything. This was what I'd wanted to happen when I'd burned her clothes from her body. The intention was to humiliate her, though it seemed to be having the added side effect of gaining way more male appreciation for how fucking hot she was than I would have liked. But I wasn't saying a word about it. I didn't need to. The gossip was in the rumour mill now and unlike me and the rest of the Heirs, the Vegas weren't used to everything about them being scrutinised in the public eye. This was a regular occurrence in the lives of the most powerful people in our kingdom and they needed to learn that before they got carried away with fantasies of how much fun it might be to claim their crown.

Ruling this kingdom wasn't fun. It was gruelling, never ending work and political minefields which needed constant monitoring and navigating. It was an art me and the other Heirs had been learning since the day we were born, and it was one that two girls who'd grown up with mortals would never be able to learn adequately. They didn't even know the names of the different parts of the kingdom, let alone how to manage them and help them thrive. The idea of them coming into power was as ludicrous as it was dangerous. Especially with the Nymph situation worsening every day.

Father might have ordered me to get rid of them, but I knew well enough for myself that they could never be allowed to rise up above us regardless. It wasn't just about pride or entitlement. They may have been more powerful than the four of us, but they didn't have the knowledge it would take to rule this kingdom and there was no way they'd ever be able to learn all of it either. You couldn't make up for the years they'd missed out on living here and learning about what it took to rule. So they would never be fit to in my mind no matter how strong they were.

I needed to bring them to heel. And as I thought over the defiance I'd seen in Roxy's eyes, I found I liked the idea of that a whole lot more than I should have. Just like I'd enjoyed looking through the pictures Milton had sent me of her standing naked before me in this very room. It wasn't even the images of her naked flesh that had caught my attention. It was the fire I could see burning between us as she'd glared up at me and I'd loomed over her. She was challenging me to make her bow and I was aching to do it in more ways than one.

I unbuttoned the top of my shirt as the heat of my magic made my skin prickle and I got a little carried away with the idea of making Roxy Vega bow for me in my own mind. I wanted my hand fisted in her black hair, her mouth on mine and her naked flesh pressed up against me as she gasped my name like a prayer to a god and I ruined her like a demon born to sin. But I needed to stop those thoughts in their track. Not least because I wasn't ever going to be able to indulge in them. By the time I was through with her, she'd hate me far too much for her to ever consider parting her thighs for me. *More's the pity.*

Marguerite appeared out of nowhere, jerking me from my fantasies about Roxanya Vega and dropping into my lap where she gasped as she found the hardness of my cock driving into her ass.

She leaned in to kiss me and I dragged her closer, kissing her hard and grinding her down over my cock to try and gain some relief from the ache in it.

I closed my eyes as I kissed her hard, sinking my tongue into her mouth and thinking of a girl with dark hair and fire in her soul. But as she mewled like a kitten and melted for me, my fantasy was somewhat ruined. I may not have known Roxy well, but she didn't seem like the kind of girl to melt into a puddle when I kissed her. No, she'd be all fire and spite and the kind of lust that burned the roof from houses while her fingernails gouged lines in my flesh.

I tried to push that thought out, gripping Marguerite's ass and rocking her back and forth over my cock, but I was fighting a losing battle because she was mewling again and her limbs were going as floppy as my dick was becoming as she instantly let me take control.

I released my grip on her waist, sighing as I pulled back and let her start sucking on my neck while I just looked up at the ceiling and waited for it to get more interesting again. Or maybe for it to just stop.

But before I could make a decision on that, Milton's voice drew my attention to the other side of our group and I instantly perked up at his words.

"Oh hey, it's Tory, right?" he asked and I nudged Marguerite aside to look over at the girl in question where she stood before him as she raised her hand and a tsunami of water slammed into him.

The attack sent him flying back off of his chair and slamming to the floor, but my gaze was fixed on her furious features and the curl of those full lips as she glared at him. My pulse picked up as she blasted him with more water which rolled him across the wooden floor before pinning him to the wall.

The group surrounding me all leapt up in shock and I almost dropped Marguerite on her ass as I stood too.

Roxy glanced at us for a moment like she expected someone to attack her, but that wasn't how this worked. It was Fae on Fae. She'd started this fight and it was down to her or Milton to end it. No one would be stepping in. But I'd sure as fuck be watching the show.

The power spewing from her was so ferocious that it made the hairs along the back of my neck stand on end and a shiver track down my spine. I wanted to step closer, feel more of it, dive into the depths of its potency and see what it made of me when I emerged on the other side.

Milton was shouting something unintelligible through the water that was damn near drowning him and she lowered the deluge so that it slammed into his chest instead, keeping his arms pinned so that he still couldn't fight back while allowing him to speak.

Clever girl.

She may not have been using any kind of finesse, but brute force was clearly enough to get the job done here and as the floor began to flood and a chair floated away from us towards the stairs, I had to wonder how long she could keep this up before she tapped out.

"Delete the picture," Roxy snarled, grabbing Milton's Atlas and holding it out towards him with the hand that wasn't controlling the flow of her water magic.

"Piss off," Milton bit out and I almost laughed at him, trying to sound intimidating while an untrained freshman handed him his ass in front of the entire House.

Roxy flicked her fingers, switched to air magic so seamlessly that I had to work to keep the surprise from my face. Milton was lifted upright and pinned against the wall by a force of wind which seemed just as powerful as the water she'd been wielding a moment before.

I pushed a couple of the other members of our group aside as I moved a little closer to watch her, fascinated by the fury in her gaze and how certain she seemed of herself despite his refusal to do as she said.

She stalked forward, grabbed Milton's hand and jammed his thumb down on the Atlas to unlock it before opening his photo album finding the pictures he'd taken of her. There were a bunch more than just the one he'd shared to FaeBook and she casually deleted all of them before removing them from his trash folder too, like restraining a trained Fae with air magic was a totally normal occurrence to her and it meant nothing at all.

But it wasn't nothing. It was something. This was her, this show of undeniable power which went on and on. She was a hurricane trapped in a jar and this was only the beginning of the storm. The longer I watched her, the clearer it became. I'd known that these girls were dangerous, but the punishing force of her power was immense and she had barely even begun to learn how to wield it. It was my duty to make sure they never did.

Roxy released Milton and he stumbled forward, raising a hand to fight back and my lips twitched as I waited to see him put her in her place. Because he would. She was powerful but he had two years of training on her and now that she'd made the mistake of freeing his hands-

Before Milton could do so much as summon a spark to throw at her, Roxy's hand snapped closed into a fist and her eyes flared with power once more. Vines sprang to life all around Milton, snaring him in their hold as they grew so fast that it was impossible for him to even attempt to burn them away. They pinned his arms to his sides and even gagged him before he overbalanced and fell to the wet carpet with a resounding slap.

Roxy's magic fell still and it was like static settled in the room as the press of it dropped away, making my skin prickle with the desire to feel it again. Silence surrounded us as all eyes stayed glued on her and I realised that this was most definitely a bad thing. Everyone here had seen that, seen her rise up and overpower a student who she never should have been able to match let alone beat with as little training as she had. There were whispers which would spread from this, rumours of her power and the potential she held. And that couldn't cause anything good.

"You need to learn to respect women," Roxy snarled, looking like she intended to kick him or spit on him before she just whirled away and stormed towards the exit without so much as a glance at me.

But that wasn't gonna work for me.

"He sent me copies of those photos, you know," I said calmly, my voice carrying over the calm room and shifting the focus onto me.

Roxy stopped abruptly and turned to look at me, a shock of connection burning through my chest as her defiant green eyes met mine.

"Teach her a lesson, baby," Marguerite cooed, making me bristle at her interruption, but I held my tongue as Roxy's attention shifted to her.

"You're Marguerite, right?" she asked, looking decidedly unimpressed and tossing me a look that seemed to cast judgement over my choice of hook up. "Or do you go by muff scruff now?"

I almost laughed aloud as her comment took me by surprise, biting down on my tongue to hold the noise in and barely suppressing a smile.

Roxy looked to me again and I had to force my expression to tighten, offering her the mask I wore for my father and letting her see nothing of what I thought about her behind it. Because the things I was thinking weren't likely to be what she expected and as my gaze dragged over the bronze expanse of thigh beneath the hem of her skirt and the way her shirt clung to her chest, I was finding it hard not to get caught up in the fantasy I kept having of her either.

Marguerite started forward like she thought she might step in, but this was between me and Roxy. The Fire Heir and the lost Princess. I didn't want her involvement and she should know better than to assume it was her place to offer it. I flicked my fingers at the irritation and she jerked to a halt, instantly falling to heel and backing away to leave me and Roxanya to it.

"So are you going to try and make me delete my copies?" I pressed, taking my Atlas from my pocket and holding it out in a dare for her to try and claim it. And I really hoped she'd try. Just to give me the excuse to put her in her place right here where everyone could see.

Roxy looked from my face to my Atlas, the desire to just snatch it from me written plainly across her features, but she held herself back before shrugging like she didn't even give a shit.

"Keep them," she said dismissively, her eyes flicking over me like I was nothing more than an annoyance to her. "If you're that desperate for material to jerk off to then be my guest."

"As if he'd be turned on by pictures of you!" Marguerite spat furiously as her words took me by surprise again.

I'd been so sure I had her. So certain she wouldn't be able to resist trying to claim them from me when they'd clearly pissed her off so much. But she'd turned the tables on me again in an instant and somehow I was back on uneven footing, not knowing how best to strike at her.

"Don't worry, Marguerite," Roxy said with a taunting lilt to her seductive voice. "It's not your fault that he needs them to get his motor going. I'm sure your hairy bush does it for him once you start bouncing about on his lap."

"You jumped-up, two cent alley-whore!" Marguerite screeched but I cut across her before she could continue with her dramatics, shutting her up the moment I spoke.

"I can have any girl I like," I said, not liking the implication in her voice or the way some of the people in the room were sniggering at our exchange. "Why would I be interested in looking at images of *you*?"

Roxy raised her hands innocently, giving me wide, mocking eyes that set a fire burning in my veins with the desire to put her in her fucking place.

"Hey dude, you're the one with naked photos of *me*, not the other way around. And you can't have *any* girl you like. Because that's a hard no from me. But you may as well enjoy the fantasy you're creating with those images because I can assure you that you've got zero chance of getting your hands on the real thing."

A smattering of laughter broke out as I ground my teeth, thrown off by her line of attack and not managing to find the words to toss at her before she backed out of the room with a taunting grin at my expense and disappeared out of sight.

My fist tightened at my side, not least because that mocking rejection actually hit the mark and a growl tumbled through my chest as I turned back to look at the rest of the idiots in the room.

"Clean this shit up," I barked at them, pointing at Milton who was still wrapped in vines on the floor among the puddles of water that were covering the carpet.

The laughter in the room died a quick death and everyone scattered to do as I said while I strode away to get my bag from my room.

I opened my Atlas as I went, pulling up the naked photos of Roxy at her initiation and deleting all of them with a hiss of irritation. I wouldn't be jerking off over some shitty photographs of a girl who drove me insane, and I wouldn't give her the satisfaction of believing I was either.

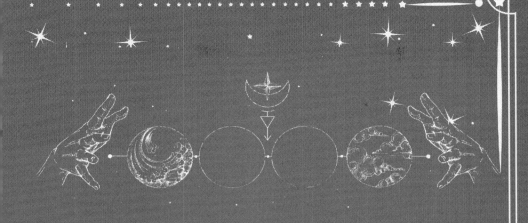

ORION

CHAPTER TEN

I stood under a tree near The Orb, dusk colouring the sky deepest blue and the first glint of the stars appearing within the murky sea of the heavens. I had a concealment spell around me so students didn't notice me as they walked by and I took some pleasure in tripping up any asshole who was wearing their uniform wrong. Duck-tailed shirt? *You're on your ass.* Blazer sleeves rolled up? *Straight in a ditch.* Not wearing a uniform at all? *It's after hours, but fuck it, you can fall flat on your face.*

"Whhhy?" wailed Tyler Corbin as I sent him spiralling down the path on a furious breeze and crashing into a bush. *Because you're an irksome little shit, that's why. If you can't handle that, wait until you reach Hell Week.*

"That Washer guy is gross," Tory Vega's voice caught my attention and my head snapped sideways as I spotted her and Darcy walking down the path with Geraldine Grus in tow.

"He's the most bothersome babbalumbaduke I ever saw," Geraldine agreed.

Tory rolled her eyes, looking away from her, clearly not enjoying the girl's company nor in any mood to indulge it. And I knew exactly why. Darcy on the other hand, gave Geraldine a polite smile and answered her. Ever the sweetheart. *You won't be so sweet when you embrace your inner Fae, Blue.*

"What's a babbalumba-thing?" Darcy frowned and Geraldine flapped her arms and gasped like someone had just dropped dead in front of her.

"You haven't heard of a babbalumbaduke!? My queen-"

"Darcy," she interjected and my brows arched at her dismissal of the royalist's bullshit.

"Pish-posh!" Geraldine waved a hand. "A babbalumbaduke is the most creepsome creature you can imagine. It crawls from sewers and pulls unsuspecting virgins into its grasp, never to let go. The legend says it feasts upon their innocent flesh with nothing but its two-pronged armensprout."

"To be fair, that does sound like Washer," Tory said with a smirk.

"Yeah, but what's an armensprout?" Darcy wrinkled her nose and my lips twitched up at the corner at how fucking cute she looked. Then I murdered that lip twitch and gritted my jaw, replacing the curiosity within me about her with a healthy dose of hatred. She was a Vega. Their name alone was a curse on this land.

"My good lady!" Geraldine wailed. They were close now, about to pass me by on the path as they circled The Orb, probably headed for dinner. "An armensprout is a dilly dongle. A war-willy wingle. A goblin of the grouse. A terrible Leroy."

"A dick?" Tory guessed and a snort escaped my lips that made Darcy's head snap around to look into the trees. My heart bolted up into my throat even though I knew she couldn't see me. But I swear her eyes found my fucking soul anyway.

"Wait, that monster thing eats people with its dick?" Darcy snorted.

"Why yes! That's what I've been trying to tell you!" Geraldine guffawed.

Darcy suddenly tripped over her own feet and almost went flying to the ground, but my fingers flicked and I cast air magic before I knew what I was even doing, catching her so she didn't hit the ground. She looked confused as hell and Tory chuckled, linking her arm through hers and pulling her along.

What the fuck did I just do?

I'd just spent the past ten minutes tripping up students and Darcy hadn't even had her shirt tucked in. So why hadn't I taken the opportunity to send her flying into the mud?

"Come on, clumsy butt," Tory said and Darcy laughed.

"Are you okay, my sweet lady?" Geraldine gasped, hovering around her and Darcy's cheeks pinked as she waved her away.

"Yup, just hungry," she said brightly and the only way I could describe Geraldine's next movement was a high-kneed gallop as she beckoned the girls after her down the path.

"Make way – make way!" she cried at the other students, blasting some of them off the path with her water magic. "The true queens are coming through!"

Tory whispered in Darcy's ear and I tuned my senses on them to catch it. "Do you think we can outrun her if we turn back and skip dinner?"

"No chance. Look at those legs go," Darcy said and they both fell into silent laughter, leaning on each other, their bond shining clearly between them.

My heart tugged violently as I stared after them, remembering having that bond with my sister Clara before she'd died. Before Lionel had killed her. My throat tightened and suddenly I couldn't breathe all that well as I shut my eyes and felt darkness licking at the edges of my flesh.

My ears hummed with energy and it felt like the stars were peeling back a layer of the world for me. I lived in that sensation for a moment, feeling closer to Clara like she was standing at the edges of my consciousness.

The scales are tipping, Libra. You must soon choose.

A howl cut through the whispers in my mind and my eyes snapped open, leaving me unsure if I'd really heard those words. The stars spoke so rarely to people, I'd only ever experienced it a couple of times in my life. The first time being when my father had died and the words, *claim his place* had echoed in my head. Since then, it seemed like they were always more present, like they were watching me. And it made every one of my choices seem far more important than I liked them to be.

But I hardly thought I had some important role to play here. And I wasn't sure what their messages even meant. You must choose? What choice could there be to make? I couldn't understand it, just like I hadn't understood the message they'd sent when my father died. But I'd tried to do my best to embody everything he was all the same.

I taught an Acrux dark magic, which had been a big part of his life work, though I wasn't as adept as he was at creating dark spells. Experimenting with dark magic always seemed like a dangerous idea to me. And risking Darius's life with something untested was unthinkable. So I stuck to what my father had taught me and hoped it was enough to give Darius the edge he would need against his father in future, putting them on a more level playing ground. Because Lionel Acrux would not be above using dirty tactics to beat his son if it came down to it. And dark magic could be very subtle, undetectable.

My father had warned me away from using some kinds of it, not even teaching me anything that could cause me permanent harm. Like Dark Coercion. Unlike normal Coercion, it couldn't be fought off with mental shields or any spell I knew. It was as binding as a death vow and that made it terrifying. It took a soul sacrifice to achieve such high levels of dark magic. If your soul wasn't intact when you died, it could forfeit your place among the stars, they could cast you into eternal damnation and suffering. And nothing that happened in this life was worth being cursed for eternity by our celestial rulers.

I focused back on the reason I was waiting here and the heaviness lifted from me a little as I stared at the curving golden wall of The Orb ahead of me. At the end of last term Darius had stolen all of the diamonds that were embedded in the constellations marked on the outer walls of The Orb. Lionel had funded them like a prime asshole and yeah, I'd helped Darius gather them all up for his little treasure stash in the dead of night to piss Lionel off.

I smirked at the memory, but sadly new gemstones now filled their places, cast there by the Earth Elemental Professor Rockford this afternoon. And as Darius was definitely going to be distracted by those twinkly stones, I was planning a surprise attack. It was my way of teaching him to always keep his guard up, and it fed my inner Vampire as I enjoyed hunting one of the most powerful Fae in the kingdom. Though real hunting was strictly forbidden, I indulged in this little game, walking the line of what was really acceptable. But I wouldn't bite him. If I did, I could get a taste for the hunt and then I really would be in trouble.

The source of the howl that had drawn my attention belonged to Seth Capella as he walked down the path among the other Heirs. People were leaping out of their way or gathering at their backs as they fangirled over the four of them and I resisted the urge to roll my eyes at their kiss ass bullshit.

Seth was loudly telling anyone who'd listen that he'd just been awarded Wolf of the year in Make You Howl Magazine, waving the thing in everyone's faces to point out his photograph.

"You think that's good? I got awarded hottest water Elemental of the year twice in a row. You might be hottest of your Order, but I'm hottest out of an entire Element," Max said smugly and a few girls around them giggled and tried to catch his eye.

"Well it's bullshit I didn't get hottest air Elemental anyway," Seth said with a growl. "Why would someone pick a washed up professor who tossed away his Pitball career as the winner, even if he is hot?"

"Don't talk about him like that," Darius snarled.

"Oh come on, let's just all admit Orion isn't *me* hot. Look at my hair." Seth shook his head so it rippled in the sunlight. "Look at that gleam. He doesn't have a gleam like that."

"I dunno, he's pretty gleamy," Caleb taunted and Seth lunged at him, the two of them instantly starting to wrestle.

I clenched my jaw. I did not read bullshit magazines like that. I had however, had my entire classroom plastered with photos of me hitting the number one spot in Elemental Weekly last term after I'd won that stupid title and with the skill they'd been stuck to my wall, I had to suspect an Heir. Or all of them. When they banded together, they got up to so many pranks, we practically had to have a team at Zodiac Academy employed entirely to rectify the chaos they caused. And because of their status, no one was allowed to give them any kind of decent time in detention. Even me. Elaine Nova was very clear about that. *Suck up.*

Darius seemed distracted and I smirked as I realised why. His eyes were fixed on the gemstones in the Capricorn constellation near to me and he trailed to a halt while the others all kept walking.

"I'll catch you later," he muttered to them and they waved goodbye, heading off down the path and taking most of their fan club with them.

Darius chased off the few who remained by baring his teeth at them and the path cleared out as he stood there, glancing around for any teachers before creeping closer to the wall. I supressed a snigger as he reached out to stroke his fingers over the lowest gemstone, his head cocking left and right as he examined it.

"Mine," he said, the word low and I only caught it because of my Order gifts.

I took the pouch of stardust from my pocket and shot forward with the speed of my Vampire, a grin splitting over my face as he didn't move a single muscle. Then I slammed into him, throwing stardust at the same time and we were torn away into the ether, a surprised yell escaping him as my laughter echoed around us.

We landed in a woodland and went tumbling down a steep bank among the fallen leaves as Darius started punching me, a Dragon's roar leaving his throat. I cast a solid air shield against my flesh to stop his blows from touching me and I landed on my back beneath the bulk of him, his hair falling into his eyes and his face twisted in a vicious snarl that reminded me all too much of his father for a second.

"It's me," I said quickly, my heart hammering, the game suddenly not so funny anymore.

His brows drew together as he took in the culprit and his whole body sagged with relief.

"What the fuck, Lance?" He shoved off of me, getting to his feet.

"You've gotta stop leaving your guard down on campus," I warned as he offered me a hand and pulled me to my feet.

"No one on campus can challenge me but the Heirs, and they're hardly gonna do that," he said, brushing some leaves from his hair.

"Don't get cocky," I said, shoving his arm. "Skill can outmatch power."

He released a breath that was tangled with smoke then he lurched forward and wrapped his arms around me. I hugged him back, sensing something was troubling him, but then again something was always troubling him lately. And I knew the feeling.

The bond between us thrived and the relief I got from being this close to him helped soothe the worst of my anxiety, and I guessed it helped him too.

He started chuckling and I joined him as we broke apart.

"You fucking asshole," he said, a smirk pulling at his lips.

I gave him a mocking shrug. "You're just salty because you know you'd be dead right now if I was your enemy."

"Lucky you're on my side then," he said with a grin. "And speaking of sides, how's the Vega watch going?"

I frowned. "Nothing really to report. They're still vulnerable. But it's not gonna last forever."

He nodded seriously. "Do you think they're cracking? Should we push harder?"

I eyed him closely. "What exactly are you and the Heirs planning to do them?"

"Whatever it takes," he growled. "Father's been threatening Xavier again and I just..."

I rested a hand on his shoulder, feeling his pain over that as it mixed with my own. "We'll figure this out. I swear."

"Any ideas on their Orders?" he asked.

"I think Darcy might be a Siren," I said and his brows arched.

"Oh yeah? Why do you think that?" he asked.

"It's just a vibe. Like she's trying to manipulate my feelings or something," I muttered and he nodded slowly.

"Yeah now you say it, Roxy could be one too," he said thoughtfully.

"Really? You felt it from her as well?" I asked hopefully, latching onto this explanation with both hands.

"Yeah, like a sort of pull..."

"Exactly," I agreed and relief fell between us.

The heaviness lifted from his expression. "So where's my hatchet?" he asked like a kid asking for candy and I smirked.

I took out the sun steel sword I'd concealed as a switch blade in my pocket along with Darius's hatchet which currently looked like a tiny green Dragon keyring with a dick for a head. I may have gotten carried away with the concealment spell on that one, but my last lesson had been a senior class who'd spent the hour practising levitation, so I'd had time to work on it.

I tossed it to Darius and he snorted as he looked at it. "Nice."

"Do you think your father would approve?" I asked with a grin.

"He'd probably roast you in the kitchen fireplace and eat you for a snack," he said with a laugh.

"Worth it," I murmured and he released a note of laughter.

"What's the plan then?"

"I think we have a lead," I said with a grin. There was nothing like the thrill of the hunt to make me forget the rest of my shitty life. I lived for this, defying Lionel, battling monsters. It was about the only thing that reminded me I still had a beating heart in my chest these days. "There was a Nymph sighting near here reported to the FIB and I think it might belong to the group we were tracking."

Darius's face brightened at those words and my chest warmed at being able to give him some good news for once. I took out my Atlas, checking the coordinates Francesca had sent me. She was strictly not allowed to give me any locations for Nymph sightings, but she still did, risking her job for the sake of knowing more Nymphs were being dealt with by us. The FIB were stretched too thin to deal with the mounting problem of Nymph attacks, but they wouldn't admit there was a problem and build a bigger taskforce to fight them.

They were afraid to scare the public by announcing there was a crisis going on in the kingdom, so Francesca sent me the reports that came in whenever they were ignored. It was hard, bloody work but I relished every second of it. Teaching all day wasn't natural to me. I needed a purpose and this gave me one. And I knew Darius needed it too. It was an outlet that also made us feel useful in this world, like we were actually making a difference. Would I have gotten in serious trouble with Lionel if he knew I was bringing his son out on dangerous, illegal Nymph hunts? Absolutely. Did I give one Tiberian Rat dropping of a shit? Not one.

Especially because this Nymph sighting had occurred here in Tucana, only a stone's throw away from Zodiac Academy. And that was not to be taken lightly.

"Come on, this way." I slid the concealment spell off the switch knife with my thumb and it expanded into a full sized sword.

We delved deeper into the woods and clouds drew in as we walked, rain soon drizzling down from the canopy above. I cast an air shield around us to keep us dry, but it made sounds more difficult to catch as I listened to a million drops of rain slapping against leaves and branches, sending my senses into overdrive.

We reached the edge of a large property where the Nymph had been sighted by some old guy who lived in the ancient farmhouse surrounded by grassy fields. Ferris Pike had made the report, but according to Francesca he was an unreliable witness due to his drinking habit. He cried wolf down in a local bar and had been laughed out of there. The only reason Francesca had taken it seriously was because of the photograph he'd managed to take.

I checked that very picture now on my Atlas and showed it to Darius. It was of this exact spot, though the angle was too low to see any of the Nymph's upper body. It was hard to distinguish, but between the two trees where we stood now, there were long, barky legs that melded in with the woodland. It could easily be dismissed as part of the trees, but standing here confirmed what it was. Because there was no sign of them now.

"You see that scar on its right leg," I said, pointing to it and a grin split across Darius's face.

"That could be the one that had a limp. The chances of a Fae having an unhealed injury is pretty damn unlikely," he said excitedly. We'd only seen the group we'd been tracking out of their Nymph forms, so we couldn't be one hundred percent sure they weren't Fae. But one of them had had a bad leg, and this Nymph seemed to have an old injury in the same place. It was really possible that this could prove those people we'd tracked were Nymphs who were part of a nest. And if we could figure it out once and for all tonight, we could go after them.

"My thoughts exactly," I said darkly, but then Darius's face fell as he realised what that meant.

"You think the nest is this close to Tucana?"

"Could be," I muttered, not liking the idea of that. We'd suspected the nest was further out based on the sightings we'd had of the group, but maybe we were wrong.

I dropped down to the ground and as I pushed away some of the fallen leaves, I found large footprints in the mud.

"Which way do you think it went?" Darius asked as he dropped down to a crouch too, pushing more leaves away around us to hunt for more footprints.

"There." I pointed as my keener eyesight locked on more prints just beyond where he was looking.

He stood up, following the prints along the wooden fence that circled Ferris's property and I headed after him, keeping my ears trained on the woodland in case anything approached us from the dark.

The rain was picking up in ferocity and I cursed as it became even more difficult to distinguish sounds among the pattering raindrops that filled the world. But one thing cut through it at last that sent a shiver of dread racing up my spine. A scream, the blood-curdling, terror-filled kind.

My head snapped around to look at the farmhouse where it had come from and in an instant, I grabbed Darius, throwing him over my shoulder and leaping the fence. I shot at full pelt towards the house and reached the front door just before it exploded off its hinges and fire magic bloomed in my vision.

I threw out an air shield as we were knocked to the ground and Darius gained his feet before I did, releasing a battle cry as the keyring in his hand shifted into a hatchet and he leapt at the giant Nymph as it stepped out of the house. My gaze locked onto a pendant on a chain around its neck, the black gemstone swirling with shadow and exuding a power so dark it sent a dagger of fear into my chest.

His hatchet sank into its arm as it tried to shield itself and I leapt up to help, shooting forward and slashing at one of its legs.

It shrieked in fury then stolen earth magic exploded from its body in a furious blast that tore the ground apart beneath us.

I fell with a gasp of panic and Darius fell with me, my air magic catching us before we hit the rocky ground at the bottom of the pit.

The Nymph leapt over the hole above us and I flew us up there as fast as

I could with a storm of air beneath us.

"I'm gonna shift!" Darius cried as we landed on the muddy ground outside the house and my gaze locked on the Nymph as it fled in the direction of the trees, a slight limp to its gait that made me almost sure it was one of the people we'd been tracking. But unless we could get hold of it and force it to shift, there was no way of proving it.

"No, we're too close to town, you'll be seen," I barked, grabbing Darius's arm to halt him as he went to pull his shirt off. The Nymph leapt the fence and immediately melded into the woodland as it disappeared between the dark boughs.

"Then run us over there!" he demanded, but a wave of heat behind me made me turn to look back at the house. Fire was blooming within it, consuming it fast.

A siren rang out somewhere in town and my heart leapt as I realised we were in trouble.

"We have to go," I growled, reaching for the stardust, but Darius shook his head.

"Are you crazy? We need to chase it. Destroy it." His face twisted in rage, his need for this kill clear.

"It's too late," I snapped. "We have to go."

"Then *you* go." He ran off across the grass and I swore, running after him as I refused to leave him behind.

The Nymph made it into the trees and my Atlas started buzzing in my pocket.

Darius was almost at the fence when ten FIB agents appeared there via stardust, looking directly at him and making my stomach clench.

I acted in an instant, shooting away with the speed of my Order and jumping the fence further up the field. I darted into the cover of the trees, watching as Darius raised his hands in surrender, the hatchet no longer in sight.

"Stay where you are!" a large male agent boomed.

Fuck, fuck, fuck.

I snatched out my Atlas, finding a message from Francesca that said nothing but *RUN*.

I noticed her among the agents as they climbed the fence and surrounded Darius, all of them wearing their black jumpsuits.

I trained my ears on them as my pulse jerked violently in my chest.

"A man's been attacked by a Nymph," Darius said loudly, pointing to the house. "He needs help."

A few of the agents ran that way, quickly dousing the flames and heading inside. It wasn't long before they reappeared carrying a body behind them on air magic and laid him on the grass.

"He's been killed. Could have been the fire, it's hard to tell without a proper examination," one of the agents called.

"Dragon fire?" another asked sharply. *Shit.*

"It was a Nymph," Darius said firmly, but no one seemed to be listening.

Francesca gave him a look that told him to be quiet and he locked his jaw tight.

An agent quickly pulled Darius's hands behind him and snapped magic blocking cuffs onto his wrists, making my panic go from a hundred to a thousand.

I did the only thing I could do, because this was bad. Like going to prison bad.

So I called the one person in the world who could smooth this shit over, tasting bile in my mouth as I did it. The call rang and rang and I cursed him with every name under the sun as I waited for him to pick up.

"Yes?" Lionel answered curtly.

"Darius is being arrested for a crime he didn't commit," I let the axe fall all at once and a stretch of furious silence followed.

"Send me your location." He hung up and I texted him the coordinates, praying Darius wouldn't fucking hate me for this.

But I had to protect him, and this was the only way to do it. Because if the FIB took him in, they'd find that hatchet, they'd use a Cyclops to search his memories. They'd see everything we'd been up to, and not just the Nymph hunts, they could see that I'd been teaching him dark magic too, that he was planning to take on his father. And I couldn't let that happen.

I took a moment to conceal my sword once more, sliding it into my pocket in the form of the switch knife.

Lionel stardusted into existence just beyond the agents and one of them got such a fright that he fell right onto his ass.

"What in the stars' names are you doing to my son?!" he boomed and Francesca rushed forward to answer.

"Lord Acrux, sir, he was found at the scene of a crime," she said hurriedly. "We need to bring him in for questioning. But not to worry, I'll interrogate him myself and I'm sure that will clear everything up."

I could see what she was doing. She was a Cyclops, and if she conducted the interrogation then maybe she really could protect him. But if she was questioned, or if someone higher than her ordered someone else to do the interrogation…

"You will do no such thing," Lionel snapped, his eyes two pits of hellfire. "My son is not a criminal, are you boy? So explain to the FIB agents what exactly it is you are doing here." He stared at Darius, clearly curious as to why he was here too and fuck if we could ever let him find out.

"I was out flying and I saw the fire," Darius said confidently. "I landed here to check what was going on."

"Then why are you wearing clothes?" some helpful little bastard of an agent demanded.

"Ever heard of a Pegobag, dipshit?" Darius growled. "I left it over there." He pointed in the vaguest direction across the field. "Want me to go get it?"

"Ye-" the guy started but Lionel cut over him.

"Of course you won't ask him to do such a thing. You aren't really suggesting my son could be responsible for this house fire?" he demanded and the agent looked uncertain, glancing at his colleagues for backup, but they were all looking pretty sheepish now.

"It's our job," the guy piped up.

"He is to be a High Lord of the Celestial Council," Lionel scoffed. "So do you really believe he is responsible for this?"

"Of course not," the agent backtracked. "But it's protocol. We must take him in for questioning. Once we've confirmed his story we'll-"

"Agent Blakely," Lionel said coldly, his eyes dipping to the FIB badge on the guy's chest and I swear I saw him trembling. "I suggest you think very carefully about your next move. If you arrest my boy, you are ensuring the whole kingdom hears about it in the newspapers. You will be soiling the grand name of Acrux, one of the rulers who ensure the FIB are so well provided for."

Blakely slowly nodded, anxiously running his fingers through his hair. "Well I...perhaps this once we could...alter protocol considering...the circumstances."

"Yes, yes," Lionel said brightly, clapping Blakely on the shoulder so hard I swear he sank an inch into the mud. "That's more like it. A little respect. I appreciate that, I truly do. Your division will be handsomely rewarded for your hard work here tonight. I will see to it myself."

By the stars, I hated that asshole. But hell did he have the sway of a god when I needed his help.

"We'll get out of your hair and leave you to your investigation. And I expect my son's name to remain anonymous in all this, hm?"

"Of course, your Highness, I mean my Lord, I mean-" Blakely babbled and Lionel knocked him out of his way as he approached his son.

Francesca took the cuffs off of Darius and Lionel caught hold of his arm as the agents all headed over to the body and the crime scene awaiting them. Lionel spoke in a low voice that was meant for my ears.

"I shall escort you both to the academy." Then he stardusted away with Darius and I rubbed a hand over my eyes before doing the same.

I was pulled through the endless spiral of stars and landed on the tarmac outside the huge gates of Zodiac Academy.

Lionel had a deadly air of rage about him that made my skin prickle and I glanced at Darius, an apology on my lips, but he shook his head, his eyes telling me he didn't blame me for what I'd done.

Lionel flicked up a silencing bubble around us, a sneer pulling at his mouth.

"Explain. Now. And do not dare lie to me."

"It was like I said," Darius said firmly. "I was out flying and I saw the fire."

"Then explain your clothes to me, because my son does not wear a *Pegobag*. Dragons do not fly with clothes stashed in some disgusting backpack created for lesser Fae," Lionel spat.

"I was running along beneath him," I said. "I had his clothes. I gave them to him when he landed. Then when the FIB showed up, I ran off so I had time to call you."

Lionel fell silent, looking between us, hunting for the lie. Fear rippled up and down my spine, but I didn't let an ounce of it show on my face.

"Tell me the truth, boy," he said as he fixed his gaze on Darius. "Did you set that house fire? Did you use your Dragon fire? Because there are tell-tale signs of Dragon fire which will be harder to keep under wraps if you did." There was a glitter in his eyes that gave me a horrible, gut-churning feeling that Lionel was hoping his son would say yes. That he had killed that man in cold blood.

"I didn't," Darius swore, his brows pulling tight together.

"I won't be angry," Lionel said, his voice softening to a tone I had never heard from him before. "Ferris Pike was a powerful Fae, but he was also a vile Sphinx. A hoarder of knowledge. Did he offend you somehow? Because there is honour in such a kill."

"No," Darius snapped. "I didn't kill him."

Lionel sighed, looking disappointed. "Fine," he bit out. "Well you're going to pay the price of what I just did for you. It will cost me a substantial contribution to the FIB to keep your name out of the press."

"Okay," Darius agreed, jutting his chin out as he waited for the punishment. But Lionel wasn't going to lay into his son right here at the gates of Zodiac Academy. "Get it over with."

"No, boy." Lionel stepped closer to him. "I will punish you when I see fit."

He snapped his fingers at me like I was some obedient guard dog. "Take my son back to his room, Lance."

"Yes, Uncle," I said, my tone dry as usual, but he didn't seem to notice.

He threw stardust over himself, disappearing from sight and a breath of relief left my lungs. Darius stalked through the gates and I headed after him, watching him in my periphery as I cast a silencing bubble around us.

"We'll have to lay low for a while. Stop the Nymph hunts," I muttered.

"What?" he snarled, rounding on me. "I was about to suggest the exact opposite."

"It's too risky," I hissed. "Don't you understand what would have happened if the FIB had taken you in for questioning? They could have found out everything we're planning, not to mention all the illegal shit we've been up to."

"But they didn't," Darius snapped. "And we can't stop hunting the Nymphs just because of the risks. We knew the risks before we started and they're worth taking if we can stop the Nymphs before they pose a real threat to the kingdom."

"I'm not saying we stop forever. But for now-"

"No," he gritted out stubbornly. "You don't get to tell me what to do. You're not my father, Lance."

"No, but I am your friend," I pushed.

"Because he made you be," he sniped. "This is your Guardian bond speaking, not you."

"Fuck you," I grunted, his words stinging more than I liked. "It's not the bond."

"It is. You can't even differentiate it from your real feelings, that's how it works. Because the real Lance Orion would stand at my side fighting Nymphs until the end of time, but this guy demanding I stay out of trouble was put in you by my father," he said and before I could contradict him, he took a right fork in the path and murmured goodnight to me, heading in the direction of his House.

I stood there for a long moment, tempted to go after him, the bond urging me to. But his words were circling in my head and I forced down the lump of pain burning in my chest over leaving him when he clearly needed me and made my feet walk in the opposite direction. Because maybe he had a point. Maybe I was just a dog on a leash when it came down to it. And I didn't want to do what the bond begged of me even though it felt like my ribcage was being cleaved apart.

I looked to the stars, needing direction but finding them sparkling quietly, having nothing to say. So I'd turn to a darker source for my knowledge tonight and read the ancient bones I kept hidden in my closet. They'd give me something to go on, a path to take, and confirm if it was a good idea to stop the hunts for a while or not.

But as I walked further and further away from Darius Acrux and the Guardian bond flared so hot it burned, I had a feeling protecting him was going to be my choice no matter what fortunes I could read. Because Darius was right, my choices were made for me when it came to his safety. And there was nothing I could do to fight it, even if it put the entire kingdom at risk.

DARIUS

CHAPTER ELEVEN

I strode out into The Wailing Wood with my mind on the Nymph attack and my attention on my Atlas.

Lance was ignoring my texts and I was getting pretty damn pissed at him over this whole thing. We'd been so close to discovering something important with the Nymphs and yet now he was actively blocking me from pushing into this investigation.

There was a damn good chance that there was more than just that one Nymph hiding out in plain sight, pretending to be Fae right on the edges of the closest town and it was pretty clear to me why. At this academy there were plenty of young Fae with newly Awakened magic who would be prime targets for the Nymphs to strike and steal power from. Especially the two ultra attractive prospects of Roxy and Gwendalina Vega.

If I was a Nymph, I'd have been sorely tempted to try my luck at stealing their power while they were untrained, easy targets and now we knew for a fact that those creatures had been close to the academy.

But with my father's interest in our after class excursions officially piqued, alongside the fact that the FIB were now at the very least connecting my name to a man who had been killed by the creatures we'd been hunting, Lance was insisting we lay low.

I got it on one level. He was my Guardian, blood bound to protect me and keep me safe as well as my best friend who was concerned for my safety. And between the threat my father posed us and the threat the FIB could pose if they decided to look into us any more closely, he had reason enough to be concerned. We were wielding dark magic as well as conducting illegal Nymph hunts in our free time, but I just couldn't bear to back down on our goals now. We were so close.

Not to mention the fact that hunting the Nymphs was one of the few things I got to do that helped me relieve some of the tension which was always compounding inside my skull. I needed the release of heading out into the fight. Call it bloodlust or adrenaline highs or just plain running away from the shitty reality I lived in a lot of the time but there it was. I needed it and I wasn't willing to back down. Especially not while we had some of them within reach and the threat they were posing was so close.

"Darius!" Max's voice drew my attention and I looked around to find him jogging towards me, a wide grin on his face as he caught up. "I thought that was you brooding your way along the path."

"I'm not brooding," I muttered, tightening up my mental shields so that he couldn't call me out on my bullshit, but he'd obviously already gotten a sense for my mood anyway.

"Sure. Just like you're not pissed as all hell at Orion over something. Because sitting with you in Cardinal Magic today was kinda like sitting there listening to teeth grinding while I was saturated in all your rage."

I rolled my eyes but didn't deny it. I didn't elaborate either and that made me feel kind of shitty. The other Heirs were always so open and honest about everything they had going on and I...wasn't.

The worst thing about that was that they got it. They didn't know the details about what went on in my father's household, but they got the gist even if I couldn't tell them. Sometimes I wished I could, but other times I figured they were better off not knowing. It would only burden them with worry over something they were powerless to change. The only way out of the cage my father had created for me was by defeating him. And I was the only one who could do that. Once I was strong enough to beat him, I'd take him down, claim his place on the Celestial Council and banish him from my life for good.

Or at least that was the pretty fantasy Lance and I lived for because without that, I basically had no hope at all of ever getting out of this hole and actually waking up looking forward to my life.

Max gave me a concerned look and pushed some happy vibes my way, causing me to swipe a hand over my face before slapping on a smile for him.

"Shit man, I think I'm just feeling sorry for myself today, ignore me," I said, giving myself a mental shake and forcing my thoughts away from my father and his hold over my life.

Things tended to get dark for me pretty fast when I let myself dwell on that crap - which was kinda easy to do as he had almost full control over everything important in my life and monitored my every move constantly. Still, I had a lot more freedom here at the academy than I had at the manor, and I had friends I would die for, so it wasn't all doom and gloom. I just needed to buck the hell up and stop moping like a little bitch.

I lowered my mental barriers a bit, letting Max perk my mood up with his Siren gifts and he smiled in relief as some of the tension fell from me.

A low howl drew my attention to the path and I looked up just as Seth leapt from the trees in his Wolf form and pounced on Caleb as he rounded a corner up ahead. The two of them fell to the ground wrestling as Seth shifted back into Fae form so that he could use his fists.

Max and I wordlessly broke into a sprint and dove into the fray, my heart thumping as we all scrapped in the mud like a pack of mutts.

One of them punched me in the kidney a moment before I caught an elbow to the chin and Max cried out in horror that Seth's dick had slapped him in the face. Before long we were all cursing and bleeding and laughing as we fell in a heap beside each other, looking up at the moon through the trees.

"I love you guys," Seth said and the rest of us all punched him a few more times before he started licking any of us.

"Put your dick away, dude, you're making this weird," I told him, flicking his nipple and making him yip in pain.

"You know, every once in a while, you guys could all just get your dicks out instead of making me put mine away," he joked as he rolled over and got to his feet, heading off into the trees to find his clothes.

Caleb shot to his feet then offered me a hand and I let him pull me upright before healing the bruises and scrapes I'd gotten in our brawl, the smile on my face sticking this time as I let myself live in the moment and just have some fun with my friends.

Once Seth returned wearing his clothes with his long hair tied up, the four of us headed on down the path, moving to one of our favoured spots in the trees where we could hang out away from all the other students. We were used to being followed around by adoring fan types all the time, but it got tiring pretty fast and we liked to escape into the company of each other as often as we could so that we didn't have to feel like we were out on show all the damn time.

"I need a piss," Cal muttered, moving into the trees as we closed in on our destination and the three of us carried on without him.

"I heard something pretty interesting today, Darius," Seth baited me as he led the way into the clearing, dropping down on a stump which formed part of a circle.

"Hang on a second," Max said as we followed Seth into the clearing and I got the feeling he already knew what was going to be said. "If you're going to get emotional over this then I want in on your pain."

"If you must," I said, trying to sound pissy over it, but I didn't really mind letting him regenerate his power from me.

We took a seat on two stumps which were sat close to each other as Seth practically bounced up and down in anticipation of sharing whatever he wanted to say to me. Max threw an arm around my shoulders so that he could syphon my power more easily.

"Well," Seth said, pausing dramatically. "I heard that you've promised Marguerite a meeting with your parents the next time they come for a visit."

I choked out a laugh at that suggestion, leaning forward and resting my elbows on my knees. Max was forced to shift with me to maintain the contact between us. "Well she can certainly come up with some creative stories even if she's less imaginative than a potato in the bedroom."

The thought of me introducing her to my father as if she were my girlfriend or something was more than a little ridiculous. For a start, the conniving bastard wouldn't give a shit, not least because he'd already decided on how my romantic life would play out for me. And secondly, if I really was going to attempt to introduce anyone to him, it would only ever be if I was blessed by the stars and somehow found a single, pure blooded hot Dragon girl who I could offer as a real option. So basically, it wasn't ever going to happen.

Seth barked a laugh at Marguerite's expense and Max grinned as he got to feed on my amusement even if it was tinged with bitterness.

"Still all set to marry your cousin then?" Caleb joked as he emerged from the trees, zipping up his fly.

I growled at that joke because ha fucking ha, my life was just so amusing. I knew they didn't really mean anything by the teasing at my expense but for the love of the stars, sometimes I had to think I'd been cursed at birth.

"I'm not marrying my fucking cousin. Besides, she's my second cousin," I muttered. Not that that would stop them from just calling her my cousin all the star damned time.

"Okay then, are you all set to marry your *second* cousin? And did she ever manage to get rid of that growth on her face?" Caleb jibed.

"What growth on her face?" I asked, a flicker of amusement finding me because if there was one thing I didn't mind doing then it was mocking my bride to be. At least until I actually ended up marrying the beast...and having to consummate the damn union. *Fuck my life.*

"No, Caleb. That growth *is* her face. Remember?" Max joked and the three of them fell about laughing while I tried not to join in because we were literally laughing about my fucked up reality. But if I was being honest, the whole thing was so shitty that if I didn't laugh about it I'd probably just lose my sanity altogether so I couldn't help but break a laugh too.

"Ah, your joy tastes so much better than your rage," Max said with a satisfied sigh as he tugged me closer and yanked me into a headlock.

"I swear on all the stars I've never seen an uglier girl," I chuckled as I shoved Max off of me. He released me from the headlock but kept his arm around me so he could still replenish his magic from mine. "And I'm *not* marrying her. I'd sooner give up my claim."

The threat may well have been an empty one but I sure as hell hoped it wasn't. Because looking down the barrel of my life and seeing myself tied to that ogre of a girl throughout it and having to make fucking babies with her made death seem a whole lot more preferable. Of course, Father probably wouldn't let me have any kind of choice in it and I knew well enough that he could force the matter if he wanted to and I'd be helpless to prevent it. Though the heavens only knew how I was ever supposed to get my cock hard for her.

"I'd argue with you on that, but I've seen her and I think I'd give up my claim to save you from that marriage too," Seth joked. "So maybe you *will* be presenting Marguerite as an alternative after all?"

I rolled my eyes. "No chance of that. Can you really see my father going for a Sphinx as an alternative? They're ten a penny and half useless in combat, plus she's only a level six in fire. No secondary power at all. Besides, I prefer my women to present more of a challenge and she's far too...ordinary to make the cut long term."

My situation with Marguerite wasn't one that had been going on for all that long and I was already growing bored of her. Especially since Roxanya Vega had come bursting into my life full of fire and temptation in all the best and worst ways. I was pretty sure I'd be ending things with Marguerite officially soon, especially if she was spreading bullshit rumours about me introducing her to my family.

"I can't feel my left butt cheek," Max announced, ending their mockery of my life. "Can one of you make these stumps more comfortable if we're going to be sitting here?"

"Don't look at me," Seth said. "I'm tapped out until the moon rises." He glanced up hopefully but there was no sign of it in the sky.

Max turned his gaze on Caleb hopefully, but he shook his head in refusal too. "No can do, I rinsed my power in training tonight. Unless one of you wants to donate to the cause?"

"Not me," Max said, his grip on me tightening defensively and I growled to warn him back. I wasn't a chew toy for him to guard like an overprotective dog. "I'm still getting my own fix."

Seth shrugged, like he wished he could offer Cal a top up and Caleb shifted his gaze to me with a hungry look in his eyes.

"I'm already feeding one parasite tonight, you're not seriously going to ask me to feed two are you?" I asked reluctantly.

I wasn't exactly at full charge myself, but if he really needed the fix I'd let him have it. I'd be sleeping in a pile of gold tonight to replenish my magic either way.

Cal sighed dramatically as he dropped down onto a stump of his own. "I *had* planned on topping up from my Source at dinner but the Vegas never showed."

"You could bite any idiot in the school," I said, rolling my eyes and trying to ignore the sting of irritation in my gut at the thought of him putting his mouth all over my fucking girl. I wasn't even sure why him doing it was pissing me off so fucking much, but every time I saw him bite her or heard him go on about how great she tasted, I was struck with the urgent desire to punch his pretty face for it. "Why didn't you just get your top-up elsewhere?"

Max arched an eyebrow at me like he'd just caught a taste of that anger and possessiveness from me and I fought to get my feelings under control again before he read into it too much. I didn't even understand it myself so I wouldn't be able to explain it to him anyway.

"You know I like my power how I like my spirits," Caleb replied dismissively. "Top shelf or nothing. I enjoy the way Tory tastes, she's got more power in her blood than even you assholes."

We all shifted uncomfortably at that comment because although we all knew it was the truth we didn't fucking like it and Caleb shrugged, running a hand through his blonde curls.

"There's no point in denying it," he said. "We all know what their potential is."

"Which is why we need to make sure they fail The Reckoning," Max growled.

"It's all in hand." Seth shrugged, not taking this seriously because he never took anything seriously. He just assumed everything would all work out and we had to hope he was right about that. "We can come up with some more ideas back at King's Hollow. I think tomorrow should be a big day for those twins. And if you wanna come for a run with me at midnight then I'll let you feed on me," he added to Caleb.

Relief filled me for a moment at that suggestion and Max shot me another confused look as he registered it. I cursed myself internally and forced a sentence past my lips which my tongue hated the taste of.

"Or you can meet me at Ignis House in the morning and wait outside Tory's room to surprise her," I suggested with a smirk I painted on. Even calling her that sounded wrong in my mouth. Tory was a girl who I could want in all the ways my body was begging me to want her. Roxanya was a princess poised to destroy everything we were. Which was why I called her by that name because no matter how much my dick might have wanted me to, I couldn't let myself forget that for so much as a moment. "If we get really lucky, we might find out that she sleeps naked." There went my damn mouth, running off with the train of thoughts my dick had started and I cursed myself again for voicing that errant thought. I needed to stop giving Max access to my emotions, it was making me looser with my mouth than I should have been.

"I'm surprised you haven't found that out already," Max said suggestively and my lips hooked up into half a smile before I could stop myself. He'd already felt my lust anyway and it wasn't like any of us were trying to deny how fucking hot the Vegas were, so I might as well just own it. Because yeah, I'd more than enjoy getting her acquainted with my cock if I got the chance, but no, I didn't really think that was ever going to be happening. Not with what we all had planned for the two of them.

"Yeah... I might just take you up on that," Caleb said, his own smile widening as he gave some thought to the idea of Roxy sleeping naked too and the urge to punch him rose up in me again like an unfettered beast. Damn his pretty fucking face, if he got in her panties I really was going to break it for him.

"Why don't we all show up?" Seth added excitedly. "We can give her a wakeup call she'll never forget."

"Sounds good to me," I said, getting to my feet and knocking Max's arm from my shoulders because I had the sudden urge to tell them I'd changed my mind and wanted to deal with her myself. I was done with letting him get a glimpse into my inner turmoil for one night. And to make it worse, first urge was followed by the second urge to head over to her bedroom right now and see if I could convince her to spend the night coming all over my cock before we had to go back to hating each other again. *Bad idea.* "I'm going to head to bed."

I bit down on my tongue as I tried to block out that oh so tempting mental image and remind myself of the way she'd very publicly shot me down the last time we'd come face to face.

"You're not coming to the Hollow?" Max asked with a pout.

"Nah, I'm beat. I'll see all of you in the morning then? Wanna say six? She never gets up early." I was getting her routines pinned down pretty well now and I was telling myself that was because my father had commanded me to watch her. But I didn't know Gwen's routines. And I had to admit to myself at least that I just liked watching her. Figuring her out. She was a puzzle that may have been bordering on an obsession or at the very least a dangerous kind of fantasy, but I found I didn't have it in me to stop. Besides, I was only watching. So far.

"Alright, we'll work on something special for our Vega fun," Seth said and he had that look in his eyes which always meant someone was going to end up hating him.

He got to his feet and yanked me into a hug, pushing his fingers through my damn hair and messing it up until I growled a little to make him back off. He grinned at me then headed out of the clearing with Max and Caleb following him, both of them clapping me on the arm in goodbye.

I didn't immediately follow, pulling my Atlas from my pocket as I waited for them to leave and turning my attention back to the issue that had been bothering me all day.

I gave it a few minutes to make sure the others were gone, not wanting Max to sense any of my emotions over this call as I felt my anger growing by the second now that my focus was on the issue again.

Fucking Lance. I was done with his shit, and we were going to have this conversation now whether he wanted to or not.

I clipped an earpiece in before dialling his number and shoving my Atlas back into my jeans pocket.

I ran my fingers over my jaw as I waited for the call to connect and my brow dropped into a frown as he let it ring. Asshole was a damn Vampire, he could get to his fucking Atlas fast enough if he wanted to. He was making me wait, no doubt muttering curses at me and sinking bourbon while he let my call ring on.

"Yeah?" Lance answered at last and the pissy tone to his voice got my back up right away.

"Took you long enough," I growled irritably. "I need to talk to you in person."

"Darius, we've been over this. I'm tired from teaching snot nosed little brats all damn day and I don't really want to get into it with you now. Can't we just do this dance tomorrow when I'm a bit more sober?" he asked, but my patience with this was wearing out and I was already feeling pissed about having to spend my morning watching Caleb suck on Roxy Vega's fucking neck, so I wanted this dealt with.

"No, not tomorrow; *now.* This situation is going on too long, we should have dealt with them by now. I think we need to escalate the plan," I said firmly.

I knew he was just trying to look out for me, but the Nymph problem was the one thing I had in my life which I felt like I could take control over. They were a threat, they were close by and I was just certain they were fucking up to something. The Nymph we'd tracked down at the start of the summer had been in possession of a dark artifact and Lance himself had told me he could sense disturbances in the shadows which suggested they were gathering more of them. And nothing the Nymphs could be planning with objects laced with shadows could be good. But we could stop them, and it was my duty to Solaria to do so whether the people knew about me doing it or not.

"Darius," Lance growled. "We've been over this. The people we were tracking might not even be Nymphs at all. Our evidence is thin at best and more of a guess than a definite fact. If we just charge in there-"

"Just stop," I interrupted him because I could see this wasn't getting me anywhere, so I was going to see him face to face and make him see sense. "I'm coming to yours now."

I killed the call as he tried to protest and got to my feet, scowling up at the rising moon. It was damn tempting to just shift and fly over to his place but I could admit that that would be about as subtle as a ton of bricks turning up and landing on his roof, so I decided on a pissed off walk instead.

I moved out of the clearing and turned right, setting a fast pace as I headed for my destination. I needed to get my way with this. Lance was just going to have to accept that I'd made my decision on it. And if he wouldn't then maybe I'd just have to proceed without him.

I kept up a brisk walk as I cut through earth territory, following the path towards Asteroid Place where the teachers lived. Lance had made it more than clear on several occasions that I was only ever to come here if he could check there was a clear route in and out for me without many of the other teachers around, seeing as students were strictly forbidden from entering the teacher's living quarters. We tried to keep our bond a secret as much as possible, not wanting too many questions into why we would have agreed to such a permanent, outdated tradition which tied our lives to one another so irrevocably because the answer was, we hadn't. And the less people who knew about it the better so far as we were concerned. But that didn't matter to me tonight because right now I was more interested in getting back out there and dealing with the fucking Nymphs.

I made it to the edge of The Wailing Wood, hesitating before a wide clearing as I sharpened my eyesight with my Order gifts to look out for any teachers who might be close by.

A prickle up the back of my spine niggled at my senses and I had the sudden feeling that someone was watching me. I straightened sharply, turning to look back into the trees where I felt almost certain that I could feel eyes on my flesh.

I peered into the woods, looking for a sign of anything out of place. The moon cast enough light for me to see by well enough and though I scoured the trees all around me, I failed to spot anything untoward and eventually I banished the notion.

I was just on edge over this whole disagreement. I needed to see Lance and make him change his mind, then all would be well again. Aside from the shitty reality of my life beneath my father's control that was, but I was used to that by now.

I gave the trees one last look before shrugging off the feeling and turning away from them. No one would dare follow me anyway. My wrath would be enough to terrify any and all Fae who even got the notion to pry into my business.

I headed out into the clearing beyond The Wailing Wood and approached the gated complex of chalets where the professors all resided. It was one of the most strictly held rules that students were never allowed to come here, but I wasn't a creature born to follow the rules of others and tonight I didn't even give a damn if Principal Nova herself spotted me.

I wasn't a fool though, so instead of striding through the gates and letting everyone who might happen to be hanging around get a good look at me entering the complex, I swung right and began to follow the wrought iron fencing which surrounded it.

A text came through on my Atlas as I walked and I pulled it out to read it.

Lance:

Don't be an idiot. Stay away from here tonight. I don't need the headache of getting caught with a student and Washer is having a fucking pool party.

The anger in me built at him trying to tell me what to do and boss me around like I was just some fucking student to him. No Lance, I was not going to stay away. And if he wanted a headache, he could have one of those too.

I stopped abruptly and shoved my Atlas back in my pocket before grabbing hold of the bars of the fence beside me. Fire magic flared in my palms and a grin filled my lips as I melted a big ass hole right through the fence so that I could climb inside.

I took a photo of it then sent it to Lance with a message of my own.

Darius:

How's that for a headache, asshole? I'll be at the back of your place in 30 seconds

I kept walking, skirting around the back of the chalets, but before I could make it that far, Lance shot towards me from the shadows and skidded to an abrupt halt in front of me. He threw a hand out behind him as he came to a halt in front of me, casting a silencing bubble in the direction of the rest of the professors' houses before snarling at me and shoving me hard in the chest.

"What the fuck, Darius?" he demanded.

"You wouldn't talk to me all day, what did you expect?" I demanded, shoving him right back and he bared his fangs at me in warning.

"I'm the one who could get into serious shit for having you here. You'll just get a little talking to - but I could end up sent to Darkmore Penitentiary if they got the idea that you were here for sordid reasons."

"Oh please, I'm out of your league. No one would believe I was here to suck your cock," I taunted and he almost laughed for a moment before frowning again.

"How the hell am I supposed to explain what you did to the fence?" he demanded.

Yeah, that was a dick move, but I was still pissed at him for shutting me down all day so I just shrugged which clearly only got him angrier.

"I dunno. You'll figure it out."

"I told you not to come here," Lance snarled, stepping right up into my face and snatching hold of my grey t-shirt, bunching the fabric in his fist. I could smell the bourbon on his breath as he growled at me and I wasn't surprised to find he'd been drinking again. His life was probably even more fucked up than mine and if I wasn't so angry I might have backed down, but as it was I was almost hungry for a fight with him. "If someone were to see you-"

"I think you're forgetting who you're talking to, *sir*," I snapped, shoving his chest hard enough to make him stumble back a step so that he was forced to release me.

We didn't often disagree over things like this, but when we both lost our tempers it was hard to rein ourselves in.

We glared at one another for a long moment while we decided whether or not to let this descend, but in the end our bond won out and some of the fire between us died as the tension relaxed just enough for us to have a conversation over it.

"You know how much I care about this," Lance said, reminding me that I wasn't the only one who lived for our hunts together and I knew that was the truth. "I just don't want us to fuck it up when we're so close."

"So why are we waiting? We know where they are. We could go there now and find them while they're sleeping - end this once and for all," I pressed, trying to subdue my temper so that we could actually discuss this which was damn hard when I had a Dragon pacing violently within my flesh.

"Not yet. If we're wrong we could end up taking innocent lives," Orion insisted and I balked against that idea. I was certain we were right about the Nymphs we'd discovered, especially after we'd seen that one with the limp. They may have been hiding in their Fae like form, but I refused to believe the hints we'd found could mean anything else. "It's too hard to be sure with the information we have. Just give it a few more days. I'll see her again, I'll confirm our suspicions."

I knew he wanted to meet with his FIB informant before we acted, but I was worried that every day we let slip by only gave the Nymphs more opportunity to strike at innocent Fae, to steal more magic from them and become an even bigger threat.

"In a few days they could be even more powerful. You've seen what's happened since the start of term. The longer we give them to adjust to their power, the more chance we have of them figuring out how to harness it and turn it against us. If you're afraid that you aren't up to the job then let me call on the others for help. You know they want to destroy them almost as much as we do."

The one advantage we had over the Nymphs who stole magic from the Fae they killed was that they were untrained in how to use it. It was why academies like Zodiac were guarded closely, so that the knowledge of how to wield our power stayed locked away from the eyes of our enemies. It was bad enough that the Nymphs could steal the power of the Fae they killed, we couldn't risk them learning how to harness it and use it against us too.

I was pushing him by threatening to involve the other Heirs. We'd had this discussion plenty of times before and had always come to the conclusion that it was best to keep them out of our secret Nymph hunts, but sometimes I questioned that choice.

Lance ran a hand over his face, shaking his head and I knew he was afraid that the Nymphs we were hoping to uncover might just be exactly what they were pretending to be - a family of Fae who liked their privacy. But there were too many signs to say that wasn't the truth. I was certain they were Nymphs in hiding and I wanted to remove the threat.

"It's too risky," Lance said, addressing the issue of the other Heirs. "Seth can't keep his mouth shut, he'd tell every member of his pack before sunrise and Max's powers soften him to others no matter how much he might deny it's true."

He had a fair point there, but they weren't the only Heirs and he knew it. He just hated Caleb on principle because he didn't like there being a Vampire more powerful than him running around campus and challenging him for the best blood sources.

"What about Caleb then? Or is your petty rivalry too keen for you to look past, even with the threat we face here?" I demanded, starting to pace as I fought to contain the anger of my Dragon and keep a clear head over this.

"It's not about rivalry," Lance spat, though we both knew it had a lot to do with that whether he wanted to admit it or not. I'd long since given up any hope of him and Caleb putting their Orders aside and finding a way to be friends. They were just too damn competitive for that. "It's about strength. You know him better than me but I'd judge him to be too impulsive for this. If he were to strike too soon then all the work we've done to get to this point will have been for nothing. The same goes for if *we* try to kill them now. While we still aren't sure. What if we fail and they manage to escape us? Or we succeed but we miss something vital and it sets something greater in motion-"

"You've been consulting with those damn bones again," I muttered because the authority in his voice told me he thought he already knew something and that meant some form of divination had warned him about this.

"I have," Lance agreed darkly. "And though they aren't revealing many answers to me, one thing is clear. This is *not* our moment."

I fell still, releasing a long breath through my nose which was laced with smoke as I worked to rein in my Dragon and think on this rationally. "Sometimes I wish we didn't live in a world where everything was mapped out for us as if our lives are nothing more than pieces in some greater fucking puzzle and we get no say at all."

Lance sighed, moving closer so that he could place a hand on my shoulder and the animosity between us slipped away as the Guardian bond urged us together as always. Besides, I hated feeling angry with him. He was the one person in this world who truly knew me. "Is this about your father? Is he still putting pressure on you to-"

I didn't want to talk about the damn Vegas or my father's continued demands for me to deal with them right now, so I cut him off.

251

"Of course he is. It's all he ever thinks about. It's like he hasn't even noticed that the world we live in could be teetering on the edge of chaos." I shook my head before shrugging Lance's hand off of me, not wanting him to worry about me any more than he already did. "Don't worry about my father, I'll bear the brunt of his wrath as always. Once the other Heirs and I sort out that situation, he'll back off anyway. You just focus on confirming everything so that we can act."

"I'm meeting with her again in a few days. I'll do a reading. Make sure that we have every piece of the truth," Orion replied with a firm nod and I knew once he met with Francesca he'd be more amenable to us heading out on the hunt again and that was all I needed to know.

"And then?" I pressed, wanting him to say the words.

"And then...well then we'll do what we have to before anyone finds out it was us," Lance agreed and I could tell he was still concerned that they really were Fae. But I knew in my gut that they were Nymphs, so I was more than ready to act.

"Good," I replied grinning at him in a feral way which promised more bloodshed soon.

Lance almost broke a smile in reply and I turned away, heading back the way I'd come and feeling a little bit shitty about fucking up the fence. He'd probably just leave it though and pretend to know nothing about it when one of the other professors discovered it. No big deal.

I was going to sleep well tonight and in a few days time, we'd be back on the hunt again.

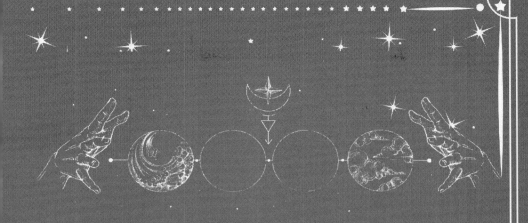

ORION

CHAPTER TWELVE

I shoved the door open and strode into the classroom, my mood hitting an all time low. I was exhausted and pissed off. I'd been up half the night talking to Francesca on the phone, trying to convince her to get the FIB to search the outskirts of Tucana for the nest Darius and I were pretty sure existed. I needed definitive clarification they weren't Fae. Because if we were really going to spring an attack on them, I could not risk them being innocents. And if Darius wet his hands in the blood of our kind, he was going to pay the price of that.

I was not in the mood to deal with insolent students today, so anyone that got on my nerves was going to regret it. I hunted the room for the inevitable. Someone would be up to something and I'd take out a little of my rage on them to sate the furious beast in me this morning. My gaze locked on Kylie Major with a bunch of freshman party leaflets in her grip and satisfaction filled my chest. *Perfect.*

"*No,*" I snarled, waving a hand so every single leaflet in the room swept toward me on a violent breeze then slammed into the trash can beside my desk.

Kylie froze, looking to me in alarm, her face draining of colour fast. "Sir, I-"

"Miss Major if you ever hand out garbage in my classroom again you'll be banned from attending a single one of this year's formals," I bit at her, relishing the way she seemed to grow smaller before me.

Her mouth dropped open and I could tell she wasn't the type to shut up even when she knew she was beat.

"But sir!" she gasped.

I flicked my hand and the remaining leaflets were snatched from her grip and torn to shreds, cascading over her in a shower of pink confetti. *But nothing, you insufferable flea.*

Laughter rang out through the room and my ears picked up a small snort of amusement from Blue, making my mouth almost quirk up at the corner. Well at least she had semi-decent taste in the company she kept. Though why she kept Polaris around, I'd never know. *The way he looks at her...*

My gaze fixed on the hat-wearing shitbag and how his eyes kept flitting to Darcy then to Tory beyond her. He looked sweaty. And sweaty people weren't my kind of people. Especially sweaty people who looked too closely at girls they had no right to look at. What did he want anyway? A leg up in this world? Yeah, that was it. He was obviously a leach. And I'd seen enough of them come through this classroom in my time to know that leaches were one of the most dangerous friends you could keep. Weaker Fae who couldn't make it on their own, but knew how to befriend the right people, offer out the right favours. Then bam. They'd bend you over, fuck you in the ass and take your glory.

I slammed my coffee cup down on the desk and the room fell quiet as I stared at the sea of concerned faces before me. My eyes moved automatically to Darcy and she raised her chin, not looking away as I tried to glare her in to doing so. The challenge in her gaze made my inner Fae roar and I ground my teeth for a moment as the rest of the room seemed to fade away. Why did she unsettle me like that? She was just a girl. Even if she was a Vega. And her mouthy sister didn't get me riled the way she did. No...it was something in the way she looked at me, like she could see beneath my hardened steely exterior that kept most other Fae out. Darius and Gabriel were among the very few Fae who could get beneath it with ease. But with her, it didn't feel like that. It was like she was prying my ribcage open and wrapping her hand around my heart, one firm squeeze away from destroying me.

I turned to the board, snatching up my digital pen and writing across it with today's daily reminder.

YOU ARE NOT UNIQUE.

I snapped around to face the class again, finding them all looking glum at that. Good. They should feel glum. Because they were all fucking useless and needed to try harder. "Every star sign in the Zodiac holds its own attributes. Good and bad. They can influence your nature. But they do not make you different or special. They make you Fae." I tapped on the board to activate the slides on their Atlases and everyone looked down at their screens, saving me from Blue's intense stare.

"All Fae are a part of this," I continued, trying to rein in the worst of my rage in case I lost my shit entirely today and ended up with Uncle Lionel paying me a visit. *Fuck that.* "And we all share two defining celestial beings in common." I pointed at the centre of the Zodiac. "The sun and the moon. They bind us. And no Order, no eyeliner, or blue hair-" I gave Darcy a pointed look as I stepped into the closest aisle and she pursed her lips at me, giving me a kick over riling her. "Or beanie hat." I took a swipe at Diego's hat, but he grabbed hold of it like it was the fucking Holy Grail, glaring up at me in a challenge. *Well hello, little Fae. Did you crawl out of your scaredy hole at last?*

I smirked at him, glad to see he had some semblance of a backbone after all. It wasn't like I wanted this bunch of freshmen to be useless. In fact, I thrived most on teaching when they started pushing back. It almost made me enjoy the job then. Not much, but it was something. Seeing the new generation realise they were some of the most powerful beings in the kingdom and figuring out they didn't have to stand for everyone pushing them around all the time was sort of gratifying - if you gave a shit about stuff like that.

"Makes you different," I finished, walking further into the classroom and checking everyone was paying attention. "There are twelve signs, I expect even our royal Vega Heirs know what they are. So let's hear them." I shot up behind the two twins, placing a hand on each of their shoulders. My grip was firmer on Darcy, my fingers curling around her possessively and my fangs tingled with the memory of her blood in my mouth.

Blue turned her head to look up at me and I saw a wild creature lurking in her eyes, one I was curious to see on the outside of her flesh. Where my hand lay on her, energy thrived. It felt like gravity, drawing me in, rooting me to her more fiercely than the pull of the earth rooted me to the ground.

"Go ahead, Miss Vega," I commanded.

"Which one?" she and Tory said at the same time.

"Blue." I tapped her on the shoulder. "Vega number two can come with me." I nudged Tory and she rose to her feet with a frown, casting a look at her sister. But no one was going to save her. I led her to my desk, sitting in my chair and holding out my hand. Prestos had been a useless fucking Liaison to Tory so far as I could tell, and though I'd insisted she send over Tory's power rankings to me, she still hadn't done it and frankly I was done waiting.

"Palm," I ordered and she hesitantly placed her hand in mine. I started reading the markings on her hand, wondering why her flesh didn't affect me the way her sister's did. It wasn't unheard of for twins to Emerge as different Orders, though it was quite rare. If Darcy was a Siren, then I'd guess from the temperament of this girl that she was a Dragon, though she was so petite it didn't seem likely. Of course, her father had been a Hydra, so what was to say she or her sister wouldn't be one of those too? I couldn't rule out anything.

"I don't hear Zodiac signs filling my ears," I sniped.

I felt Darcy's irritation with me as the sound of giggles carried from Kylie and her friends, but that wasn't really my problem. She either participated in my class or she could get the hell out of it.

Darcy called out the names to me in a flat tone. "Aquarius, Pisces, Aries, Taurus, Gemini, Cancer, Leo, Virgo, Libra, Scorpio, Sagittarius, Capricorn." Astrology had leaked into the Mortal Realm after Fae had conducted experiments there a long time ago, trying to work out if humans were affected by the stars too. It seemed there was some amount of influence, though their lack of Elemental magic and Orders meant they were affected to a far lesser extent than us. It seemed some humans were more gifted than others when it came to predicting their fates or reading the signs from the stars though, which suggested there was some magic of old at play. Though nothing conclusive had ever really come of it. Interesting though.

"Good, five points to House Aer," I said and I could almost feel Darcy's shock over that. *Yes, Miss Vega, you do actually get rewarded for effort in this class, or what would be the point of it?*

I studied the Mount of Jupiter line on her index finger, surprised by how different her markings were to her sister's in some ways. This line indicated confidence, leadership and ambition, but there was a smaller line intersecting it that spoke of a deep-rooted fear holding her back in all of these areas. One glance up at her made a frown pull at my brow. I could see the hardness in her, but there was something underneath it all and I only had to think of the shitty place they'd come from in the Mortal Realm to be sure both of these girls had suffered in life. They were both wearing armour, but in different ways and the clues within their palms was making it all too clear to me that their suffering ran deep enough to affect their fates. Fuck, I didn't wanna care. It wasn't my job to care. I'd seen suffering first hand. I *was* suffering half the time. But I'd never been poor or gone hungry. That was a kind of reality I imagined left wounds that would never heal.

I focused on her power rankings and jotted them down on a notepad, feeling Tory squirming over how long I was holding onto her for. She didn't trust me, that was obvious. I could practically feel her magic trying to force me out, but I was surprised by the comparison that gave me to the way Blue's skin had felt when it had been in contact with mine. I hadn't noticed before how much her magic had been calling to me within her veins, but now I could feel the exact opposite of that within her twin, I was sure it was true. But what the fuck did that even mean?

I finally released her hand and passed Tory a slip of paper. "These are your Elemental scores. The higher the number, the stronger your power. Your principal magic is fire."

"Oh...right." She nodded, moving to walk away but I made a sudden decision, needing to compare her sister's blood with hers, to be sure I wasn't going insane and imagining the way everything about Darcy seemed to draw me in. If Tory tasted the same, had the same affect, then that settled it. There was nothing to worry about. There was no hidden connection between Darcy and I, it was just a power lust thing which I could compartmentalise when I fed from her next.

I caught Tory's wrist, dragged her forwards and dug my fangs into her skin, making her gasp in horror. Her blood washed over my tongue, a wave of magic crashing along with it that felt like the dark and enchanting power of the moon. She tasted good, really fucking good, and her power was just as immense as her sister's. But that was where the similarity ended, because feeding from Darcy had felt like drowning in everything she was and aching for more. It had tasted like her sweetness, her fucking light had been flowing directly into me and begging me to bow to everything it was. Tory tasted like a dream, but not my dream. And that was something I wasn't sure I even understood.

"Oh my stars, sir!" Kylie gasped, but I ignored her, continuing to feed, to try and find in Tory what I'd found in Darcy, to prove I was wrong. That it was just Darcy's blood that caused me to crave her and nothing else, but the more I drank, the clearer it became to me that I wasn't going to find that same unending desire for Tory's essence. It was just blood. Really nice blood. Like bottle it and guard it forever blood. But not *her* blood.

"Stop it!" Blue snapped at me, but Tory warned her off with a look and I finally tugged my fangs free of her skin in my own time.

She moved away, glaring at me and I shut down every crazy thought in my head, getting to my feet and continuing with the lesson.

Whispers broke out behind me about some FaeBook post that had gone live and I growled, turning to face the room and finding everyone looking at their Atlases.

I was about to announce a mass detention when the door flew wide open and Caleb Altair sprinted into the room, diving over my fucking desk. He slammed me against the board and a collective inhale sounded around us as I took in the complete rage in his eyes.

I blasted him off of me with a snarl and he tumbled backwards, his head slamming into the desk and sending a crack splintering up the middle of it. My instincts flared at the challenge in his eyes as Caleb lunged at me with a fistful of flames. He was the only Fae I'd ever met who sent the beast in me spiralling as easily as this. Caleb was the one Vampire I knew who was more powerful than me, which meant the competition between us could never be settled in a way which would fully satisfy my impulses to challenge him and in that moment, I lost my head entirely as everything inside me simply screamed for his destruction.

I was about to intercept and attempt to fucking destroy him when I remembered I was a teacher and he was an Heir and there was more at stake here than this fight was worth.

"Enough!" I bellowed before Caleb could try and land the strike.

The Terra Heir paused, clearly forcing himself to consider our situation over his own instincts too and the students all fell still as they watched our interaction.

Caleb extinguished the flames in his palms, a low growl rolling from his throat. "She's my Source. Touch her again and you're dead. Professor or not."

A flicker of surprise fell through me as I realised exactly why he'd come tearing in here like someone had stuck a burning poker up his asshole and told them it was my fault. I didn't exactly pay a lot of attention to student gossip and seeing as Darius and I had had our own issues recently, I guessed no one had managed to pass on the memo that Caleb had claimed himself a Vega for a Source which meant that me biting her had absolutely warranted his psychotic attack on me...and I probably couldn't even give him detention for it. *Dammit.*

I wasn't just going to apologise like some weak ass Fae though, so I decided to own my actions and enforce my authority over him as his teacher.

I snatched the front of his shirt, pulling him within an inch of my face. "Get out of my classroom."

"Not until you swear it," Caleb spat, wheeling a hand around to point at Tory. "She's mine. Keep your teeth out of her."

"I don't belong to anyone!" Tory snapped and Darcy nodded her agreement. *You do until you can fight us off.*

I tried to work out how to deal with this without falling into a full-on fight with an Altair. There'd be news reports, fucking journalists at the gates. And as much as this rivalry which hung between us begged for it, it really wouldn't be a good look for either of us. It would probably rile up those anti-Vampire lobbyists who were always trying to claim that Fae of our Order shouldn't hold positions of power because we were too easily ruled by our instincts too. Fuck those guys.

Caleb pushed me off of him so hard my back smashed into the board and I bared my fangs, fighting my instincts to kill him for that.

Tense mutters broke out in the class and I felt Darcy's eyes boring holes in my head. A wild decision formed in my mind that fixed my issue with Caleb and simultaneously sent all my plans to keep my distance from Blue spiralling down the drain. But I was already saying the words, each one falling from my lips and not letting me go back on them. Because I didn't want to, not even a little bit. Besides, I was a Vampire and I had a right to do this. The Vegas were the most powerful magic Sources in the kingdom. And I had a chance to claim one of them as mine. The one who tormented my fucking soul.

"Fine," I said in a deadly tone. "But the other Vega Twin is mine."

"Excuse me?" Darcy gasped, but neither Caleb or I acknowledged her as we eyed each other.

Caleb grumbled, starting to stalk back and forth before me like a caged lion. He was clearly trying to decide if he should just challenge me for ownership of the two of them. But he knew as well as I did that it wasn't a good look for him to be fighting with one of his professors, which was why we tended to avoid each other and the conflict which arose from the nature of our Orders whenever we could.

"*Deal*," he finally forced out then marched from the room, slamming the door behind him. The insult didn't pass me by. Then again, I probably would have done the same in his position. I was going to work extra hard at finding something to give him detention for this week though.

A breath left me that was tangled with relief. Because now I had her. And it was the best damn feeling I'd experienced in a long time. But I wasn't going to let the class see how much my mood had just brightened, so I straightened my shirt and turned to the board, a smile tearing across my face where they couldn't see it as I continued with the lesson in a flat tone.

"Aries are ruled by Mars so they can be particularly impulsive and often aggressive when..." I went on autopilot as my heart drummed to a hammering beat and my inner Vampire bellowed his victory.

But I was fucked, so fucked because I knew this was about more than her blood, some deeper connection forged by something intangible. But screw it. Because I actually wanted something for the first time in too many years and now that I had it, I wasn't letting it go. Darcy Vega was my Source. Mine.

And no one else in the whole damn kingdom could have a taste of her but me.

"Don't we get a say in this?" Darcy hissed to her sister and my smile dug deeper. *No, Blue, you don't.*

"Not unless we can fight them off," Tory said in anger.

"Which you won't be able to do unless you listen in class!" I grabbed a book from my desk, hurling it at them and making them leap apart to avoid being hit. "One more word out of either of you and you'll be in detention for the rest of the year."

Their glares were venomous and I stared coolly back, wating for either of them to go against my word. But they kept their mouths shut at last and I went back to teaching the class.

"When you're Awakened, you will always obtain the Elemental power linked to your star sign. For example, as a water sign, all Pisceans are gifted with the Elemental magic of water. Those who gain more than one Element are usually gifted this way because they are linked to more than one constellation." I tapped the board and a chart appeared which showed every constellation in the sky. "As you can see, there are hundreds of combinations. The powers gifted to you by the stars are very elusive. Little is known about how or why some Fae are born with more than one Element. But we do know that genetics play a role and so does your Order." I glanced at the Vegas, trying to assess if my judgements on their Orders were correct. Darcy looked me dead in the eye with so much hatred that it made my skin itch. I approached her with a cruel smile curling up my lips, happy to make my enemy squirm.

"Can you name some of the constellations which aren't linked to a Zodiac sign, Miss Vega?" I asked.

"Um..." She cleared her throat. "The little bear?"

"Correct." *Damn.* I pointed at Diego Polaris beside her. "Which is also known as?"

"The little dipper, sir," he supplied.

"I bet Diego's got a Little Dipper," Tyler Corbin snorted from the front row.

"Five points from Terra," I snapped at him and Tyler huffed.

"And the Latin name?" I pointed at Sofia Cygnus who turned pink-faced as she answered.

"Ursa Minor?" she squeaked.

"Ten points to House Ignis." I strode away and started writing on the board again. "So if you are an Aquarius but are also linked to Ursa Minor which has the power of earth, you will possibly be gifted with two Elements."

"Possibly, sir?" a girl with a long braid of raven hair asked from the second row.

"The stars can be unpredictable," I explained. "Their nature must compliment ours for everything to align." I folded my arms. "So, what does your Zodiac sign mean for you personally? Does anyone know?"

A few hands rose and I picked out a boy in the row behind the Vegas. "It tells you your nature."

"Inaccurate," I said in exasperation. "Try again."

"It er..." the boy glanced around for help, but no one had any to offer. He cleared his throat then shrugged. *May the stars have fucking mercy on me.*

"Anyone?" I growled in annoyance.

"It influences your nature, sir?" Sofia offered. *Oh thank the moon, there's someone here with more than two brain cells.*

"Correct," I said brightly, moving to lean back against my desk. I pointed at Jillian Minor who had an expression like a slapped ass this morning. "Miss Minor, what are the other three things that influence a Fae's nature?"

She turned the colour of a beetroot, looking to her useless friend Kylie who sighed dramatically.

"Order," Kylie offered for her.

"And?" I pressed.

"Er...genetics?" she guessed.

"Correct. And?" I demanded.

She fell quiet and I could hear her brain rattling around in that air head of hers.

"Anyone?" I asked, gazing over everyone disappointedly. I wasn't sure I'd ever taught a freshman class as ill-prepared for life at Zodiac Academy as this.

"Life experience, sir?" Blue's voice caught my ear and my gaze snapped onto her like I'd been trying to resist doing before now. Seeing as my eyes were there, I let them roam, taking in her large eyes and perfectly bronzed skin which spoke of her ancestry. Her mother had looked like that, born to the Voldrakia kingdom where the sun always shone and the Fae were very different to those who lived in Solaria. Some called them savages due to their rather feral practises. Murder was perfectly legal there along with most other crimes. They fought for power in ways our kingdom tended to be more civilised about, and the royals who ruled only encouraged more cruelty by making a sport out of it. They hosted violent games where the prizes included wealth, status and even marriage. The Vegas' father may have had a reputation for brutality, but their mother had been forged in it. Though by all accounts, once the Savage King had married her, he had become slightly less ruthless, so it seemed she may have curbed the death toll in our kingdom a little.

Wait a minute, what did Blue say? Did she actually have the right answer?

"Correct," I said in surprise, striding down the aisle and halting in front of her desk. She fell entirely within my shadow and I liked the way she set her jaw and stared up at me unwaveringly. "Also known as?"

"Nurture," she said, her throat bobbing in the most tempting way I had ever known.

"Good. See me after class." I marched away, my pulse flickering and my fangs sharpening to points.

I berated myself internally for all the good it did, but nothing could

266

stop the buzz of adrenaline sweeping through me over soon having her alone. It was wrong. All of these thoughts were, this craving. But I couldn't seem to stop them. And now I'd branded her as my Source, I had inadvertently made things even more difficult. Because my nature was to protect her now, to keep her as mine, to ensure no other Vampire stole her blood from me. And as good as it felt to know I had that claim, it was also going to make things far more complicated when it came to getting rid of her.

What the hell are you playing at?

I don't know, but I can't fucking stop.

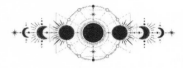

I sat behind my desk at the end of class, my gaze fixed on my Atlas as I waited for everyone to leave. Everyone but her.

I had a message from Francesca which I was debating how to answer.

Francesca:

So when are you free for drinks, you said you'd let me know when you were around this week..?

When wasn't I free for drinks? I mean, technically I had a bottle of bourbon on the go at all times. I was in the most committed relationship of my life with booze. Although, as Darius pointed out sometimes, it was more like a toxic partner I couldn't get rid of. But whenever he tried to stop me drinking, I would spiral into depression and functioning became nearly impossible. So if that wasn't a merry little reason to keep feeding my liver the good stuff then I didn't know what was. It kept me peppy. Okay, not peppy. But somewhere around the not-suicidal line, which was a place where I gave just enough of a fuck about things to keep being useful to Darius. And as that was my only goal in life these days, it seemed like the perfect place to be.

I really needed to meet with Francesca and discuss the Nymph issue. There was too much at stake when it came to that nest.

Lance:

Friday night?

It would be good to see her regardless. She was a friend, even if that friendship came with benefits sometimes. Francesca was working her way up in the FIB ranks and she didn't have time for a steady relationship, and as I would be about the most useless boyfriend imaginable and I could barely stomach most people's company, it suited me perfectly too. Only, since I'd gotten back from the Mortal Realm, I hadn't felt like hooking up. Most nights I either wanted to be alone with whiskey or with Darius. I missed Gabriel too, but he had his own life, his own family. And I didn't like him seeing me when I was in a slump, because I knew I couldn't hide anything from his Sight. If he saw me up close, he'd start trying to guide me towards a better fate in riddles I couldn't solve. But we'd played that game too many times, and I knew there wasn't a better fate waiting for me. The best I could hope for was that Darius defeated Lionel, then maybe I'd get some peace of mind.

Francesca:

Perfect! I'll book Andromeda Place for eight o'clock.

The class had emptied out and I didn't even have to look up to know I was now alone in a room with Darcy Vega because the energy in the air had just intensified tenfold. I could feel her presence like a living thing in the room and I didn't entirely hate that feeling.

I kept my gaze on my Atlas, mulling over what exactly I was about to say to her. I had to keep it professional. That was key. And maybe if I put some boundaries in place, I could keep this shitshow from becoming a shitparade.

"How's the Coercion shield coming?" I asked, still not looking up. If I did, I wouldn't stop looking. And if I looked, I'd move closer. And if I moved closer, I might bite her again. And if I bit her again, well….let's just say I might have to start punching myself in the dick pre-bite in future. But I couldn't just stare at my Atlas forever.

"Better. I've been practicing with friends," she said.

I nodded, glad she was trying. Not that I wanted her to do well obviously, but freshmen who didn't make an effort to Fae up made me sick. "You should be spending every free moment on it." I swung around in my chair, biting the bullet as I let my eyes lift to meet her gaze. Fuck, she looked edible. "It's imperative that you can throw off basic Coercion. Do you understand how vulnerable you are while you're unable to?"

I was saying this partly because I'd made her my Source. I needed her to be able to protect herself from rogue Vampires who tried to Coerce her into letting them feed from her. I couldn't have that. I'd snap their fucking necks if they tried. But the other reason was that if any Nymphs with control over their stolen magic had learned Coercion, she'd be easy prey for them. And if her magic got into one of their hands, the consequences were unimaginable.

She nodded, still standing near the door like she didn't want to be anywhere near me. It was a fool's hope now she was my Source. We'd be getting much closer in future. And my dick was decidedly happy about that, though it would absolutely not be joining the party.

"Yes, sir." She was scrutinising me and I grew desperately curious about what she was thinking. Her dislike for me wasn't surprising, but there was more to it than that. There was suspicion in those captivating eyes of hers and I didn't much like it.

"Good." I broke a smile that felt more natural than I'd intended. "So, I wanted to be clear about what it means to be my Source."

"I don't want to be your Source," she said immediately, revulsion in her voice that made my hackles rise. But she had a furious look on her face that was so damn cute, and I quite enjoyed getting under her skin like that.

"Until you manage to stop me, I'm afraid that's not your decision." I gave her a bemused look and she scowled back, but all that anger wouldn't do her much good unless she channelled it into studying.

I got up, moving around my desk to stand before her, closing the gap between us and thirsting to get even closer.

"You will tell me if any other Vampire bites you. That is non-negotiable, Miss Vega. I will make it known to the academy that you're mine and that should save us any more incidents like today. I am not likely to be challenged by anyone except Caleb, but now that has been settled we should have no more issues. However, if another Vampire happens to take a liking to you ...you *will* tell me."

"How often do you expect to feed from me?" She folded her arms and I was surprised by how against this whole idea she was. There were freshman who would have killed to have a Vampire as powerful as me claim them as their Source. It gave them a shield from all other Vampires. She wouldn't have to be pinned down and bitten in the hallways. Unless of course, *I* came across her and fancied a taste. I practically salivated at the thought of that.

"Once or twice a week." I shrugged. "But if I become drained then it may be more."

She nodded stiffly, clearly pissed about this whole thing. Then her features hardened and I felt the challenge rolling off of her, telling me this girl might just be an Alpha deep down. Though it didn't look like she knew it if she was. And I'd be sure not to point it out and to leave her confidence down in the gutter.

"One day, Professor, I'm going to be strong enough to fight you off," she said, her voice ringing with power for a moment and making me pause. *Oh fuck, why is that so hot?*

I took a measured breath, fighting the urge to rise to that challenge, because she'd end up trapped beneath me and I was supposed to be professional right now. But there was no harm making her aware of that.

"I know," I said, enjoying this game. "But until that day, you're mine, Blue."

I swear she shivered a little at those words, but her eyes were a menacing wall that forced me out.

"I don't belong to anyone," she said, her voice a deadly whisper.

I stepped closer, wanting to reach out and wrap my fingers around her throat, pin her to my desk and drive my fangs into her. Then she'd learn that she was very wrong about those words.

Be professional, for the stars' sake.

"Belonging to me is a far better fate than most could wish for in their first week at Zodiac Academy," I said coolly and she bristled.

"I'd rather be bitten by every Vampire in this school until I can fight them off than have one monster like you trying to possess me."

"Careful, Blue," I warned. "Remember who you're talking to."

"How could I forget, *sir*?" she said lightly, batting her lashes like she was oh-so-innocent again. But I could see that her innocence didn't run as thickly as it first appeared. And the idea of there being a wild, untamed beast living within her only made me want to coax it out and feel the slash of its claws.

I closed the distance between us, gazing down my nose at her and consuming her breathing space. A nervous tremble of her lower lip gave me a rush, showing me that she knew exactly who held the power right now. "You may hate me, Miss Vega, but you will learn to respect me."

Her eyes were a storm of swear words, but she didn't let any pass her lips. I'd unnerved her now and that was what I wanted. I needed her fear. And her hate. Because we were on opposing sides of a war she couldn't even comprehend yet. And when Darius forced her to bow and sent her and her sister running from this academy, I'd be there to watch her go with a smile on my face. And surely the taste of her blood couldn't come close to the taste of that victory.

She nodded, backing up and tucking a lock of hair behind her ear. Then she turned her back on me and was gone before I could reprimand her for it. I realised my hands were balled into fists and I slowly uncurled them, the raging thump of my heartbeat seeming to echo into every part of my body.

You're playing with fire, Blue. And you won't like it when it burns.

DARIUS

CHAPTER THIRTEEN

The stardust spat me out like a bad tasting snack and my feet hit the ground hard as I came to a stop before the gates to my family's manor.

Lance appeared at my side a breath later and we exchanged a loaded look before starting towards the gate.

I didn't bother to say anything to the men guarding the entrance as we strode inside and started up the sweeping gravel drive. My mind was too consumed with the weight of this place for me to spare a moment on pleasantries.

We kept our silence as we closed in on the hulking property and my gaze swept over it without me really seeing it at all. It wasn't a house. More like a museum where the attractions contained snapshots of fear and misery which adorned the walls like the blood which had been spilled inside it had never been scrubbed clean.

Sometimes I tried to remember a time when the scent of fear hadn't hung in the corridors and I could almost remember laughing here with my mother and Xavier, playing hide and seek in the huge house and feeling the touch of love I'd always craved from my parents. But I was almost certain that was just a pretty lie I'd painted for myself long ago and convinced myself to remember.

Catalina Acrux was as cold and uncaring as her husband. Though my mother's form of parenting failures could mostly be accounted for as neglect or a general lack of interest in her sons. The only thing she seemed to give any real care to was her own appearance which was the epitome of polished perfection. Father liked to boast that she was the most beautiful woman in all the kingdom like he was trying to take the reputation of the Savage King's wife and paste it onto his own in her absence.

I wasn't saying it was untrue, but I hated the way father claimed my mother's beauty as some kind of accolade of his own. Not least because he was intent on marrying me off to a girl with a moustache and a Faeroid addiction which meant her muscular bulk rivalled my own.

We reached the enormous door which sat proudly front and centre of the extravagant property and the smaller door set into it swung wide before we could so much as pause our stride.

Jenkins peered out at us like we were an inconvenience to his life despite the fact that welcoming guests into the Acrux Manor was practically his entire job description. The old butler was a sycophant for my father's cruelty though and certainly no friend of mine, so I didn't pay him any attention as I stepped over the threshold of the house I'd grown up in.

Gold adorned a lot of the interior, the bannister for the sweeping staircase ahead of us glimmering in the light as I felt the presence of so much treasure feeding my magic reserves merely from standing within this gilded cage.

"Lord Acrux is finishing up his meal with Lord Rigel," Jenkins announced. "He requests that you await him in the smoking parlour."

I exchanged a glance with Orion who gave me a flat look which spoke of our shared hatred of these power plays and I sighed.

"Is Mother home?" I asked, flicking a glance at the old bastard of a butler which made it beyond clear how much I loathed him.

"She is also dining."

That meant Max's mom was here too, but I didn't hold out much hope of their presence doing me any favours. Father would just make me wait until they were gone before dealing with me. And I knew that I wasn't here for anything good. He'd tasked me with removing the Vegas and they still remained at large within the academy. But I wasn't really sure what he expected me to do. I couldn't exactly demand they fight me Fae on Fae - no one would accept me beating them and outcasting them as a true win when they hadn't mastered their magic yet.

The pranks and ostracising might have made weaker Fae crack and quit the school, but not those two girls. Their backbones were strong, and their wills were fierce. They wouldn't be pushed out by a little bullying and it was hard to do more than we were without compromising our own reputations. Some testing of them was to be expected, but all out war with untrained Fae would just make us look bad in the press and Father didn't want that either. It was an impossible task but that wouldn't make the blindest bit of difference to my father of course.

"And Xavier?" I asked which was what I'd wanted to know from the beginning anyway.

"In his rooms. But as I said, you are to wait in the-"

"Yeah, yeah, I'll be there shortly." I headed straight up the stairs without caring how pissed Jenkins was over my dismissal. I didn't answer to him and he could go tell tales to my father all he liked. I was already in for it with him anyway, so it wasn't like it made much difference to me.

We headed down familiar corridors past oil paintings and tapestries all depicting the greatness of Dragons and we were soon climbing the spiralling stairs which led up into the tower which held Xavier's rooms.

I pushed the door open without bothering to knock and my little brother raised his head from the Xbox game he'd been playing at the sound of my arrival.

"Hey!" he said enthusiastically, jumping up and tossing the controller on the couch before hurrying over to greet me. "I didn't know you were coming back tonight."

I pulled him into a hug, ruffling his unruly dark hair as I did so and making him curse me as he shoved me off again. My relief at finding him uninjured and in a good mood was palpable and even though I knew I could only spare a moment here, I'd needed to be sure that he hadn't been punished for my failure with the Vegas.

"Last minute visit," I explained and his gaze darkened as he realised I'd been summoned but he didn't comment on it, turning to greet Lance next.

"Hey, man, how are you?"

"Stagnant," Lance replied in a droll tone. "How about you? Any sign of your Dragon Emerging yet?"

"Not yet," Xavier sighed. "I wish it would hurry up. I just wanna go flying in the clouds and learn to do a bunch of tricks and flips."

"And the breathing fire," I teased and he nodded.

"Yeah, sure that too. But mostly I just want to be out there, spreading my wings and feeling free."

I nodded my agreement to that sentiment though I resisted the urge to point out that it wasn't true freedom, only an illusion of it. Because here I was, back under this roof, awaiting the axe to fall once again.

"How's high school? Are you enjoying your last year?" I asked before he could pick up on my train of thought.

"Same old, same old. I wish Father would just arrange to have my powers Awakened early like he did for you. I can't wait to get my fire magic and find out if I have anything else." The excitement in his eyes brought a smile to my lips.

"Well it's not all perks being the Heir," I reminded him and he grimaced.

"I know, but Father is making me take all kinds of political courses and all of that boring stuff you had to do just in case I'm ever required to step into the role. But I don't get the added advantage of having my magic Awakened early." Xavier pouted, dropping back down before his Xbox and I chuckled.

"Sorry to be the one cutting this short, but..." Lance looked at me and I sighed, knowing he was right. If I made Father wait for me, it would only be worse.

"I'll try and come see you after," I promised and Xavier's eyes clouded for a moment.

"Do you want me to come with you-"

"No," I barked firmly. "Stay away from him tonight. Promise me."

His gaze sharpened and I noted the tremor in his hand before he fisted it. "I hate just sitting up here hiding while he-"

"It's a thousand times worse for me if you're involved," I gritted out. "Honestly, I don't care what he does to me. But if he lays a finger on you then I just..." I took a moment to draw in a breath then moved forward and placed a hand on my brother's shoulder. "Please promise to stay away tonight," I implored him and after another moment of that defiant look in his eyes, he finally dropped his head and nodded.

I gave his shoulder a quick squeeze then turned and left him there, following Lance from the room. But as I closed the door I heard his murmured parting words and they gave me the strength I needed to walk away with my head high and my resolve firmly in place.

"Thank you, Darius."

Lance's jaw was set so tightly as we headed back down the stairs that I was surprised he hadn't cracked a tooth. I knew the Guardian Bond must have been plaguing him, the need he felt to protect me at all times making it close to impossible for him to walk me towards the danger of my father the way he was. But we both knew the real danger would come in me defying him, so he didn't speak a word against it.

I wished I could have left him out of this, but that was just another one of my father's commands - Lance was always supposed to be close to me. It was the whole point of the bond that he had forced upon the two of us, making certain that he be near me in case I needed him to protect me, which meant he was also forced to endure my father's company almost as often as I was.

We made it into the smoking parlour only a few minutes before the Lord of the manor strode in.

Father didn't so much as greet me, the door banging closed behind him as he stalked across the room to a cabinet and took his time selecting a cigar from his collection before pouring himself a measure of whiskey from a gold rimmed decanter.

I eyed the muscular expanse of his back as he kept it to us, giving us a clear insult as he refused to even look our way. His suit was tailored and expensive, the scent of cologne and smoke hanging around him and his blonde hair quaffed back carefully.

"I do not take kindly to failure, boy," he said in a low tone while I just stood there, waiting. "And I made myself perfectly clear when it came to the matter of the potential usurpers."

I exchanged a look with Lance but kept my mouth shut, knowing he wasn't done.

"I had been starting to think you held the potential I required," he went on, carefully clipping his cigar before raising it to his lips and lighting it with a spark on the tip of his finger. "Yet you have managed to disappoint me severely in this."

Father inhaled deeply and a few moments later, yellow cigar smoke billowed from his lungs to cloud across the ceiling.

"They're tougher than we expected," I began and he turned to face me abruptly, his eyes flashing with green reptilian slits which betrayed his anger.

"The time for your excuses is past," he said, slowly plucking the cigar from his lips and setting it down on a crystal ash tray beside him. "Failure demands consequence."

"I understand," I said, my voice unwavering though my muscles bunched.

Father watched me for several dragging seconds and I could practically feel the rage vibrating off of Lance as he remained rooted to the spot on my right.

Eventually, the man who had given me life seemed to find what he'd been hunting for in my gaze and he nodded once before clicking his fingers and pointing at a spot on the floor in front of him.

"Kneel," he commanded in a bored tone which claimed he took no pleasure in this, but I could see the truth in the depths of his dark eyes and I knew that wasn't the case at all.

I swallowed a lump in my throat and stepped forward, but before I could do as he'd asked, Lance's hand locked around my arm and he jerked me to a halt.

"Uncle Lionel," he began in an attempt at a placating tone. "The Vega girls are ignorant, untrained and-"

"Enough," Father snapped, flicking his fingers and sending a tremendous force of air magic crashing into Lance's chest so that he was thrown back across the room and pinned against the door by it, unable to move a muscle.

I looked to my friend in apology, knowing he'd feel every moment of this through our bond and hating that he was forced into punishment with me every time I fucked up or failed at some impossible task.

Wordlessly, I dropped to my knees where I'd been directed to and I fixed my gaze on a clock on the far side of the room. It was nine o'clock exactly and my eyes locked on the movement of the second hand as it continued to tick.

Lance started cursing as he tried to fight against the air magic pinning him to the door, but my father just threw a silencing bubble over him so that he didn't have to listen to it.

I remained where I was, not reacting as my father slowly moved around the room and shrugged out of his jacket.

"You will work harder to achieve this goal in future," he said. Not a question, so I stayed silent. "You will make a concerted effort not to disappoint me again."

He picked up his drink and took a sip, letting the tension coil in the room, toying with me while I waited for the inevitable.

I used to be so afraid of him when he got like this, used to work tirelessly to do all I could to please him. But that was before I realised it was impossible to please him. I could achieve all he wanted and he would punish me for being cocky about my accomplishments.

This wasn't about me failing at anything. It was about power just like everything in my life was. I was his Heir, set to take his place as one of the most powerful Fae in the kingdom one day and as much as he wanted me to be strong, he was never going to tire of proving he was stronger. This was him asserting his dominance over me. So now that I knew my fear was pointless, I'd let it go. I didn't fear being at his mercy like this. I was just numb to it. Not to the pain of the blows I was waiting on, but to the hurt or feelings of betrayal my younger self used to feel. To the sense of injustice or the jealousy I felt when I saw the love other families held for each other.

That wasn't my life. So it didn't matter. This right here was my reality and fearing it didn't change it. But I hadn't accepted it either. For every second that ticked by on that clock I wouldn't cringe or cower, I'd rage and plot and wait. Because his day was coming. He may have been enforcing his position above me for now but one day I would rise up out of his shadow and show him the monster he'd made in me.

One day he'd be the one kneeling before me.

Father set the glass down and removed his belt. The buckle was a gaudy golden Dragon with spiked wings and a pointed tail. I'd felt the bite of it before and I clenched my jaw as he moved to stand behind me.

"It has been nine days since I told you my expectations in this matter," he said but I didn't react. "So we will say one for every day you've failed me."

Still I remained silent. I'd learned a long time ago that it didn't pay to try and delay the inevitable.

My father was a big man, the Dragon in him clear for all to see and his muscles bulged across his huge frame. He made no attempt to rein in the full force of his strength with me so as the first strike of the belt crashed across my spine, I almost crumpled at the agony which ripped across my flesh.

A growl of pain lodged in my throat and I forced myself upright again, my fists bunching at my sides as I locked my muscles and tried to remain upright.

The buckle tore into my back as the second struck blew and the wet splatter of my blood hit the wall as he raised his arm again.

On the fifth strike the agony was so intense that a curse fell from my lips, inciting a furious snarl from my father.

The sixth stroke knocked me to my hands and knees and my arms trembled with the effort to hold myself up as the blinding pain consuming my body sent tremors racking through every inch of me.

I wasn't sure how I managed to hold myself in that position while the final lashes struck across my flesh and my blood ran thick and wet down my spine, dripping down my sides and splashing onto the carpet beneath me. Bile rose in my throat and sweat coated my skin in a sheen as the Dragon within me paced back and forth furiously, wanting to rip and bite and destroy.

But I held it at bay through pure force of will, raising my head to the damn clock on the wall as its golden minute hand slid past the number one and the punishment finally ceased.

Six minutes. That was all it had taken for him to rip the flesh from my spine and leave me shaking at his feet.

I tried to push myself up again but found my body locked in its position on my hands and knees, the tattered remnants of my bloodstained shirt hanging down around me as I remained stuck there, prostrated at the feet of the man I hated above all others in this world.

"Get up," Father sneered as I fought against the shaking in my arms which threatened to give out and pitch me face first onto the floor. "On your feet, boy, or I'll bring your brother down here to join in the lesson."

Those words cut through me like no other. He'd found my one weakness in my love for Xavier and he knew it. Ever since he'd come to realise I was willing to put myself between his wrath and my younger brother, he'd been using it against me, mocking me with it, adding another string to his bow.

My vision darkened and a snarl of agony escaped my lips as I managed to grip the table beside me and haul myself to my feet.

Every movement sent more pain lancing down my spine and as turned my head, I managed to see some of the shredded flesh and muscle which had been my back in the mirror which lined the wall to my left.

I swallowed down my pain and raised my chin until I was looking my father in the eyes.

I didn't make any attempt to hide my hatred for him as I glared, my eyes shifting to reptilian slits and letting him know in no uncertain terms how hungrily I ached for his death.

"I see you still haven't gotten the message," Father tutted, drinking more of his whiskey as he surveyed me. His pale shirt was speckled with my blood and the veins in his right arm bulged from the exertion of wielding his belt against me. "So I will leave you to think about it tonight."

I frowned, not knowing what he meant by that as he stepped closer to me and took my hand in his.

"You will swear not to heal yourself or allow yourself to be healed until dawn," he growled, showing me the Dragon in his eyes too and making it clear he would happily teach me this lesson as a beast if I challenged him to.

The words stuck in my throat as the agony of my injuries consumed me, but I heard the veiled threat there. If I didn't do this then he would find another way to punish me and with Xavier's safety on the line I had no choice but to agree.

"I won't heal myself or allow myself to be healed until dawn," I gritted out and magic flashed between our palms as the star bond was struck between us.

In the corner of my eye, I could see Lance thrashing and straining against the magic which still immobilised him while his roared protests were silenced by Father's power too.

If I broke my word and healed myself then he would feel it happen and I'd also be cursed by the stars with seven years bad luck.

"I will speak with you in the morning once you've had time to think on your failures," Father said, looking me over once more with a feral satisfaction in his gaze which said he was getting off on this. On the power, on the pain he'd inflicted, all of it. "Take him back to the academy, Lance, and be sure this remains private."

Father turned and walked from the room, using a door on the other side of it and making us wait several more seconds before the magic he was using to contain Lance was dispelled.

My strength failed as he shot towards me and I grunted as he caught me, slinging my arm around his shoulders and holding me up.

"Darius..." Lance's wild gaze met mine and I locked my jaw at the agony I found swimming in them. The bond between us meant that he had felt every strike of that belt against my flesh and even now I knew his instincts would be tearing him apart with the need to heal me.

"I'm sorry," I muttered, dropping my gaze and hating that he was always dragged into this, that he'd been forced to be a part of it and his entire life had been stolen for it.

"I hate it when you say that," he snarled and I nodded but I always said it anyway because it was true. I was sorry, more so than I could ever express for the life that he was never going to be allowed to live because of his bond to me. "I'm getting you out of here. I'll be as fast as I can."

I couldn't find the energy to say anything but he didn't wait for me to, his grip on me tightening until he was lifting me against him then he broke into a sprint and shot out of the room.

The world blurred around us and I was fairly sure I blacked out because the next thing I knew we were caught in the grip of the stars, travelling across Solaria and landing with a thump in my bedroom at the academy.

Lance moved me to my bed, his eyes dark and jaw gritted as he helped me to lay down on my front on the golden sheets.

He shot away again and the burning pain in my flesh consumed me for several long minutes while I just lay there in the dark, my gaze locked on the glow of the dying fire in the grate beside my bed as I prepared myself for a long night.

When he returned, he pressed a bottle to my lips and I almost choked on the bourbon as it spilled into my mouth.

"Drink," Lance commanded. "If I can't heal you, the least I can do is get you shit faced enough to pass out."

I couldn't deny his logic so I swallowed the burning mouthful of liquor followed by another and another until the bottle was drained and my head was spinning.

I could still feel the pain of my wounds but as the booze settled into my limbs, it started to feel separate from me somehow, almost like something that had happened to someone else and not me.

Lance climbed into the bed beside me, a shuddering breath passing his lips before he spoke into the dark.

"We will end him, Darius," he swore. "No matter what it costs us, we will see him fall."

I grunted some kind of agreement, but my words were as slurred as my mind was beginning to feel and I let my eyes fall closed instead, urging oblivion to take me as I waited for dawn and the end of my fucking punishment.

286

I woke to the feeling of Lance pushing healing magic into my flesh and cracked my eyes open to see the sun rising over the hills in the distant view through my window.

"Thanks," I mumbled, swiping a hand down my face while I tried to ignore the feeling of his fingers moving down my spine as he pushed the ragged strips of skin back together before healing the damage done to me.

Lance grunted, continuing his work while I just watched the golden rays spilling over the ground outside and lighting the academy up inch by inch.

I could feel the press of gold against my skin and the bed jingled softly as I repositioned myself, signalling the treasure which Lance had clearly placed around me while I slept to help me replenish my magic.

He sighed as he finished, sitting back and giving me room to sit up beside him.

I glanced down at the bloody scraps of fabric which had once been my shirt before tugging it over my head and off of the arm it had still been hooked around before tossing it into the fire.

I swept a hand up the back of my neck and over my head, casting water magic in my palm and using it to clean all of the blood from my body before sending it flying towards the bathroom where it sloshed away down the sink.

"Good as new," Lance said gruffly, his brow pinched as he looked at me and I noticed his gaze lingering on my neck for a moment.

"Same shit, different day," I agreed and silence hung heavily as neither of us mentioned the latest fucked up thing we'd endured at the hands of my father.

Lance's gaze dropped to my neck again and I tilted my head to the side.

"You know you want to," I said as he held himself back, his gaze darting out of the window.

"I should top up from my Source," he hedged.

"I'm the reason your power is running low," I pointed out. "Besides, it's not even six in the morning so unless you plan on breaking into Gwen's bedroom and pouncing on her in her bed-"

"Of course I don't want to do that," he snapped, his gaze meeting mine as he snarled at me and I caught a glimpse of his fangs.

"Well if you aren't going to be creeping into any other students' beds tonight then you should probably just-"

Lance pounced on me with a growl tearing from his lips, his weight knocking me back against the headboard and his hands slamming against my shoulders as he straddled me before sinking his teeth deep into my neck.

I cursed him, muttering a warning about him remembering who the fuck he was chomping on but he just growled again, drawing my blood out of me and making my back arch as the bond drew me closer to him.

There was a damn good reason why we tried not to do this too often and as my hand moved to the back of his hair to tug him closer to me and a sigh escaped my lips, I was forcibly reminded why.

It felt too good to please him like this. Much better than it did when I let Cal bite me. The bond wanted us to be close, as close as possible and as much as it drove him to protect me, it made me want to keep him strong and his magic replenished too. It made him biting me feel way better than it should have and forced thoughts and feelings into my mind which I had to work hard at remembering weren't my own.

Lance drew back with a groan, his dilated pupils meeting my gaze as he shoved on my shoulders and sat back on his heels, looking down at me with my blood still staining his lips.

"I think I should go before I start trying to dry hump you," he joked and I laughed pitifully, hating this fucking curse my father had put on us. It twisted the essence of our friendship and muddied our own feelings to the point that we had to force distance between ourselves while knowing we'd be pining for each other at the same time.

"Why couldn't you just be a girl?" I replied, shoving him out of my lap and raising my own fingers to heal the bite wound left on my neck.

"Oh please, even if I was a girl I still wouldn't let you fuck me." Lance hopped up and grabbed his shirt which he'd tossed on a chair beside my bed, yanking it on before heading towards my window. "Are you alright?" he added, glancing back at me and my muscles tensed at the implication that I might not be.

I pushed myself up and out of bed, stopping by the floor length mirror which stood by my dresser and looking at the perfect flesh of my back in it. Even my tattoo looked flawless and I flashed Lance a tight smile as I pointed it out to him.

"Looks fine to me."

He hesitated a moment longer and I knew he wanted to point out that he hadn't meant the question in the physical sense, but I gave him a hard look until he dropped it.

"Good. You have no excuse to be late to my class then so be prepared for me to dock House points if you are."

I breathed a laugh and he gave me a sad kind of smile before pulling my window wide and leaping out of it.

I moved closer to watch as he used his air magic to guide himself down to the ground before shooting away with his Vampire speed and disappearing in the direction of Asteroid Place.

I stood there for a while longer, watching the sun rise and wondering if it was worth me going back to sleep before giving up on that idea and moving to change into my running gear instead.

I wasn't going to be able to sleep with the echoes of the sound that belt had made slashing against my skin ringing in my ears, so I'd just drown it out with exercise before grabbing some breakfast and heading to class.

By the time tonight rolled around again, I would have successfully buried any lingering memories of last night deep enough in my subconscious to sleep like a baby once more and everything would just go on as usual.

I headed out for a long run, my feet pounding around the footpaths which crisscrossed the entire academy until I was panting and sweating and had no more room inside me for feeling anything at all, let alone fixating on my father and his constant attempts to control my entire life.

I ducked into The Orb and grabbed myself a couple of slices of toast and some coffee, heading back out again before anyone could spot me or try to draw me into conversation.

I ate as I walked back to Ignis, my gaze trailing over the students who were heading in the opposite direction, searching each of their faces for several seconds before I realised who I was looking for.

Roxy Vega had been curiously absent since Tuesday and though I'd had plans with the other Heirs to take her by surprise early in the morning on the days since then, we hadn't managed to catch her. I'd been looking out for her ever since and had started to get the feeling she was avoiding me. The idea of that pissed me off because if I couldn't find her then I couldn't exactly work on my plans to get rid of her. But more than that, I just wanted to see her, maybe even hear her call me an asshole. It was fucking strange, but I had the feeling it would help shake up this mood I was falling into and give me something a little more interesting to concentrate on.

By the time I made it back to Ignis House, scoured the common room and made it back up to my bedroom, my mind was on the Vega twin who was alluding me and firmly diverted from the arguably more pressing issues in my life.

I stripped off and showered quickly, my mind slipping to her more than once as I tried to figure out where she might be hiding.

By the time I'd dressed in my academy uniform and was heading back out of the House, I decided to shoot Seth a message to check up on the other twin.

Darius:

Any sign of my Vega crashing in your House?

Seth:

I've been balls deep in my beta for the last few hours so can't be sure? Do you want me to go check or can I come first?

I took a selfie of my seriously unimpressed face and shot it to him. He responded with a selfie taken from above his head while grinning big as he fucked a girl from behind as another naked girl sucked on his neck.

Darius:

Thanks for making me wanna puke up my coffee

Seth:

Thanks for helping me finish - knowing I was performing for an audience helped tip me over the edge. Breakfast in ten? I can check my House for Vegas on the way

Darius:

I already ate mine. Keep me posted on the Vegas. See you in class, asshole

I still had almost half an hour before my first class of the day, so I decided to head to the Pluto Offices to collect the post I'd been putting off retrieving. It wouldn't be anything interesting, probably just some fan mail and requests for interviews, but I made an effort to check through it whenever I could in case there was anything that needed my attention.

A couple of people called out to me as I crossed campus but I wasn't in any mood to entertain them so I just kept walking, the scowl on my face enough to give them the message about leaving me be.

Just as I reached the door to Pluto Offices, my Atlas rang and I pulled it out to answer it, my gut sinking as I saw my Father's name on the caller ID.

For a moment, my back blazed with the pain of his belt ripping the flesh from my spine and I closed my eyes as I got a hold of myself before answering the call and continuing my walk into Pluto.

"Father."

"I trust you spent the night thinking on your actions," his curt voice greeted me and I ground my teeth at the effort it took me to remain civil with him.

"I did," I agreed, though I didn't point out that the actions I had been focusing on while I writhed in drunken agony all night were the ones I intended to carry out against him in the future when I beat him down beneath me and stole my fate back from his hands.

"Good. Then you can focus your efforts on ridding us of the Vega infestation at your academy. If you fail to do it soon then I may have to get more involved. Perhaps I should be arranging a meeting with them of my own?"

My skin crawled at the idea of him throwing his weight around with the twins and I bristled at the implication that I couldn't handle this myself. If I had anything to do with it, he would never get within a mile of the Vegas and if they had any sense, they'd be thanking me for shielding them from him and running the fuck away before I stopped managing to do so.

"I'm confident that you shouldn't have to bother yourself with this, but if you really feel it's necessary then fine. But I assure you I have it all in hand," I said, trying to keep the bite from my tone and failing somewhat, but I didn't care. What the hell did he expect after what he'd done last night?

I pushed the door to the mail room open and stepped into the tall space which was filled with racks and racks of shelves which towered up to the ceiling several floors above.

My step faltered as my gaze fell on the girl I'd been hunting for all morning and I barely covered my surprise at finding her in this unexpected place as she raised her chin to look me in the eye.

I drank in the sight of her, my gaze clinging to every inch of her body and I swear that she'd somehow gotten even more enticing in the time since

I'd last laid eyes on her. Her expression blazed with a determined kind of rebellion and her full lips pressed into a faint pout which somehow seemed like a challenge of their own, making my attention linger on them for far longer than it should have.

My father was speaking again and it took a wrench of determination for me to pay attention to what he had to say.

"I'll be the one to decide whether or not I get involved with them personally," he said with a lash of authority to his tone. "You just concentrate on doing your part in this and don't presume to question mine."

"As you wish," I said, paying lip service to his bullshit while keeping my gaze riveted on the intoxicating creature who was looking at me with utter dislike in her green eyes. "I'll get it done. Is Xavier there?" I added, wanting to check in with my little brother to make sure Father's anger hadn't moved onto him after I'd left last night. I hated that I hadn't even said goodbye to him, but I knew it was best that he hadn't seen the results of my discussion with our father. But instead of replying to me, Lionel cut the call, the dead tone ringing in my ear and sending a spike of anger through my limbs. "Hello?" I shot a look at my Atlas before releasing a breath of irritation and shoving my earpiece into my back pocket.

My scowl darkened as my anger over everything I'd endured last night and the constant shit I had to deal with because of my father built up yet again before I remembered that I had company.

I raised my eyes to look at Roxy Vega, finding her wary attention still very much fixed on me and liking that a little too much. What was going on beyond those big green eyes? What thoughts filled that pretty head of hers when she set her gaze on me?

"Just get it over with then," she said with a sigh, the pout to her lips increasing just enough to make me stare at her mouth again. Why was she here now? And where had she been since the last time I'd seen her? I got the feeling she was running rings around me and I was equally pissed off over that idea and amused by it.

"Is this where you've been hiding then?" I asked, ignoring her little outburst as I forced my attention from her mouth and the filthy things I'd like to do with it as I quickly tapped on my Atlas and used it to order the room to retrieve my mail.

"What do you mean, hiding?" Roxy asked innocently, but that tone just didn't sit right on that mocking little tongue of hers. No, Roxanya Vega may have been a lot of things, but innocent was most definitely not one of them. She'd been avoiding me alright, she just didn't want to admit to it.

"I haven't seen you at the House or The Orb since Tuesday," I replied, playing along with her innocent act as I tried to figure her out but as she narrowed her gaze on me, I looked back to my Atlas like I couldn't care less what she was up to. Like I hadn't been thinking about her far more often than I should have. Like my thoughts hadn't been about doing plenty of things I shouldn't have wanted to do with a girl who was supposed to be my enemy. And most definitely like I hadn't been picturing her pinned beneath me every time I stroked my cock since the moment I'd laid eyes on her, thinking how slick and tight her pussy would feel wrapped around my length or how much I'd enjoy silencing that smart mouth of hers by fucking it roughly with my fist in that ebony hair.

"I didn't realise you were so obsessed with me," she quipped, and I almost showed my hand then, almost reacted and let her see that that guess wasn't as far from the truth as it should have been. "Am I expected to run all of my movements past you? Or are you just disappointed that your cunning plans to surprise me when I woke up yesterday with your little friends didn't work out?"

My gaze snapped up to hers in surprise and she tossed me an insolent smile. *Oh you really shouldn't taunt the beast in me, baby.*

"How did you find out about that?" I asked, making no attempt to lie about it because it was no secret that we were after her and her sister.

"I'm used to looking out for myself," she replied smugly. "Not all of us grew up with Daddy's money keeping us safe and warm at night-"

"You don't know shit about my father or the way I grew up," I snapped, taking a step towards her automatically as she struck a chord I didn't want her to pull at.

A flicker of fear danced through her eyes for a moment and I stilled, not wanting her to look at me that way for some reason. Like I really was the monster my father had made me.

But just as fast as that fear had appeared, she banished it, her gaze hardening as she held my eye, raising her chin and daring me to do my worst. And I could have met that challenge head on but as I looked at her, I found I didn't want to. Not today. Not on his command. No, I didn't want to hurt her or scare her, but I wasn't entirely sure what I *did* want from her either.

"Just like you don't know the first thing about *me*," she replied and I had to agree that she was right about that. But it didn't mean I didn't want to know more. In fact, I was starting to think I wanted to know a whole lot more about her and where she'd been for the last eighteen years. She was a mystery and I wanted to unravel her. "I've met much meaner bastards than the four of you before and come out swinging. And I've learned a thing or two about the way basic bastards like you operate; you're not very original. And you don't frighten me," she said firmly, but I was pretty sure she didn't believe that anymore than I did.

She said it with such conviction though and such raw challenge that I couldn't help but find it amusing. I didn't know any other woman who would dare speak to me the way she did and yet she didn't seem the least bit inclined to back down even though she could clearly tell what a dangerous game she was playing by baiting me. A breath of laughter escaped me before I could help it and I felt my mood lifting in a way that shouldn't have been possible after the night I'd just had.

"You've got balls, I'll give you that," I muttered, dropping my eyes to my Atlas before I started doing something truly insane like grinning at her and hitting the button to get my mail.

The shelves before us began to move, shifting left and right, up and down, making way for the compartment which held my mail to slide down from its previous position near the roof. It fell still and I stepped forward to grab the contents of the shelf, flicking through the handful of envelopes addressed to me before stuffing them into my blazer pocket when I failed to spot anything interesting.

I probably should have been making good on that promise I'd just given my father to do something new to fuck up Roxy's life and make her want to run from here but as I considered it, my gut twisted and my lip peeled back.

Why the fuck should I be working so damn hard to appease a motherfucker who wanted to grind me down beneath his heel anyway? Why should I do anything he wanted after what he'd done to me?

I made a snap decision and turned for the door, not wanting to do a damn thing to Roxy Vega on his orders. Why should I anyway? She was no real threat to me. Not yet. And probably never would be. Even if she was more powerful, I had five years of expert magical training on her and I was never going to stop working to master my power. So how was she ever supposed to catch up to that? Besides wouldn't the truly Fae way to deal with her be to just let her challenge me if she wanted to? Then I'd prove beyond a doubt that I was the stronger one and we wouldn't need to waste time trying to drive them out like we were afraid of what they might become if they stayed.

I passed Roxy who seemed all too pleased to let me leave, but as I reached for the door, I couldn't help but look back over my shoulder at her.

She wasn't looking my way anymore, instead frowning up at the shelves lined with mail and glancing between them and her Atlas in confusion.

My fingers locked on the door handle as I prepared to leave her there to struggle, clearly not knowing how to work the system to get her things, but then I changed my mind.

I sighed heavily like this was such a burden to me and moved back towards her, pulling her Atlas out of her hands.

She looked up at me angrily, reaching out to snatch it back but I ignored her, opening the app she needed and selecting 'Mail Retrieval' from a list of options.

I caught her hand in mine without really thinking about it and my fingers flexed against her soft skin as the feeling of it against my own made all the fantasies I shouldn't have been having about her move firmly to the forefront of my mind.

"It needs a thumb print," I explained as she began to tug her hand back out of mine and she relaxed just enough to let me press her thumb to the screen so that the shelves beside us started moving.

I released her despite feeling the urge to tug her closer and tossed her Atlas back to her, making her scramble to catch it as I tried to convince my feet to step back while they remained firmly planted exactly where they were.

A big compartment stopped before us, stuffed full of bags and boxes with labels from all kinds of clothes stores printed on them and I looked to them with interest.

"Thanks," Roxy muttered, sounding like she wished she didn't have to say it as she placed her Atlas back in her satchel and moved to gather her deliveries. But I wasn't done with her yet and I moved to grab one of them before she could, smirking at the slogan of a lingerie company which was stamped to it.

"Looking to burn even more of my clothes?" she asked in a dry tone.

"I could be persuaded not to," I replied, my mouth hooking up at one corner in amusement as I remembered just how good she'd looked naked. Not that I'd be opposed to seeing what she looked like wearing the contents of this package too.

"Just do what you've gotta do, dude. I can't stop you." Roxy folded her arms and gave me a look that said she didn't even give a fuck if I really did burn all of it.

"You're really sucking the fun out of this, you know that, right?" I commented, preferring it when she bit at me, this vaguely pissed off acceptance wasn't giving me a look at the fire I liked so much in her. "How about you give me a fashion show wearing the contents of this box and I'll let you keep your new wardrobe?"

She rolled her fucking eyes at me and turned away, dismissing me yet again and making the heat of my fire magic flare in my skin.

I caught her wrist before she could leave me hanging like that, tugging her back to face me again and feeling her pulse jump beneath my fingers. She glared at me and yanked her arm out of my grip but all I could do was smirk at her because she might have been trying to pretend she didn't give a fuck about me, but I'd just felt the evidence against that for myself. Her pulse had leapt at my touch which meant I was under her skin just like she was under mine.

"Keep your shit, Roxy," I said in a voice that matched her bored tone just to see how she liked it. "Ruining your clothes was last week's fun. I can do better than that next time."

I tossed the box of lingerie back into her hands then strode out of the room with a smug fucking grin on my face. Because not only had I ignored my father's request to attack her at every given opportunity, but I'd also just found a pretty little fix for my festering mood. Roxy Vega might just have been right about becoming my new obsession, because I had never found anyone who could light me up the way she did with a glare and a hostile comment. And as her parting words caught up to me, my smile only deepened.

"Pleasure seeing you as always, asshole!" she called loudly, making sure I heard every word.

And for some strange reason, her calling me an asshole was the highlight of my damn week.

CALEB

CHAPTER FOURTEEN

I stood with Seth to the side of the huge cavern where our earth Elemental lessons were held as we watched the Vegas take their first little Bambi steps into our underground world. Geraldine and her band of Royalist sycophants were gathering all around them, gushing praise and squealing any time one of them glanced their way. The twins were lost amongst the middle of them and my fangs were prickling while I watched. I didn't like the idea of my Source being manhandled and I was on the lookout for any other Vampires who might have been dumb enough to come sniffing around her.

"There's something about them, isn't there?" Seth said, sidling closer to me so that his arm grazed mine while I nodded.

"It's their power. It's magnetising."

"We're plenty magnetising," Seth muttered irritably and my lips quirked with amusement.

"Jealous?"

"Of the two shiny new toys who everyone is fawning all over while we stand here abandoned in a corner like a pile of forgotten rocks? No."

I laughed and he grinned.

"Well if you want the fangirls to come make a fuss over you we could just step out of the shadows," I pointed out because we had purposefully chosen this spot to avoid the other students when we'd arrived which was fine by me, but it seemed to be bothering him now.

Seth huffed then dropped his head on my shoulder. "You're fangirl enough for me, Cal," he said in a resigned tone and I shook my head at him as I let him stay there, his skin warm where it pressed against mine.

Geraldine was squealing something dramatically and I tuned my gifts on them so that I could pick out her words.

"I would be boundlessly honoured to even be considered as a candidate for your friendship!" she gushed, throwing her arms around Darcy and looking like she was about to start sobbing.

"Perfect," Tory said, backing up a little to keep herself free of the hug zone. "Now that we're all friends, I'm just going to go for a little explore."

She started backing away from the group of royalists and I nudged Seth to draw his attention to her.

"Looks like a fish just swam out of the barrel."

"Can we play with her?" Seth whispered excitedly, pushing himself upright again and bouncing up and down on the balls of his feet as he stared at her like she was a stick and he was just an excited puppy waiting for someone to toss it.

"It would be rude not to," I agreed and the two of us moved out of the shadows as Tory began to cross the cavern, heading towards one of the side tunnels there like she was just looking to be caught alone or something.

We stalked along after her, silently following as she moved further down the darkened tunnel where the glimmering blue lights which illuminated the roof of the cavern were fewer and father between.

Seth hid our approach with a silencing bubble and the Vampire in me lit up with the excitement of the hunt as we followed her further into the dark while she had no idea at all that there were monsters at her back.

Seth lunged forward, grabbing her shoulder to make her flinch, though sadly she didn't scream the way I'd been hoping she would.

I shot around her before she could spot me and stayed at her back while Seth took up her attention. He pushed his face into her hair, inhaling deeply while she recoiled but his arm slid around her shoulders to keep her close.

"Where have you been hiding, little Vega?" Seth asked, ignoring her as she tried to push him off.

He'd told me and Max over breakfast about Darius searching for her and I was curious for the answer to that question too. It was actually quite impressive that she'd managed to avoid all of us so successfully.

"I think we've established I'm not of your Order," Tory growled shoving his chest harder to try and make him release her. "So how about you cut the touchy-feely stuff with me?"

"You know, I could take offence to that," Seth said dramatically, catching the hand she was using to push him back and linking his fingers through hers instead. "Order shaming isn't cool."

Tory yanked her hand away and shoved him hard enough to force him off of her before taking a step back which almost had her bumping into me, though she hadn't realised that yet and I got a little thrill from it. "It's not Order shaming. I just prefer to keep my body to myself unless *I'm* the one choosing to share it."

"Is that an offer?" I purred behind her, making her flinch in alarm as I reached out to run my fingers down her bare arm.

"No, it wasn't," she snapped, sidestepping so that she could glare at both of us at once.

Seth closed the gap between us instantly, brushing his arm against mine as we looked down at our little plaything and we tried to decide what to do with her.

"What do you want?" she asked, taking a step back like she thought she might be able to escape us. But that wasn't going to happen. I had her at my mercy now and I found I liked the way she looked there.

"We've been looking for you," Seth said. "Poor Caleb has practically starved to death without his little lunchbox on tap. You really should have come begging for his forgiveness after letting Orion put his mouth all over you like that."

"Forgiveness?" she scoffed, looking to me like she didn't even think there was a problem with her allowing another Vampire to bite her and a darkness trickled through me at the idea of that. "You can be assured that I have zero interest in *any* Vampire feeding from me but if I do decide to let a man put his mouth on me, I won't be asking permission from *you* for it. You don't own me."

"Wrong," I said darkly, the warning in my tone clear as my anger rose. "I claimed you. Which makes you mine, we're bonded you and I. It's your responsibility to remind any *lesser* Vampires of that fact if they try to feed from you again. And if you don't want to agree to that then we could always try out the old fashioned way of marking you as my Source."

Seth chuckled as Tory frowned in confusion. "What's that supposed to mean?"

"Years ago Vampires would mark their Sources with a tattoo right in the centre of their forehead." I reached out to poke her between my eyes and she flinched, making adrenaline spike through me. For some reason, I really liked making this girl squirm and the desire to bite her rose in me like a demon. Or better yet, maybe she'd like to try her chances at running from me first? "It helped them to avoid little accidents like your run-in with Orion. If I can't trust you to make other Vampires aware of my claim then maybe I should consider it," I said convincingly and she blanched in alarm like she thought I might really mark up her pretty face like that.

"If you come anywhere near me with a needle I'll drive it through your fucking eye," she snarled. Fuck me, this girl had grit.

"So can I assume that I have your word to announce my claim to any other Vampires who show an interest?" I pressed, wanting her to say those words with a feeling akin to desperation. She was mine. All mine. And I wanted her to speak it out loud.

"Fine," she said though she didn't seem entirely pleased about it. "So long as you keep any ideas about permanently marking my body off of the table, I'll tell all your little buddies that my blood is spoken for."

"You do realise that there are a lot of people who would kill for your position, don't you?" Seth asked, taking offence at her clear reluctance for her position as my Source. "Being the Source of Caleb Altair is an honour."

"Well they're welcome to have it. By all means, find another girl or guy to suck on and I'll be on my way." Tory tried to sidestep us but we shifted as one so that we were blocking her way.

"I own you. I wanna hear you say it, Tory," I pressed, eyeing her mouth and hungering for those words to fall from her full lips. "Who do you belong to?"

"Go screw yourself, I don't belong to you." A growl built in my throat but before I could let that anger grow, she went on. "But the Tory blood-bar is closed for all other business and I'll pass the message on to any parasites who come my way."

I smirked at her in satisfaction, my fangs tingling as I eyed her throat for a moment and she barely suppressed a sigh as she caught up with my train of thought.

"Fine. Bite me then if you have to," she said, holding out her wrist without any kind of fight at all. She was beating me at my own damn game, refusing me the fight and the fear she'd obviously realised I liked when I bit her and now she was ruining my damn meal times.

"It's not as much fun if you just accept it willingly," I complained, wondering if I could convince her to play with me the way I wanted her to. Just a little running and screaming before the bloodshed. Was that too much to ask?

"Well why don't you find someone else to suck on if you're looking to get your kicks from fear? And I can assure you I'm *not* willing, I'm just practical. I can't stop you so I just have to endure it."

Ergh, did she just say *endure?* Having me bite her wasn't supposed to be a chore, it was supposed to be an adrenaline filled, fight or flight experience that ideally got her all kinds of turned on once I had her pinned beneath me and my mouth was on her flesh.

"You're making it sound so boring," I muttered. "But you are right about one thing. You *can't* stop me."

"Yet," she replied icily. There was the fight I'd been hunting for.

"Confident little thing, aren't you?" Seth murmured, taking a step towards her.

She stayed where she was, though she didn't try to hide her distaste for my brother as he closed in on her.

"I think this little Vega needs reminding who she's up against," Seth purred, running his hand down my back and making my skin prickle at the contact.

I liked the sound of that plan.

Before Tory could do more than glare, I shot forward and wrenched her off of her feet, tossing her over my shoulder and shooting further into the tunnel while she swore and punched me, making me laugh.

We made it into a cavern further down the tunnel where the rest of the class would be unlikely to venture, the wide space glowing with blue and silver light that glistened wetly. Seth howled behind as he raced to catch up and I set her down with a grin at the game as she scowled up at me.

"You're stupidly strong," she grumbled, pushing me back as my hands lingered on her waist.

You like that, do you, sweetheart?

She looked away from me to glance over the ledge to our right. We were standing above a cavern filled with sparkling stalagmites around ten meters below us, their sharp points glinting threateningly as we looked down.

Tory shifted away from the edge uneasily and I began to get an idea about how I might earn that scream from her after all.

"I am," I agreed with her assessment of my physical prowess, flexing my arms a little to draw her attention back to them. "And that's only my second best attribute."

"What's your best?" she asked, her assessing gaze flicking over me and making my dick get all kinds of interesting ideas as she wet her lips.

"That would involve us ditching our clothes," I said, dropping my voice and letting my gaze drink her in and I wondered if she might bite.

For a moment, her attention dropped down to inspect my body and I was almost certain that it was going to be on between us, but as her dismissive gaze flicked back up to mine I realised she wasn't going to make it that easy.

"Well I won't be putting that claim to the test," she assured me, sounding almost bored. "Why have you brought me here?"

"I thought you might like a look at the view," I said, prowling towards her as I decided to get that scream from her if she wasn't going to be giving me a kiss.

She glanced at the drop to our right then shifted away from it a little more. "Er, yeah. It's great, thanks. But I really should be getting back to my lesson."

"Don't you want a closer look?" I pressed, moving right into her personal space so that I could inhale her air.

"I can see it just fine from here," she insisted, staying where she was instead of backing up any more.

Pounding footsteps approached and Seth burst from the tunnel behind us with a howl which echoed off of the cave walls.

"Like the view, little Vega?" he asked, shaking his long hair around his head in a way that let me know the Wolf in him was aching to come out to play.

His excited gaze met mine and my lips twitched as we silently agreed to keep playing this game. "I think she needs a closer look."

"Yeah, you can't really appreciate it from way back here," I agreed.

Tory backed up and my fangs tingled at the look in her eyes, my cock throbbing with the thought that she might be about to run. If she did, I absolutely shouldn't chase her because Vampires seriously weren't advised to indulge in the hunt, but I knew I would. I was hungering for it with an ache I'd never felt before. I wanted her to run and scream and try to escape me while I chased her down and stole the blood I thirsted for from her. But that was likely to end terribly so I forced myself to take control of the situation before it could even begin.

I shot towards her, shoving her chest so that she was thrown backwards towards the edge, a beautiful scream tearing from her as the razor sharp stalactites beckoned her to her death.

I caught her hand easily, my speed making it as simple as breathing and Seth managed to catch her other hand too.

Her sneakers scrambled against the edge of the drop off and fear flared in her dark eyes which made my pulse race and a laugh fell from my lips as we held her suspended like that, at our mercy. Seth and I always had made the perfect deadly team.

"Pull me up," she demanded, the breathy note of fear in her voice giving me the kick I'd been looking for from her since this whole game had started.

"Solaria has been much better off since the Vegas left the throne to the Celestial Families," Seth growled, and I glanced at him, remembering this was supposed to serve the purpose of chasing them out like our parents wanted. Though I doubted a few silly tricks were going to be enough to do that. "Since our parents took up the throne that yours left cold, our world has been a better place. We don't need you to come back here and claim it for yourselves. We don't want you to."

"We didn't ask for this," Tory breathed, her fingers gripping mine like a vice but she didn't need to worry, I was never going to let her go. "We don't want it. You can keep your stupid throne and your power!"

I was surprised at how honestly and easily she tossed those words our way, but it just made it all the clearer how little she understood our world.

"That's a beautiful offer, sweetheart, but it doesn't change the facts," I told her, trying to make her see why these games were necessary, though I was pretty certain she was having as much fun as me even if she didn't seem to fully grasp the rules. "Your blood-right means the throne belongs to you so long as you prove yourself capable of taking it. And there are enough people who would support your claim to cause a civil war over it."

"But we don't want it!" she insisted, her feet scrambling against the ledge again as she fought to try and pull herself up, but that was in our hands, not hers. Seth's fingers had already twitched, casting a barrier of air beneath her to catch her if she fell, but my grip was iron and I wouldn't be letting go. "How can anyone seriously expect us to rule over a nation we know nothing about? It's insane!"

A touch of pity nudged me at her words, and for a moment I wondered if she really was that naive, if she really thought this could all be solved with something as simple as her and Darcy just saying no thanks. And hell, maybe it could be if they truly meant it, if they publicly renounced their claim. Did we really have to chase them off if they didn't even want it?

"Look, all we want is to learn how to control this magic inside us and get our inheritance. That's it. We grew up with no one and nothing. Before we came here we weren't even sure if we were going to be able to keep a roof over our heads for the winter! I swear we have zero interest in claiming any throne or taking your places."

I glanced at Seth, not liking the way her words struck a chord with me and wondering if he was feeling the same as me. But one look at the wild excitement in his eyes said that wasn't the case. He was still fully on the get-rid-of-the-princesses train, and with the clarity of our parents' wishes on the matter, I couldn't exactly question it. Especially not with her here.

"I say we drop her," Seth said with a shrug that unbalanced her and made her grip on me tighten with panic.

I could see the wild look in my brother's eyes and decided to put aside any sneaking little doubts I may or may not have been experiencing in favour of us just finishing this game of ours and sating that hunger in his eyes.

We looked between one another, considering our options here while we let the princess dangle at our mercy for a bit longer, but before we could decide what to do with her, she spoke in a tone that snapped through my mental barriers like a whip and had me falling at her command instantly.

"*Pull me up,*" Tory demanded, her tone fierce and thick with Coercion which we hadn't been expecting.

We heaved her up over the edge to safety before we could even try to shake off the command and shock spiked through me at the display of her power as she scrambled away from us and backed up towards the wall.

"Shit," Seth muttered, eyeing her with a whole lot more caution than he'd been using before, but I didn't know why he was surprised by this. I'd been warning them all about the level of power these girls held since day one.

"I told you how strong they were," I said, fortifying my mental shields as I eyed her and tried to predict her next move. This game had just taken a much more interesting turn than I'd been expecting and the way my heart was pumping made it more than clear that I liked it at least as much as I was concerned by it.

"*Stay away from me,*" Tory commanded, trying her little party trick again.

I glanced at Seth as I deflected the command easily enough now that I'd been expecting it and he smirked as he clearly did too. My fangs were aching now, the fight in her making me all kinds of thirsty and my patience for this game of cat and mouse was officially running out.

"Nice try sweetheart, but you aren't going to slip past our defences so easily a second time," I said.

Her lips parted on an angry retort, but she didn't manage to voice it before I shot towards her, my hand hooking around her back as I dragged her entire body against me and sank my teeth into her neck.

A groan escaped me as I held her there, her body tensing in my arms as her power flooded my senses and I swallowed down as much as I could with an electric sense of satisfaction.

She tasted so fucking good that my entire body hummed with delight at the sensation of her blood sliding over my tongue and down my throat and it was hard to imagine anything better in the entire world.

Seth moved closer and brushed his fingers against Tory's arm, sending my instincts into a blinding rage as he closed in on my damn meal. A menacing growl of warning rumbled through me as I tightened my hold on her, my fingers moving to knot in her hair while my other hand grasped her waist and pulled her entirely flush with my body.

My cock was thickening in my pants as I felt the press of her flesh against mine combined with the intoxicating flavour of her blood soaking my parched throat and her power spilling into all the dark places inside me.

Her hands landed on my biceps like she was going to try and push me back but she didn't, her grip firming and only enhancing all of the filthy thoughts which were beginning to circle in my mind over her. If she gave me half a chance, I could show her exactly how good it could feel for me to bite her when she let her inhibitions go.

"Sorry," Seth said innocently, stepping back like he hadn't known touching her would piss me off.

I drank down a few more heady mouthfuls before the swelling of my cock meant I really had to draw back before she would feel it. I was all up for letting her know I wanted her, but I figured I could be a little more subtle than just driving my hard on into her out of the blue.

I released her with a wrench of determination, taking a measured step away before cutting a glare at Seth. "Don't touch my Source while I'm feeding."

Seth grinned, letting me know he was up for a fight over it if I wanted one and my gaze lingered on his throat as I considered teaching him a lesson about Vampire feeding with my damn teeth.

"I'm still here, assholes," Tory snapped, but our attention was locked on one another so we continued to ignore her.

"You know I'm not going to bite her, what's the big deal?" Seth asked innocently, baiting me and I half considered just lunging at him to remind him what my teeth were for before the tingling of Tory's power within me distracted me from that idea.

I decided against teaching him that particular lesson right now, cracking a smile at him while warning him with my eyes not to do it again.

"I just don't want your paws all over my food while I eat," I said, knocking my shoulder against Seth's just hard enough to make my point while still keeping it more playful than hostile.

"Wanna go finish this lesson with a contest?" Seth asked excitedly, seeing the challenge in my eyes and knowing how to satisfy it as always. Because yes, I did want to take him up on the offer of beating his ass in a competition, that was exactly what I needed.

"Only if you don't mind getting your ass whipped," I replied.

Seth barked a laugh then took off, howling loudly as he led the way back to class and we left Tory behind as I raced after him, ready to beat him down publicly and bathe in the glow of victory at his expense.

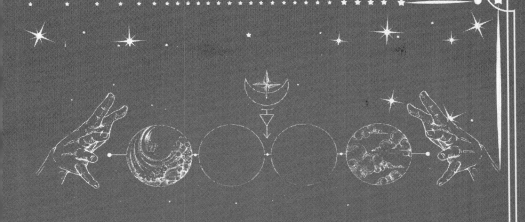

ORION

CHAPTER FIFTEEN

I shot back to Asteroid Place after my last class on Friday afternoon, a weight seeming to press down on me like the stars were reaching out from the sky and shoving me towards the ground. I'd been consulting with my tarot cards at every chance I got today, but their answers weren't clear. I needed a fortune told that wasn't in damn riddles all the time.

As I walked through the gate, someone shoulder barged me from behind and Astrum stalked past me, his red robes whipping out behind him as he went. For an old asshole, he sure had a lot of backbone.

"You wanna watch where you're walking," I called after him as my fangs extended in preparation for a fight, my fingers tingling with magic.

He glanced back at me, looking sort of nervous and distracted.

"Your aura's dark today, Lance," he said, his tone taking on a low, mystical quality that he often used in his classes.

"Sorry I'm not exuding sunshine and rainbows like my usual self," I said dryly, hounding after him as he upped his pace, continually glancing back at me like he thought I was about to pounce. And maybe I was.

He reached the pool and stepped around a sun lounger, strategically putting it between us as he turned back to face me. As if that would keep me away though.

"When I taught you at this academy, you had so much potential," he said, shaking his head like he was disappointed in me and I frowned, caught off guard by that comment.

"So what? Were you a Pitball fan or something? Because if you're pissed I gave up my chance to join the League then maybe-"

"That's not what this is about," he tsked. "You know nothing about anything."

"Enlighten me then," I growled.

He glanced around like a jittery little house cat and smoothed down his long grey moustache. "I've *seen* things," he whispered, his throat bobbing and sweat starting to bead on his brow. "Something is coming."

I momentarily became distracted from my anger as I took in those words, because I'd been feeling that way for a while now and every reading I did confirmed it. Plus, I may have hated the old guy but he'd worked as a consultant to the Vega Queen years ago and I knew his Sight was powerful. Maybe he'd been able to grasp more than I could from the stars about what was coming.

"What've you *seen*?" I demanded, taking a step closer.

He shook his head, eyes darting left and right again like he expected an enemy to appear from thin air, but there was no one here.

"The dice is already rolling," he hissed. "And I fear it's too late."

"Too late for what?" I pressed, searching for answers in his eyes.

"Yoo-hoooo!" Washer's voice cut through the air and Astrum turned tail and scarpered away like a rat down a drain.

I gritted my jaw in irritation, my head snapping around to where Washer was approaching the pool with a bright pink flamingo ring around his waist, and as I looked at the transparent pink plastic, I saw his cock squashed up between it and the ring. *No, by the stars no.*

I physically jerked away from the sight as he waved enthusiastically at me. "Join me for a dip in the pool, Lancey boy. We can have a good chat you and me. A real cosy catchup before we head out on the town for the night. We can enjoy getting wet together and if you let your guard down, you can let your worries be *Washered* away. How does that sound?"

Like my own personal hell.

He chuckled, his Siren gifts swirling around me, trying to feed on my frustration, but he couldn't have it.

"Can't. I'm going out," I said and his eyebrows shot towards his hairline.

"Oooh with Franny, is it? You two always did make a saucy couple. She was always such a gushing student."

I almost snapped at him for that last comment before I remembered his weird sliding scale of ranking students. Ergh.

"We're not a couple," I muttered, though why I was bothering to explain myself to him, I didn't know.

"Will you bring her home tonight? You, me and Fran could have a midnight tipple. Just the three of us getting wet and wild in the hot tub, what do you say?"

I say I'd rather cut my own hand off and feed it to an unwilling crow.

"I'm staying at hers tonight," I lied and his eyebrows somehow went higher. Though why that was a lie, I wasn't sure. I just knew I'd be sleeping alone in my own bed tonight.

He shook his hips left to right and his skin rubbed against the rubber ring, making a creaking sound. "Oh I see. You two little lovebirds want some rompy pompy, do you? A teeny weeny bit of the old hanky panky." He started thrusting his hips as he laughed, making the flamingo's head bob and I swear it looked distressed.

I grimaced, about to snap at him when a Harpy landed right between us, their black wings folding behind them and slapping Washer in the face.

"Noxy." I beamed in surprise, finding my friend Gabriel grinning at me with a takeaway bag in his hand. His dark hair was ruffled by the flight he'd taken and his muscular bare chest was exposed, the myriad of inked symbols on his body on display.

"Hey Orio," he said, continuing to flap his wings so Washer got a face full of feathers and started spluttering as he tried to back away. "I brought dinner."

"Thank you," I said seriously and he smirked in a way that told me he'd *seen* this already and had planned his Washer intervention.

I strode past him, leading him to my chalet and a splash told me Washer had jumped in the pool. I never went swimming in there. It wasn't sanitary with how much time that over-tanned creep spent in the water with his floaties. I swear I should just pop them all to save them from the molestation. They'd probably thank me for it. That was no life for a happy little blow-up creature.

I unlocked the door with my magic and led the way inside, a breath of relief leaving me as Gabriel came in and I shut the door behind him. I let the professor mask fully slip from my body. It was my favourite moment of the day, just letting go of the fakeness I had to put on beyond these walls.

I rubbed my eyes wearily then turned to my friend and he moved swiftly forward and wrapped his tattooed arms around me.

"You look dead on your feet," he said as he let his wings shift away.

"I'm dead off them too," I said, conjuring something of a laugh but it didn't sound right. "What are you doing here?"

He released me and dropped down onto the couch, placing the bag of food on the coffee table.

I joined him, shedding my blazer and putting my feet up on the table as I loosened my tie from my throat. I swear that thing felt like a noose put there by Lionel Acrux most of the time.

"Just checking in," he said, frowning at me as I leaned forward to grab my bourbon off the table. "I had a vision about your drinking habit."

My fingers grazed the bottle and I huffed internally, sitting back in my seat and leaving the bourbon there. "I wouldn't call it a habit, more of a necessity." I smirked, but he didn't smile.

"How are the Vegas?" he asked, changing topics faster than the wind.

I shrugged. "Powerful.

"Tell me about them," he urged, looking genuinely curious. "One has blue hair, right?"

"Yeah, so?" I said sharply, the words coming out defensive and I cursed myself internally.

I didn't want Gabriel noticing anything about my behaviour when it came to Darcy. He could use his Sight to try and *see* more. Too much. Not that there was anything to *see*. I hadn't done shit. And I wasn't going to. So how could he *see* anything anyway? There definitely wasn't a future where I acted on these crazy feelings, so I was a hundred percent safe from his visions. Even though I trusted him with my life, no one could know this. It was just a blip. Something to do with her Order for sure. She was just a Siren. Just a harmless little Siren.

Gabriel scratched at a tattoo of three intertwined wings on his collarbone. "Just tell me about them," he laughed and I relaxed a bit, telling him everything I'd learned so far about the two lost princesses as we ate the tacos he'd brought - barring the part where Blue tasted like the best dream of my life and had made me so hard I couldn't think of any other girl lately.

His grey eyes glazed for a second as he fell into a vision and when he refocused, he glanced at the back of the couch like he'd *seen* something there and surprise crossed his features. "Blue means you...holy shit," he muttered under his breath.

"What?" I demanded, my heart thrashing irrationally.

"Nothing." He cleared his throat. "Look, I came to talk to you about something in particular," he said seriously, darkness crossing his eyes. "I've been getting some strange visions lately. It's like there's walls stopping me from *seeing* something. Like a dark cloud barring my way. I try to push through it but it's impossible. I'm not sure what it is, but I...I think it's bad, Orio. And it fucking scares me because if I can't *see* the danger, then I can't protect my family from it. I can't protect *you* from it."

"Shit," I breathed, pressure mounting in my head again. "I dunno what to say, man. Maybe you could consult with some other Seers, find out if they're struggling too?"

He nodded vaguely, still staring at me with concern in his eyes. "Have you been acting on what I said to you the other day? You need to follow the light, Lance. It's important. More important than I can really say."

"I don't know what that means," I said imploringly. "What light, Noxy? There is no light. This world is so fucking grey sometimes I just..." My gaze drifted to the bourbon again, thoughts twisting in my head over Darius, his father, that fucking beating he'd taken the other day. I only had to close my eyes to feel the lashings of that belt on my back. On his back. It made me sick. Fucking literally. The moment he'd passed out in his bed the other night I'd thrown up in his golden-seated toilet as I fought the urge to heal him. I hadn't slept, knowing he was suffering and not being able to do a thing about it. It was an agony I couldn't even describe, and the worst thing was I knew Lionel could do it again at any time. And there was nothing I could do to protect Darius from him. Just like I hadn't been able to protect my sister from him.

Clara was gone because of that fucking monster and every day that passed without her reminded me how helpless I was to his power. If I'd only acted sooner, spoken to her about Lionel and realised how deeply he had her under his control, maybe I could have gotten her away from him...

Gabriel reached out and rested his hand to my shoulder. "The past is gone. There are no more paths for you there."

"I know," I bit out, my mind descending into a dark, all-consuming pit.

"So take a new path," he urged. "You can be happy, I know you can."

"You've *seen* it?" I asked, begged really, because I couldn't see any path in my future that led to happiness. Though maybe destroying Lionel would bring me that. Maybe that was what Gabriel could *see*. And that gave me hope, because if he could *see* Lionel falling then it meant it was really possible.

He nodded, a promise in his eyes. But I didn't have his gifts, I couldn't perceive what he'd *seen*. So I was just a gambler, blindly placing bets and I didn't know where to put my money.

"The answer is in the path of least resistance," he said and I sighed.

"Well, it must be at the bottom of my bottle of bourbon then," I said sardonically, swiping it up from the table at last and giving in to my craving for numbness. I twisted the cap off, taking a swig out of it and felt Gabriel's eyes on me. He wasn't judgemental, that wasn't his style. But sometimes I thought about the guy I'd been when I first met him and wished I could still be that for him. This alcoholic asshole I was now was probably far more than he'd bargained for as a friend. But we weren't normal friends, we were Nebula Allies, which meant I was star-chosen for him and him for me. No escaping that, sadly for him.

We chatted about Gabriel's family and I basked in the happiness of his life, trying to steal some of it for my own as I forgot about my problems.

After a while, my Atlas buzzed and I found a message from Francesca telling me she was about to leave and I cursed, shoving to my feet. I was still wearing my professor bullshit and had totally forgotten about meeting her.

I scrubbed a hand over my face as Gabriel pushed to his feet too, already *seeing* what I was about to say.

"I'll see you later. Have an interesting evening," he said with a knowing grin and I frowned at that before he headed to the door, letting himself out and flying off towards the horizon.

Damn cryptic oracle man.

I shot to the shower, pulling off my clothes as I went and quickly washing before tearing back to my room and throwing on a nice shirt and some smart pants. I dried my hair, styling it fast, glancing in the mirror and figuring that'd do before pocketing my stardust, my sun steel sword concealed as a switch knife, my Atlas and my wallet. Then I shot out of the house, locking up in record time and throwing stardust over me as I went. Being a Vampire really had its perks when you were as useless at time keeping as me.

I was cast among the stars, my soul seeming to scatter before being drawn back together as I was transported onto a street in Tucana outside a bar called Andromeda Place. Francesca was already there, wearing a fitted dress with her hair styled to perfection. She looked good, but somehow as I took in her curves which usually seemed appetising to me, I didn't really feel much of anything. I blamed it on the shitty day I'd had and hitched on an expression that was less end-of-the-world and her face split into a smile as she spotted me.

She jogged over on her high heels, wrapping her arms around me, her lavender perfume surrounding me. I gave her a one armed squeeze and she clung on a little tighter, leaning back and pressing her mouth to mine. I blinked in surprise. It wasn't like we hadn't kissed before, but we usually only did it at my place, or hers. This was very…public. Not that I cared what anyone thought, but we'd never acted like this outside of the bedroom before and it left me vaguely stunned.

She leaned back, threading her fingers between mine and scoring her thumb across my lips to wipe away the lipstick she'd left there.

"Why do you look like I just punched you in the dick, Lance?" she snorted and I made a vague attempt to rearrange my features.

"I just didn't realise we were kissing in public now," I said with a frown.

"Is that a problem?" she asked.

Was it? No. Not technically. Except I'd made it clear I didn't want any kind of serious relationship with Francesca. But she'd said that too. So maybe I was just overthinking this. The thing was, it wasn't her kissing me that was really the problem, it was that the second her mouth had touched mine, I'd thought of someone else. And I'd felt the weirdest fucking sense of betraying her.

I cleared my throat - and my thoughts for that matter - tightening my hold on Francesca's hand and leading her into the bar. I felt the security spells washing over me, checking my identity and the cool sensation of a silencing bubble barrier filling the place. Most bars didn't allow silencing bubbles because they ruined the atmosphere, but there was enough chatter here that it didn't much matter, especially as I couldn't see any Vampires that could potentially tune in on our conversation.

We headed over to the end of the bar, sitting side by side and Francesca's knees pressed to mine as she turned to face me.

"How's your week been?" she asked.

"Dreadful," I deadpanned. "Yours?"

She laughed, swatting my arm and I frowned. She wasn't usually like this. Normally we chatted about Pitball scores and Nymph attacks, not small talk bullshit.

We ordered drinks and my attempt to steer the conversation to Pitball somehow kept ending up back at weird topics.

"You never really speak much about your mom," she said, reaching over to squeeze my arm as I drained my second whiskey.

"That's because she's a royal cunt," I said flatly and she laughed again, her hand sliding higher and squeezing my bicep.

"You must love her though. She's your mom," she pressed, a frown pulling at her brow.

I shrugged, tapping the bar so the bartender immediately replaced my drink. "Love's a word I reserve for few and far between these days."

"Like for me?" she asked playfully, tossing her hair.

I snorted. "Yeah," I said and her eyelashes fluttered. "You, Darius, Gabriel. My Nebula Allies." I shrugged. "That's about it."

Her lips turned down at the corners as she sipped her wine and nodded, seeming sad about something though fuck knew what.

323

"Did you see the last Skylarks game?" I asked as my gaze hooked on a TV screen beside the bar playing the highlights. I'd missed watching it live thanks to fucking Lionel, but had managed to catch up during my lunch hour today. "I swear Altair is made for scoring Pits. She's like a rocket on the field, especially when the Lion starts knocking everyone over." I grinned. Man, I loved Pitball. If there was one thing that could still get my heart racing these days, it was that. That and a blue-haired Vega apparently. *No, I'm not thinking about her tonight. In fact, no more Darcy thoughts for the rest of the weekend. And by Monday, I'll have a clear head and a no-bullshit attitude towards our relationship.*

Francesca's hand dropped onto my thigh and I turned back to her in surprise.

"I don't wanna talk about Pitball tonight," she said huskily, wetting her lips.

"Oh," I said disappointedly, trying to look back at the screen, but she caught my chin and yanked my head around. "Are you okay? You're acting weird."

"I'm fine," she said, laughing girlishly again and leaning back in her seat.

She sipped her wine and her hand slid off my thigh, making me feel strangely relieved. It wasn't like she hadn't touched me intimately before. It was just odd. Here. In a bar. And my cock definitely had no interest in it.

My Atlas buzzed and I took it from my pocket, finding a photo sent from Gabriel of a snake with a top hat on and a tiny rose between its teeth. I started laughing, showing it to Francesca but she didn't even crack a grin. That shit was funny, man, what was her deal?

"Lance, can we talk about something?" she asked seriously and I nodded, placing my Atlas down on the bar and leaning in closer.

"Is it about the Nymphs?" I asked, hoping she had some information for me on that nest.

"No," she said in frustration. "It's about us."

I frowned, waiting for an explanation, but as she went on a flash of blue in my periphery made my eyes whip over her shoulder to the door as it opened. Darcy Vega walked into the bar with her sister and a couple of freshmen including the smart Cygnus girl and the hat guy who tasted of feet. My breath stalled in my lungs. Blue looked fucking radiant in tight fitting jeans and a black cami that dipped low enough to show off her cleavage in a lacy bra that had my cock's full attention. *Oh fuck no. Why is she here? Of all the fucking places in Tucana, she chose to come here?*

The stars really couldn't give me a break. And I was still staring. Even right now, when I knew I needed to look away, I was still. Fucking. Staring.

"-and I feel like there is something special between us, don't you?" Francesca was saying and I grunted some sort of affirmation, not really taking in what she'd said as I stared at the girl who seemed to carry the sun with her wherever she went. It felt so much warmer in here now, so much brighter. I was gonna turn to ash in that light, like Vampires from the mortal stories.

"You do?" Francesca asked excitedly.

"Uhuh," I said vaguely, my eyes still locked on Darcy.

"Isn't that Professor Orion?" Sofia Cygnus asked as I trained my ears on them too and my gaze immediately snapped back to Francesca a heartbeat before Darcy looked this way. *Shit, she could have caught me staring like a fucking creep.*

My heart was pounding furiously and my breaths were coming unevenly. What the fuck was happening to me?

Francesca smiled at me with a glint in her gaze while I kept my ears firmly on the Vegas. For research purposes, obviously.

"Could be," Darcy said lightly like she didn't really care and my neck prickled irritably.

I couldn't pick up her heartbeat with so much chatter in the restaurant part of the bar, so I couldn't be sure if she was having any reaction to my presence at all. Not that it mattered.

"This way," the waitress said to them and they were seated at a table that was right across from us. *Perfect.*

When Darcy sat exactly in my line of sight, my stomach rippled with heat and I fought a satisfied grin as she immediately hid behind a menu. She definitely knew I was here and she was definitely affected.

When she ordered a whiskey and coke, I swear my dick did some sort of salute. Whiskey girl? *Dammit, why are you doing this to me stars?*

"So do you think we should?" Francesca asked and I realised she'd continued talking while I'd been staring at the forbidden fruit in the room.

"Hm?" I asked, forcing my eyes back onto her.

"You know…" she said, biting her lip. "Should we try?"

"Er, yeah," I said, figuring it was fifty-fifty odds on whatever I was agreeing to being the right choice.

"Are you sure?" she asked excitedly as I tried to get the bartender's attention again.

"Uhuh," I said, flicking my fingers and sending the best bottle of whiskey in the bar down to take the place of the one the bartender had been about to use to make Darcy's drink while he fetched a glass.

He poured the one I'd chosen without even noticing the switch, making Darcy's drink ten times better than it would have been with the piss water he'd been going for – and ten times more expensive than he realised. Though the coke would likely ruin it anyway.

I watched as she was brought her drink, waiting for her reaction as she took a sip and switching the bottles back so no one noticed. But as she did so, her eyes locked on mine, catching me clean off guard and making my heart slam into my ribcage. Blue promptly started choking on her drink, coughing like mad and I got out of my seat, worrying I'd just killed a fucking Vega before she managed to rein it in and Tory shot her an amused smile.

"What are you doing?" Francesca asked in confusion. *Good fucking question.*

I dropped my ass back onto my seat and focused on my friend in front of me, done with acting like a crazy person and absolutely done with looking at that girl.

The bar was pretty busy now and no one was paying us attention so I decided to force the topic of conversation at last. "Did you get any new information on the nest?"

Francesca frowned. "Yes...I'm almost certain it's Nymphs."

Relief washed through me. "That's good. Can you keep tabs on them for now? Darius needs to lay low for a while since he was almost caught."

"Well if we're lucky, Captain Hoskins will deal with them for us. I sent the information to him to see if he'll send a taskforce after them. But if not, we'll have to take them on together, all three of us," she said. "But you just need to relax tonight. Have some fun and we can talk about this in the morning," she said, cocking her head to the side. "We always have so much fun together."

"I'm not sure many people think I'm fun," I said with a breath of amusement.

"Well I do," she said, grinning. "I know you, Lance. I know you better than anyone."

Not true, but I didn't wanna be rude so I just took a swig of my drink. Francesca was a good friend and I trusted her, but there was a lot she didn't know about. Like my dark magic habit.

"Remember when we went on that field trip to Sunshine Bay in our senior year?" she asked.

"It rained the whole time," I said, nodding. "That's about all I remember of it. The endless rain."

"That's the only thing you remember?" she balked.

"Um...oh there was that Turtle Shifter you thought was just a normal turtle and he crawled into the girls' tent and saw you all getting changed," I laughed and she slapped my thigh.

"What about when we kissed?" she said, her cheeks reddening slightly.

"We kissed?" I frowned in confusion, not remembering that at all.

"*Yes*. Under those giant leaves which you said looked like Dragon dicks."

"Oh yeah," I chuckled as I remembered them. "They really did look like Dragon dicks."

"And then we kissed," she pressed and my features twisted as I tried to recall that part.

"Are you sure it was with me? Didn't you have a thing with Jessie Starhole that semester?"

"It wasn't Jessie fucking Starhole, it was you!" she snapped and I stared at her in shock at her outburst. "Don't you remember the Faeflies? And the way the sea was lapping at our feet? And that pod of glimmerlight jellyfish that were out in the water so it was all lit up in a thousand colours? And our lips tasted like the rain..."

"Um..." I scratched my jaw.

"Let me find the memory." She reached out to touch my temple but I caught hold of her wrist, not wanting her to feast on my memories tonight.

It was how Cyclopses recharged their power, and usually I gave her access to my old school memories, especially the ones where I won Pitball games, liking reliving those while she recharged her magic. But my head was fucked this week and I couldn't be sure I'd be able to keep out thoughts of Darcy Vega and let slip my nightmare of a secret to her.

"I remember now," I lied, placing her hand back in her lap. Still had zero memory though, which was weird considering I didn't drink back then.

She smiled at last and I guessed I'd dodged the bullet. "That was a fun trip."

I nodded vaguely, my gaze slipping back over her shoulder to Blue who was chatting with her friends. She was laughing, enjoying herself and seeming to exude purest energy from her flesh.

I'm thirsty. So fucking thirsty I should just go over there now and bite her.

There were a lot of people looking at the Vegas from around the bar, though they didn't seem to notice the attention they were garnering. I even caught a few people snapping subtle photos of them and some protective part of me wanted to shoot around the room, smash all of those assholes' Atlases and lay them at Darcy's feet. *Because that made total sense.*

Francesca leaned sideways to get back in my line of sight and I cleared my throat. "What are you looking at?" She glanced over her shoulder then her head snapped back around, her eyebrows shooting up. "Holy shit, is that the Vegas?"

"Yeah," I said, my throat tightening like a python was coiled around it. "Strange how inoffensive they seem, isn't it?"

"I wouldn't be fooled by that," she said. "I've arrested people who seem so small and innocent, you'd never suspect they could murder a whole family or cause destruction everywhere they went."

I nodded, knowing she was right and needing to keep my guard up because of it. "I'll never underestimate them."

"Good," she said. "We really can't afford to have some girls on the throne who don't know anything about Fae. The kingdom is already in enough trouble as it is," she murmured and I firmly agreed with that. "Oh no," she groaned suddenly, her gaze on the entrance and I followed it to where Washer was leading a line of professors into the bar - including my biggest fan, Ling Astrum.

"For fuck's sake," I muttered as they swept through the bar and Washer instantly spotted us.

"Franny!" he cried, hurrying over to hug her and she was practically pulled off her stool as he pressed her against his flowery shirt. "Oh how I've missed seeing your pert little...face around campus." He grinned, looking over her shoulder at me and winking.

I bristled, tugging her out of his arms. "Have a good evening, Brian," I said curtly and he gave me another wink.

"Don't mind me, I won't interrupt your little tête-à-tête," he said, though it sounded more like he said titty-tit. "I'm sure you're going to have a hard, firm talk tonight," he said as he wet his lips, his eyes dipping down my body for a second and I felt his Siren powers trying to push some lust into me, but I locked down my mental shields before he could get any hold over me. The guy was such a creep. I'd put him through a wall if it wasn't for the priority of keeping my damn job.

He headed off and Astrum shot me a scowl, making my jaw tighten before I lost sight of them as they moved to sit in a booth with the other professors.

My ears involuntarily picked up the conversation at the Vegas' table again and I kept my expression neutral as I listened.

"Washer is a total perve," Sofia whispered then giggled as if she shouldn't have said it.

"Is that why we have to wear bathing suits that barely cover our asses in his class?" Darcy asked, her nose wrinkling and making me want to cast an orb of water around Washer's head and watch while he drowned.

"I'd bet on it, chica," Diego Polaris laughed, nudging her in the ribs. *Did she ask you to touch her, fuck face?*

The bourbon was starting to make me irrational, but I quite liked this place in my head where the part of me trying to fight this wild possessiveness was now knocked out unconscious.

The Vegas and their friends seemed to be on a mission to get drunk as they ordered more and more drinks to the table and I had to fix my attention on Francesca for a while to stop her from noticing where my attention really wanted to be. She reached out, gripping my fingers and drawing my hand onto her knee as she leaned in closer to whisper to me.

"You look thirsty, Lance. Haven't you fed lately?" she asked, dropping her hand and leaving mine in place on her bare flesh. It would have been awkward to remove it straight away, but it felt odd putting my hands on her outside of a bed. And I really wasn't feeling a hook up tonight, though I didn't know why. She looked amazing, I just felt so...distracted.

Gah, fuck Blue and her fucking mind tricks. Why shouldn't I hook up with Francesca?

"Oh about that," I said as I realised I hadn't told her something. "I kinda claimed a new Source."

"You did?" she balked, anger colouring her features. "Who?"

"It's no big deal."

"But *I'm* your Source," she growled. "How's it not a big deal?"

"It's not personal, Francesca, I just claimed someone more powerful," I said with a shrug and her lips parted indignantly.

"But Vampires can have multiple Sources, you can just keep me too," she said, but somehow, I didn't find that idea very appealing.

"I know...it's just their power is so strong I don't think I'll ever really crave yours again. Not that there's anything wrong with yours. It's great. Just not...theirs." Damn, that was not tactful and her face said she was not pleased.

"Who is it?" she demanded in a hiss. "Darius wouldn't let you claim him officially even if he does let you feed occasionally."

"It's not Darius," I said, heat rising in my veins as I thought of who it was. Of how fucking good she tasted. How much I wanted to get out of my seat, go over there and drink from her right now in front of everyone to show them who she belonged to.

"Then who?" she bit out.

"Darcy Vega," I said lightly, trying to play it off with a shrug, but Francesca looked ready to decapitate me. I mean, yeah, she liked me biting her when we fucked but that wasn't a reason for me to keep her as a Source. And she knew she wasn't the only one I fed from either. That wasn't how it worked. I could have anyone I could catch, my Source just couldn't be bitten by another. So what was with the jealous look?

"Come on," she said, shaking her head in disbelief. "This is a joke. You're joking." Her lips quirked up as she prodded me in the chest, waiting for me to admit it was, but it wasn't so...

I shrugged again.

"I thought you liked biting me," she said, her voice full of some plea I didn't understand.

"I did," I said. *Shit, past tense.*

"Did?" she snagged onto that little slip. *Fuck.* "So my blood's not good enough for you anymore?"

"I didn't say that," I sighed. "I'm a Vampire, I have to claim the best Source available, it's my nature. And the Vegas are the most powerful Fae in our kingdom, how was I supposed to pass up on the opportunity to claim one?" Especially *that* one.

She pouted, looking away from me and I took the opportunity to slide my hand off of her knee.

"If you enjoy being bitten, you could always find another Vampire to claim you as a Source?" I suggested.

"I don't want another Vampire, Lance. I thought you..." she trailed off, downing her drink.

"I had to have her," I admitted, the words rolling from my tongue like a cardinal sin. "You don't understand what it's like to crave another Fae's power. It's how I'm made. And she's fucking made to tempt me. I mean, her *power* is made to tempt me," I backtracked quickly and she sighed.

"Fine, but you owe me," she muttered, turning her attention to the bartender to order us more drinks.

"Shots!" Diego announced, rising from his seat and drawing my eyes to him.

"Yes!" Sofia hooted, looking drunk already as she swayed in her seat.

Darcy and Tory laughed as Diego strode away to the bar, looking pretty half cut themselves. They looked so happy, it made me envy them. Their bond. Their joy. The fact that they didn't feel this constant weight driving down on their shoulders because they'd lost the other half of them. I'd give anything for one more night laughing with my sister.

"Oh no," Tory said suddenly, sinking low in her seat.

"What is it?" Darcy whispered and I followed her line of sight to the window.

Geraldine Grus was crossing the street with a paper bag in her grip and a peppy expression.

"Hide," Tory begged her friends, grabbing up a menu and burying her face in it.

I watched, intrigued as Darcy pulled her hair over her shoulders as if trying to hide the tell-tale blue in the ends.

"Just ignore her," Tory hissed and as Sofia raised a hand to wave, Tory took a swat at her with her menu.

"We can't," Darcy said with a pained expression.

You're too sweet for this world, Blue. Someone's going to eat you up. And it will most likely be me.

Unsurprisingly, their piss poor efforts didn't deter Geraldine who spotted them instantly and came prancing into the restaurant and rushed over to them. "Well bless my cream crackers! I thought you were staying at The Orb?"

"We changed our minds," Darcy said innocently and I ran my tongue over my canines. *If you don't like Grus, force her to leave.*

I was morbidly fascinated by her politeness. All freshmen turned into monsters eventually. This one though…her monster was hidden deep so I was really fucking curious to see her embrace it.

"Oh." Geraldine's confusion melted into a bright smile. "Well why didn't you call me?" She dropped into Diego's chair, placing a paper bag on the table. "You're going to *love* these, I just got them made."

She tipped the bag up and a pile of sparkly silver badges fell onto the table with the letters A.S.S inscribed on them, my keen eyesight picking out the word immediately. What in the love of f-

"Lance." Francesca snapped her fingers in front of my face and I blinked, clearing my throat as I paid her attention again. Shit, my mind was not in gear tonight. "Are you even listening?"

"No," I admitted. "Sorry, what were you saying?"

She started talking again but so did Blue and my ears chose for me as I concentrated on my Source.

"Um Geraldine," Darcy said gently as I kept my gaze firmly locked on Francesca's lips, not hearing a word leaving them.

"Yes?" Geraldine asked brightly.

"It's just...that acronym, it kinda spells *ass*."

A laugh tumbled from my chest and Francesca gaped at me.

"How's that funny? My colleague *died*, Lance," she said in horror.

"Right yeah, it was just how he died that was amusing," I tried to cover my ass.

"Being blasted to pieces in front of his family by a maniac?"

Great. He had to die horrifically, didn't he? Couldn't have died drowning in a whirlpool of Griffin shit. Selfish bastard.

"Er-" I drained my whiskey. "Another drink?"

"Sure," she said, eyeing me in confusion like she couldn't work out what was up with me tonight. That made two of us.

I noticed Diego by the bar, gathering up four bright green shots and spending a lot of time jiggling them between his hands as he arranged them in his grip. He was literally an air Elemental and could have used his magic to assist him easily, so this display was painful to watch. He eventually headed over to the table and I took a moment to order Francesca and I more drinks. My head was getting fuzzy now and I knew I should really sober up a bit, but I was enjoying the feeling of all my worries vanishing from my mind. Especially as the guilt was temporarily gone, switched right off and waiting to haunt me tomorrow. But right now, I was free. And I was using that as an excuse to watch Darcy Vega as much as I could get away with. It was like feeding a secret drug habit that no one could ever find out about.

Geraldine darted off out of the restaurant and I gave Francesca my undivided attention in a bid to make up for being completely absent with her all evening. It was far more difficult than I cared to admit, but I didn't let my eyes or ears stray to Blue again.

After a while, Francesca got a message and checked her Atlas, her brow dipping as she read the words. "Fuck," she hissed. "Captain Hoskins has denied my request to send a taskforce to investigate the suspected Nymph nest."

"What?" I growled in frustration. "Does that asshole not understand how serious this is?"

"He thinks I'm mistaken." Her lip curled in anger as she looked up at me. "The Nymphs are getting out of hand. There's more reports every day."

"I know," I muttered, tension knotting my muscles.

"It's all moving so fast. We should do something about it tonight."

She squeezed my arm.

"No. It's too soon. We have to wait," I said, thinking on this. Darius needed to lay low for a while, it was too soon to go on another hunt. Dammit, was her captain a fucking idiot? The threat they could pose was unimaginable.

"It will get out of control, Lance. It has to be tonight. I can't wait any longer," she pushed.

"That's not what we planned," I hissed. "If we try to kill them now we'll draw attention to ourselves."

Francesca's eyes suddenly slid over my shoulder and reflected in the glassy surface of them was a girl with blue-tipped hair right behind me.

I swung around with the speed of my Order, grabbing Darcy's arm before she could escape and yanking her closer as fear blossomed in her eyes.

"What did you hear?" I growled and she gasped, trying to prise my fingers off of her but there was no chance of that. The contact between us was like a flash of lightning crackling directly beneath my flesh and I inhaled sharply. *Holy fuck.*

"*Lance,*" Francesca warned, but a Vega was the last person on earth I could risk nosing into my business on this. She couldn't know the illegal shit I was up to; it could jeopardise everything Darius and I had worked for.

"I didn't hear anything," Darcy insisted and I released her as Francesca's' fingers dug into my leg.

I watched as Blue darted away, her heartbeat so loud it thumped like it lived on the inside of my skull even after she walked into the women's restroom.

"I'll deal with this," I told Francesca, getting to my feet and feeling the thrum of alcohol still burning in my chest.

"Just don't do anything stupid. Remember who she is," Francesca said, concern lacing her voice and I nodded as I walked to the restroom door and shoved it open.

Darcy was clinging to one of the basins and fear trickled into her face as she spotted me. I pushed the door shut, locking it tightly and feeling the pull of her yank on a vital piece of me. She started backing up and as she opened her mouth to yell for help, I stole the air from her throat, keeping her silent. Keeping her trapped. *This is what happens when you go looking for trouble, Blue. It finds you.*

Her heartbeat thundered in my ears as her spine hit the far wall and she raised her hands with a determined flare in her eyes. I allowed some air back into her throat, just enough to breathe a whisper.

"Stay back," she hissed.

"What did you hear?" I demanded, fury scoring through my veins. "*Tell me everything.*"

My Coercion ran over her and the truth immediately fell from her lips. "That you're planning to kill someone. And I know it's us. You want us out. You don't want me and my sister ruling Solaria, but you can't really think you'd get away with killing us in a restaurant do you?"

Well fuck me. That was quite the accusation.

Hatred poured from her eyes and I ground my teeth as I stared at this girl who thought I was out for her blood. And alright, I was. But only to drink it. I wasn't a fucking murderer. Though I guessed her thinking I was didn't do any harm. In fact, I quite liked her looking at me like I was capable of her complete and utter destruction. It made feel like one hell of a powerful asshole.

She raised her palms higher, her teeth bared and so much passion in her eyes that it made me think forbidden thoughts. I wondered what she'd looked like panting my name. My real name. No more sirs or Professors, just me and her fighting for dominance and seeing who could break the other first in my bed. The alcohol in my system made it hard to feel bad about that image in my head.

Fuck, if her hate makes me this savage, one drop of her love would corrupt me to my core.

I waved a hand and forced her arms to clamp to her sides, stopping her from casting any magic against me.

"That's it?" I asked, my tone softening.

"Yes," she spat. "Isn't that enough?"

I blew out a laugh, staring at her and desperately wanting to crawl inside her mind. I was half tempted to tell her the truth, but I was content with her despising me. It made our relationship far simpler. And if the Heirs didn't find a way to make them bow out of our world soon, then this girl was someone I'd have to teach for the next four years. But that seemed like a long time to harbour this craving for.

Damn, why did I have to feel this way about a girl I couldn't have? Maybe in another life I might have leaned into these impossible urges. But not this one.

"Go home, Blue." I unlocked the door, forcing myself to move, leaving her there and dropping the magic binding her in place as I left.

The air was thinner beyond that room and I felt myself draw in a breath that wasn't laced with her scent, her aura, and I instantly missed her. No, it. The blood. Not her. *By the stars…*

I returned to Francesca, muttering to her that the problem was dealt with.

Darcy appeared from the restroom, her jaw set and her chin raised as she walked past me without offering a glance my way. She re-joined her friends and I looked down at the new whiskey poured for me, snatching it up and knocking it back in one go, hoping the burn that surged down deep into my chest would drive away the ache living in me over that fucking girl.

"Let's go," I growled, tossing a wad of auras down on the bar to pay our bill and Francesca eyed me curiously as I led the way from the restaurant.

I didn't look at Darcy again. I was going to three wise monkeys the fuck out of this problem. Because I was officially going to see no Blue. Hear no Blue. Speak no star damned Blue.

DARIUS

CHAPTER SIXTEEN

I sat listening to the sound of the other Heirs laughing and joking between one another around the table we'd claimed for ourselves outside one of our favourite haunts in Tucana, but I wasn't really paying attention anymore.

No. My attention kept wavering back to the text Lance had sent me fifteen minutes ago and my gaze kept crawling along the street as I hunted for the subject of it with a mixture of hope and confusion.

I glanced at my Atlas for the hundredth time, not even sure what I was expecting from it as I read over his message again.

Lance:

The Vegas are in town tonight.

That was it. One dumb sentence. Yet it was all I could damn well think about as my gaze slid past the groups of girls trying to garner our attention in search of the only one whose interest I was looking to grab.

But she wasn't here. I was tempted to ask Lance where exactly he'd seen them, but I had no good reason to do that. Maybe I could convince the other Heirs to come searching for them with me, but I wasn't really looking to spend the night terrorising them. I just wanted to see *her*. By the stars, what was I even doing? I kept fantasising about her, dreaming about her and jerking off over imagined scenarios of me dominating her with every inch of my body and now I was hoping to see her on a night out like some desperate little fan boy hoping to try my luck. Who even was I right now?

Seth made some joke which had the others cracking up and I forced my attention back onto them as I grinned like I was in on it and drank a healthy measure of my beer.

But as if my wandering thoughts had summoned her, a sudden commotion and rush of movement drew my attention across the street to an alleyway as the Vega twins came tearing out of it looking utterly terrified for some reason.

A few people called out in surprise as they spotted them too and the rest of the Heirs swivelled in their chairs to take in the sight of them racing across the road.

I drank in Roxy's long legs clad in jeans that looked like they were little more than a second skin with a low cut cami that drew my attention straight to her tits as they bounced while she ran across the road, her hand locked with her sister's.

I lost sight of them as they joined the crowd in front of the bar and Seth flashed a malicious grin at the rest of us.

"Looks like our night just got a whole lot more interesting," he said.

"Why don't I invite them to join us?" Max offered with a dark grin as he got to his feet and I felt the allure of his Siren gifts flooding over me as he kicked them up to the top setting in preparation of luring a couple of Vegas our way.

My night had just taken a decided turn for the better, so I smiled into my drink as I took another mouthful and waited for my girl to come to me.

"Hell yes, this is going to be all the right kinds of fun," Caleb said as he leaned back in his chair and tried to get a look through the crowd to see where Max had gone. "I've been looking forward to seeing what Tory looks like when she cuts loose."

The upturn of my mood took a hit at his words as I realised I wasn't the only one of us looking forward to spending more time with my Vega, but I wasn't going to be letting him steal her from me without a fight.

Mine.

"Well I doubt she feels the same, seeing as she's clearly not a fan of the whole biting kink you go in for," I said, setting my drink down and draping my arm over the back of my chair.

I looked the epitome of relaxed, but the look I shot Caleb's way made it clear I wasn't going to be backing down over this easily.

The asshole raised his chin at the challenge and Seth chuckled.

"I wonder if Darcy's a real screamer in the sack?" he mused. "She has that deadly kind of calm about her which just promises to be all the right kinds of interesting when she's naked."

"I don't get the impression she's a fan of orgies," I pointed out because there hadn't been a single rumour of the Vegas hooking up with anyone since they'd arrived at the academy which was a pretty sure sign that they hadn't. Those kinds of secrets spread like wildfire around here, especially if they were to do with someone interesting like those girls.

"I can go monogamous," Seth said defensively. "One night at a time anyway. For the right Fae." His eyes slid to Cal who was tussling his hair with the hand which wasn't holding his drink and I had to fight a scowl at his dimples.

"The day you go monogamous will be the day I start sucking cock," Caleb joked and I laughed along while Seth pouted indignantly.

Before we could continue that riveting conversation, Max reappeared with two stunning princesses in tow, and we quickly shifted our attention onto checking them out.

Roxy was wearing a pair of killer heels which did all the right things for her legs and I couldn't help picture them wrapped around my head while I made a feast out of her which would make her scream so loud she'd lose her damn voice.

Seth made a show of pretending to be shocked by the arrival of the twins and we played along, acting as if we hadn't been expecting them as Max kept his arms around the two of them and herded them right up to our table.

"Look who I just found running from shadows," Max said, his arm dropping down to Roxy's waist and making a snarl build in my chest, but she shrugged him off before I let the noise escape me.

"We weren't running from shadows, someone was chasing us," Gwendalina said, eyeing Seth warily as he leaned closer like he was planning on sniffing her.

"You really must be scared if you thought we were a better option," he teased.

"They are. I can taste their fear," Max said enthusiastically. "And they were just about to tell me all about it."

Caleb released a breath of laughter, running a hand through his blonde hair and heaping on the charm as he gave the two girls flirtatious looks. *Stupid pretty boy.*

Max dropped back into the only free chair at the table and yanked Gwen down into his lap, pulling her against his chest as he leaned close to her ear and made sure she was well and truly locked in the grip of his Siren gifts.

"What was the worst part?" he asked, his gifts flooding over all of us and bringing a smile to my lips as I watched these powerful girls fall under his sway oh so easily.

"They kept making this horrible noise," Gwen replied. "Like a growl or a rattle..."

I leaned forward, my brows lifting with interest as looked from Gwen to Roxy, taking note of the genuine fear that was clinging to them and remembering how suddenly they'd burst out of that alleyway.

I glanced across the street cautiously, my mind going to the Nymph we'd seen close to town the other day as a growing sense of dread pooled in my gut. We still had damn good reason to think there was a nest close by and if I found out there really had been one of them trying to prey on Fae in town, then I was going to be seriously pissed at Lance for stopping our hunts.

"We aren't staying," Roxy said sharply, leaning forward to pull Gwen out of Max's grip, but that wasn't going to work for me.

"Hold on a moment," I said, snatching her wrist into my grasp and causing her to whip around and look at me instead of trying to pull her sister free of Max's hold.

She turned to meet my eyes with a glare and my heart leapt as I found her so close to me, the fire of her aura wrapping around me and drawing me closer as I breathed her in. She looked ready to bolt, to curse me out and to head off somewhere for the night which was anywhere other than here. But I didn't want that. Especially not if there really was a chance there had been a Nymph close by. But even if there wasn't, I still wanted her here, her lips close to mine, skin hot where I held her.

"What if we call a truce on our issues? For one night only," I offered, my fingers shifting on her wrist like I just couldn't get enough of the feeling of her flesh brushing mine.

"Why would we believe that?" she asked dismissively, but there was something in her eyes which almost seemed to challenge me to convince her.

"We just want a fun night," Caleb added, his gaze landing on the place where I still held Roxy's arm. "We can leave our political situation out of it."

"Our political situation?" Gwen echoed with a frown.

"Yeah, you know. The little issue we have with you rocking up out of nowhere to steal our birth right and upsetting the balance of power in the entire kingdom," Caleb teased.

"We don't want your stupid birth right," Roxy muttered bitterly before trying to jerk her hand out of my grip. But she was going to have to try harder than that if she expected to break free of a Dragon's strength and I smirked at her before tugging her right back.

She gasped as I knocked her off balance in her towering heels and in the next moment, her ass landed in my lap and the beast in me raised its head in contentment as I claimed the treasure I'd been aching for.

Mine.

Caleb met my gaze with an irritated scowl and I gave him a taunting grin as I wound an arm around her waist and repositioned her so that her ass was firmly seated on my crotch and her side pressed to my chest.

I laughed as she gripped my thigh in an attempt to balance herself better and her back arched against me at the sound, giving me even more ideas I shouldn't have been indulging in over her. But that was damn hard with her round ass currently grinding against my cock and giving it plenty of encouragement.

"Drink with us," I insisted, moving my mouth to her ear and feeling her shiver as my stubble grazed her neck. I waved at the bartender through the glass window beside us and the girl who had assigned herself as our personal bartender for the night nodded to show she'd seen me. "I swear we won't lay a finger on you unless you want us to," I added to Roxy in a low voice, letting my mouth graze against her ear for the briefest moment and loving the way I felt her body react to that despite her trying to hide it.

"Well I didn't want you to drag me into your lap but that didn't seem to stop you," she muttered, but she wasn't going anywhere and I wasn't holding her tight enough to force her to stay if she didn't want to.

I laughed again and she glanced up at me from beneath dark lashes like she wasn't sure what to make of me when I wasn't scowling and working to intimidate her.

I could feel Caleb's attention still on us and I suppressed a growl as he moved closer to us, reaching out to brush his fingers against her arm, despite the fact that I'd clearly beat him to claiming her tonight. *Asshole.*

"I'll even promise not to bite you tonight if you want?" he offered and I scowled at him while he flipped me off behind her back where no one else could see. I was going to punch him for that later.

Roxy looked across the table to her sister, the two of them entering into some kind of silent twin communication and I took the opportunity to slip my Atlas from my pocket and shoot Lance a quick message.

Darius:

The Vegas just showed up here looking terrified and saying something was chasing them. They said they heard a rattle too.

Lance:

Stay with them. Keep them safe and I'll scout the area with Francesca.

I wasn't going to complain about staying as close as I needed to to the girl currently perched on my ever more solid cock, so I slipped my Atlas back in my pocket and turned my attention back to the girls.

"I guess we could stay for one drink," Gwen said hesitantly as Max stroked her arm, his gifts pushing against all of us as he worked to make them feel amenable to the idea.

I shifted Roxy on my lap before she got a really clear idea about how much I wanted her to stay from the feeling of my cock trying to punch a hole in the ass of her jeans and she released a shaky breath as my skin brushed against hers.

"One drink then," she agreed finally and I relaxed as I got what I wanted just as easily as that.

The bartender appeared with a smile and a notepad ready to take our order and Seth perked up with a look in his eyes which promised he would be getting utterly shit faced tonight.

"Better make it a big one then if you'll only stay for one," Seth said as he ordered for all of us.

I leaned back in my chair, pulling Roxy closer so that I could steal a moment with her for myself and brushing her hair away from her ear so that I could speak to her alone.

She leaned in to listen to me and my grip on her waist shifted so that I could hold her even closer, the fingers of my other hand stroking against the bare skin of her shoulder where I'd smoothed her black hair aside.

"Do you want to tell me about what happened in that alley?" I asked, wondering if I really should have been worrying about Nymphs or not.

A shiver moved across her skin and I was filled with a protective kind of anger as I felt that echo of her fear.

"Is this the part where you laugh at us for falling for some prank you set up?" she asked. "Was that one of your friends back there? Did you get someone to send the messages too?"

I was tempted to push her for more information, but Lance and Francesca were already hunting for any signs of a Nymph and I didn't want to fall into the trap of arguing with her again while I was holding her like this. I just wanted to steal this moment from the universe and forget about all the shit that was hanging between us outside of right now.

"I don't need to recruit anyone to do my handy work," I replied dismissively, dropping the subject. "Maybe I'm concerned for your wellbeing."

She snorted in disbelief, shifting away so that she wasn't pressed against my chest anymore and I fought a sigh at how quickly I'd managed to fuck that up. Though as she was currently still in my arms, I had to think it wasn't a total lost cause yet, not that I had any real idea what I was trying to achieve with her here.

The bartender returned and I pulled a roll of auras from my pocket which was more than enough to cover our tab, pressing them into her hand as she finished laying the drinks out for us. We'd been planning to move on after this drink anyway and I was keen to get Roxy and her sister away from the place.

Roxy reached out to claim her drink, my gaze moving to her mouth as she lifted the glass to it and tipped the whole thing back, swallowing over and over until every last drop was gone.

"There you go," she announced. "One drink."

She pushed out of my lap so suddenly that for a moment all I could do was blink up at her in confusion before my brain caught up to what was happening and I reached out to pull her back again. But she stepped aside, offering me a mocking smile which made it more than clear how much she disliked me.

Darcy smirked as she got to her feet too, not even bothering to touch her drink. "See you later, guys," she agreed and the two of them turned to walk away.

Caleb shot into Roxy's way with his Vampire speed before she could actually escape and I was glad when she cut him a glare just as acidic as the one she'd offered me, even while he tried to throw the pretty boy charm on with his gleaming smile.

"I guess your word means shit then?" she demanded as he gave her throat a look which said he was thinking about biting her.

"No. I said I won't bite you tonight and I meant it," he promised, acting all alluring and pissing me the hell off as she hesitated. "I'm just wondering where you're going now?"

"Dancing," Roxy replied moving to brush past him, her hands landing on his waist for a moment as she nudged him aside and irritation flared through me at the contact. "You can always join us if you think you can keep up."

My anger grew as she offered him that invitation and I scowled at the two of them openly, wondering why she was so much more willing to fall for his bullshit than she was for mine.

Roxy gave Cal a flirtatious look and I ground my teeth before shoving to my feet the moment she was out of sight.

My fist slammed into his bicep as he turned to look at me and he barked a laugh as he shoved me in return.

"Come on, assholes, if the two of you waste time in a dick measuring contest then we'll lose them before you finish," Max said.

"Especially when Cal starts sobbing inconsolably," I added, making Seth laugh loudly while Caleb cursed me out.

We headed into the club after the twins and I looked around at the packed room, spotting them over by the bar with a couple of douchebags closing in on them.

"Me and Darius will go get the VIP table, you two go fetch the Vegas," Seth said, catching my arm as I made a move towards the bar and practically dragging me in the opposite direction.

"Get off of me," I growled but he didn't, leaving Max and Caleb to go get rid of the assholes closing in on my girl.

"No. You look about ready to start a bar fight and as fun as that might be, it would also be a whole scandal and my mom has said I can't go on my family moon march next week if I get wrapped up in any more scandals this month."

I gave in reluctantly, my gaze following the others as they cut off the men who had been introducing themselves to the girls and Seth tugged me into our VIP booth.

"Is this because of that story they ran about you peeing on that parking warden's car last week?" I asked, tearing my eyes from Roxy as I took my seat and trying not to give too much thought to what her and Cal were saying to one another. He was probably being all 'do you like my dimples?' and hopefully she was responding like 'no, they look like two buttholes on either side of your face.'

"I told you guys, I thought it was a lamppost," Seth huffed.

"It was parked on his drive, dude and it was the middle of the day."

"Well maybe if he doesn't like things being put on his car when he parks it, he shouldn't do it to me," Seth retorted, his indignation over that whole thing clearly still fresh.

"It was like fifty auras, why do you even care?"

"It's not about the money, it's about the principle of the thing. He told me to pay the fine and I told him to make me. He couldn't. So why the hell should I have to pay it? Are we Fae or field mice?" Seth shrugged, still maintaining his innocence on that basis.

I shook my head and glanced away, catching a glimpse of Roxy and Caleb through the crowd but it was so brief that I couldn't get a read on how it was going. On the one hand I wanted him to convince her to join us again, but on the other I didn't want her coming over here for his benefit.

"What do you think he's saying to convince them to come over here?" Seth asked. "He's probably just saying 'come on, I'll buy you a drink then you can be *my* drink.'"

"Roxy isn't into him biting her," I grunted.

"Yet," Seth said, rolling his eyes at me. "Think about it, he's grabbing her all the time, his mouth on her neck, pinning her up against things. It's only a matter of time before he's slipping more than his teeth into her-"

A growl escaped me and I shoved to my feet, done with waiting around for Caleb and Max to bring the girls to us. There was a good chance that there could be a Nymph hanging around here which meant I was supposed to be sticking close to the twins and that was exactly what I intended to do. In fact, I'd probably have to shove Caleb out of my way so that I could get closer and make sure he didn't accidentally put them in danger of having their magic stolen by a dark creature determined to destroy us all. He might even fall against a table and break his pretty nose. Doing so was basically me saving the whole of Solaria from the wrath of the creature in question though, so it was my duty to do it.

But as I looked across the top of the crowd to where they'd all been standing just a few moments ago, I only found Max and Caleb there, no sign of the twins at all.

I mouthed 'where are they?' to Max and he rolled his eyes before pointing to the dance floor.

Roxy and her sister were in the centre of the floor, arms in the air and bodies moving to the beat of the music as countless Fae closed in on them from all sides, some of them seeming to have realised who they were while a few guys just seemed interested in them for reasons of their own. Or reasons of their dicks.

No. No fucking way.

I shoved away from the table and strode across the room, sensing Seth on my heels as he joined me in my Vega hunt.

I made it to the dance floor and people backed away, giving us space as we strode through the crowd towards them.

I fell still as we found them there, my intentions to drag them back over to our table whether they liked it or not falling away as my gaze found the movements of Roxy's body and fixed on them instead.

Her eyes were closed, head tipped back and body moving to the seductive beat in a way that had me drawing closer automatically. I should have just been grabbing her and towing her away, but instead of doing that, my fingers brushed over her waist instead, the rough skin of my hands meeting the softness of her flesh beneath the hem of her shirt.

She turned her head to look around at me, her eyes fluttering open and surprise filled her gaze for a moment, but I just held her eye and tugged her closer.

Her blood red lips parted and I fully expected her to tell me to fuck off, but instead the barest hint of a smile tugged at the corner of her mouth and she inclined her head just a little as if to say *okay.*

I tugged her body against mine, tits pressing to me and damn near making me groan with longing before she slid her hands up my chest as we began to dance with one another.

My body fell into a rhythm with hers so naturally that I swear even my heart was pounding to the tune. Her chest brushed mine, fingers skimming up my neck as my hand fell to the round curve of her ass and I tugged her closer.

My gaze was on her mouth as the heat between us built in time with the movements of our bodies and our breaths mingled in the small space left dividing us. But just as I was starting to give serious consideration to an absolutely terrible idea, she turned in my arms, her ass pushing back into my crotch as she hooked one arm around the back of my neck.

A real growl escaped me then as she ground herself against me, making my cock swell and my thoughts scatter as I lost all sense of everything other than this fucking girl in my arms as we danced together.

I was vaguely aware of Seth dancing with Gwen beside us, but I couldn't tear my eyes from this perfect temptation in my arms.

It was hotter than any sex I could ever remember having and neither of us had removed so much as a single item of clothing.

Roxy kept dancing with her hand clasped around the back of my neck, the arch of her spine giving me a view down her shirt which I was having a damn hard time tearing my attention from. The fabric shifted and slipped across her skin, offering me the barest glimpse of her hardened nipples with every thump of the music and I licked my lips with the desire to suck on them.

My dick was definitely letting itself be known as she continued to grind herself against me and as much as I was enjoying that friction, I really needed to make some effort to control myself.

I grasped her hip and turned her around, the beast in me purring as she instantly looped her arms around my neck to draw me closer.

I didn't even know how many songs had played while we'd been dancing and I didn't care because I knew it wasn't enough. Not nearly enough.

My gaze met hers and the fire in her was enough to set me alight too as she tilted her chin up and bit down on that full bottom lip. My attention was instantly hooked on her mouth, our bodies still moving together in this hot, endless friction which was begging for some relief.

My resolve was snapping, all the reasons I had to pull away falling from my mind like flakes of snow trying to land on an inferno and I found myself leaning in, devouring the distance that parted us like I wanted to devour this beautiful creature in my arms.

I tightened my grip on her waist, letting her feel the throbbing press of my dick driving into her and making it more than clear what I wanted to spend the rest of the night doing to her. I didn't care if she was a Vega, a princess, the architect of my fall from power, none of that mattered. Because all there was in that moment was her and me and the press of the heavens above us driving us together like we might burn up in the fire which blazed between us if we didn't just dive into it now.

I slid a hand up her spine, moving it towards the back of her neck as I watched her mouth and prepared to claim it. Claim her. Claim everything that went with that choice, because it didn't even feel like a choice at all, more like an urgent need which demanded to be answered.

"Drink!" Caleb demanded suddenly from beside us, snapping the tension that had been building and destroying the moment before I could claim her in any of the ways I ached to.

Roxy turned away from me to accept the shot he was holding out for her and I took mine without once looking away from her face, tipping it down my throat and wishing something else was gracing my lips.

There was a question hanging between me and her. A want which we both felt and ached to satisfy. But there was a whole chasm full of reasons for us to deny that need too. Not that I gave a shit. Because every fibre of my being was screaming for me to claim her and make her mine with an urgency that made my head spin. I swear I could practically hear the universe holding its breath like there was so much hanging on the choice we made now. But before either of us could make it, Caleb interrupted again.

"Orion's looking for you," he said to me, pointing back over to the bar where I had to assume Lance was. "Something about an assignment you haven't handed in. I told him to chill the hell out and enjoy his drink but he gave me that look, you know the look where you're not sure if he's trying to set you alight with the power of thought alone or if he's just super constipated, so I said I'd tell you."

Roxy snorted a laugh, and as she looked away to search the crowd for Lance, the spell between us was broken.

I scrubbed a hand down my face, wondering what the hell I'd been thinking. The girl might have been hot. Scorching fucking hot and endlessly intoxicating. And I might have wanted to fuck her more than I think I'd ever wanted to fuck any girl I'd ever met. But she was a star damned *Vega*. And that meant me and her were over before we could ever even consider beginning.

"I guess I'd better see what he wants," I said, knowing that the moment I stepped away from here would be the moment this opportunity left us. I cast a final look at Roxy, not really knowing what I expected to find there but she seemed to have forgotten me already as she moved away to place her empty shot glass down on a table.

A growl rumbled through my chest and Caleb grinned widely, slapping me on the shoulder as I passed him and making me want to punch his fucking face all over again. No doubt Lance's appearance had made his fucking night. And it had definitely ruined mine.

ORION

CHAPTER SEVENTEEN

My right hand was locked so tightly in a fist, it was starting to shake. My gaze was riveted to two people on the dancefloor, and it was taking every ounce of willpower I had to remain standing there in favour of destroying the man touching Darcy Vega.

Seth Capella's hands were roaming all over her as they danced like there was no one else here but them. They were staring at each other, exchanging flirtatious smiles and their mouths were getting all too close all too many times.

Through the thump of the music and clamour of voices, it was difficult to focus on the words that passed between them, but I managed to catch a couple of sentences.

"Fuck being enemies, I wanna be your friend tonight," Seth purred·in her ear, his fingers twisting into the blue ends of her hair and making me spit a snarl.

Darcy laughed, clearly drunk as her fingers slid down his arm while his other hand dropped onto her ass, drawing her even closer and squeezing hard.

No.

"What kind of friends act like this?" she laughed again and he nuzzled the side of her head, a carnal look entering his eyes that made my canines sharpen.

All rational thought was exiting my mind until I was nothing but an animal about to attack. I knew in that second I was going to do it. I was going to shoot over there, tear Seth Capella off of her and make him bleed for touching her like that. She was my gir- *Source.*

"The best of friends," he answered with a wolfish grin and I took a step forward, but suddenly Darius was there with a scowl the size of a Dragon's tail, blocking my line of sight.

"Well?" he demanded irritably like I'd just punched him in the cock.

"Well what?" I sniped back and he frowned. "Oh right, yeah. We need to go hunting."

I gritted my teeth, crushing them to dust in my mouth as I forced my feet to move towards the exit, refusing to let myself look back. Darius walked stiffly at my side, seeming as pissed off as I did to be leaving and judging by how hard he'd been grinding himself against Tory Vega, I had to wonder if she was the reason. I glanced at my friend and caught him looking back.

"What?" he snapped and I looked away again.

"Nothing," I grunted. "I'm just in the mood to kill something."

"Same. Let's find the fucking Nymph and make it suffer." His eyes turned to reptilian slits and a group of guys in our way scarpered aside as they saw us coming.

We made it outside and Francesca nodded to me further up the road, beckoning us towards an alleyway there.

I uncurled my still clenched right hand, my knuckles white as I flexed them and brought magic to my fingertips. *Is she gonna go home with him? Is she gonna fuck him?*

She can't. He's a fucking Heir. The worst fucking Heir.

The urge to go back was rising in me and I had to force my legs to keep moving away from that nightclub. There was a Nymph out here somewhere, that was my priority. Not whether or not Darcy Vega chose to fuck an Heir. My heart thumped a painful tune in my chest, continuing its plea with me to go back. To stop her from making the most stupid decision of her life. She was too good for that Wolf asshole. Too sweet. He didn't deserve to get his hands on her flesh. I pictured her pinned beneath him and stopped dead in the street.

"Lance," Francesca hissed frantically as Darius glanced back at me. "I spotted it. It's gone this way." She pointed down the alley and my mind shifted back into gear.

I kept going, taking a breath to clear my head and trying to force all thoughts of her out. But she wouldn't leave.

A scream pitched through the air that made my blood chill and suddenly I was running, tearing along with Darius and Francesca into the alley behind the nightclub.

I put on a burst of Vampire speed, shooting down into the darkness and feeling the rattling suck of a Nymph's presence just before I saw it. Its hulking form was hunched over a girl on the ground, its probes in her back, the red glow of its eyes igniting the side of her face.

Geraldine Grus.

She looked unconscious and panic slashed through my chest as I took the switchblade from my pocket, removing the concealment spell so it grew to a large silver sword in my hand. I leapt forward and slammed it down into the Nymph's back with a surge of energy, aiming for its heart with one powerful strike but a shriek left the monster as it jerked aside before I could hit my target. *Shit*.

It swung around and I blasted a furious wave of air magic at it before it could lock my power down with its rattle and cursed as I realised how low on power I was running.

The Nymph's rattle filled my head and worked to shut down everything

359

I had and I snarled, running forward and stabbing my sword at its chest instead, using my speed to outmanoeuvre it this time and slamming it hard and deep into its heart.

The Nymph exploded into ash and shadows before my eyes and relief fell over me as I won the fight.

"Darius get out of here!" I barked at him, turning back to find him running up behind me.

"But-"

"No fucking buts," I snapped as I fell to my knees to try and heal Grus. "You can't be found at the scene of another attack. Even your father can't save you from this if the FIB find you again. Francesca get him out of here."

She grabbed his arm, obeying immediately and Darius swore as he stared at me before giving in to my glare and running back down the alley. I kept one hand pressed to Geraldine's back as I did my best to heal the holes carved into it by the Nymph and pulled my Atlas out with the other, dialling star-star-star.

"Stay with me, Grus," I barked.

"Babbling brooks, don't kill me you fantagoon," she mumbled before passing out again.

"Come on, wake up," I growled.

My magic poured out of me in wave after wave as I gave her everything I had left, fighting to keep her alive as the well inside me hollowed out and left me utterly drained. The wound had been deep and it still wasn't close to healed. She needed a special healer for an injury placed there by Nymph probes and she needed them fast. I couldn't do it myself but I was sure as fuck going to try.

"What's your emergency?" a woman answered.

"Nymph attack. Havenfire Street, Tucana," I barked. "Hurry."

"A team have been dispatched via stardust, they'll be with you in three…two…one. May the stars be with you." The call disconnected and I shot a warning message to the professor group chat I was a part of to ensure the students in town got rounded up ASAP. This Nymph might have been dealt with, but we still had a suspected nest close by and what was to say there weren't more of them on the hunt tonight?

I scooped Geraldine into my arms as she started to come round again, a breath of relief leaving me.

"Goldfish in a ganderbush," she mumbled, pawing at my chest. "What muscular beast has me in its grasp?"

I shot out of the alleyway, finding an ambulance there with paramedics spilling onto the street and rolling a stretcher towards me as I came to a halt. I laid Geraldine on it and her fingers curled around my arm.

"Where are my queens? Are they safe? Tell me my dear queens are safe from harm and I shall go into the stars' embrace without fear." She looked delirious, staring up at the sky like she really was about to die.

"What happened?" a paramedic demanded of me.

"A Nymph," I growled under my breath and his eyes widened in shock as he nodded, hurrying to attend her with his colleagues.

A shriek sounded from behind me and I glanced around, finding Marguerite Helebor there with a couple of dolled up junior girls while people started pouring out of the nightclub behind her. "Oh my stars! Geraldine Grus is dying!"

"Calm down," I barked. "No one's dy-" I tried, but she was already running into the nightclub, screaming out, "Geraldine Grus has just been attacked! They're saying she might die!"

For fuck's sake.

A crowd made up of mostly Zodiac Academy students and some professors was growing on the street and I backed up as Geraldine was cared for by the paramedics, my heart rate slowly coming down.

"Oh sweet mother, I am coming to you. My darling dote of a damselfly, how I've missed you," Geraldine said in a shuddering voice, passing out as one of the paramedics injected her with something. They lifted her into the back of the ambulance and some of them climbed in after her and pulled the door shut.

"You saved her life," one paramedic said to me. "It's a good thing you found her before her attacker could finish the job."

"I was only just powerful enough. I haven't got a drop of magic left," I muttered. There were too many witnesses to say more than that right now; it would cause a mass panic, but I knew it wouldn't be long before the report came out that this was a Nymph attack.

The paramedic moved away, giving me a line of sight into the crowd and my gaze latched onto Darcy. I was so starved, I moved before I was even aware of making the decision, colliding with her and driving my fangs into her neck.

She squealed in fright and I growled deeply as I drank the sweet nectar of her blood, shutting my eyes and enjoying every second of it. She felt connected to me by it, her spiking pulse seeming to thump within my own body and I relished the feeling of having her power in my grasp. I lost all sense of everything as I fell into the needs of my Order and the desire to devour this girl's magic. I wanted every last drop. I needed more of her. Everything.

She clawed at my arm and I enjoyed the contact, holding her firmly against my hip as my cock began to throb. I was in the middle of a crowd of students and this was the wrong fucking time to get turned on for so many reasons. But hell she tasted so good. And it was more than that, I had her in my arms again and I didn't want to let go. She was the summer sun after the longest winter of my life and all I wanted to do was bask in her glow. Especially after I'd seen Capella touching her. This girl didn't belong to him. I'd staked my claim and maybe that should have only been about her blood, but it was becoming clear to me that it was far more than that. I didn't want anyone but me getting this close to her. And I'd fight any rival I had to to keep it that way.

"*Hey,*" Tory snapped, shoving me roughly to try and force me off of her sister but I was in a frenzy and I couldn't stop. "That's enough!"

I released a growl in warning for her to back off, but then she shoved me with fire in her palms, the power behind the blast sending me staggering backwards and freeing Blue from my hold. My head was spinning with so much power I felt drunk and my breaths came heavily as I realised how much blood I'd just taken. Far too much.

There were two hand marks singed into my chest, my shirt smoking and my flesh reddened, and Tory looked ready to burn me alive if I took so much as a step closer to her sister again.

"You've had enough!" Tory snarled and I bared my fangs at the challenge in her voice.

"Maybe you want to donate to the cause then?" I snapped, but I was just trying to deflect from how much I wanted her sister, how every student close by had witnessed me go fully savage on Darcy Vega like I had no self control at all.

Caleb appeared, dropping an arm around Tory's shoulders and releasing a deep growl in the back of his throat. "You might want to rethink that statement, *Professor.*"

I stared at them when I really wanted to be looking at Darcy, but I feared if I did, I'd lunge at her again. And I wasn't sure I'd stop this time. *Fuck. What's wrong with me?*

I shook my head to try and clear it, taking a breath as I realised my magic reserves were full and I didn't need any more blood. This craving left in me wasn't anything to do with my power reserves. It was purely about the girl I could see glaring at me in the corner of my eye. I couldn't believe what I'd just done. I'd taken too much blood and it was wrong. It went against the Vampire Code.

I swallowed the lasting taste of her and finally glanced her way, finding so much hatred in her eyes it scolded me.

"I haven't been drained that low in a long time. I shouldn't have tried to take so much all at once," I muttered, wanting to apologise but not quite finding the right words beyond that statement.

"Well feel free to just steal all of mine then," Darcy spat icily, clutching her neck tighter. I had the urge to heal her, but knew if I tried to touch her again, she'd only recoil.

The ambulance pulled away and I glanced around, double checking Darius wasn't here and I was glad to find he'd listened to me for once. That was something anyway.

"Come on, I can drive you girls back in my car," I offered. I'd left my Faerrari parked at the Acrux Hotel when I'd last visited Tucana, opting to stardust home because I'd been too drunk to drive. But I hadn't had any magical drinks tonight, so I'd healed myself of the effects of the whiskey I'd consumed before coming to get Darius from the nightclub.

Tory's lip curled back as she glared at me with poison in her gaze.

"We're not going anywhere alone with you," Darcy said bitterly, distrust in her eyes.

"Don't be ridiculous," I snapped, stepping forward to get hold of her. I'd protect her tonight whether she liked it or not.

Tory moved to intercept me and Caleb joined her too like a prime asshole.

"You don't fucking touch her again," Tory growled.

I narrowed my eyes at her, about to object, but as my gaze slid to Darcy over her shoulder and I saw the wall in her eyes that told me to get fucked, I knew I wasn't going to win this fight.

"*Bastard*," Darcy hissed at me, looking woozy. Shit, I needed to heal her. And I could get her a blood replenishing potion back at the academy.

"Come on, girls. The bus is gonna leave soon," Caleb said, tugging Tory after him but she dug her heels in, waiting for Darcy.

I opened my mouth to try and find the words that would convince Blue to stay with me, but she walked straight past me with her cheek turned and Tory threw me one more filthy look before they all headed down the street to the bus stop where mountains of students were gathering. Professors were among them and I knew they were safe enough in numbers, but my feet were still rooted to the pavement as I watched Darcy leave.

You drank way too much. You have to get a grip. How are you going to keep feeding from her if you act like a monster every time your teeth are in her?

I'd never had this problem before. The only thing I could compare it to was when my magic had been Awakened and my Order had Emerged. That first feed had made me feel like a ravenous beast with a bottomless stomach, and yet it still didn't have a pinch on what it was like to feed from Blue.

Caleb led Tory and Darcy past the queue straight onto the bus and my hackles rose as they joined Max and Seth on the back seats. And as Seth pulled Darcy close to him and nuzzled against her cheek, that feral animal in me awoke once more.

I took out my Atlas and shot an update to Francesca, anxiously scoring my fingers through my hair.

Just as the bus pulled away and rounded a corner, the FIB appeared on the street and I was immediately surrounded by three agents with dark frowns on their faces.

"Lance Orion, you need to come down to the station and make a statement," Captain Hoskins said and I sighed, knowing it was going to be a long ass night.

I agreed and as I was stardusted away to the precinct, my heart was tugged in another direction, nearly forcing the stars to guide me elsewhere. But the captain ensured I made it to where he wanted to take me and I made a silent prayer to the stars that Darcy wouldn't end up in Seth Capella's bed tonight. Because I wasn't sure I could control the demon in me who'd want his head for that.

DARIUS

CHAPTER EIGHTEEN

66"**M**y source told me they're up in a house on the hills just outside of town," Francesca told me as we ran together down side streets and back alleys and my pulse raced with the thrill of the fight.

We made it to the edge of the town and paused in the shadow of a tall building there, looking out towards the rolling hills beyond.

"Just a sec, I'll find the coordinates." Francesca muttered, tapping away on her Atlas.

I let my head fall back against the brick wall behind me, trying to take long breaths of the cool air to still the spinning in my skull. Fighting Nymphs while half cut wasn't the best idea I'd had in my life and even though I'd been healing myself of the effects of the alcohol I'd consumed on and off ever since I'd left the bar, it still wasn't entirely gone from my system yet. I really should have known better than to consume so many magical drinks for this very reason but when Seth bought a round of shots it was damn near impossible to refuse him.

I unbuttoned the front of my shirt, letting the air caress my heated skin and concentrating on that sensation as I forced my thoughts into line.

Francesca cleared her throat and I cracked an eye open to look at her as she held out her Atlas for me to see. Her cheeks pinked as she glanced down at my bare chest for a moment but I ignored the attention, focusing on the marker she'd placed on a farmhouse out there in the dark.

"The mountain rise is just beyond there," I said, easily picking out the location from all the time I'd spent studying maps and arial photographs of the kingdom. Part of my training to become one of the next leaders of Solaria included me knowing each and every part of the land we were destined to rule over. It was just one in the list of thousands of pieces of knowledge which the Vegas could never hope to learn the way we had, and yet another reason why they'd never be capable of ruling.

"Yeah and the trails through the pass head north towards the land where we've long suspected the Nymphs have their bigger nests," she agreed. "It's a pretty good place for them to set themselves up."

"It's a good few miles to get up there, we can take my bike," I said as I considered it. It was tempting to shift and fly but if we wanted to remain inconspicuous then it was better if I stayed in my Fae form this close to the town.

"I parked it outside the club-"

"I'll go grab it for you," Francesca offered. "No one will question me, but they were rounding up the students and bussing them back to the academy last I heard from Lance so it's probably best you don't go in case they try to make you head back too."

I suppressed a sigh as I took the key from my pocket, holding it out for her. I didn't really want anyone else driving my bike, but her argument made sense and with a bit of luck she might even be able to pick up Lance along the way.

Francesca darted away back down the alley in the direction we'd come and I quickly shot Lance a message.

Darius:

Everything good your end?

Lance:

Yeah. Grus should be fine. She's being healed then she'll be taken to the Uranus Infirmary. Nova has specifically requested to speak with me once I'm done with the FIB though, so I'll have to just see you tomorrow. Are you heading back to your dorm now?

I read over his words, knowing that would be the sensible thing to do, but as I looked out into the darkness beyond the town, the fire in my veins seemed to light with the desire to head out there and track down the monsters who were encroaching on my people.

Lance wouldn't like it but he was my Guardian, not my keeper. Besides, I'd be done with this and back in my bed before he'd ever find out a thing about it.

Darius:

I will soon. See you tomorrow.

I flicked my Atlas onto silent, knowing he'd probably read between the lines of my words and be all kinds of pissed at me for heading out without him. But he didn't know where we were going and he was stuck between Nova and the FIB anyway, so he wouldn't be able to stop me anyway.

The roar of my bike's engine caught my ear as I pushed the Atlas back into my pocket and I pressed my fingers to my temple again, using some more healing magic to banish the dizziness from my skull.

Francesca pulled up beside me and I less than subtly pushed her to the back of the bike before climbing on to drive myself. I cast a silencing bubble around us to hide the sound of the engine as Francesca shifted behind me like she was trying to figure out how she was supposed to stay on the back of the bike without falling off.

She muttered a low apology as I revved the engine before hesitantly winding her arms around my waist and the moment she was holding on, I took off.

The bike tore out into the night and I left the headlights off while using my Dragon eyesight to pick out more details in the terrain than I could with my Fae eyes.

The wind whipped around us and helped banish the clinging effects of the booze from my flesh as it woke me up and my adrenaline began to rise at the prospect of the coming fight.

It took us a little under half an hour to make it out to the farmhouse Francesca had pointed out and I parked in the cover of some trees before cutting the engine and climbing off of the bike.

"Nice ride," Francesca commented, looking at my bike as she took the helmet from her head and hung it from the handlebars. "I might have to get myself one of those."

"It's a limited edition," I muttered. "They only made thirty of them."

"Oh..."

I walked away before she could waste any more of my time with small talk, raising my hands and drawing the shadows to me as I worked to conceal myself in the darkness. Luckily the moon was hidden beyond the clouds tonight and it was easy enough to hide myself from any prying eyes as I approached the dark farmhouse.

Francesca hurried to my side, my instincts prickling to tell me she was there, though as I looked her way I could see nothing but shadow either.

I wished I had my hatchet with me, but I was more than capable of matching these monsters with magic and my Order form anyway.

My heart beat harder as we made it to the farmhouse and I led the way to the front door, reaching out with my power to try and sense any traps or magical locks in place, but there was none.

I stepped over the threshold and paused in the dark, cold room, casting an enhancement spell to draw any sounds to me from close by. There was a repetitive drip coming from one of the rooms upstairs and the faint scurrying of little claws against wood made me think there were rats living in the walls, but that was it. The place seemed abandoned.

"I'll check it out to make sure," Francesca's voice came from beside me and I muttered my agreement.

"I'll circle the house and look for any signs of where they might have gone," I replied before stomping back out into the crisp night air.

I made a quick circuit of the building while using magic to hunt for anything I could along the way, but there was no taste of power on the air. Chances were if there had been Nymphs here then they didn't have any magic anyway. And even if they had managed to murder some innocent Fae to steal some, they wouldn't have the training required to create anything as subtle as a trap for me.

I huffed in frustration as I failed to find anything outside, stopping beneath the shadow of the closest mountain which rose up beyond the rear of the house. There were more like it to the north, a whole belt of monstrous mountains which I had flown across more than once in my Dragon form. It was a beautiful, merciless part of Solaria and it was utterly uninhabited due to the ferocious snowstorms which plagued it. Uninhabited by Fae anyway.

"There was nothing inside," Francesca's voice almost made me flinch and I turned towards the source of it, finding her standing there, her concealment spells abandoned. I guessed she'd used her psychic abilities from her Cyclops form to figure out where I was, and I dropped the concealment spells around me so that we could talk.

"Can you sense anything out here? Any trace of where they might have gone?"

Francesca hummed in concentration and a moment later she shifted, her two eyes merging into one big eye which dominated the centre of her forehead.

I cursed as the force of her gifts struck against my mental shields, a wave of nausea passing over me before I managed to lock my mind up as tight as a fortress to keep the effects of her psychic abilities fully out of my head.

It took her a few minutes but she suddenly raised a hand, pointing towards the mountains as she strode away from me and I followed close behind.

We made it to a dirt path at the foot of the mountain which headed towards the pass and she dropped into a crouch, brushing her fingers against the mud before straightening again.

"Something with a complex mind passed through here several hours ago," she announced. "Several of them...I'd say six if I were pressed. It could have been animals but the only things with a brain big enough to leave these kinds of psychic echoes don't live around here. Maybe Heylic Wolves or Tangarian Moose but it's pretty far south for either of those. Ghost Hounds don't travel in groups this large, so I'd place money on it either being a group of Fae or-"

"Nymphs," I finished for her in a growl. "If it's been a few hours then we aren't going to be able to catch up to them on foot and my bike won't be able to cope with that path."

Francesca eyed the rocky dirt track like she wanted to protest that claim, but it was clear from the sharp flints and thick mud that a super bike wasn't going to make it far up the mountain pass.

"We're far enough from the town now," I pointed out, glancing over my shoulder at the glimmering lights of Tucana in the distance. "I can shift."

"Okay...so how am I going to keep up, could you carry me? Or maybe I could ride on-"

"Dragons are not pack mules," I snarled in an angry bark which my

372

father would have been damn proud of. His laws on Dragons not allowing other Fae to ride them were more than clear enough and Lance was the only one I'd ever break that law for, and even then I'd never be letting anyone know about it.

Francesca stumbled back in the face of my anger and she almost fell on her ass as she tripped over her own feet. "Sorry," she gasped. "I know that. I didn't mean...It's probably best if we just leave hunting them until-"

"You wanna do something useful?" I asked her as I shrugged out of my unbuttoned shirt and unbuckled my belt.

Francesca's eyes fell to the movements of my hands for a moment before she snapped her gaze back up to meet mine. "What?" she breathed.

"Take my clothes and put them by my bike. I assume you can get yourself out of here without it?"

Her lips popped open like a goldfish, and I could tell she didn't much like me telling her what to do, but as I dropped my jeans and kicked off my shoes, she seemed to be distracted by my cock and didn't protest fast enough to stop me from tossing my shit into her arms.

"I'll get Lance to let you know how I got on when it's done," I added.

Francesca's eyes widened indignantly but I turned away from her and shifted before I had to endure any attempts to change my mind.

My enormous golden Dragon burst from my flesh and I leapt into the sky while the shift was still taking place, my wings beating hard as I raced up towards the clouds.

I flew above the mountain pass, my wings carving through the frigid air as I ate up the distance and I relished the feeling of my Dragon fire flooding my body.

Further and further the pass crept up into the mountains and I had to bank hard between sheer rock faces and narrow crevices to make sure I could keep my gaze fixed on the trail below.

Hours passed me by but still I flew on, determination burning through me as hot as my Dragon fire.

Finally, as I was soaring between two behemoth mountains and beginning to give up hope of finding anything out here in this dark wasteland, movement caught my eye from below.

Fire burned a trail up my throat as I spotted the Nymphs racing across the ground beneath me. Six of them, just like Francesca had thought. And better than that, one of them was limping.

A roar bellowed from my lips as I let them know their death had come for them and they cried out in furious shrieks and rattling death calls which sent an ache through my bones as they fought to disable me.

But with my Dragon blazing with power and my inner beast on full display, I was easily able to shake off the pull of their debilitating power and as I roared again, a torrent of Dragon fire burst from my jaw.

The Nymphs shrieked and screamed as I circled around them, fire raining down from the heavens to consume them without mercy. But I was no heavenly creature sent forth to do good work for some supreme lord, I was a beast built of wrath and hatred, moulded into the image of a man I despised and full of so much anger that it was enough to set the whole world on fire.

Smoke and shadows billowed up to me from below as the Nymphs were destroyed and I roared my triumph to the stars whose knowing gaze was always watching.

A metallic glint caught my eye as I wheeled around above the area where the Nymphs had been and I tucked my wings tight to my body as I dove toward the ground to check it out.

My claws dug deep into the mud as I landed in the ring of charred earth where my fire had destroyed the Nymphs and I huffed out a lungful of smoke as I looked down and found the necklace we'd seen that limping fucker wearing before.

I could taste dark magic and shadows writhing around it and I hated to think what foul purpose these creatures had for coveting such things.

I drew in a deep breath then bellowed a roar filled with the fury of Dragon fire directly down on the necklace, blasting it with all I had and hearing the echoes of screams raking through my ears as it was destroyed.

When the flames finally burned out, nothing remained on the ground and the shadows were slipping away like ants scurrying from a flooded nest.

I made certain that nothing of it remained then took off once more, carrying on up the mountain trail, bloodlust fuelling my actions as I flew on and took up the hunt. Because those Nymphs hadn't been aimlessly running into the mountains - they'd had a destination in mind. And that could only mean one thing. Out here somewhere were more and more of them. Perhaps even the mother nest we'd feared was out here for so long. And I was on the scent.

I beat my wings hard and roared with all the fury I possessed as I let them know I was coming for them and hoped they were trembling in fear at the prospect.

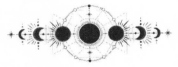

Dawn began to crest the horizon by the time I gave up my hunt and headed back to the farmhouse where I'd abandoned Francesca.

I was dog tired, my wings flapping like they were weighted with lead as I took every opportunity I could to glide rather than beat them.

I hadn't found anything else in the mountains. One trail splitting into another and another until there were far too many for me to track and I was flying through snowstorms and losing all visibility anyway.

I was irritated by my failure but pleased to have destroyed the six Nymphs who had been trying to flee at least. I could only hope that now they might think twice about coming close to Tucana again too.

I landed heavily in the clearing beside the trees where I'd abandoned my bike and shifted back into my Fae form with a sigh of relief escaping me and thoughts of my bed drawing me on.

I found my clothes neatly folded on top of my bike and dragged them back on, lacing my shoes just as my Atlas began to ring.

I answered it without looking at the ID, knowing Lance would be all kinds of pissed at me right about now for pulling a disappearing act and going after the Nymphs alone.

"I'm fine, stop worrying," I said distractedly, rubbing at my eyes in an attempt to make myself wake up a little more.

"I'm not certain why you think I would be concerned for your welfare, but I assume it is because you are already aware that it is in jeopardy," my Father's voice bit against my ears like the crack of a whip and I cursed myself for not checking the damn caller ID as I swallowed the words which came to mind and forced myself to consider them better.

"Sorry, Father, I thought Lance was calling me. You know how he can be because of the bond."

"Hmm."

That was it. All he offered me, and my skin prickled at the implications of that one simple sound.

"Is there something you needed from me?" I asked.

"You will come home now. You and I need to have a conversation."

Dread pooled within me and my grip tightened on my Atlas, but that was all he offered me before the line went dead.

Fuck.

I pulled up Lance's number, wanting to check in with him and see if there was any light he could shed on why Lionel Acrux wanted to see me so damn desperately. But before I could even hit call, my fucking Atlas flashed with a battery warning and the damn thing died on me.

I swore as I pressed the heels of my hands into my eyes and tried to figure out why the fuck my father wanted to see me and what the hell I'd done to piss him off now. But my mind was just coming up blank, offering me nothing and I knew I couldn't keep him waiting any longer or I'd only make it worse on myself.

I kicked my leg over my bike and sat down on it heavily before pulling a pouch of stardust from my pocket and tossing it over me, bringing the bike with me as I was wrenched through the sky to Acrux Manor.

I started the bike up as the men on the gates saw me and swung them open to let me in and I tore up the gravel drive at full speed with my mind still racing as to what this was about.

I parked up and strode to the door, wrenching it open before Jenkins could manage and cutting a dry look at the butler as he scowled at me.

"Lord Acrux awaits your attendance in his office," he said, his eyes lighting with the kind of glee I'd come to associate with my father's fists landing against my flesh.

I didn't bother to reply, taking off up the stairs and trying not to cringe at the fact that I was showing up here in last night's dirty clothes with bags beneath my eyes from my sleepless night and fatigue hanging heavily over me.

I knocked on the door as I reached it and my father's clipped voice came in reply.

"Enter."

I pushed the door open and stepped inside, keeping my chin high as I crossed the threshold and closed it behind me once more.

Father sat behind his desk, his suit crisp and blonde hair perfectly styled despite the fact that the clock said it wasn't even six yet.

His gaze roamed over my dishevelled shirt and unkempt appearance with distaste before he slowly reached for his Atlas and began to read from it.

"Is there love in the Heir for our returned Princesses?"

My heart plummeted as I realised what this was and he continued to read aloud from the article on his Atlas without a flicker of emotion on his cold face.

"Darius Acrux seemed more than enamoured with the beautiful daughter of the Savage King last night as he wrapped his arms around her and danced provocatively with her for the entire world to see. Members of the public who witnessed the scene of seductive dancing and unbridled lust said he seemed entranced by the girl in his arms and made his intentions to claim her fully clear by growling like a beast at anyone who drew close to them."

The television behind his desk flicked to life and I fought a cringe at the sight of countless images and videos of me dancing with Roxy, our bodies pressed together, eyes fixed on one another, hands roaming, lust burning right out of the screen. My blood heated just from looking at them and I couldn't help but think of how fucking good she'd felt pressed against me like that even as I fought to stamp down any reaction I had to seeing those images.

Father placed the Atlas down with a sharp click and I caught sight of one of the most provocative images of the two of us enlarged on the screen of the device.

"The article goes on to detail how Seth Capella was equally keen to get to know her sister better. Then there are photographs of Caleb Altair with his hands all over this one after you apparently 'left in a hurry.' It seems Roxanya was happy enough to trade your attentions for his the moment you were gone."

A growl fought to rumble its way out of my chest as I was gifted a look at images of Caleb dancing with my girl after I'd left and rage flooded through my skin. Though as I looked at them it was clear things hadn't gotten as heated between the two of them as they'd been with me and her.

Father switched the images to a series of Seth and Gwen as he looked about five seconds from fucking her right there on the dance floor and I was at least a little relieved to see that I wasn't the only one caught up in this damn scandal.

What the hell had we been thinking doing that in public where anyone could photograph us and sell it to the highest bidder? I should have known that this would happen and been prepared for this confrontation with my father at the very least.

"Though I suppose your behaviour is preferable to the things Max Rigel got up to," Father added with a slight curl of his upper lip.

The images changed again and I really had to fight my surprise as I caught sight of Max standing on the bar with his shirt off and the navy scales of his Siren Order coating his dark skin. He had his pants unbuckled and his cock in his hand as he used his water magic to make it rain over himself like he was taking part in a porn shoot.

I wasn't sure if I'd left before that or if I'd just been so fixed on Roxy Vega that I'd failed to notice it, but I cleared my throat uncomfortably as I forced my gaze back onto my father.

"We all had rather a lot to drink," I said in explanation but I knew it was a pathetic excuse that wouldn't fly with him for one moment. We weren't idiots. We knew what it was to be constantly scrutinised in the public eye and we'd had more than enough training on our behaviour in public to know better than to get wasted and let our behaviour get out of hand like that.

Silence rang between us for so long that it was all I could do not to fidget.

"Did you fuck her?" my father asked, his finger skimming over the photograph of me and Roxy, brushing against the curves of her body in a considered caress that made my hackles raise. "Did you at least let her feel the full power of a Dragon between her thighs and the dominance of our kind bending her to submit to your will? Did you take her body and use it like the beast you were born to be and force her to understand what it is to be owned by the king of all Orders?"

"We were just dancing," I ground out, hating the way he was talking about her and the lust filled look in his eyes which went with his words.

"So you're telling me you had that girl panting for you like that and you didn't even make use of her willing body? You didn't take the opportunity to use her like the disposable creature she is and show her exactly what position she is good for in this kingdom?"

"And what position is that?" I snarled, the Dragon in me raising its head with a rage I wasn't even sure I fully understood. But the longer he kept speaking about her like that, the more urgently I felt the need to rip his head from his shoulders rippling through my body.

"Well if she's lucky then she might make a good whore for the Fire Heir to fuck. You know it wasn't so long ago that the rulers of this kingdom used to keep such pets - pretty, useless little Fae who were only good for one thing kept close to their more powerful counterparts so that they could provide pleasures of the flesh whenever it was wanted. Perhaps when you finish breaking the Vega twins you and the other Heirs could make use of them like that. Show the kingdom time and again that the only thing the daughters of the Savage King are good for is servicing their betters."

Bile stuck to the back of my throat at the gross reality of his words. It wasn't the first time I'd heard him wax lyrical about the ways the kings and queens of old had run Solaria and I knew if he had his way we would return to many of those outdated and fucked up practices.

He'd be in favour of keeping power slaves, stopping inter-Order relationships and of course he'd be all for having a harem of pretty, vapid girls to service his cock alongside his wife. He'd been cheating on my mother for years even if he had managed to keep most of his sordid affairs out of the press. She cheated on him too, though it was only ever with men who he wanted some kind of political alliance with and as much as I didn't like to give much thought to that, Lance and I had long since concluded that she likely did it under Father's encouragement.

But Roxanya Vega and her sister were not and never would be the kinds of girls who could be forced into that kind of position even if he really did want them to be. They were forged in fire and ice with the determination of a hurricane and the strength of the earth beneath our feet. Making them bow was never going to be as easy as he kept making out it would be. And even the idea of me using Roxanya for my own personal whore was laughable.

"I didn't fuck her," I snapped, not wanting to hear any more of his lecherous words about her.

"So where were you all night then?" he demanded. "Because the scandal of the Grus girl's attack has also broken and if Lance was on the scene then I have to assume you were close by too."

"He told me to leave before anyone saw me," I admitted. "Seeing as the FIB already tried to arrest me once, it seemed like the better option for me to leave before they arrived at the scene of another attack and found me there too."

"Well I suppose you aren't entirely useless then," Father mused, leaning back in his chair and stacking his hands over his chest as he fell into silent thought.

I resisted the urge to shift uncomfortably before him, remaining still and unwavering as I waited him out.

"So what you are telling me is that not only are the Vega twins still very much enrolled at Zodiac Academy, but that rather than working to get rid of them as I tasked you to do, you spent the night dry humping one of them in front of an entire room of witnesses for...*fun?*"

I cringed at the word but what could I say? I hadn't done a single thing to Roxy since the last time I'd been here at his mercy. I couldn't even really say why not. I just hadn't wanted to bow to his will over yet another thing. I'd wanted to figure this out and fix it in my own way without having to just blindly bow to his rule. And yeah, if I was honest last night had been about more than just me keeping her close in case there were any Nymphs lurking nearby. I'd wanted to be close to her for my own reasons. I'd felt my skin burn in her presence and had felt more awake, more alive than I had in a long damn time while I held her in my arms.

I hadn't wanted to fuck her because of the twisted reasons my father had hoped I might have done. I'd just wanted her. Plain and simple. But that was beyond foolish of me and I knew now that I was going to pay the price for giving in to my selfish desires. I didn't just get to find a girl I wanted and have her. Not in any real way. I had a fiancé who I would be forced to marry and even if there was some miraculous way around that for me, it would only come in me happening to find an elusive purebred Dragon girl. And as far as I knew, there wasn't one of those anywhere in Solaria or in any of the other kingdoms - I'd checked. Even if there was some skewed version of my reality where I could have picked a girl I wanted for myself, there was one girl it could never be no matter the circumstances and that was a Vega.

It didn't matter if I watched her and hungered for her and lived for the moments when I captured her attention and she brought me to life with her sharp tongue and total lack of tolerance for my bullshit. Because she was a princess, the Heir to the Savage King and no matter what I wanted with her, I couldn't have it. Even if she turned out to be a Dragon, I still couldn't have it.

"I see." Father turned off the screen behind him but left the one of me and Roxy dancing together alight on his Atlas. He reached over to the other side of his desk and pressed a button there which I knew would call Jenkins and I had to fight against the urge to ask why he was calling on the old butler right now.

Silence stretched between us and though my throat burned with a hundred excuses or apologies, the look in his eye said none of them would help with this at all so I forced myself to remain still and silent where I was.

When the door finally opened again, my heart sank like a stone in my chest and I couldn't help but lurch forward as Jenkins showed Xavier into the room with us. He was in a pair of black sweatpants and a white t-shirt and he looked like he'd been dragged straight from his bed to attend this meeting, his eyes blurring with sleep and dark hair dishevelled.

The door clicked shut as the old bastard of a butler slipped back out again with amusement touching his lips and a snarl echoed through the room as I moved to stand between my brother and my father.

"Why is Xavier here?" I demanded, ignoring the way my brother caught my elbow and tried to tug me back again.

I wasn't going to be moving a damn inch. I'd take five times my father's fury over letting him suffer a moment of it.

Father watched the two of us without saying a word, his finger tapping on the solid wood of the desk before him like he was thinking about what best way he could punish us.

"Xavier has nothing to do with this," I ground out, unable to hold my tongue. "I get it. I fucked up. Punish me - do whatever you have to. But leave him out of it. It's not his fault that I did this."

Father pushed to his feet slowly, lifting the Atlas with him as he did so and looking down at the photograph.

"I haven't heard any reports on your efforts to rid us of the Vega problem since the last time we spoke," he said slowly, placing the Atlas down and leaning it against the lamp on his desk so that the photograph was aimed our way. "And now I see this, I have to assume I know why."

"It's nothing," I protested, grasping at straws as I tried to cover for why I'd been denying him. "Like you said, I just wanted to fuck her. Let her see what it was like to be owned by a Dragon and then toss her away so she knew how little she meant to me. It was a dumb idea. I'll just-"

Father flicked his fingers at me and I flinched as fire magic flared through my skin, but it wasn't any use against the subtle spell he cast to block off my airway.

I gritted my teeth as my lungs tightened with the feeling of the oxygen being stolen from them and he leaned back against his desk, folding his arms as he watched me impassively.

The desire to strike at him with my own magic was like a roaring monster inside my own mind, but my fear for my brother and my understanding of my father's power held me in check.

If I struck at him, then all bets would be off. Whatever he was planning right now would be a thousand times worse if he felt the true need to crush any ideas of rebellion from me.

My fists bunched at my sides as my lungs began to burn and black spots sprang to life before my eyes.

I stayed on my feet for as long as I could before my vision darkened to the point of me almost blacking out and I crashed to my knees with my lungs constricting painfully.

Xavier gasped as he lurched towards me, half catching me as I pitched over onto my side, his terrified gaze meeting mine for the briefest of moments before he was yanked away from me forcefully with my father's magic.

I fought against the uselessness of my body as I tried to fight through the lack of air in my lungs and push myself up to help him again, but my limbs felt weighted by shackles of iron and I could hardly even raise my arm in his direction.

Darkness enveloped me and stole me away from the moment as my heart thundered with the terrified pace of a thousand stampeding horses.

I hung in the darkness for what felt like an eternity, but it must have only been a few seconds before I sucked down a lungful of air and my eyes snapped open again.

Xavier's screams tore through my ears and I scrambled to my hands and knees, my muscles shaky as I continued to suck down as much oxygen as I could while trying to make sense of what was happening.

"You are strong, Darius," Father sneered as he still stood before his desk, his eyes fixed on me while a ring of fire surrounded his youngest son and his screams of agony filled the room and tore me apart from the inside out. "So strong that I think my punishments have become little more than a nuisance to you recently."

"They're not," I gasped, managing to get to my feet and lurching towards my brother before slamming into a solid barrier of air magic. "Please, stop, please just-"

"So it occurred to me that you don't care enough for your own hide to do all it takes to keep it safe anymore. But the weakling..." He cast a sneering look at Xavier who I could barely even see beyond the ring of blazing red fire as he screamed and screamed. "For some reason, you seem inclined to try and defend him. It isn't very Fae of either of you, but I suppose it serves a purpose."

"Tell me what you want," I gasped as the pitch of Xavier's screams sent agony of my own spiking through the marrow of my bones and pierced me through to my core. "Anything. I'll do anything."

"You will strike at the Vegas harder than you have been," Father said in a dark tone. "No more tricks or games or trying to hurt their precious little feelings. I want them tested, pushed beyond the limits. I want you to strike at them hard enough to either force them from the academy or make it clear beyond the point of doubt that they are Fae enough to stand against you. Either way we need to know. And either way you will do what it takes to achieve that goal. Do you understand me?"

"Yes," I gasped, though my heart twisted with the words and I felt like the stars themselves were kicking me in the gut over choosing to obey this monster yet again. But it wasn't a choice. Not with Xavier on the line. He was the only pure thing I had, the only piece of real goodness I knew. I'd sacrifice all I had and all I wished to be for him and Father had clearly figured that out too.

"Good."

The magic fell away and I stumbled forward as the barrier I'd been hammering with my fists disappeared, swiftly followed by the ring of fire which had been burning Xavier alive.

A choked sob caught in my throat as I took in the sight of my brother's burned and blistered flesh, the scent in the room enough to make me gag as I scrambled towards him on my hands and knees.

Xavier cried out again as my hand landed on the charred flesh of his shoulder and I clenched my teeth so hard that I was surprised they didn't crack as I sent waves of healing magic into his body.

I closed my eyes to concentrate on what I was doing, focusing on throwing as much magic as I could into the spell so that I could fix him as quickly as possible.

Xavier continued to scream at first but that fell away into sobs and gasping breaths before a hand finally landed on my arm and I peeled my eyes open to find him gazing up at me with so much gratitude in his watering eyes that I had to look away.

He shouldn't have been grateful to me. He should have been furious. Because this was my fault. I'd brought this upon him with my selfish actions and my childish attempt at defiance. I was just as bad as the creature who had done this to him and the guilt clawing its way through my soul felt powerful enough to consume me.

"Get out, Xavier," Father said dismissively and my brother flinched at his words, looking to me with concern in his gaze.

"I want to stay with-"

"Go," I barked at him, hating that he flinched then too, knowing he could see that monster in me as well in that moment. Knowing he could see how much of me was just as rotten and vile as the man who had created us. But I had to be. Because it was the only way that I could even hope to protect him from this ever happening again.

A tear slipped down Xavier's cheek as he looked at me, but luckily Father didn't notice it before he turned and fled from the room. It cut into me though. That tear. That pain and fear in his eyes which had been all for me.

I didn't even bother to try and defend myself as Father's fist collided with my jaw and when he knocked me to my back and started kicking me, I did nothing other than take it. I deserved every bite of agony, every moment of pain. Because I'd failed my brother tonight and I was never going to be able to undo what had just happened to him.

"Tell me what you are planning for the Vegas," Father growled as he finally finished his assault on me.

"Whatever it takes," I breathed, hanging my head in defeat and trying not to think about those big green eyes which seemed to look right through me. Trying not to feel the twist in my chest as I accepted what I had to do and feel the burn of reluctance over what I knew it would make me into.

But if I had to become my father so that I could save my brother from him then I would do it. I would do whatever it took and become whatever I had to. And there was no turning back now.

Father was clearly satisfied by my reply because he nodded firmly then strode to the door. "Clean yourself up and get back to the academy. Those girls must be tested. If they manage to prove themselves strong enough to remain at Zodiac after the four of you have done your worst then we will have to reassess our plans for them. I have no more time to spare for your failures."

The door clicked shut behind him and I drew in a deep breath which made every bruise and cut he'd placed on my body ache, but I didn't heal them. I was fairly certain I had some cracked ribs too, but the agony of my flesh was nothing compared to the hurt I felt over causing Xavier to suffer for me. It was the least I deserved.

I stood, glancing down at my shirt and finding my father's spotless shoes hadn't left so much as a footprint on it despite how many times he'd slammed his foot down on me and only the traces of blood seeping through the fabric gave away what he'd done to me.

I glanced at the Atlas he'd left propped up on his desk, the image of me dancing with Roxanya Vega seeming so far from reality that I could hardly believe it had only been last night.

I forced myself to look at her and feel the pain of my injuries, to recall my brother's screams and breathe in the air which was still laced with the scent of his burning flesh. I focused on what that moment of pretending in her arms had cost me and cost my brother. Then I turned away and headed for the door.

I should have gone to see Xavier. To apologise, explain...something. But I was too ashamed, too fucking cowardly for that, so I headed for the door instead.

I used my water magic to remove the blood from my clothes, but I didn't heal my wounds because I didn't deserve to just rid myself of that pain after what I'd caused.

The moment I made it beyond the gates, I tossed a handful of stardust over my head to take me back to the academy. But just as the stars ripped me into their grasp, I thought of her. The girl with the fire in her soul and the power to destroy all I was.

When the stars spat me back out of their embrace, I didn't find myself in my own room. I found myself in hers.

I sucked in a sharp breath of surprise as I stood there, looking down at her sleeping form, the covers kicked aside and her bronze legs drawing my attention beneath a black silk teddy which had my inner animal screaming *mine* so loud it deafened me.

She was so beautiful, so serene in sleep and so innocent looking for such a destructive force of chaos.

I wondered how different our lives might have been if the Savage King had never been killed. If she'd been brought up right alongside me and I knew her as intimately as I did the Heirs. I would have been raised to serve her instead of raised to rule in her place. And maybe to someone else it would have seemed like we should be preparing to serve them again instead of planning to do all we could to stop them, but it wasn't that simple.

Firstly, there wasn't a sensible Fae in the kingdom who would want rulers like the Savage King to return to the throne, to have to fear the brutality of his reign and the atrocities he'd committed being repeated by his offspring. But even if we didn't have to fear that, there was something so much more dangerous about these twins who could have been my queens in another lifetime.

They were ignorant. And an ignorant leader would always be the worst kind of leader. They understood nothing about this kingdom, our people, the ways to rule or the threats we would have to face to keep Solaria prosperous and its people safe and happy. And there was no cure for their kind of ignorance, no way they could ever learn all the things we had spent our lifetimes learning. Without that knowledge, the kingdoms surrounding us could easily take advantage, the Nymphs could close in or at the very least, our own people would suffer for their badly informed decisions. It was unthinkable even without my father driving me to fight against it.

I wasn't determined to keep the throne from them for his sake or even for my own. I knew first hand what it was to suffer beneath the rule of a powerful tyrant and I refused to let our people suffer that too. I'd sworn an oath with the other Heirs a long time ago to become the best rulers our kingdom could wish for, and we had worked tirelessly our entire lives to make sure we became that. No matter their intentions, even if they were as pure as a virgin beneath a blood moon, they'd never be able to rule the kingdom the way it deserved to be ruled. And I would never rescind my promise to give Solaria the best leaders it could get.

I wasn't sure how long I stood there, watching her sleep and letting myself feel all the lust and longing and desire I held for her. I didn't understand why she drew me in the way she did, but I had to mark this as the end of it. I wasn't going to let myself look at her like this again. I wasn't going to be thinking about her with anything other than the coldness I required to do what I had to.

She had been a pretty dream for a foolish moment, but now I was waking up to my reality and the bruises staining my flesh were a stark reminder of what that was.

The Vegas had to go.

And I had to make that happen.

I turned and let myself out of her room, the soft sound of the door clicking closed behind me sounding like a thunderclap in my ears as the urge to turn around and open it again swam through me like liquid gold trying to gild me from the inside out.

The hunger I felt for her was like an ache in my soul and I could have sworn I felt the world tipping, leaning so that gravity was trying to tug me back through that door into that room. I wanted to wake her up with the kiss I should have given her last night and forget everything the two of us were while I lost myself in the feeling of her body giving in to mine.

But as Xavier's screams echoed inside my skull, I let that daydream burn away and ignored the feeling of wrongness which resounded through my body with every step I took away from her door.

I made it to my room and stripped out of the clothes I'd worn to the bar last night, pausing to take in the blue and green mottled bruises which were raising angrily all over my torso. I let all of my thoughts focus on them and I left them marking my flesh to be certain that with every bite of pain, I wouldn't forget.

I had a job to do. And I'd let my heart burn in payment for my brother's soul if that was what it took.

SETH

CHAPTER NINETEEN

I woke to tight lips around my cock and a groan left my lips as I thought of the girl I'd planned on bringing to my bed last night. I'd walked her upstairs, my hand on her lower back, her body leaning into mine. It had felt right in ways I was never gonna understand. Me and her were something special. I couldn't figure out what it was yet, but I planned on fucking her fifty ways under the moon to get my answers.

Unfortunately, when we'd made it back to her room and I'd gone in for a kiss, she'd scruffed my hair like I was a dog, slipped through the door and slammed it in my face with a wild laugh.

She was a challenge. And Caleb was all for fucking Tory if she would give in to him, so why shouldn't I have some fun with Darcy? Cal had the right idea. Fuck 'em, break 'em, dump 'em. Then the two of us could run off into the sunset together. Not as a couple obviously. Unless… I pictured Cal's mouth on my cock in place of the one currently sliding up and down it with enthusiasm and a growl rolled through my throat as I reached under the covers and fisted my hand in the hair of whoever was working me over. Short hair. Like Cal's.

Fuck, hangover brain was being wild. But it was just a little fantasy. No harm in that. Everyone had fuckfest fantasies about their besties, right? Totally normal.

So I let myself indulge in the idea of Caleb's mouth wrapped around my dick as I thrust my hips and worked on choking him with it, the idea getting me so hot that it ended when it had only just begun.

I groaned as I came, spilling myself down the throat of whichever one of my pack was working to please their Alpha, my head tipping back against the pillow as a sigh left me.

I cracked my eyes open as Frank crawled out from under the covers with a roguish grin on his lips, falling down beside me on the bed as a few sleeping bodies shifted to let him in. His hard on drove into my thigh as Alice started kissing his neck and caressing his chest and I tipped him a salute as I got up, crawling over the sea of bodies, the heat of so much flesh making my skin burn.

I needed a shower. And food. And...Darcy. Yeah, I wanted to see Darcy. For a morning cuddle and a bagel. Nothing suss about that. Except I was definitely supposed to be working harder at getting rid of her. But my brain was a fuzz of hangover and I wasn't gonna heal that fuzz away because I kinda liked it here. And fuzzy me wanted Darcy. Maybe I could shove her face into her bagel or something, so it'd be like a compromise. Yeah, Mom would totally approve of a bagel bashing. And if she didn't, well...she wasn't here. So I could do what I liked.

I wasn't the only Heir who'd been dry humping a Vega last night anyway, so why not cosy up to her for a little longer? Maybe I'd find out something that could help destroy her long term, maybe not. Maybe I didn't really care. Just because we were one day going to fight for the throne didn't mean we couldn't be breakfast buddies in the meantime. Yup. Decision made.

I headed into my en-suite, finding Ashanti pinned to the wall by Eric as he thrust into her and I whistled a tune as I joined them in the heated flow of water, grabbing the body wash and soaping myself up good.

Ashanti kept pawing at me, trying to draw me into their fucking but I was hungry and I wanted to get downstairs to wake up my new friend. She kept at it though, so I gave her a filthy kiss to tip her over the edge, tugging her lower lip between my teeth as she came with a loud cry. Then I headed out of the shower, brushed my teeth and dried off with my air magic, heading back to my room where a full on orgy was breaking out in my bed and across the floor.

I had to step over several grinding bodies as I walked to the closet and when I pulled on my clothes, howls of disappointment echoed around me.

"Join us, Alpha," Nessa begged, gripping the waistband of my jeans, but I pushed her hand off.

"I'm hungry," I growled and she whimpered in complaint.

"We'll bring you some food," Tina offered from where she was pinned beneath Geoff on the bed, her head hanging upside down over the side of it.

"Nah, you guys have fun." I grinned, making my way towards the door through the orgy maze as howls of sadness followed me. But I had stuff and things to do today. And I was craving the company of the Heirs. I loved my pack but sometimes I needed a break from all their pandering and pleasing. With my boys, I could just be me. An Alpha among Alphas.

I pushed a hand through my long hair as I made it down to Darcy's room, hesitating there for a second. After last night, I liked her way more than I'd admit out loud. Maybe all this enemies stuff needed to be resolved by a good old fashioned fuck. In fact, I was willing to bet all issues in the world could be resolved with sex. I was so good in bed I could probably get her to renounce her claim while I was deep inside her, and she'd hail me as her king for good measure. *Definitely plausible.*

I lifted my hand to knock on Darcy's door, but it opened before my knuckles touched it and my eyebrows arched in surprise. She wore a black sweater and jeans, her eyes squinty with her hangover and she looked cute as all hell as shock dawned on her features.

"Morning, babe." I smirked as I thought of her hands all over me last night, hoping we could get back on that train pronto.

"Hey," she said tersely, tucking a damp lock of hair behind her ear.

"Let me help you with that." I raised a hand and cast heated air to dry it for her, stepping forward and pressing my nose into it as I took in the scent of her shampoo. It tasted edible and had my mouth watering as I wondered if I should just skip breakfast and have a feast on her instead.

"Cherry, my favourite. Speaking of cherries, has yours been popped yet?" I threw a glance into her room in case she'd invited any big-dick-Daniels or bouncy-titted-Tammys over after I'd left her here last night, but her room was empty. She jammed her shoulder against the door to keep me out, her expression growing fierce and making my gut tug. Why was she so angsty this morning?

"That's none of your business," she hissed.

"Can I make it my business?" I purred, wrapping an arm around her and yanking her into my chest. Was she really a virgin? She hadn't fucked anyone on campus yet, and she'd been at Zodiac nearly a whole week. I'd fucked a whole marching band in my first three days here. I quite liked the idea of her being untouched though, because I had so fucking much to teach her if she offered her unclaimed pussy to me. I swear Venus herself had imbued my cock with her gifts.

"What the hell are you doing?" She pushed me back and a whine built in my throat that I didn't let out. What was her deal? I thought she liked me. I was fucking loveable when I turned the charm on and last night I'd given her the charm and ground my dick against her multiple times, so what wasn't to love?

"I thought we were cool now...you know, after you sucked on my lower lip then whispered dirty things in my ear," I taunted. Okay, so maybe what she'd whispered to me was that I was an arrogant fuckwit with a god complex, but she'd been grinding on my cock at the time so I'd taken it as a compliment.

"I don't recall any whispering." Her eyes dipped to my mouth, giving away that she did remember the lip-sucking part.

I chuckled darkly. "Do you remember this bit too?" I moved my mouth to her ear, about to draw it between my teeth and get this breakfast party started when she yelped and forced me back.

I gave her a wicked grin, enjoying this game as she stepped out into the corridor with me and pulled the door shut behind her. *Alright, I guess she'll play with my balls after we eat then.*

"Come on, I'll walk you to breakfast." I slung my arm over her shoulders and she wriggled a little, but not really enough to say she wanted me to let go. I kinda liked this cat and mouse game we played although my little mouse really would have done well to remember that in the end the cat would always get too hungry and the game would end in bloodshed.

"Why are you pretending to be nice to me? We've played this game before and I'm not falling for it, Seth," she warned and my dick jerked in my pants. Wow, she just screwed the hell out of my name with her tongue.

"*Fuck*, do that again," I said, biting down on my fist.

"What?" She stared up at me with a frown.

"The part where you say my name like you're mouth-humping it." I grinned tauntingly.

"That's not a thing." She shook her head, making another vague attempt to escape and failing. "I need to go and see Geraldine," she said anxiously, glancing at me for a reaction and my gut dipped. Darius had texted us last night after he'd disappeared to tell us she'd been mauled by a Nymph. And that Nymph attack was on my list of things to talk to the Heirs about today, but my hangover brain was keeping me from worrying about it too much. No doubt my mom would be losing her shit over it and there'd be a whole statement from her and the other Celestial Councillors in the news today. *Food first, work later.*

"Yeah, sounds like the poor chick got seriously messed up," I said. Grus was an eleven on the crazy royalist scale, but she was an alright girl. She could play Pitball like a damn warrior and I respected the hell out of that.

"Lucky Orion was there to help," Darcy said dryly and my rage spiked as she said his name like that. Like it was a sweet as fuck candy she was rolling over her tongue.

"Woah." I turned her to face me, hunting her eyes.

"What?" she gasped.

"We have a serious problem, babe," I growled.

"What is it?" she asked in alarm.

"You just mouth-humped another guy's name," I accused, wanting this girl's attention all to myself.

We could bring in a fuck buddy or two into the bedroom once I'd had her to myself for a while, but Professor Orion was off the menu. She got that right? He was like one hundred percent taboo. He was great to look at, I even had a memory of him in my spank bank where he'd nearly choked me out for burying a student fifty feet underground after they'd called the moon a whore and punched me in the throat. But that memory only came out to play in my mind, there was no acting on it. He was off limits.

Darcy's lips parted and her cheeks turned pink, giving away all of the truth over her little crush to me. It was hardly surprising, there weren't many girls who didn't notice Orion was hot as fuck. "Are you kidding me right now?"

"This is no joke. You know you can't date teachers, right? Them's the rules. And I'd appreciate if you didn't mouth-hump his name in front of me," I said, tightening my grip on her.

"Can you please stop saying mouth hump? It's not a thing," she said, her nose scrunching adorably. *Mmm, little mousey I'm going to eat you soon.*

"It is a thing." I said with a shrug. "I just made it a thing."

"You're impossible," she sighed, pulling free of my hold and marching away from me in frustration.

"Wait up," I called, a doggish whine in my throat as I ran after her and caught her hand, winding my fingers between hers. I didn't want her to run away. In fact, I wanted to go back to last night where she didn't look at me like I was the Devil. "Look, I know I mess around a lot and I've been an ass, okay?"

She turned to me, looking shocked as hell by that statement, but it was the truth.

I took a deep breath, wanting to soften that glare she was giving me and earn myself a snuggle instead. "I'm sorry, alright? For your first night... for trying to make you cut your hair off and then covering you in mud with my mates and posting it online....and then leaving you in The Wailing-"

"I got it," she cut over me, making my chest yank at the venom in her eyes. "I remember it all pretty clearly."

She tried to pull her hand free, but I refused to let go. It was just fun and games. I wanted her to bow to me, but she didn't have to hate me. We could work this out. We could be frenemies with benefits.

"I just thought...after last night." I cleared my throat, feeling weirdly vulnerable as I tried to bridge this shit between us. Last night had felt so right. All six of us together, hanging out. I always felt unequal around other students, the way they revered me or feared me, it made it difficult to form any equal relationships outside of the Heirs. But with her and Tory, they just...fit. "I just thought things had changed. But clearly I was wrong." I released her hand, hoping she might contradict me as she aimed a hard scowl my way. Not even a teenie weenie contradiction? Just an itty bitty one?

"Last night we were drunk," she said and I fought back a huff.

"I know but..." I shrugged. "So what? I still know how I feel this morning, don't you?"

My heart beat madly as I bared my soul to her and felt vulnerable for one of the first times in my life. Me and her, there was definite attraction there. I knew it was complicated but...it didn't have to be. We could set our politics aside for now and explore each other's bodies with our tongues. Why not? What harm did it really do? Just a little nipple sucking and finger fucking before breakfast.

She shook her head, suspicion in her deep green gaze that I supposed I couldn't really blame her for.

"I don't trust you," she admitted warily and my heart lifted, because trust issues were totally my bag. I was the best friend anyone could have, she'd see. She'd get it if she gave me a chance.

"Can I try to make you trust me?" I asked.

She pressed her lips together and brushed her fingers through the blue tips of her hair.

"No," she whispered and kept walking, leaving my heart on the ground behind her, stomped on and kicked like an old tin can. I stared after her for two endless seconds as I fought the urge to howl in mourning of that single word then ran forward and planted myself in her way. I had one more card up my sleeve. The one thing the Heirs could never resist. That no one could ever resist.

I gave her my puppy dog eyes, my biggest, most gleaming doggish expression that made anyone melt for me. I. Was. Adorable.

"Ergh *fine*," she gave in, a smile playing around her lips and I almost bounced with joy.

I grinned from ear to ear, playing it cool instead. "Kiss?" I leaned in for one and she jerked backwards in surprise.

"No! Are you crazy?" She shoved me back and I started bobbing on my heels, loving this back and forth. This challenge. She wanted me. Drunk her had said it all. So if I had to coax out her wild side and earn her trust, then fine. I'd do it. Then I'd get all the sober kisses I wanted from her.

"Crazy for you," I said with a stupid smirk.

"That is the cringiest thing I've ever heard," she laughed.

"Yeah actually, don't repeat that to anyone, babe. Street cred and all." I winked, snatching her hand again and tugging her along. *I'm on a trip to breakfast with my breakfast buddy.* I sang the made up song in my head, a wide smile on my lips. *Breakfast, breakfast, have you seen my buddy? Oh there she is, there's my breakfast buddy. Just me and her for breakfast-*

"You're not coming with me," she said firmly, dousing my mood in gasoline and setting it alight as we stepped into the stairwell.

Oh.

A couple of freshmen approached us, one with a beanie hat on and the other a petite little blonde thing.

"See ya." Darcy pulled her hand free of mine, moving to join them and she shot me a glare that told me to stay back.

I stared at her, rejection stinging and raw in my chest as her eyes shut me out and told me to get fucked. I ran my tongue over my lower lip as I fought back the Fae in me who wanted a fight, but I decided I didn't want to beat her down right now and forced myself to walk away and head downstairs.

I took out my Atlas with a pout, finding a bunch of missed calls and texts waiting for me. Half of them were from Kylie demanding answers for a video that had been leaked online of me and Darcy dancing at the club, and my gut sank as I realised the other half were from my mom and there was a bunch of notifications telling me I'd been mentioned in all kinds of articles online and FaeBook.

Shit on the moon, I'm in trouble.

I headed out of Aer Tower and bolstered myself up as I walked to the cliffs to make this call, casting a silencing bubble around me. When I made it to the very edge, I sat down on a large rock jutting over the cliff, letting my legs hang down as I stared at the bright blue sea below and hit dial.

My mom answered immediately, her voice cutting into my brain like a knife.

"Seth Capella where have you been?!" she barked and I flinched from her furious tone.

"Sleeping," I said innocently.

"Sleeping?" she snarled. "While the world is crumbling at your feet, you've been sleeping?!"

"It's not crumbling-" I started but she cut over me.

"There has been a Nymph attack on a Zodiac Academy student outside a club that you were at last night, and do you know how I found out about that? Through a call in the middle of the night from Gus Vulpecula asking me for a statement on why my son was witnessed with his hands all over a Vega while an innocent student was being attacked by a Nymph right under your nose."

Oh fuck.

"Mom, if you just-"

"I will not just anything. You are in serious trouble, you reckless little pup."

Oh no. She was pupping me. This was bad. Apocalypse bad.

"This is on the verge of being a full blown scandal," she went on in a snarl that made me whine. "And the other Heirs are not even close to innocent in all of this, you understand? There are photographs and videos all over the internet of you all flirting with the Vegas – do you have any idea how damaging this could be to your reputation?"

"I know, Mom, but they're just girls. And they're kind of cool. Isn't it a good thing that we're showing how amicable we can be with our enemies? I mean, we only have to beat them down and take the throne from them, and we've been training for years, they can't even cast any simple spells yet, what's the big deal?"

"The big deal?!" she roared, making my heart hide behind my lungs. "The big deal, pup, is that you look weak in those images. You look like the girls are in control, leading you all along by your willy winkies-" By the stars, I hated when she called my dick a willy winkie "-Do you have any idea of the compromising position you've put us all in? Of the damage control needed here to rectify this?"

"I don't see the big deal," I pushed, my blood rising with frustration.

"You are an Heir. Born to rule. And the Vegas are your enemies," she snapped. "You cannot be seen fraternising with them, especially not when they distract you from detecting a Nymph in your near proximity. Do you know how bad this makes you look?"

"How am I supposed to detect Nymphs? I don't have Nymph radar in my head, Mom," I growled.

"Don't you get clever with me, pup," she hissed and I gritted my teeth. "You are to get rid of those girls, do you understand me? You will work to undo the damage you have caused. You will show the world that those twins are beneath you, that you could crush them easily, that you are the true power in this kingdom and that you will rise up to claim the throne the Vegas have come back to steal."

"I can beat them any time I like, anyone with a brain knows that."

"They do not, in fact, know that. The news needs to be full of stories that counter this scandal, Seth. You have severely disappointed me."

"But Mom-" I tried.

"No buts. I've had enough of your arrogance. You need to understand the important of this, the magnitude. So I have no choice but to punish you to drive the point home."

"Punish me?" I balked. "Why? Because of some Nymph attack out of my control and because I danced with a Vega?"

"Exactly!" she boomed. "Because if you will not take this seriously then I shall force you to. You are officially banned from attending the family moon march and you cannot come home again until you have made extensive efforts in rectifying this failure."

My breath stalled in my lungs and I shoved to my feet in horror. "What? You can't do that."

"I just did," she snarled. "Do what you must to fix what you have broken, or there will be further punishments, and I guarantee you they will make this punishment seem like a dream by comparison." She hung up and I felt choked, unable to breathe as I stood staring at the sea and my pulse skittered everywhere under my flesh.

She couldn't do this. She couldn't. I needed to see my family like I needed air to breathe. I went home every week to see my brothers and sisters, my cousins. I needed their bond, it was one of the most important needs I had. And to ban me from the family moon march was like cutting off a lump of my soul. It was a Capella tradition. I hadn't missed a single moon march my entire life. It was a huge party held under the moon on the shore of Lake Questos. We remained in our Order forms all night and slept out beneath the rays of the moon, bathing in its light. And now I wouldn't be there to take part. I wouldn't get to swim in the cool waters gilded in moonlight and feel the lunar power rippling through its depths. I wouldn't hear the chorus of my family's howls rising to our celestial goddess in the sky. I'd be here. Alone. Without them.

My breaths came furiously and my hands began to shake as panic set in. She couldn't do this. How could she fucking do this?

My Atlas started ringing and I found the one person I craved to talk to above all others calling.

"Cal?" I croaked as I answered.

"We're fucked," he gritted out and I took a moment of relief knowing that at least I wasn't alone in this. Though it was short lived. "Come to the Hollow."

"Okay," I rasped. "We'll figure this out, won't we?"

"We always do," his tone softened a little. Caleb was always so calm in the face of chaos; he had this way about him that grounded me and I needed that more than ever right now. He hung up and I turned and started walking in the direction of The Wailing Wood, my limbs heavy and numb, the only thing I could feel was the pained thump of my heart in my chest.

What are we gonna do? How are we gonna fix this?

I trailed along the path in the woods, staring at the ground as my mind ran at a thousand miles an hour, trying to find a solution. But there was too much panic in my head to let in anything logical. I needed a hug. And a coffee. And a snack.

A freshman boy bumped into me and I shoved him to the ground in anger.

"Capella," a harsh voice made my head snap up and I found Professor Orion stalking into my path, aiming a hard glare at me. "Was that really called for?" He jerked his chin at the freshman who scrambled upright and sprinted away down the path, weaving left and right like he thought I might start firing magic at his ass.

"He got in my way," I snarled.

"Is that how you plan on ruling the kingdom?" he asked icily. "Forcing anyone down who gets in your way?"

"What's it to you?" I snapped, losing my shit. I didn't need him riding my ass this morning. What did he want anyway? It was a Saturday, shouldn't he have been off being an asshole elsewhere today?

"Watch your tone," he warned, prowling closer until he was right in my path, his fangs bared.

I glared at him, wondering why he was targeting me right now. It was the wrong fucking time to mess with me.

"Or what?" I hissed, unable to rein in my temper. I needed an outlet, and maybe starting a fight with a teacher was a shitty idea considering my current situation, but I'd never had much impulse control. So I squared up to him and his eyes darkened with the challenge, like he was as keen as I was for this fight.

"What's got you in such a foul mood, Capella? Get shot down last night?" he taunted, his eyes glittering with malice.

"I don't get shot down, *sir*," I spat. *Except by Darcy Vega apparently.*

That seemed to get him even angrier and he stepped closer, his chest brushing mine and I wondered if I really was going to dig my grave deeper today.

"So you think the best way to claim your throne is by dating a Vega?" he asked, his voice cold and his eyes flaring. I guessed he had his own investment in my actions. He was firmly team Heir and Darius's little bestie – not that I was jealous. Except okay, maybe sometimes I wished I could get in on their cuddle parties.

"I'm not dating her," I spat bitterly. *And it looks like I won't be now either.*

His brows arched and I sighed, a whine leaving me as I looked away from him.

"Have you seen Darius?" he muttered. "I can't find him and he's not answering his Atlas."

I frowned, shaking my head even though I imagined Darius would be coming to King's Hollow. But if he didn't want to be found then I wasn't gonna rat him out.

Orion sighed, rubbing a spot on his chest as his eyes splintered with some need.

"Are you…okay?" I asked and he frowned at me.

"Fine," he snapped.

"*I'm* not okay," I mumbled.

I didn't know why, but suddenly I started splitting apart in front of him and I just needed a hug so bad. So I lunged at him, wrapping my arms around his neck. "I don't know what to do. What do I do?"

"Get off of me," he grunted, shoving me back, but I held on like a limpet. I bet he gave great hugs, I just needed to hold on until he gave in. "*Capella.*" He blasted me away with a gust of air and I tipped my head back and howled to the sky before running past him, tearing off the path into the trees, needing my brothers more than anything in the world.

I made it to the huge tree that gave access to King's Hollow, darting inside, running up the winding stairway within the trunk and shoving the door open.

Caleb was there casting fire in the hearth and I collided with him, knocking him down onto the rug and nuzzling against his face.

"*Seth,*" he wheezed out as I held him down, a whimper in my throat.

He sighed, slowly closing his arms around me and I finally relaxed, burying my face in his neck.

"My mom banned me from attending the family moon march," I said into his flesh. He smelled so good. I just wanted to stay here forever where things almost felt okay.

"Oh man, I'm sorry," he said, running a hand up and down my back in soothing strokes. The tension started to leave my body as I stole comfort from him, knowing he didn't like the snuggly ways of my kind, but he always indulged me when I needed it and I couldn't help myself.

A boom sounded and the treehouse trembled as Darius landed on the roof. A beat later, he appeared through the hatch already dressed in a pair of sweatpants and a black t-shirt and I vaguely wondered why he'd carried his clothes here instead of just grabbing something from the chest like usual.

"Hi," he grunted at us and I got to my feet, walking toward him with my arms outstretched.

He turned his back on me as he started making coffee and I kept walking, my arms closing around him from behind. I rested my chin on his shoulder and watched him make coffee as I remained wrapped tightly around him. He winced a little like that hurt so I took it down a notch because I was super strong and I didn't mean to over squeeze.

"It's okay, Darius," I whispered in his ear and he batted a hand at me like I was a wasp buzzing around his head. But I knew he needed this hug. We all needed hugs sometimes, and luckily they were my speciality.

The door opened and Max strode in wearing a dark blue t-shirt and jeans, his face like thunder. "Shit, it tastes like a funeral in here."

I released Darius, striding towards Max instead with my arms wide again and he pulled me in tight, his Siren powers coiling into my chest and stealing away the worst of my anxiety.

"Thanks, bro," I murmured and he clapped me on the back before we broke apart.

"Why do you smell kind of…hospitally?" I asked him, cocking my head to one side.

"Oh…err." Max ran a hand up the back of his neck then raised his chin as he went on. "I just checked in on Grus at Uranus Infirmary this morning is all. Like…she wasn't allowed visitors and I didn't wanna make a scene, so I snuck in and checked she was still alive while she was sleeping."

"You crept into her bedroom and watched her sleep?" I asked, arching a brow.

"Only for like twenty minutes or something – just to make sure she didn't die. Because, you know, we don't need the headache of a Nymph murder right on our doorstep."

"Hail to that," I agreed with a nod, turning away from him to the couch as I found myself suddenly losing interest in this topic. I vaguely wondered if he'd just done something to my emotions to make me forget about it, but figured it was probably to do with his calming energy.

Darius brought us all coffee and I dropped down beside Cal on the couch, though there wasn't much room as Darius was beside him, so I mostly just curled up on both of their laps.

"Dude," Darius grumbled as he got my ass end and I wriggled to try and get comfortable, kicking my shoes off onto the floor.

"I'll be comfy in a second," I said, grinding my hips left and right as I worked to settle myself and Cal cursed as my head knocked into his coffee.

Max flicked his fingers, catching the boiling liquid before it splashed over me and sending it flying straight back into the mug.

"You done?" Cal demanded of me and I nodded, giving him a sad look as I rested my head down on his lap.

"So…damage control," Max said in his deep voice, placing his ankle on his knee in the seat to our left. "I did some things last night…things I'm not proud of."

"Was it the bit where you climbed on the bar and shouted hail to the

Vegas' tits?" Caleb asked with a snigger. "Or the part where you got your cock out and said you could do the Macarena with it – I was kind of impressed that you could actually do it."

"Yes, Cal," Max gritted out. "Those are the parts I'm not proud of. Especially because my fucking parents had the pleasure of watching those videos all over the damn internet."

Darius dropped his face into his hands with a heavy sigh. "We're so fucked."

"It's not that bad," Caleb tried and Darius's head shot up as he glared at him.

"Not that bad? Are you fucking kidding me? My father will destroy me if I don't do something to fix this fast. And I'm terrified he'll-" He cut himself off, sipping his coffee instead and a whine of sympathy left me.

"It's okay, Darius," I said softly, but he shook his head, his eyes wrought with some untold fears and my heart twisted in my chest. "We'll think of something."

"We need to go in hard," Max said. "When my father called this morning, I heard my mother say they should see if they can get Ellis Awakened early just in case I'm not up to the task of defeating the Vegas."

"Seriously?" I balked and Max nodded, his features drawn with worry. The more this news descended on me, the more I blamed the Vegas for it. They'd lured us in, made us want them and now look! My brothers were hurting. And no one hurt my brothers and got away with it.

"We need to make a move that shows the world they're beneath us. We've fucked up guys. Bad," Max said.

"Yeah," I agreed as realisation washed over me. Maybe I'd let my dick take too much control last night, maybe I'd been an idiot to think we could hang out with the Vegas and it wouldn't be a disaster in the making.

"I think it'll blow over," Caleb said. "My mom was pissed, but she usually forgives me pretty quick."

"You're not taking this seriously enough," Darius barked at him and Caleb sat up straighter in his seat. "This is do or die, Cal."

Caleb shrugged. "I think if we give it a week-"

"We can't," I said in a growl, panic rising in me. "My mom was clear, I can't come home until I do something to fix this."

Caleb looked down at me with a shocked frown, his fingers curling in my shirt. "Really?"

I nodded, a lump thick and unyielding in my throat. "I need them, Cal. I can't survive without my family."

He nodded, his brows drawing together.

"The pranks aren't good enough anymore," Darius said darkly, draining his coffee and placing his mug down on the side. He looked like he'd hardly slept and I moved my foot back and forth on his thigh to try and soothe him. His hand slammed down on it to stop me and I enjoyed the contact.

"So what do we do?" I asked. "Challenge them?"

"No," Max said firmly. "A beat down at this stage is pointless. They aren't trained to fight back, it would look weak on our part."

"So what then?" I pressed.

"We have to make them want to run," Darius growled darkly. "Run and never come back."

A whine left me, but I knew this was the only option. We were left with no choice. Our parents weren't going to let this lie and we had to prove to them that we were capable of being the Heirs they'd raised us to be. This was one of our first real tests and I couldn't lose my family over a Vega. So I'd become the heartless creature I needed to be to rule and cut off any ideas of a friendship with them. It had been stupid anyway. Look where it had landed me already. I was missing out on the moon march because I'd gotten stupid ideas about fucking Darcy Vega and my mom had always told me to think with my head not my willy winkie – I mean my cock for fuck's sake.

"So we need them afraid of us," I said, leaning in to the darkest side of me and making my inner psycho purr. "They need to think they can never defeat us." *You take my family moon march, then I'll take something from you, Darcy Vega.*

Darius and Max nodded, though Caleb was quiet, his brow deeply furrowed.

"I can find out what it is they fear," Max said as a dark cloud seemed to descend over the room, one tainted with the ruthlessness of our natures.

"Yes," Darius said decisively. "Then we can become the monsters that bring their fears to life."

"I dunno…" Caleb said, pushing his fingers into his hair. "Is this really necessary?"

"It's necessary," Max growled and both Darius and I nodded.

Caleb frowned, giving in, though I could tell he had reservations. But he'd benefit from this too. I wasn't gonna see his name dragged through the mud for one slip up, I'd damn well do what I had to to protect him.

My mom always told me that rulers didn't always do things they liked, but what was best in the long run. This was one of those things, and if I wanted to prove myself worthy of her seat on the Celestial Council, then I had to rise up and be worthy of the title I was one day going to claim from her. I had to show the public that I had a spine of steel and it would not be bent for the Vegas. So I'd force them down in the dirt and show the world that I was destined to rule and they were not. And even if my soul was the price I had to pay for that, then so be it.

ORION

CHAPTER TWENTY

One measly message from Darius telling me to stay away was all I'd had since last night, I'd hunted the whole of campus for him and had finally given up as evening drew in. When the moon was high and the darkness was deep, I headed down to the beach of Air Cove to consult with the shadows.

Pain was ricocheting through my body with every step I took. *His* pain. And the Guardian bond begged me to find him, to heal him, but he clearly didn't give a fuck about what I wanted.

I'd called Francesca late last night and found out exactly what he'd been off doing, but if he'd gotten himself hurt in a Nymph fight why wasn't he fucking healing himself?

I resisted the desire to call him again and glanced up and down this rocky part of the beach, knowing coming here was always a risk, but our secrets were hidden well enough and could only be unveiled with a draining dagger.

I used my blade to slice open my thumb before cutting through the spells to allow me access to the cave. I cast a Faelight as I walked inside and ensured the dark concealment closed up behind me like curtains drawing together. I sank down on a flat rock with a hiss, clutching my side where the flare of pain in Darius's flesh flared within my own. His ribs were bruised badly for sure, probably broken but this pain was nothing compared to the agony the bond was causing me over not being able to help him.

I scrubbed at my eyes then raised the dagger to the centre of my palm, wanting the shadows to draw me into them and seek their dark guidance of what was coming. Maybe I'd finally *see* something that could assist us in defeating Lionel, but part of me simply wanted to escape into their embrace. I hesitated before I made the incision, thinking of my father's advice to never slip into the shadows with a fraught mind. And my mind was particularly fucking fraught right now.

My hand began to shake and I curled it into a tight fist as anger slammed through the centre of my chest. The call of the shadows was like a Siren's song in my head, begging me to give into it, to let it take away all of my pain. And it was so star damned tempting. Maybe it would be a good thing to let them take hold of me. Maybe I'd find some peace if I just…

With a surge of willpower, I stood up, hurling the dagger with all my might so it hit the wall, the sound ringing through the air like a bell tolling my imminent fucking end.

"Darius!" I bellowed so loud I swear it ripped my lungs in two. I couldn't go on like this. I had to heal him. I had to make sure he was alright. I was losing my fucking mind and I didn't know what to fucking do. How long was he going to avoid me for? How long was I going to endure this?

I shot across the cave, snatching up the dagger and pressing it to my palm. Fuck it. *Maybe the shadows will show me where he is, or maybe they'll at least give me some relief from this torture.* I could handle them. I was trained to handle them.

Before I made the cut, Darius's voice echoed through the cave, making my heart cease to beat. "I'm here."

I swung around, dropping the dagger and shooting forward, colliding with him so hard I knocked him back against the wall at his back. A pained curse slipped from his lips as I pinned him in place with one hand, the other sliding up his shirt and seeking out the bruised flesh as I released a wave of healing magic from my body into his. He groaned, his fingers knotting in my hair as my forehead fell against his, but it wasn't enough. He didn't understand what he'd done. And now I had to fulfil this bond as fast as I could or I'd be driven to insanity. I ripped his shirt off his chest and he swore as I did the same to my own in the next second, pressing my flesh to his as my magic swelled against my skin and demanded he meet it with his own. He gave in to what I was asking, letting his magical barriers down so our power washed together in one furious storm of energy that made both of us groan.

I healed every mark I found on him, seeking out each bruise and cut, the cracks in his ribs and mending all of it while he clung to me and the tide of magic rolled between us.

"Fuck you," I said through my teeth. "Why'd you stay away? Why have you done this?"

"I deserve every wound," he said bitterly and I caught hold of his chin, searching his eyes and finding nothing but an empty grave there.

"What happened?" my anger twisted into concern and he shook his head, his gaze sliding away from me. "What happened?!" I barked, needing to know as my heart thrashed against my chest as fiercely as his own was thrashing.

"I found the group of Nymphs we'd been after and destroyed them," he said and my mind spun over that. "Then I went home and saw Father," he said simply, still not meeting my gaze and I instantly forgot about the Nymphs.

"It's more than that," I softened my voice as I realised Lionel must have done something terrible. Darius could withstand his beatings. He'd done so countless times. This was different. Something had changed, and I was terrified of what it was.

His throat bobbed as he looked back at me, looking so broken it shattered what whole pieces of my soul still remained. "He hurt Xavier."

My teeth snapped together in anger over that and Darius tried to turn away again.

I stepped back, breaking the contact between us despite my hunger to stay closer.

"He wants me to deal with the Vegas," he continued, his tone so hollow it frightened me. This wasn't my friend. This was the creature Lionel wanted him to be. His leashed monster.

"We are dealing with them," I tried, but maybe I knew that wasn't exactly true. What had either of us really done to ensure they were no longer a problem to the Heirs? I'd watched as Darius had danced with Tory Vega and I hadn't said a damn thing. I hadn't even thought of anything except my own forbidden desires for the other Vega girl. We were failing so spectacularly at trying to get rid of them that we were ending up compromised because of them. And now Darius and Xavier were facing the price of that.

"We're not," he ground out. "Not even close. But we will. The Heirs and I have a plan."

"What plan?" I demanded but he shrugged past me.

"It doesn't matter. Just leave it to us."

"So you expect me to stay out of this?"

"Yes, Lance," he growled then his features softened and I saw the friend I loved rather than his father peering at me through his eyes. "I need you to trust me."

"I do," I rasped. "But..."

"But what?" he asked sharply.

I forced myself to keep talking, walking the line of what I was really saying here. "But it's not that simple, is it? Those girls aren't savage like their father. They're just...girls." *And one of them has reached into my chest and taken hold of a cord tethered to my soul.*

"It doesn't matter what they are," he muttered. "I won't risk Xavier being tortured by my father. You don't understand…"

"I don't?" I scoffed, shooting in front of him as he tried to turn his back on me and smacking a palm against his chest to hold him still. "I watched your father steal my sister from this world." My heart shredded in my chest as I fought to keep talking. "I heard her screams and I couldn't go to her because of him. And trust me when I tell you, I will do everything in my power to ensure the same fate doesn't befall your sibling, Darius."

His features pinched and emotion blazed in his eyes. "I'm so afraid for him, Lance."

"And I'm afraid of what you'll become to save him," I said in a low tone. "Because I would have cast my soul into damnation for Clara, and I see you on the brink of doing the same for Xavier. But there must be another way."

Darius looked conflicted, hunting my eyes like he hoped he'd find an answer there. "What if there's not? We're just players in this game, and maybe it's time we admitted we're always going to lose because he's the master of it. And whatever move he wants us to make, he'll find a way to force us to make it so because he creates the rules."

"Don't talk like you're giving up," I growled, desperate to find that fire in him which always ignited in this cave. When he worked to learn everything I could teach him about dark magic so that he could one day use it against his father. But now his eyes looked empty and I couldn't see any sign of the fight in him.

"Darius, please," I said gruffly, gripping the back of his neck and yanking him closer. "Talk to me. We can find an answer together."

"There is only one answer, Lance. There always was, we were just too fucking hopeful to see it before. All of this…" He gestured to the cave, to the draining dagger on the ground. "It was a way to fool ourselves into thinking we ever had a chance against him."

"We do," I snarled because it was all I had to hold onto. Without this drive to destroy Lionel, this purpose, what did I even have? The bottom of an empty bourbon bottle staring back at me. "Please don't give up," I fucking begged, losing all dignity as I clung to this need in me, desperate for him not to take it away. My revenge plot for Clara, my reason to get up in the morning. My soul was sewn together by these final worthwhile things in my life and without them it would be cast to the wind. I'd have nothing. I'd *be* nothing. And worst of all, Clara's death would mean nothing.

He looked so defeated, it turned my heart to glass and smashed it into razor sharp shards.

"I'm sorry, Lance," he said, looking me in the eyes and clearly meaning it with all of his being. "Really. I'm so fucking sorry for everything. But I would do anything to save Xavier from my father. And this is the price."

He squeezed my arm, a war fought and lost in his eyes, then he dropped his hand and started walking away, leaving me there with my only remaining purpose in life torn clean from my chest. I was a husk with no more direction than a dandelion seed in the wind.

And I swear I could feel the stars coming loose from the sky, every one of them threatening to fall.

Sunday was a haze of booze and sleep. When I was conscious, I was drunk. When I wasn't, I was stuck in nightmares where my sister screamed for help in a room full of black veils and every one I tore down to find her only led me to another.

Monday arrived and I dragged myself through classes on autopilot, taking my rage out on my students to try and satisfy the wild animal in me. But nothing did.

I headed to Pitball practice after hours, hoping to find some joy in training, but the Heirs were sombre and I somehow missed Grus's enthusiasm on the field as rain beat down on us and I barked orders at all the players until my throat was hoarse.

Darius had descended into a dark mood that hadn't seemed to have lifted at all since our conversation in the cave and I knew there was little I could do to change that. The Guardian bond burned at me, begging me to please him but there was nothing within my power that could help. So we trudged our way through training and when everyone was thoroughly miserable, I dismissed the team and remained out in the pouring rain, gazing up at the black, unforgiving sky and wondering if the stars were laughing beyond the storm. Maybe we were their playthings here on Earth, doomed to dance in a show they called life. Their entertainment on tap.

I didn't want company, so I used the speed of my Order to shoot to the locker room and collect my bag before tearing back out of it and exiting the stadium. I shot all the way back to Asteroid Place, shoving the gate open and tearing up to my chalet. Inside, I dripped water on the floor and let my bag fall from my hand.

I grabbed the TV remote, switching it onto the news. I'd been checking all day for any updates on the attack on Grus. The Nymph attack hadn't been announced and I had to assume the Councillors had bought themselves time to prepare for the attention that would be turned their way. But it looked like their time was up because the newscaster was revealing it to the world now, interjecting it with statements from the Councillors who were promising the kingdom that the problem was a rogue incident. Which was utter bullshit, they just didn't want a panic on their hands.

My gaze fell to the empty bottles of bourbon sitting on the kitchen counter, then to the three new ones lined up beside them. The news report changed to some dull story about a Pegasus kid who'd Emerged super early at six years old. She was singing the colours of the rainbow while glitter tumbled from her hair and I lifted the remote to turn it off. "-and yellow and pink and green, orange and purple and-"

"*Blue*," I gasped, tossing the remote and shooting out of the door with a curse, tearing across campus towards Jupiter Hall.

I made it inside, slowing to a walk as I rounded into the corridor that led to my office and found Darcy standing outside it looking pissed. My heart crashed against my ribcage like a trapped animal and anger rose in me as I stared at the sum of all my problems. Her and her sister had no idea about the trouble they were causing. They'd fucked everything up and now I didn't even know what Darius was going to do to try and deal with them. It set me so on edge, I didn't know who to be angrier at or if I should just throw all of my rage at the stars and tell each and every one of them to get fucked.

I kept my eyes firmly off of her as I jammed my key in the lock of my office, pushing it open and stepping inside without a word. Screw her, dammit. Why did she have to be like this? Why couldn't she be a bitch? Or at the very least, ugly.

I stalked up to my desk, trying to block out the roaring drone in my head and wishing I'd had the forethought to drain a glass of bourbon before I'd come here.

My door suddenly flew open so hard it smashed into the wall and I didn't even bother to look back as I dropped into my ottoman chair and started siphoning the mud and water off of myself, trying to focus my thoughts so I didn't completely lose my shit.

After a beat, Darcy cleared her throat and I waved a hand, throwing the door shut with air magic, using as much force as she'd opened it with.

"*Stand on the desk,*" I commanded, my voice flaring with Coercion. *How weak are you still? Or are you finally learning to hone that power of yours?*

I looked up at her at last, finding her eyes shut as she concentrated and I stole every forbidden second staring at her face. I never got to just look at her, always having to turn away, to steal every little glance. But now I was taking what I kept craving, my eyes travelling down the smooth apples of her cheeks, the slope of her small nose, the bridge of her upper lip and the fullness of her bottom one. I tried to figure out why that face was endlessly tempting to me beyond her obvious beauty. Then I suddenly realised she wasn't moving. She wasn't obeying.

She released a long breath, opening her eyes and I swear her gaze sent a needle driving into my heart. I kept my features neutral, giving nothing away on how impressed I was at her fighting off Coercion as powerful as mine.

I clucked my tongue like it was nothing, even though it was absolutely the opposite.

"Good. Let's get on with tonight's session." I glanced at my watch to see how late I really was. *Well fuck me.* "All thirty five minutes of it."

She dropped into the seat opposite me and my jaw began to tick as her proximity felt like a vacuum drawing the air from my lungs. But there was to be no more sinful thoughts of this girl. I was done with falling under her spell. I was stronger than that. I had a will made of sun steel and no girl – no matter how alluring – would tempt me into treacherous thoughts again.

"Geraldine's doing better," she said, eyeing me closely like she thought I might have something interesting to stay in relation to that. I didn't.

"Yes, thank the stars," I said hollowly. "She can go back to annoying us all by preaching about the 'True Heirs'." I air-quoted those words, falling back on my finer talents of being an asshole. It was unfortunate such a skill wasn't a class here at Zodiac or I would have passed it with flying colours.

"Any idea who attacked her?" she asked airily. Her hair was curling from the rain, the sheen of the blue ends like nightglass. It was a rare substance made when a Storm Dragon's lightning impacted with sand. There was a place out near Alestria where it could be found, but the ruthless Oscura gang had claimed ownership of it. I possessed one piece of it though, gifted to me by Gabriel.

"Whatever I know or do not know about that incident is none of your business." I stared her down, hoping she'd flinch, but she didn't. I wanted her hate, I wanted to push her until she withdrew from me. Until she stopped sitting there with her accusing eyes.

She scrunched her fingers up in the black skirt she was wearing, drawing it further up her thighs and my gaze fell straight to her bare flesh. I pictured spreading those legs, driving her down on my desk and making her take my cock like a good girl.

Then I crushed my teeth together and leaned back in my chair as I slapped on a cool expression that gave nothing away of how much my cock was thickening at the thought of Darcy Vega laid bare for me on this very desk.

"So, how is Order Enhancement coming along?" I stacked my hands on my stomach and her eyes dipped to where my shirt was riding up above my waistband before snapping back up to meet my gaze. Fuck she was pretty when she was flustered. And I really didn't want to be amused, but a muscle in the corner of my mouth dared to twitch.

"Well I know I'm not a Werewolf," she said with a shrug, composing herself fast and that word on her lips brought my mood crashing back down to a furious zero.

"Yes, a great way to figure out if you're a Werewolf is dancing with one of them like you were paid for it." I gave her a long, hard stare that let her know I'd seen her. I'd seen and I'd heard and I knew she desired that asshole. A fact I'd made a point of ignoring ever since Friday night. But now she was here, bringing it up and my insides were on fire again, doused in rocket fuel and lit up like a bonfire.

She shifted nervously, seeming uncomfortable of my assessment. And I started regretting saying it. It wasn't professional. Why should I mention it at all? But at the same time, I was so fucking curious as to whether she'd gone through with what she'd clearly wanted from him on that dancefloor. Had they fucked? Had he had her beneath him moaning his name?

I couldn't stand the thought of it. It made me want to hunt him down and rip his head clean from his shoulders. And I knew that was irrational and so much more besides, but I was on this path and I couldn't get off it. I had to know. Had he had her? Would I have to accept that that strutting prick of a dog had laid a claim on her which I could never hope to?

Her cheeks were flushed as my gaze became no less intense and I didn't back down from the question that was hanging in the air between us. And why not ask it? Put a voice to it? It was there anyway. And perhaps I could ask in such a way that didn't hint at my interest in the subject. I simply couldn't read the answer from her expression, so fuck it, I was going to ask.

"And screwing him didn't bring out the wolf in you either?" I said completely calmly, not giving away the stormy sea inside me that brought cliffs down into its waters. It was just a simple question, meant to mock. I was an asshole teacher, that was what she'd think. Nothing else.

Her lips pressed tightly together and anger flashed in her eyes like lightning. "I didn't," she hissed. "And it would be none of your business if I did."

Relief hummed like a song in my veins. It echoed through every inch of me and I didn't let an iota of it show on my face. But I scooted my chair forward until our bare knees brushed together and the smoothness of her skin made me ache for more contact. I was supposed to be rational right now, but it was the last thing I was. This man was bordering on insanity and she was the voices in my head, telling me to do the unthinkable.

I leaned forward and her lips parted, the breath she drew in seeming to draw me in too. "It's my business as your Liaison to look out for you. The Heirs will chew you up and spit you out, Miss Vega. Just a friendly warning." I said it in a way that was anything but friendly, my fangs extending as I hoped to drive the point home. *Run for your star damned life, Blue. I cannot protect you and I wouldn't even if I could.*

She rested her palms on the desk, leaning closer rather than retreating from me and my dick hardened for her the moment her scent wrapped around me. She was the sweetest fucking fruit I'd ever seen, hanging there so ripe and appetising that my mouth was watering for a bite. Just one, lingering bite.

I trained my ears on her heartbeat, finding it pattering out a frantic tune that gave me a hit of power, helping my head clear as I realised she wasn't as confident as she looked.

"Funnily enough, sir, I've taken an interest in *your* business too lately." She didn't blink, delivering those words carefully like she'd constructed them in her mind before now. We were playing her game, but I was already crowned the winner. She just couldn't see it yet.

I cocked my head, my mouth tugging up at the corner as I enjoyed the confident look on her face while knowing she had nothing on me. "Well don't keep me in suspense, Miss Vega. I'm dying to hear the speech you've written for this occasion." I smirked darkly, knowing what she was angling at. That I was out for her and her sister's blood, that she thought me capable of murder, and of course therefore believed Geraldine Grus's attacker was right in this chair. She'd already accused me of plotting her and Tory's deaths and if I was in her shoes, I'd probably have drawn the same conclusion. But the problem with Darcy's little Poirot moment, was that she had no evidence and she clearly hadn't watched the news recently.

She eyed my expression, realising I'd already figured out what she was about to say and folded her arms as she glared at me. *Well you did have a speech planned, didn't you, Blue?*

Her eyes were full of hellfire and I had to admit I was enjoying getting her riled up like this. She raised a hand, counting off her points one at a time. "You and Darius have been against Tory and I since we stepped in the door. You meet up in secret and you talk about going on killing sprees like it's completely normal. You chat with some stupidly hot model in a bar who is apparently in the know about your killing sprees and then you corner me in a women's bathroom like a psycho. *Then* later that evening both you and Darius go conveniently missing just before Geraldine turns up almost dead in a strange attack. Oh and who happens to be the first on the scene? You. Covered in blood and smelling like cinnamon."

That was a lot to process. And my brows had taken a flight towards my hairline as I picked each of those points apart, focusing on two that perhaps should have been the least relevant, but to me were very interesting. Stupidly hot model? Am I totally fucking deluded in thinking the way she said that sounded like jealousy? And holy shit, has she been smelling me?

A grin ripped across my face, a traitor in itself but I couldn't stop it as I realised Blue might actually have some interest in me beyond her witch hunt. "Cinnamon?"

"Yes," she said firmly, but her cheeks were getting red and she was growing more flustered, more fucking edible. "Geraldine smelled it and that's what you smell like so..." She raised her chin like she'd made a great point, like this was some undeniable evidence against me, when in fact all it was was a confession that she knew what I smelled like and apparently it was worth noting.

"And how many people have you told this, Miss Vega?" I asked casually which seemed to piss her off more. I was doing it on purpose, delighting in getting under her skin. Because if she looked this cute while semi-composed, I simply had to know what she looked like when she lost it completely. And I was enjoying this so much that I didn't even let myself think of all the reasons why I shouldn't be toying with her. Not least the way the head of my cock was throbbing.

"Enough that if you lay a hand on me, the whole school will know what you're up to before midnight." Triumph spread over her face, and it was so fucking cute I almost wished she wasn't about to be cut down to size. Not enough to stop me from doing it though.

"Well it seems you've been spending a lot of your time spying on me - and smelling me apparently. But I'm still waiting for you to plant the evidence on my desk?" I gazed at her hands, pretending I was looking for it when I knew full well she had absolutely jack shit on me. "No?" I taunted. "No video, photo, audio recording? No evidence at all?"

The colour in her cheeks started to drain and I calmly took my Atlas from my sports bag, placing it under her nose and showing her the news report that had recently gone out.

Wounds on Zodiac Academy Student Now Confirmed as a Nymph Attack. Professor Orion (the head of his field in Cardinal Magic at Zodiac Academy) is expected to be awarded the Noble Crest after his act of bravery saved her moments before her death.

Her eyes fell to the words and I watched, drinking in every second as embarrassment radiated from her.

"Oh," she breathed.

"Yes – *oh*. Now can we return to your session or do you have any more wild accusations you want to throw around? Is Principal Nova dealing drugs under the bleachers at the Pitball Stadium? Or is Professor Pyro starting fires in The Wailing Wood?" I laughed at my own words, though the sound stuttered out as she shoved to her feet, knocking her chair over in her haste as she aimed a poisonous glare at me.

"You know what? I'm done with these sessions. I know what I heard, *sir*. And maybe you didn't attack Geraldine but I know you're up to something." She strode toward the door and in a split-second decision, I decided that that girl was currently the only thing making my life seem remotely enjoyable and if she left, she wouldn't come back in here. She wouldn't bring her light to me anymore. I'd be alone in the dark again and with everything that had happened lately I needed her to stay.

I flew in front of her with my speed, blocking her way out and trapping her, knowing it was crazy, stupid, a selfish desire. But I wanted her in this room. With me. For as long as I could keep her.

"Don't bite me," she snarled, stepping back in a rage. "You took almost everything from me the other day and I've only just got my full power back."

My brows knitted together in surprise as a jolt ran through me. "You got it back? How?"

She shook her head. "I'm not sure."

"Well pay attention next time." I stepped forward and she slammed a hand to my chest, the heat of her palm almost making me curse.

"Don't," she commanded, her eyes flaring with how much she didn't want my fangs in her. And I was surprised by how much that stung.

"I wasn't going to bite you," I muttered and her shoulders sagged with relief, making my stomach knot tightly. *I just don't want you to leave. Because when you do, I'll have to return to reality. And my reality sucks so fucking much, you have no idea.* I stepped back and pointed to her chair, flicking a finger to force it upright with a gust of air. "Stay. Finish the session." *Please.*

She glanced at the door uncertainly, looking unsure if she even wanted to stay. And I couldn't really blame her. I wasn't exactly a barrel of laughs. "Will you answer something for me first?"

"Depends what it is," I said in a low voice. *Because there are some secrets I can never tell. But to keep you right now, I think I'd tell them all.*

"Do you want me and my sister dead?" She gave me a hard look that spoke of how much she needed this answer, staring into my eyes as she waited to try and assess my answer, to seek the truth from my eyes.

My gaze travelled over her beautiful face and there was only one answer I could really give, because no matter what happened from here on out, I was sure that I didn't want to see her or her sister die. To see this girl perish would break something in me I didn't even know existed until I met her. "No, Blue. I don't."

Silence spanned between us and a heavy breath left my chest the same time it did hers. She frowned at me like she couldn't work out what I was thinking and honestly, I wasn't sure I even knew. My head was messed up over Darius, but it was messed up over her too. At this moment in time, I felt torn in two directions, and part of me wanted to lock the door and remain in here for as long as I could get away with. For as long she'd stay.

"So…what do you wanna teach me?" she asked, clearly still pissed at me over how her accusations had gone down.

My fingers flexed with the urge to take hold of her, but I jerked my head in a command instead, figuring it was best to keep some distance from her. "Sit down."

She did and I walked around, opening a drawer in my desk and taking out one of my favourite tomes. The Illustrated Guide to Orders and their Gifts.

The cover was hand painted, the Order constellations delicately brushed onto its black surface in gold and glittering gemstones marked the stars.

Darcy reached out to touch it, her fingers brushing mine and her eyes igniting with a spark I remembered from my days studying at this academy. She was hungry for knowledge and I had the quiet urge to feed her every scrap I had even if that was a dangerous idea. Because knowledge was power and power in Solaria was everything. Still…I was her teacher, her Liaison. So there was no harm in playing the role a little.

I slid the book towards her and she sucked her bottom lip into her mouth as she opened it, the sight doing more to me than the best porn in the world. I took the opportunity of her distraction to sit down and rearrange my dick in my shorts, shifting closer on my chair, but not close enough for our knees to touch again.

"Here," I said, my voice coming out hard and rough around the lump swelling in my throat as I pointed to the contents page, every Order laid out with a tiny symbol of their kind beside each. "These are the Orders." The list in this book was as close to a complete encyclopaedia of every Order ever known to exist as you could get. There was always a chance there could be a new, strange and rare Order form discovered, but so far as anyone knew at this moment in time, this book had it all. I'd given them a short list of some of the more common Orders to study in my Cardinal Magic class, but this right here had every single Order listed in it, which had to mean hers lay between its pages too.

"There's so many," she breathed in awe, turning page after page of the contents while I watched with rapt attention to every tiny movement of her eyes, her lips. She was entirely captivating to me and I was caught off guard again as her gaze flicked up to meet mine, a smile lifting her mouth that wasn't for me. It was for that book. And the idea that it made her happy had my heart beating to a fierce tune, demanding I show her more, every favoured one in my damn collection. Which was absurd because I coveted those books and I'd never cared to share them with anyone. But if each one delivered me a smile as natural as that then it seemed inevitable that I was going to show her them all. Not fucking sensible though.

I cleared my throat, realising she was waiting for direction and I reached out to turn the page, revealing the first Order. The Aalarian Aardvark.

On the left hand page was a skilled painting of the creature in full colour, its bronze and rust scales shimmering on the page, the artwork so realistic it looked as though it could walk right out of the book. On the right hand page were stats about its size, its needs, its gifts and what it required to recharge its magic.

I pointed to that part of the text, showing that an Aalarian Aardvark needed to curl up and roll down hills to recharge its power, silently thanking the stars I didn't have to do anything so ludicrous to recharge my own power.

"I want you to look through these pages and read each of these," I instructed. "If you find anything that resonates with you, then you will note down the Order and I shall conduct some tests to see whether we are getting closer to discovering which one you'll Emerge as."

She nodded, turning the page, her eyes widening at the Abada there, a rare Order which was like a small, wingless Pegasus with two crooked horns and a boar's tail.

"However," I continued. "It is worth noting that some Orders have little known about them because they are either too rare or extinct. There are some colonies of Muskian Tigers for example who live independent of society and covet the secrets of their Order, but what is known will be found between these pages."

She nodded, looking anxious to keep going as she turned another page.

"If you have any questions, then feel free to ask," I said, but she was lost in her own world now, turning page after page, her head cocking and her nose getting closer and closer to the book as she let it fill up her field of vision.

I let myself watch, finding peace in her naivety to our world, and with the chaos raging outside of this room, I allowed myself to indulge in it. Because this was surely the calm before the storm and I had no idea of the damage that was going to be caused when it came. So for now, I'd steal this moment of quiet, finding the ache in my soul lessening as her glow seemed to fill up the entirety of my office. It felt like a truce during a war, our weapons temporarily put down and in a moment of insanity, I wondered what it would be like to leave them cast aside.

DARIUS

CHAPTER TWENTY-ONE

I lay in my bed with gold heaped around me as I replenished my magic and music blared out through my speaker while I tried to find some semblance of peace from the warring thoughts and feelings which were constantly taking place within my skull.

I was supposed to be down in the Fire Arena now, tutoring Roxy Vega in her fire magic but I would be doing that precisely never. Professor Pyro might have asked me to do it and I might have even agreed, but when it came down to it, Roxy was going to have to force my participation if she wanted it. And seeing as she was entirely incapable of doing that, it wouldn't be happening.

I was avoiding her anyway. The other Heirs and I had come up with the start of the plans required to get rid of her and her sister for good and I was focusing on that goal. I didn't need to be distracted by my desire for her and I wasn't going to be putting myself in a position which might lead to her drawing me in again.

Lance thought they could be Sirens, but I was wondering if they weren't something more like Incubuses. The Order was pretty rare but their entire way of rejuvenating magic was based off of sexual desire and they were masters at controlling and claiming lust from others. And Roxy Vega definitely inspired plenty of lust everywhere she went. She inspired so much lust in me that I found myself entirely unable to jerk off over anyone other than her, memories of her body, her mouth or even just her calling me fucking names filling my mind the second I wrapped my fist around my throbbing cock. I'd even tried watching porn to distract myself from her but I just ended up closing my goddamn eyes and thinking of her anyway, imaging how good it would feel to be filling her with my dick instead of fucking my hand all the damn time.

But I was determined to stop thinking about her like that. To stop thinking about her at all in fact, other than with the desire to get rid of her.

I'd spoken to Xavier again a couple of hours ago and he had reassured me that everything was fine. He was doing a lot of extra work and training after school in an attempt to get ahead as well as avoiding my father by not ending up caught in his company at the manor too often.

He'd said that Mother had been sneaking into his room at night, sitting on the edge of his bed and pushing her fingers into his hair like she used to when we were children, and I knew that he was reading a lot into that. But I wasn't sure what a few gentle touches from the woman who had abandoned us to our father's tyranny a long time ago were supposed to prove. Not that I'd said that to him of course because Xavier wasn't like me. Despite the two of us being raised in the same toxic environment, he was still so damn hopeful all the time. Still seeking out light in the dark. And maybe that had something to do with me being the Heir and taking the brunt of Father's attention, lessons and punishments, but I had a feeling it was something innately him too.

Mostly I was wishing this year away so that Xavier could come and stay here at the academy with me. I'd feel a whole lot better when he was out of that house for good and somewhere that I could keep a proper eye on him at all times with his magic Awakened and his Dragon Order form released too.

My Atlas buzzed and I glanced at it, seeing the message from Lance and tsking irritably.

Lance:

Are you going to tell me your plans?

Darius:

It's better you don't know.

I still wasn't sure what the other Heirs and I were going to do to deal with the Vegas but there was a good chance that it would go beyond what a teacher should allow to happen. I wasn't going to put his job here in jeopardy for the sake of this. Besides, this was on me and the Heirs to sort out, he didn't have to be dragged into even more of my shit.

Lance:

I could help

Darius:

Your entire life is spent helping me. Go do something you enjoy for once

I looked at my Atlas for several long seconds but he didn't reply. My gut twisted, knowing that statement would have upset him but it was also the truth. Father had stolen Lance's life when he'd bound us together and I was sick of dragging him into my bullshit all the damn time. Yeah, it was nice for me to have an ally in my hatred of Lionel Acrux, but where had anything we'd been trying to do really gotten me? Lance may have been training me in dark magic, but it still wasn't close to enough to put me on an even playing field with my father so that I could take him on. And now Xavier had been attacked because of my foolish attempts at defiance. I didn't want to put Lance in the firing line too.

So he might have been hurt by me pushing him out of this, but I was just trying to protect him. Trying to keep him as far from my father's wrath as I could. And if I was being honest, I was being selfish too. Lance always wanted to see the good in me, the things that set me apart from Lionel Acrux and proved I wasn't the clone he'd tried to force me to be. But I was starting to think that had just been a pretty lie we'd been telling ourselves for the last few years because now I was going to have to be just as monstrous as him to protect my brother. And if I had to turn to the dark to achieve what my father wanted then I knew I'd do it – I just didn't want to have to face the disappointment in Lance's eyes when he saw what I let myself become.

A prickle ran down my spine and I lifted my head, looking to my bedroom door a beat before someone knocked on it.

"It's open," I called. I'd been half expecting Caleb to drop by anyway and it was probably a good thing he had because I needed a distraction from the tempest of my thoughts. "Come in."

There was a long pause then the door swung open and my heart lurched as I looked towards it, finding Roxanya Vega standing there in a skin tight sports bra and leggings combo, looking entirely too tempting while she scrutinised my room.

Her nose wrinkled faintly as her green eyes skimmed over everything, drinking in all the details of the place I called home from the yellow and orange windows which spanned across the wall above my bed to the couch and TV area I had by the far wall.

Her gaze touched on every golden item in the room, from the furniture to the clock and picture frames before falling to the chest of treasure which currently stood empty at the foot of my bed.

A protective growl built in my chest as her eyes lingered there, looking at all of my most prized possessions before she finally turned her attention to me where I sat shirtless on my bed surrounded by my gold.

"What the hell do you want?" I snarled, pushing myself up to a sitting position as I glared at her.

I'd been avoiding her for a damn good reason and as my cock jerked like it wanted to salute her in greeting, I was forcefully reminded why. I'd been making a point to keep away from her until we were ready to execute our plans to get rid of her because I didn't want a single moment of doubt to colour my decision on this.

"Do you have a pirate fetish or something?" she asked, arching a brow at my gold and throwing me off as she almost seemed amused. I'd expected her to start screaming at me about skipping our session or at least cussing me out, but instead she was cocking her head at me and looking kind of cute and confused in the face of the hatred I had decided to aim at her. I guessed she might have thought that the time we'd spent dancing together had softened some of the animosity between us, but that couldn't be further from the truth considering the cost of that moment of weakness I'd experienced in her arms.

"What?" I asked, forcing my scowl to tighten as I thought of my brother screaming in agony and refused to let her distract me from my goal.

"Well you're half naked in a bed full of coins so either you're doing something with them or putting them somewhere...*inaccessible* while fully dressed or I missed the memo about your enrolment in Captain Silver's new fleet."

Was that a joke? For a moment I didn't even know what to say to her but as she blinked at me with genuine confusion in her gaze, I realised that she didn't know what I was. Was that why she wasn't afraid to rile me up? Was that why she pushed and pushed me when any other Fae would cower in fear?

"You really don't know anything do you?" I scoffed. "This is how my kind regenerate our power; from gold."

"Oh." She frowned at the coins again and I could tell she still didn't get it. "So are you Order of pirate then? Do you transform into a one legged man with an eyepatch, a hankering for rum and a pet parrot?"

Her question caught me so off guard that I almost cracked, a laugh building in my chest which had no fucking business being there. I was forced to crush it with a firm reminder of the way the scent of Xavier's burning flesh had filled the air in my father's office and I forced myself to take back control of the situation.

"What the hell are you doing in my room?" I demanded.

"Why do you think I'm here?" she shot back instantly. But I wasn't going to be doing her the favour of making this interaction easy.

"The only possible reason I can imagine for you to be stupid enough to come bursting in here would be that you've finally come to realise who really deserves to rule Solaria. And that being the case, I imagine you're about to bow down low and praise me and the other Heirs as your kings," I said, shrugging like that seemed like a genuine guess and watching the way her eyes flared with anger at that suggestion.

"Keep dreaming," she muttered. "I'm here because you missed yet another one of our tutoring sessions, as I'm sure you're aware."

"And what if I am?" I asked, pushing to my feet suddenly and knocking a handful of gold coins to the floor. "What will you do about it? Make me bow to your will?"

Roxy lifted her chin and glared at me defiantly. "Come and do the session like you promised," she demanded.

I stalked closer to her, forcing her to look up at me as I came to tower over her, wanting to see her back down, but she held her ground and tightened her jaw instead, waiting for my answer.

"No," I breathed, every inch of my body burning with my fire magic as it raced to the surface of my skin at the challenge in her eyes. "If you want me to train you, you'll have to make me. If you really are one of our kind then you're going to need to learn quickly that Fae take what they want and the only thing that matters to us is power. So if you want me to do something for you then you're going to have to force me."

Roxy looked ready to start screaming at last, but when she opened her mouth, what came out was a mocking taunt instead. "How many Elements do you wield again, Darius?" she asked, her voice rough and low. "Two, isn't it?"

The Dragon in me roared in anger at her insinuation but I refused to let it show, keeping my face locked in the unyielding mask my father had beat into me.

"Two are more than enough," I replied simply.

"Yeah... but having all four has got to be better." She was practically smirking at me, baiting me, daring me to do my worst like she truly thought she could handle it if I did. And damn my heart to the stars, but I was tempted to do just that. Let her see the beast in me and see if she truly could handle it.

"I'm an apex predator. My kind aren't built to take orders from anyone. It's written in my DNA to rule over you. I could never bow no matter how powerful you might have the potential to be," I said icily.

"How can you know that? You don't even know what Order I am. Maybe I'm higher up the food chain than you think," she said, eyes still glittering like she was getting off on the danger of taunting the villain in me.

I scoffed, closing in on her until I was right in her personal space, the sweet scent of her skin calling to me as I leaned in close and placed my hands against the door either side of her head, penning her in and watching her with my heart racing as she still refused to flinch.

"No one is higher up the food chain than me, *Roxy*," I promised her, my gaze dropping down to drink her in even though I refused to let anything other than hatred for her and all she represented touch my soul. She was my enemy, plain and simple and I couldn't allow a single moment of doubt cloud that for my brother's sake.

She studied me while I studied her and the pull I kept feeling towards her crackled against my bare flesh like an oncoming thunderstorm. But I wouldn't bow to its desires. There was nothing left between me and her aside from the need in me to get rid of her.

"What Order are you?" Roxy breathed, her chest rising and falling with the heavy pressure of the air that surrounded us and my gaze fell to the swell of her tits in the little sports bra she wore.

"I'll show you mine if you'll show me yours," I teased, my eyes shifting to the golden hue of my Dragon, reptilian slits and all before I blinked the shift away again and watched the shock flash over her features.

"But I don't know my Order yet," she protested. "Professor Orion thinks growing up in the mortal world suppressed our abilities."

I watched her for a moment, wondering if that was really true and she genuinely had no idea what she was. And strangely enough, I actually believed her.

But if she wanted to know what breed of creature was standing before her then I was happy enough to give her a show and make her realise exactly why she should fear me.

I stepped back suddenly, snapping the band of energy that had seemed to be drawing me closer to her as I unbuckled my belt and unbuttoned my fly.

"What are you doing?" she gasped, staring at me as I dropped my jeans, knocking my boxers off with them and letting her get a good eyeful of the full length of my cock.

Her gaze stayed glued on it and blood began to rush that way at the feeling of her attention, like that part of me still hadn't agreed to my decision to have nothing more to do with her beyond making sure she left this place. I gritted my teeth as my dick continued to get all kinds of ideas about the things it could do with her if I just made her bow for me now and I tried not to let my gaze linger on her mouth while I considered how much I'd like to fuck it.

"When you stop eye-fucking me I'll show you what you're so desperate to know," I mocked, forcing her attention back up to my face and earning myself a scowl.

"People don't tend to whip their junk out in the middle of a conversation," she snapped like she was pissed at me for it. "So if you didn't want me catching an eyeful of little Darius then you shouldn't have brought him into our discussion."

I released a breath of laughter before I could help myself, my mind and dick wandering down all kinds of out of bounds roads as I gave myself two seconds to consider whether or not I could convince her to bow for me after all.

I leaned closer to her as she scowled back, but her breaths were speeding up and her pupils were wide with what I could have sworn was desire of her own.

I wanted that. I wanted it more than I could say and it was so fucking tempting to just step forward, catch her by the back of the neck and kiss her roughly until she gave in and bowed to me the way I ached for her to. I could see it in her eyes. The temptation despite the hatred and I wanted to hate fuck her so much that I almost took that final step.

But as my own pulse thundered like a war drum in my ears, I knew it wouldn't be so simple. One taste of her and I'd be addicted. And I couldn't afford that no matter how tempting a sin she might have been.

"If you come to my room uninvited again then it had better be because you're ready to bow to us or to beg me to bend you over that headboard and make you scream my name," I said with all the confidence I felt in knowing that she was getting as wet for me as I was getting hard for her.

She pressed herself back against my door, her thighs clenching together like she was trying to fight her reaction, but I felt it humming in the air between us no matter how deeply she scowled.

It was all animal and I knew it would be the best kinds of bad if we gave into it. But I couldn't.

I turned away from her suddenly then took a running jump out of the open window beside us.

Roxy gasped in alarm as I fell and I stretched my arms wide, letting the seconds tick by as I hurtled towards the ground while my Dragon rose up in me with a fiery desperation for freedom.

As the golden Dragon burst from my skin, a roar tore from my throat loud enough to rattle all of the windows in Ignis House.

Fire burst from my jaw in the next moment, the heat of it billowing back over my golden scales as I dove headfirst through the flames.

I tore away through the sky, not letting myself look back at the girl who I knew was still watching me while the feeling of her eyes on my skin scraped me raw and sent a shudder of premonition racing through me.

That girl was my downfall in the making. I just had to make sure she never reached that potential.

MAX

CHAPTER TWENTY-TWO

I sat on the edge of Aqua Lake waiting for my Siren Order Enhancement class to start with anticipation brimming through me as I watched the Vega twins stalking across the lawn towards us.

Today they were joining our class to see if there were any clues that they might Emerge as one of us, but I was seriously doubtful about that. Sirens were naturally empathetic by nature, easily locking into the emotions of others even before our Order officially Emerged. We tended to be either genuinely more concerned about the welfare of other Fae than ourselves because we were so in tune that their feelings actually affected ours too, or we were conniving assholes who abused our knowledge for the sake of manipulation.

Whichever way, I couldn't say I'd seen any evidence of either behaviour from the two girls who were on their way to join our class and I hadn't felt the sway of their own emotions trying to reach out and affect others either. So I was pretty confident in my assessment that they weren't of my kind.

That said, I was actually really looking forward to this class. The other

Heirs and I knew what we needed to do now and though Darius hadn't wanted to let me feel his emotions while we'd been discussing it, there were times that I'd tasted his fear on the air.

My friend wasn't a man who feared much in this world and though he kept his secrets about the things he endured when he was at home, none of us were stupid. We picked up on the tone of his relationship with his father. We'd been close enough to witness some of the bruises and Caleb had once overheard some of it too though none of us could do a damn thing about it to help save him from it. But Darius was one of the strongest Fae I knew. He endured all his father threw at him and even thrived despite it and despite him having his demons, I knew he'd never been broken by any of it before now. But the fear I'd managed to sense on him over the last few days was fresher and somehow so raw that it made shivers run down my spine too. So I was willing to bet all of my scales that Lionel Acrux had threatened him with something truly motivating to have invoked such a certain reaction from him.

Which meant one thing and one thing only. We had to succeed in our task now. My own father had made his wishes on the matter perfectly clear to me too. The Vegas needed to be tested beyond all matter of doubt. If there was any chance that they were weak enough to be driven out, then we were responsible for making that happen. And if we struck at them but they still found the courage and strength of will to stay...well then we were going to have to adjust our tactics. It wouldn't be about getting rid of them anymore. It would be about proving they could never match us. And that seemed a whole lot more dangerous to me than simply making them leave.

So with that plan in mind and the desire to help fix whatever was causing the turbulent emotions I kept tasting on Darius, I was willing to do anything it took to fight against the Vegas.

And luckily for me, as they were attending this class today, I would be able to get the information we needed, and later the other Heirs and I could finalise our plans.

The twins reached us and I felt their nerves as they made it to the large group, their attention flicking to me momentarily before shifting away again.

"Good morning girls, I'm Professor Undine," called the teacher who ran this class, beckoning them closer. She had deep red hair which was braided down her spine and wore a thin top and shorts despite the chill in the air, ready for us to go for a swim once the class really got going. "Come on everyone, get in the circle," she instructed.

Everyone who was still standing sat down in the grass, my little group of admirers crowding close to me as always, letting me feel their adoration, lust, envy - all nice emotions for me to feast on while inflating my ego just a little.

I sat forward to get a better look at our new arrivals, locking my arms around my knees and observing how uncomfortable they looked at being surrounded by my kind.

"I wouldn't mind feeding them a little lust and seeing how wild they can get," Lewis muttered, leaning in close beside me. The guy was a grade A ass licker who probably would have sucked my cock while polishing my shoes for me if I asked him to, but I indulged him because his family were pretty influential, and my dad wanted to keep them on side.

I smiled like I was amused by his remark, but I wasn't a fan of forcing lust on people without them wanting it. Would I fill the room with it while I was fucking a girl? Yeah, of course I would. But at that point her consent would have been confirmed and I could use my gifts without having to feel like a creep trying to force sex on someone who wouldn't have wanted it without the influence of my gifts. Lewis however was always a creep.

Undine took the emotions reader from her pocket, the silver ball hanging in a nest of wire which she set in motion by flicking a finger at it, making the ball inside start to spin. She tossed it at Kayla across the circle who caught it out of the air.

"Happy," Kayla announced, reading the emotion from the ball as it stopped spinning.

"Great," Undine said. "Who wants to start?"

I groaned, bored of this damn kids game already. I'd asked my father more than once to get me out of these classes, but he insisted that it was good for me to get to know the others of my kind so that I could build their loyalty to me within our Order. On top of that, we repeatedly ended up feeding on happy emotions which I generally didn't like to do. "Can't we do fear again, miss?"

"We did fear last week," Undine said firmly. "And besides, you spend enough of your time terrorising the other students at Zodiac to get your fix, Mr Rigel. You don't need to get it here every week too."

"For fuck's sake," I growled. It wasn't even about preferring the taste of fear, I was just so powerful that if I fed on another Fae's happiness for too long I usually ended up stealing it away and leaving them feeling empty or sad for a while afterwards. I much preferred to get my fix from taking unpleasant emotions away from them and leaving them feeling free from their burdens and happier than they'd been to begin with. Not that I ever gave out that truth to anyone. Let them think I was a monster who thrived on the taste of fear and pain - it only fed my reputation as one of the more ruthless Fae in the kingdom anyway.

"*Language*, Mr Rigel. That's five points from Aqua," Undine shot at me. "You know how much I hate the Fs and the Ss."

"What about the Cs?" I taunted with a smirk.

Undine ignored me, glancing around the circle until she fixed her attention on the Vegas. "Ah, this is a good opportunity to introduce you to our Order, girls. Come and stand up here with me."

They rose to their feet and everyone perked up as they eyed them with interest, knowing how this game went. Everyone here clearly wanted the chance to feed from the most powerful Fae in the kingdom.

"Think of a happy memory you've had this week," Undine instructed and the girls exchanged a look which seemed to suggest they hadn't been happy at all this week.

The empathy engrained in me almost made me feel bad about that, but then I focused on the need to remove them from this academy and realised it could only be a good thing if they were miserable here.

"Er..." Tory frowned and Darcy chewed her lip.

A couple of giggles sounded from the watching Sirens but I remained quiet.

"You must have something that's made you happy in the last seven days? Or the last fourteen perhaps?" Undine raised her brows, looking concerned as she reached out with her gifts to assess their emotions.

I felt the shift in the twins' emotions as they both managed to find a happy memory to focus on. "Got one," Darcy announced and Tory nodded with a grin.

"Okay." Undine picked out ten people from the circle, including Lewis who gave me a dirty grin as he hopped up and they all rushed forward eagerly while I remained where I was.

"Take your coat off," Bree urged Darcy and Simon pulled it from her shoulders, tossing it on the grass before she could protest.

"Hey!" she made a grab for it but the Sirens closed in around her, blocking her off.

"Hold that happy memory in your heads," Undine called out.

"Tell us about your memory," Bree encouraged and I could feel her trying to calm Darcy down so that she'd be more willing to share.

"I was out in town drinking with friends," Darcy said, with a smile that turned into a snort of laughter and the Sirens all chuckled along as they drank in her happiness and fed their magic reserves.

"What else?" Lewis asked, and from the smarmy lust I could feel coming from him, I could tell he was hoping for a sex story. "I can sense something else in you, tell us about the rest of your evening." He reached out to brush his fingers over her wrist and I felt his power pushing against her will as he drew what he wanted from her tongue. "I saw Professor Orion."

Kayla gasped, shooting a look at Lewis then grinning keenly as she held onto Darcy's arm.

I could taste that lust from all the way over here and I rolled my eyes. Half the girls in this school were lusting after out Cardinal Magic professor. It was kinda sad really.

Darcy frowned as she tried to pull back, but Lewis held on tight and shoved all of his will into forcing her to go on. "He was angry...he's so hot when he's angry."

A couple of the girls moaned lustily and Undine suddenly clapped her hands as she realised what they were up to. "Enough. We're not doing lust today."

The group of Sirens released Darcy and her face burned red as she seemed to realise what she'd said. Lewis returned to sit with me, grinning from ear to ear and holding out his hand for a high five.

I wasn't high fiving that shit so I pretended not to notice as I looked towards Tory who was still sharing her story with the group surrounding her, but I wasn't close enough to eavesdrop on that one.

Undine split the group up into smaller clusters and they started recounting happy memories for each other while I just lay back in the grass, cupping my head with my hands and waiting for our professor to move past this boring part of the lesson.

No one tried to force me to participate so I just watched the grey clouds rolling by and bathed in the feeling of happiness surrounding me as everyone continued to feed on that emotion and I was gifted a rare break from all the teenage angst and drama which generally filled this academy.

Undine moved to try her luck stealing some lust from Darcy and I sighed. She was no better than the rest of them for that. When I was certain she was fully distracted by whatever Darcy Vega was thinking about Professor Orion, I got to my feet and prowled up behind them.

I crept closer then pounced with a yell, grabbing Undine's shoulders and sucking the fear right out of her as she squealed in fright. My power reserves swelled and I grinned at her furious face as she whirled on me.

"We're not doing fear, Rigel," she snarled, throwing up a hand so a gust of air shoved me back a few steps.

She stalked away, checking on the other students and I turned my attention to scaring some of the others to alleviate my boredom. I got a kick from the spike of fear I could create followed by a rush as I stole it away from them and I wasn't done yet.

I got a top up from a few more victims but then Lewis found me again, bringing a couple of girls he'd snagged with lust and they giggled as they pressed closer to me.

"Hey man, these four say they wanna come party with us after this lesson is over," Lewis said excitedly, nudging me in a way that made me want to snap his damn elbow off.

"I heard you can fill a room with so much lust that a girl can come just from walking into it," one of the girls said breathily, eyeing me with a keen interest which I couldn't say I minded.

"It's happened once or twice," I admitted with a grin that made them all giggle.

"So what do you say? Shall we head back to your room after class and make a party of it?" Lewis pushed, his lust sliding over me like a greasy hand caressing a pumpkin.

"Sounds good to me," I agreed as one of the girls bit her bottom lip hopefully. But I wasn't going to be including Lewis in this party. I just had to be a little more subtle than simply telling him to fuck off thanks to dad's political agenda. But I was sure I'd come up with something.

"I am *not* a Siren," Tory Vega's voice drew my attention and I looked over to see her standing with her sister who nodded in agreement.

"I just need to have a little word with the Vegas before we head off," I murmured to the others and Lewis groaned like a dirty old lech as he looked over at the twins.

"Are you gonna get them to join us too?" he asked excitedly.

"No," I snapped. It was one thing sharing lust with this group of Siren girls who were actively adding their own powers to the mix and clearly wanted it, but I wasn't ever going to be forcing lust on a girl who didn't want it and if I ever caught Lewis trying it then I'd punish him for bringing shame on our Order, political agenda or not. Dad would back me if it came to that.

Undine clapped her hands to signal the end of this part of the lesson and everyone headed to the edge of the lake where they started peeling off their clothes and shifting to reveal the scales of our Order form coating their bodies.

Undine didn't bother with a further explanation, diving straight into the lake the moment her red scales appeared on her flesh.

"I'm not going in there," Tory said firmly, backing away from the edge of the water and a touch of fear brushed against my skin which got me all kinds of intrigued.

The rest of the class were quick to follow Undine into the lake and I tugged my shirt off like I was going to dive in too until only me and my little group remained on the bank with the Vegas.

I let the shift come over me, navy scales rippling across my flesh and coating my skin like a cool caress which instantly protected me from the bite of the cold wind.

I grinned at the Vegas as they turned their attention to me, stalking closer to them and signalling the rest of my group to hang back while I unleashed the full force of my power and prepared to get what me and the other Heirs needed to complete our plans.

The girls fell still as I caught them in the thrall of my gifts and I took their hands, using the skin on skin contact to fully immerse them in my power and make them feel calm and safe with me.

"Hi," Tory said breathily and I had to fight the smug bastard look which was crawling over my face as I took control of the two most powerful Fae in

Solaria as easily as breathing.

"How're my favourite twins?" I asked, and Lewis and the others laughed like a bunch of cronies though none of them dared approach, knowing this was my feed. "Come sit with me."

I guided the Vegas toward the edge of the lake and they sat either side of me while I kept a tight hold on their hands and made sure they remained fully under my spell. I released their hands but dropped an arm over each of their shoulders to pull them closer, sinking my power in even deeper to make sure I had them before I went on.

"What's your greatest fear, Tory?" I breathed in her ear and she turned to look up at me, her eyes widening with terror as I felt it building in her under the strength of my gifts.

I sighed softly, waiting them out as both of them tried to fight me off, but my influence was potent and lodged deep within them. With a hard shove of my gifts, I managed to force them back under my control, drawing that truth from Tory's lips.

"My ex-boyfriend was driving me home late one night," Tory whispered and for a moment the sound of shrieking tyres seemed to bounce through my skull. "We'd been fighting and he kept shouting at me. I told him to shut up and watch the road. He was driving like a maniac." Her fear increased and I held on tight, needing more than this, needing something we could use. "We were heading back from a weekend in Wisconsin. The roads were so dark but he wouldn't slow down. He took a turning too fast and..." Her eyes glimmered with tears and Darcy reached out to take her hand, making guilt well in my chest for a moment before I forced myself to focus on why I had to do this. Our parents needed us to do it. Solaria was relying on us to ensure it was ruled by the best Fae for the job. Darius needed this to happen more than all. It was necessary. And I wouldn't back down.

"We veered off a bridge and crashed into the river below. The car sank so fast and my ex...he got out. He left me. Just swam to the river bank," Tory's voice was filled with the horror of that memory and I got a few flashes of water pouring in on her, the sounds of her screams. "I couldn't get my seatbelt undone and I panicked. The air was running out and it was so, so dark." Tears ran down her cheeks and I bit my tongue against the inclination to stop, instead drawing back enough so that I didn't have to see her memories and could take in the words. "And when the water went over my head I just thought that was it. I was going to die stuck in that shitty car while my even shittier boyfriend sat on the riverbank and didn't try to help me." She swallowed thickly and I decided to release her from that moment, having what I needed anyway. "Luckily a farmer had seen us swerve off of the road. He swam out and cut the belt. He saved me. But since then I just can't go in deep water. It frightens the hell out of me." She shivered and I soothed her, rubbing her arm as I pushed calming feelings into her skin and hardened myself against any sympathy I might have been inclined to feel for her. Everyone was afraid of something. And her fear just so happened to be an easy one to make use of, so it was a good thing. I was going to keep telling myself that until I could wash the feeling of this fear from my skin and taste some happiness again.

I turned to Darcy, focusing my power on her next. "And you? What's your worst fear Darcy?"

"Every foster family we ever had got rid of us. We were barely in one home for more than a year. We caused trouble. Sometimes I regret some of the things I did so much. If I'd treated those families better, maybe they would have wanted me. That was almost bearable. I knew I was difficult to love but I didn't think I was entirely unlovable not until..." She tried to fight against my power, but I had a firm hold on her and I needed this done so I pushed until she couldn't fight it anymore.

"Go on," I whispered, lacing my tone with my gifts too.

"This guy started pursuing me in school last year. I never really spent much time making friends with people but he was nice and it felt good to talk to someone who cared. We dated for around three months and I thought for one idiotic second I was actually falling for him. I lost my virginity to him at a party and afterwards he was so cold with me. He would barely look at me and I knew something was terribly wrong. The way the air changes just before a storm, that was how it felt. He'd gotten what he wanted and he just left me there after feeding me some bullshit excuse about how he wasn't ready for a relationship."

"Darcy," Tory whispered, trying to fight my hold so that she could save her sister from recounting this but I needed to hear the end of it, so I pushed her to go on.

"He dumped me five *seconds* after he'd gotten what he wanted. I got out of there as fast as I could. And on my way home, I was crying and couldn't see properly. I tripped over on the sidewalk and bashed my right knee like the clumsy idiot I am. That night I sat in bed just staring at that bruise, wondering how a physical wound could look so bright and angry but emotional wounds stayed entirely invisible. I wanted my hurt branded on me, to remind me never to trust anyone again. So I dyed my hair the colour of that bruise. Black and blue. My own personal wound. My deepest fear is being cast aside, my heart crushed by trusting blindly again. So I'll never let anyone in again."

Silence fell between us as I tried to figure out how we could use that against her and for a moment she just cried in my arms.

I pulled my power back, hardening my heart against any foolish notions of sympathy as I focused on all the reasons I had for doing this before I stood abruptly, leaving them sitting there on the ground.

"Thanks for the meal Vegas. See ya."

I dove into the lake without a backwards glance, wanting to scrape the feeling of their fear from my flesh. But at least I'd gotten what I needed from them. And when I met the Heirs for lunch in a couple of hours, I would be able to bring the Vegas' fears to them so that the four of us could finalise our plans against them.

I didn't waste much time swimming in the lake, instead heading for the underwater entrance to Aqua House and striding up out of the water onto the small beach inside the common room.

To my surprise, the four girls and Lewis followed me out of the water and their lust washed over me as they all moved closer as I stepped onto the dry carpet.

"So is this happening?" Lewis asked excitedly, looking to me like the idea of the two of us spit roasting a girl together would be the highlight of his entire life.

The Vegas' fear was still clinging to me but as the Siren girls moved closer, fluttering their eyelashes and biting their lips with lust dancing all around me, I realised I could easily banish that feeling by taking up this offer. I could skip a few classes in favour of indulging in this to brighten my mood again.

"Yeah, come on then," I said, using my water magic to dry all of us off before striding through the common room and down the corridor which led towards my room.

The lust built between the six of us as we went and I used my gifts to stoke it, building it until I was hard as stone inside my shorts and looking forward to fucking these girls until they lost their voices from screaming my name.

But Lewis was not going to be joining the party.

As I spotted my door ahead, I pushed more lust into the guy who was walking at my side, building it up and up until he grunted.

"Fuck, watch it, Max," he gasped, fisting his hard on through his shorts. "You're so powerful, I'm going to come before I even get inside at this rate."

My lips twitched and I shoved even more lust at him, using the brute force of my power and making him groan loudly as he jizzed his pants right outside my bedroom door.

"Oh shit, sorry man," I said, faking an apologetic look as I opened the door and the four girls scurried inside with flirtatious giggles.

"Fuck," Lewis cursed, staring down at the cum stain seeping through his shorts.

"Maybe next time then, yeah?" I stepped into my room and swung the door shut in his face before he could even try to protest.

A dark chuckle erupted from me as I turned to my room and found the four girls naked on my bed already. Two of them had started without me, the brunette feasting on the other girl's pussy like it was her favourite meal and making my cock harden even more as I watched the show.

I dropped onto the bed between the other two and I lost myself in the feeling of fucking all of them one after another until any lingering guilt I might have been harbouring was well and truly gone.

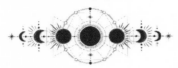

By the time I'd worked my way through all four of the girls and made them come so many times that I knew they'd never forget the time they spent in my bed for the rest of their lives, I was officially late to meet with the other Heirs.

I left the girls in a sated, sleepy heap of limbs and gave myself a slap of cold water to the face to wake myself up before tugging on some jeans and a t-shirt and heading out of the House to go meet with them.

There were a bunch of messages from Seth and Caleb warning me that they were gonna eat my pizza if I made them wait much longer, so when I made it out onto the shore of Aqua Lake, I broke into a jog.

I hurried through The Wailing Wood, heading off into the trees and passing through them before diverting to The Orb where the others were waiting for me to show up for lunch.

I headed inside, moving straight across the space to our couch. There was a stack of takeaway pizza boxes and several cans of soda on the coffee table in front of them.

"Oh, here he is," Cal mocked from his position on the couch beside Seth who had half a slice of pizza hanging out of his mouth.

"Yeah, yeah," I said as I dropped down into my spot on our red couch to the left of the fire, glancing at Darius who sat at the far end of it as I subtly tried to gauge his mood. The others were generally open books to me, allowing me access to at least the surface of their emotions, but Darius always worked the hardest to keep me out.

"Did you do it?" Darius asked, tossing a silencing bubble up around us and ignoring the others as Caleb shot away from us to get himself a drink.

"I did," I said, grabbing a pizza box for myself and flipping the lid open so that the scent of cheesy goodness swept over me and made my stomach rumble in anticipation.

"And?" Darius demanded, leaning forward and pinning me in his dark gaze as he rested his forearms against his knees.

"Tory's is easy. She's afraid of deep water, drowning, that kind of shit," I said before taking a bite out of my pizza and letting them give that some thought.

"So why don't we just toss her into the pool at Lunar Leisure?" Seth suggested with a grin like he couldn't think of anything better.

"And freeze the top over so she can't get back out," I added with a dark tone to my voice, remembering the fear she'd felt at the touch of icy water against her skin and figuring that would really ramp up the terror.

"Freeze the top over?" Darius asked, his jaw ticking. "I don't think we can actually kill one of the Vega princesses."

There was a bite of anger and maybe even pain which accompanied that statement but as I shot him a look, he slammed his mental shields up in a solid wall which wouldn't let me so much as sniff at what he was feeling. *Asshole*.

"No," Seth agreed. "But we could make her think we will. Scare her up good until she's begging us to save her then we sweep in, pluck her out of the water, give her mouth to mouth and maybe a little slip of the D when she pleads for it, then send her running on out of here away from the big bad monsters who she's just not strong enough to face. Simple."

It wasn't as simple as he was making out though. He was playing psycho since his mom had threatened him to get rid of the Vegas and I knew when he got like this he wouldn't back down until he'd gotten what he wanted.

"What else was there?" Darius demanded of me. "There must have been something else that she was afraid of. Something that's not so..."

"Nothing," I replied with a shrug. "Water is it for her."

Darius's hand balled into a fist but he nodded finally. "We can make her think we're going to push her in. Maybe the fear of that will be enough."

"And if it's not we kick her ass in and freeze the water over, yeah?" I asked, purposefully pushing at him to try and get a read on what he was feeling. Was he reluctant to go ahead with this for some reason or was this what he needed? It was infuriating not knowing and I hated that he refused to let me get a full read on him to tell.

Darius stayed silent, looking to me again like he was still waiting for another option to pour from my lips, but I didn't know what he wanted me to say. The plan seemed pretty solid to me. I'd even be able to feel her heartbeat in the water if I maintained a strong connection to it with my power while we did it. It wasn't like she'd be in any real danger. It was just about using her fear.

Caleb made it back to us, dropping a can of soda onto the table before launching himself at Seth and beginning to wrestle him over a slice of pizza despite the fact that there was plenty of pizza left on the table.

Seth growled playfully, shoving away from Caleb as he managed to finish chomping down on the pizza and Cal looked around at the rest of us as he took in the serious mood of our conversation.

"So what did I miss?" Caleb asked, leaning back in his chair with a frown.

"We're just deciding on the best ways to use the Vegas' fears against them," I said firmly.

Caleb pursed his lips. looking from Seth to me and Darius like he had something to say but he held his tongue as Seth spoke again.

"It'll be great, we'll force them to go up against the things that terrify them most and when everyone sees that they're not even Fae enough to stand against their fears, there will be no more doubts about who is fittest to rule the kingdom after our parents."

"Do you really think all this is necessary?" Caleb interrupted, pushing his fingers into his blonde curls as he looked between the three of us. "I personally feel like it makes us look kinda weak. Why are we attacking a couple of untrained girls and trying to chase them out? If we really believe they'll never be able to outmatch us in skill, then why not let them attend the academy? I don't feel like they're ever going to claim the throne from us anyway. Not if we keep building on our knowledge and refining our magic. How could they ever catch up to us in skill? And it's not like our power is that much lower than theirs."

"You're only saying that because you want in Tory's panties and you know you won't get in them if you fuck with her like this," Seth scoffed.

Darius growled in a dark warning, his gaze narrowing on Caleb who didn't even bother to deny it.

"So what? I like the taste of her blood and I wanna taste a bit more of her too. Doesn't mean I'm suddenly a royalist. Besides, I stand by what I said, and my mom agrees too. Them staying on here isn't the end for us and if anything, it would only offer us up more opportunities to prove that our superior skill and knowledge outmatches their brute strength."

Caleb looked between all of us in aid of an ally, but Seth seemed more interested in grabbing another slice of pizza and I was just happy to follow my dad's plan to try and squash this problem now. If it didn't work then we'd be doing what Caleb wanted anyway.

"No," Darius barked, speaking for all of us and causing a ripple of tension to pass through the group for a moment as the Alphas in all of us bristled against the idea of him trying to take charge. "I just need this over. We have to do what our parents want and that's the end of it. I can't afford to go against my father on this."

A beat of silence passed where we all read between the lines of his words, and I caught the barest hint of desperation coming from Darius. In fact, I was almost certain there was reluctance there too but it was tempered by a steely determination which I knew wouldn't be swayed. He wasn't even giving his own feelings on this any kind of consideration, he was clearly just focused on fulfilling Lionel's wishes and I had to assume that if he didn't do so the consequences would be something he couldn't stomach.

I glanced at the others, knowing they'd picked up on that too even if the subtleties I was partial to thanks to my Order gifts had been lost on them. But it was clear enough that Lionel had made some threats over this being done and none of us wanted Darius to face his wrath over any kind of failure on our parts.

"Okay," Caleb conceded though he didn't look all that happy about it. "If you're all determined to go ahead then you know I'm with you like always."

Darius nodded in satisfaction, leaning back in his chair and sighing, letting a few tendrils of smoke pass between his lips. "So what about Gwendalina?" he asked, looking into the fire instead of at us.

"Hers is a little more tricky," I admitted. "She's got this deep rooted kind of fear of rejection. Of trusting someone, opening herself up to them and having them betray and humiliate her, that kind of thing."

I looked between the others as they all frowned at that, as lost for a way that we could turn that against her as I was. She wasn't even seeing anyone who we could force to turn on her and the only person she really cared about was her sister.

But the bond between the twins was ironclad and I knew there was no way we'd be able to force a wedge between them, especially on such a tight timescale.

"What if someone were to make her like them?" Seth asked thoughtfully.

"You know, get her all tingly and excited for the dance, take her as a date then pull a full Carrie on her."

"You want to dump pig's blood all over her head?" I scoffed. "Isn't that a little overdone?"

Seth shrugged. "Maybe something a little better than that, something more personal, something that would really hit hard and-"

"Her hair," I blurted as the rest of what she'd said came to me and I realised what we'd need to take from her if we really wanted to hit her hard. "She dyed the ends blue to remind her never to trust anyone ever again. So if she were to trust someone and then they cut it all off..."

Seth clapped his hands excitedly, waving a hand in the air. "I volunteer as tribute! I'm gonna make her fall in love with me so hard that she'll be panting all over my cock by the night of the party. Then bam, like a ninja with more than just a single weapon between my thighs I'll strike and cut her hair clean off. Bye bye hair, bye bye dignity, bye bye Vega."

Darius's lip curled back like he was disgusted by that idea and Caleb didn't seem to like it much either but neither of them spoke out against it.

"It will work," I said confidently, because I'd felt those fears in the girls and I was certain that if anything would be enough to break them then this would be it.

"Let's do it then," Darius said firmly, shadows flickering behind his eyes as he turned to look at us again.

"On the night of the dance?" Seth suggested, his head whipping back and forth between us eagerly like this was the best game he'd been invited to play in a long time.

"Yeah," I agreed and Caleb nodded though he still seemed reluctant.

"Let's figure out the details then," I said firmly. "It's time to get rid of our Vega problem for good."

"You guys figure out the details without me. But speaking of our Vega problem..." Cal nodded towards the door and I turned to watch as the twins walked into the room, looking tired from their lessons and probably still pretty drained after spending so much time among the Sirens earlier.

They crossed the room, choosing to join a couple of their friends tucked away in one corner rather than sit with the Ass Club today and the four of us watched them go with a silent kind of anticipation.

Tory's gaze scoured across our line up and as she landed on Darius, her upper lip peeled back in clear dislike which caused him to tense up irritably.

Seth grinned widely, shooting his hand in the air and waving at Darcy like they were best buddies but she just turned away.

"And let the fun commence," he said, digging around in his pocket for a scrap of paper and a pen before scrawling out a note which the rest of us read over his shoulder.

Be my date for the dance.

"You've got no chance, dude," Caleb said with an amused look but Seth just hid the note in his hand and pushed himself to his feet.

"Err, yeah I do - I'm crazy hot, stupid sexy and every girl and guy in this room can tell with one look that I know exactly how to make them howl if I want to. And even through the haze of disdain Darcy Vega throws my way, I just know there's a whole heap of curious vagina waiting for my attention."

"Fifty auras says she turns you down flat," Caleb said with a shake of his head.

"A hundred," Darius upped the bet and Seth gasped as if he was offended.

"Just because you guys were hoping I'd ask you to the dance with me doesn't mean you get to be salty little bitches over me asking someone else." He turned and strode away purposefully and I chuckled as I watched him go.

"No fucking way he can pull this off," Caleb muttered, watching him too.

Darius dismissed the silencing bubble which surrounded us as our conversation about the Vegas came to an end.

Seth looked as confident as ever as he just strode on up to the Vegas and dropped down into the free chair beside Darcy, causing her little friends to pretty much recoil in horror while Tory just scowled at him.

I couldn't tell what they were all saying from way across the room, but it looked like Seth was getting shot down.

"Do we need a new plan for her?" I asked the others dubiously as Seth got to his feet again.

"Nah, he's got her interest piqued," Caleb pointed out and I gave them my attention again as Seth leaned down to speak in Darcy's ear before dropping his note in her pocket.

He strode away from her, returning to us and I watched as Darcy's cheeks pinked while she watched him walk away.

"I think it might actually have worked," I said in surprise though Darius didn't look convinced.

Just as Seth made it back to us, Marguerite appeared too, her school skirt hiked up to her ass and lust pouring off of her like syrup as she moved to drop into Darius's lap.

"Don't," he barked, catching her hips and redirecting her to her feet.

"Don't what?" she asked in confusion, batting her eyelashes as she gazed down at him.

"Sit your ass on me," he replied in a flat tone. "In fact, I'd prefer if you didn't place any part of your body on me again, okay?"

Marguerite spluttered in confusion as a few of her friends drew closer behind her like a pack of hyenas scenting a kill while trying to cover it with an act of concern.

"But sweety, you and me are rock solid. I don't understand-"

"Let me paint it out for you then," Darius replied in a bored, flat tone as he leaned back in his seat and regarded her like she was nothing more than an irritation in his life.

That shit was cold. And Caleb was raising his eyebrows at me as if to say *holy fuck, Darius is savage.* I could tell from the twinkle in his blue eyes.

"You and me were never officially anything anyway," Darius said. "And now we're officially nothing."

"You're breaking up with me?" she gasped, her hand flying to her heart as several people glanced our way.

"No," Darius replied and she sagged in relief but I winced because I could already tell what was coming next. "You were never my girlfriend so we can't break up."

"W-what?"

Darius sighed and I could tell he was done with this. I probably could have stepped in to help move Marguerite on or something, but I was an asshole and I was enjoying the drama as much as Seth who had actually managed to find a bag of popcorn somewhere which he was munching on as he watched the show.

I reached over and he let me take a handful and I pushed it between my lips as Darius delivered the fatal blow.

"We hooked up a few times, but it got dull fast," Darius said. "Maybe go try out some new tricks with someone else or something, I don't really care. Point is, we're done. If you wanna believe I'm breaking up with you, then fine - I'm breaking up with you. Got it?"

"You can't!" Marguerite shrieked so loudly that the entire Orb fell silent and everyone swivelled to look our way.

"It's over, move on," Darius said loud enough for everyone to hear before looking away from her in dismissal.

But the poor, desperate fool just couldn't let her shame end there and she lunged forward, snatching his hand into her grasp and tugging on it as she began to sob.

"Darius, baby, how can you throw away everything we have?"

Darius chose not to validate that with a response and focused on reclaiming his hand instead, the flicker of irritation in his gaze letting me know that he was fighting the urge to make more of a scene, no doubt not wanting this to be spread across the tabloids tomorrow.

"Darius!" Marguerite shrieked desperately and fire burst to life in her palms as she lost her shit.

My amusement fell away in an instant and I shot to my feet alongside the other Heirs, Seth's popcorn tumbling to the floor as a snarl escaped him. Nobody made a threat against one of us and got away with it.

Darius stepped forward with a challenge in his eyes and Marguerite backed down instantly, a whimper escaping her lips as she extinguished the flames in her hands and murmured an apology.

The circling girls moved forward to tug her away and she let them pull her back while she continued to sob dramatically.

Darius was clearly much more irritated over the display than he was over the loss of his most recent fuck buddy and I clapped a hand on his shoulder, offering him some chilled vibes though he didn't accept them.

"This is about *them*." Marguerite fell still abruptly and pointed across the room at Tory who to her credit only arched a brow in response. "Ever since they arrived you've been acting different."

"Stop embarrassing yourself," Caleb said, rolling his eyes. "You just can't deal with the fact that Darius got bored with you months ago. Move on, find someone else to screw. From what I've heard, it sounds like you need the practice."

Marguerite looked back to Darius in horror but I couldn't feel much heartbreak coming from her, more like dashed ambitions and unfulfilled lust. "But you love me."

Silence rang out and Darius's blank mask shattered as he looked between me and the others with cruelty in his expression and I knew she'd gone and pushed him too damn far.

"Love you?" he laughed, turning to look at her with contempt. "At what point in our once a week bed parties did you get that idea?"

Marguerite blushed furiously and her friends tried to pull her away like they could see that this was only getting worse for her if she didn't quit now and me, and the other Heirs rallied around Darius.

Seth started laughing at Darius's words and Kylie puffed her chest up as she glared at him. "You're no better! I saw that video of you and Darcy fucking Vega at the bar last Friday."

Seth pressed a hand to his heart, gasping dramatically. "Sorry, babe, did I forget to ask your permission? You know I'm totally polyamorous right?"

She looked about two seconds from shifting into her Medusa form as fury burned through her expression and her hands balled into fists. "No Seth, you have *never* told me that."

"No?" he questioned, leaning his shoulder against mine. "Well you can't go poly-shaming me now can you?"

"You're a liar," she hissed and that dangerous kind of silence fell again at that accusation.

I stepped forward, cracking my neck. "Wanna say that again, peaches?"

Kylie backed up, fear sweeping through her expression. "He's not polyamorous, Max, he's just cheating on me."

I almost felt sorry for her if she really believed that.

Darius was clearly done with the whole show though so he moved to walk around Marguerite but she grabbed his arm, holding on tightly as she forced him to look at her. "Please," she begged.

"Let go," he said in a deadly tone and I could tell that he was doing all he could to restrain himself as the Dragon balked at this public fucking mess taking place around him.

She flinched back, seeming to finally grasp how deadly serious he was being and the four of us strode through the crowd of girls as we headed out of the room and left the drama behind us.

"That was fun," Seth grinned. "You know what you should do now to really piss her off, Darius?"

"What?" he asked, still looking irritated as hell.

"Fuck Tory Vega. Do it without a silencing bubble so the whole House can hear her screaming your name and then-"

"I'm going flying," Darius snapped, dropping his bag and starting to strip quickly. "Will one of you wait for me outside Cardinal Magic with my shit?"

"Yeah, brother," I replied, grabbing his clothes and stuffing them in his bag before he shifted into his Dragon form and took off without another word.

"Poor big D," Seth sighed. "He really needs to have some decent sex. That frustration is gonna eat him alive if he doesn't dick it out of him."

I tutted and smacked him around the back of the head. "He doesn't need to get laid," I said firmly. "He needs to get rid of the fucking Vegas so that his father doesn't follow through on whatever threats he's clearly worrying about."

"Oh," Seth said, a soft howl escaping him as he looked up to watch Darius disappearing into the clouds overhead.

"Yeah. Oh."

"Let's just do it then," Caleb said, sounding resigned. "Then after the party we can all get back to normal again."

We all agreed to that and headed away to enjoy the rest of our lunch break in peace. But I was pretty sure the only real peace we were gonna find was when the Vegas renounced their claim to the throne.

CALEB

CHAPTER TWENTY-THREE

I sat in the classroom that had been allocated to me to conduct my one on one sessions with the Vampire who had been assigned as my own personal pain in the ass freshman. It was an annoying as hell tradition my family had started years ago which said that the older Vampire students in the academy should take on a freshman to teach the ways of our Order. It was necessary as our kind Emerged the moment our magic Awakened and we needed to learn fast how to contend with the bloodlust.

In theory that all sounded great. But in practice I found it boring as hell.

I had however taken advantage of having this space to myself for the hour before Teddy was due to show up just so that I could have a little alone time to chill out.

The door to the classroom banged open suddenly, interrupting my internal musings over what we should do about our Vega problem and, lo and behold, a Vega herself appeared like my mind had conjured her.

Even better, it was *my* Vega. Though she didn't seem to have noticed I was even here yet as she leaned close to the door she'd just thrown shut and listened for sounds beyond it.

I trained my gifted hearing beyond the door and heard angry shrieking and cries of vengeance coming from the other side of it as what sounded like a stampede of girls tore past the door.

"Hiding from someone?" I asked in amusement as Tory continued to listen at the door well after they'd passed her by.

Tory's heart leapt in surprise but she covered it with a scowl as she spun to find me there with my feet on the desk at the back of the classroom. I smiled at her to combat the death glare she was offering and she sighed.

"Well damn, I've run straight from a pack of hyenas into the mouth of a crocodile," she muttered.

"Not a lion?" I teased, staying exactly where I was because we both knew I had her now. She wasn't going to be leaving this room until I decided to let her.

"Oh no, they hunt together, you don't strike me as the type to need any help in cornering your prey."

My smile widened at that assessment.

"Sometimes it comes right to me without me having to do a thing," I agreed, my gaze trailing to her throat as the thirst rose in me. I'd been intending to try and track her down after my session with Teddy, but this little game of the spider and the fly was much more alluring.

"Shall we just get this over with then?" she asked, stepping towards me with a sense of resignation hanging about her that took all of the fun out of the hunt.

I looked to her neck again but then a better idea came to mind as I let my gaze roam lower, drinking in her body and finding myself hungering for a taste of something sweeter before the main course.

I pushed myself to my feet and she fell still just far enough away that I couldn't quite reach out and grab her as she looked up at me with enough heat in her expression to make me wonder if we weren't both considering the same thing.

"You know, I can feel your power," I breathed, staying where I was and watching her as she hesitated there, unsure how to react to my behaviour, but I was done dancing around this. Besides, if we were successful in driving her out of here at the dance then I might not get another chance with her.

"Any idea on what I am then?" she asked, biting her lip and looking so damn hopeful that I actually felt bad about not being able to shed any light on that for her.

"Sadly not. I can only feel the depth of your power, the strength of it. And you're *strong*. Once you learn to harness it, I have the feeling that I won't be able to take an ounce of it from you without permission." My mouth slipped into a smile and her gaze dropped to trace the movement, making my dick get all kinds of hopeful ideas.

"Why the hell would I ever give you permission?" she asked, arching an eyebrow at me like the idea of that was so absurd, but I was pretty sure I could convince her to enjoy my bite if only she'd give in to the urge.

I reached out and brushed my fingers across the pulse point at the base of her throat, enjoying the feeling of her heartbeat against my skin.

"You're an Heir too," I pointed out. "If you make it past The Reckoning and complete your training here at Zodiac then the chances are that we will be in each other's lives for a very long time."

"I thought the whole point of your little boys club was to make sure my sister and I *didn't* make it through The Reckoning? Don't you want us gone?" she challenged.

I shrugged a single shoulder because sure, that was the plan. But I actually kinda hoped it wouldn't work. I relished the idea of the challenge this girl and her sister could present to us. The thought of really having to fight for my right to claim the throne was exhilarating. If they weren't driven out, if they made it through The Reckoning, then I was excited to see what they would become and what it would take to stay above them in the food chain.

"I'm interested to see how this whole thing will play out," I admitted. "Perhaps you'll fail and be gone by the end of the semester. Or perhaps you'll rise up and claim your birth right. Before your parents were killed our families were their Councillors. We always would have held the power beneath you if things hadn't gotten so messy with The Savage King. So maybe you'll fail The Reckoning and be sent back to your boring, mortal lives or maybe the trials you're enduring now will only make you stronger in the end and you'll pass."

"So in other words, you're just going to keep going along with the other Heirs and their stupid stunts and whenever you're feeling peckish I'm still fair game," she snapped and shit she was hot when she was angry.

"Pretty much," I chuckled, knowing it would piss her off more and enjoying that for some fucked up reason.

"Can you just get this over with? I have a lot of studying to do." She tilted her chin in the angriest offering I'd ever seen but that wasn't going to cut it today. What would it even take for her to want me to bite her? I'd have given a whole lot to hear her beg me for it that was for sure.

"Don't you want to hear my proposition, Tory?" I asked in a seductive tone as I shifted closer to her, wanting to feel the heat of her body against mine.

"I can't imagine anything that you could offer me to make me a willing participant in your dinner schedule," she deadpanned.

"There may be one thing," I said, teasing her, tempting her.

Her eyes lit angrily and I could tell she was about to start cursing me or something equally aggressive, so I took a final step forward, caught her chin between my fingers and pressed my mouth to hers.

Tory sucked in a breath of surprise and I slid my tongue between the opening in her lips, kissing her roughly and dominating her mouth in a demand for her to give in to me.

She raised her hands to my chest, palms flat against my pecs and for a moment I was sure she was going to shove me back with either her strength or her magic.

But then the moment passed and instead of fighting, she surrendered, her hands caressing instead of pushing me away, tongue moving with mine and lips devouring. And she tasted so fucking sweet.

I groaned deep in the back of my throat as I dropped my hands to her waist and walked her backwards until her ass hit the desk there.

I lifted her up easily, parting her thighs as I stepped between them and my cock throbbed as I drove it against her panties, stealing a little friction and loving the way she arched into the movement like she was aching for more of me.

Her hands banded around my neck and she pulled me closer, kissing me hard and heatedly as her hips flexed and she ground herself against my solid cock

I moved my hand to her knee, tracing a line along the top of her long socks with my thumb before shifting it up her silken skin.

Tory kissed me harder, her fingers pushing through my hair as she moaned between brushes of our tongues as I kept moving my hand higher, half expecting her to stop me while my heart thundered harder for every second where she didn't.

I pushed my fingers beneath her skirt and she moaned again, her other leg hooking around my ass and dragging me nearer in a demand I was more than willing to give in to.

I grinned against her lips, loving how quickly she'd fallen to my desire, but the moment I did, she sucked my bottom lip between her teeth and bit down hard to remind me of exactly what kind of animal she was.

I jerked back before she could spill my blood, laughing at the fire in her and pausing with my hand almost grazing her panties and the temptation of what lay beneath them.

"Why?" she asked breathlessly, suspicion colouring her green eyes and making me want to offer her the truth. "You can just take what you want from me. So why kiss me?"

"I can take your blood and power from you," I agreed as I let my gaze wander down her tempting body. This wasn't some game or anything to do with me being an Heir and her being a Princess. I just wanted her. Simple as that and I really wanted her to want me too. "But I desire more than that. And I'm a Taurus; when we set our minds on something it's not easy to turn us from it."

She scoffed, still giving me that suspicious look, though I was hoping I could convince her to trust me, at least for long enough to let me make her pant my name the way I ached to hear.

"You didn't seem so against the idea the other night," I urged while she stayed quiet.

"That was drunk Tory," she said firmly. "She's notorious for making bad decisions so I wouldn't get too excited about anything you think she might have done with you. You shouldn't presume anything that happens when I'm wasted will have any bearing on sober Tory."

"And you think I'd be a bad decision?" I teased because she might have been right about that, but I still wanted to be one she made.

My lips twitched and I was almost certain I had her convinced.

"I've been with enough bad decisions to recognise one when I see them," she said.

"How many, exactly?" I asked, leaning in to kiss her neck, my stubble grazing against her skin as I fought against the urge to take a bite.

"Enough to let me know that it's a terrible idea." Her breath caught as I reached the corner of her lips with my kisses and I paused to hear her decision, though if the way she was pulling me closer again was anything to go by, I was pretty sure I was about to get my wish. "Probably not enough to put me off entirely."

I chuckled darkly, leaning back to gaze into her deep green eyes. I wanted her to say it, beg for it. Though that may have been a little ambitious with this particular princess.

The words didn't escape her full lips, but as her gaze darkened with desire, she reached out and unhooked the top button of my shirt, making her decision clear.

I held myself still as she worked her way down every single button until she pushed her hands inside my shirt and dragged her hands across the hard lines of my muscles.

A shiver raced through my skin and my dick was working really hard to bust right through my fucking fly, so I stopped beating around the damn bush and claimed her mouth with mine once more.

I could feel the tension leaving her as she gave in, her kisses rich and consuming as I explored her mouth with mine.

I moved my hand that final inch, my thumb dragging its way up the centre of her panties until I found her clit and pressed down, making her gasp in pleasure.

I began circling my thumb against her through her panties and she arched her back, her thighs widening further to give me all the access I wanted to destroy her.

I kissed harder as I began to unhook her shirt buttons with my free hand, wanting to see those fucking tits I'd been jerking off over in the flesh.

Her hands continued to move across my bare skin as I kept working her clit and I gave up trying to take my time with her as she started panting with need. I shifted my hand, pushing her panties aside and growling with desire as I found her pussy soaked and ready for me and I immediately sank a finger deep inside her.

Tory moaned, her voice rough and breathy and so fucking sexy that I had to fight the urge to drop my pants and drive my cock into her here and now so that I could hear what it sounded like when I really made her scream.

But thanks to fucking Teddy, I knew I didn't have time to fuck her the way I ached to and I didn't want to rush through something I'd been daydreaming about for so long. So I was going to feel her coming for me like this, take control of her pleasure and leave her wanting more so that she was aching for me as much as possible the next time we found ourselves alone like this and I could really show her what I was made of.

My other hand found her tit and I squeezed it through her bra, groaning at the fullness in my palm and breaking our kiss as I worked my way down her body to better service her hardened nipple.

Tory leaned back, giving me a perfect fucking view of her with her shirt swinging wide and her skirt hitched up around her waist as I drove my finger in and out of her tight pussy.

I yanked her bra down, my dick jerking at the sight of her pink nipple before my mouth descended on it and I sucked it between my lips, coupling the move with the addition of a second finger driving inside her.

She moaned even louder, her pussy tightening like a vice around my fingers while I sucked on her nipple and felt her body surging towards its climax like I was playing the most exquisite instrument in the world.

The moment I felt her coming for me, I reared up and kissed her hard, swallowing her cries of pleasure and tasting her lust as I dragged my tongue over hers.

My dick was fucking aching and I growled with a desperate, needy plea of my flesh which I knew I didn't have time to answer as the heat of our kisses softened and I slowly drew my fingers back out of her, fixing her panties into place again.

I broke off our kiss with a surge of effort, mentally planning to give Teddy the lesson from hell for forcing me to cut this shit short after I'd waited so long to claim it.

Tory blinked up at me in surprise and I had to fight the urge to pout like a bitch as I read the desire in her body and knew she'd been hoping to come all over my cock again after that stunning first round.

"I have a student coming in a minute to learn the art of Vampirism from an expert," I explained, wishing I could just cancel the damn thing, but my mom had already been calling me out on not attending a bunch of these sessions and as our family name was linked to them, it was a bad look for me to miss any more of them.

"So that was purely for my benefit?" Tory asked in surprise as she began to re-button her shirt.

My jaw ticked with frustration, though I couldn't claim she was the only one of us who had gotten something out of that.

"Oh no, I got plenty from that too," I promised her, my gaze sweeping over her body appreciatively as I began to mentally plan all the things I wanted to do to every inch of her if I was lucky enough to get to do this with her again.

I buttoned my own shirt reluctantly though there wasn't much I could do about my throbbing hard on aside from plan a trip back to my room as soon as I could possibly get out of this training session so that I could jerk off repeatedly with all of the new spank bank material she'd just gifted me.

Tory remained on the desk in front of me and I was hoping that was because her legs weren't working right yet.

The thirst prickled at me again as I eyed her throat and she sighed loudly as she noticed.

"You're still going to bite me, aren't you?" she asked, her fingers curling around the edge of the desk.

"You could look at it as rewarding me for my efforts," I teased, because there was no fucking way she was getting out of here without me drinking from her and we both knew it.

"Well that makes me feel a little better about leaving you with blue balls," she taunted and I almost groaned in frustration as my dick throbbed in agreement.

"Next time, I'll be sure to carve out a few hours to dedicate to you," I told her. "And then neither of us will be left wanting."

"Next time?" she asked, raising an eyebrow like that wasn't at all likely to happen. But I could hear her heartbeat pounding and I knew she was wondering how hard I could make her come with several hours at our disposal and my cock a whole lot more involved in the act.

I found myself smiling again but then my mood dipped as I realised there wasn't likely to be a next time if the other Heirs succeeded with their plans for the dance. I didn't even really want to go along with the damn plan and in a moment of madness, I suddenly wondered if I could just save her from it. They would still strike at Darcy and maybe that would be enough to force the twins to leave the academy. But if I was being honest, I didn't even really want them to leave anyway.

I moved closer to her again, tucking a lock of dark hair behind her ear. "Are you going to the dance on Friday?" I murmured and her pulse scattered, making my smile deepen in satisfaction.

"Err, yeah," she said, that suspicious look returning to her eyes.

"Why don't you blow it off?" I suggested, wondering if I could just convince her to stay away from it all together. She was my Source after all so the others couldn't even really get mad at me for protecting her - that was kinda in the job description anyway. She blinked at me in surprise and I realised she'd probably thought I was going to ask her to go to the dance with me as her date. But I couldn't do that, if I wanted to save her from the other Heirs and their plans then I needed to keep her away from the whole thing.

"What possible reason would I have to do that?" she asked, shifting just enough to make my hand fall from her face.

I felt the rejection before she could even voice it, but I wasn't going to give up that easily.

I ran my dislodged hand down her arm instead, raising goosebumps along her skin and hopefully reminding her of just how good I'd made her feel with these fingers. "Because then I could sneak out and come to your room. We could have the whole House and an entire evening to ourselves."

"That's pretty presumptuous of you, Earth boy."

"Earth boy?" I asked in amusement, refusing to back down no matter how hard she was trying to resist me.

I held a hand out to her, bringing earth magic to my fingertips and causing a dark blue flower to blossom in my palm. Girls fucking loved that trick.

"Perhaps I've gotten what I wanted from you now," she said, shifting forward to get up without reaching for the flower.

Okay, so maybe this girl didn't love that trick after all.

I let the flower dissolve into nothing again and stepped forward to stop her from getting to her feet, smiling darkly.

"I'm confident you'll come back for more," I promised her and I could tell she was at least a little tempted by the prospect.

The door opened behind us and Tory looked around as fucking Teddy strode on in without even knocking. Gah, I was going to make his life hell today. His eyes widened as he looked between me and the girl I had half pinned to a desk and I leaned forward, covering for what we'd really been doing by taking what I'd been waiting for anyway.

My hand fisted in Tory's hair as I held her exactly where I wanted her, sinking my teeth into her skin and her entire body tensed as the pure adrenaline rush of her blood swept over my tongue and down my throat.

Fuck she tasted like a rainbow of blood on a damn ice cream smoothie.

I drank deeply, relishing the taste of her power as it flooded into me before pulling back with satisfaction burning through me as I forced my gaze from the beauty before me and onto fucking Teddy.

"Lesson one for today, Teddy," I said. "Always prey on the most powerful creature you can overpower. Tory here hasn't got a lock on her powers yet, so she's currently fair game. Although unluckily for you, I've already claimed her as my Source so keep your fangs off."

Tory got to her feet, nudging me back a step before grabbing her satchel from the ground beside us.

"Lesson two," she added coolly, glaring at Teddy as he eyed her hungrily.

481

"Don't underestimate the depths of vengeance. My sister and I have more power than the lot of you, and you'd be fools to think we won't remember what we went through while we were getting to grips with handling it."

She shoulder checked Teddy as she passed him and he stumbled aside while I laughed at his expense.

She pulled the door open and I called out after her before she could leave.

"Until next time, Tory!" I promised and as I listened to her pulse pounding harder, I had to hope I was right about there being a next time, and a time after that, and then another time again because I wanted to do that as often as I could.

"So what's the plan today, Mr Caleb?" Teddy asked perkily.

Well, Teddy I'm about to give you the day from hell for cock blocking me and you won't even know which way is up by the time we're done.

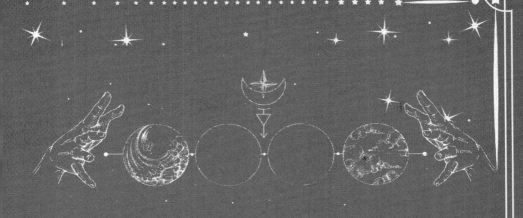

ORION

CHAPTER TWENTY-FOUR

S pending the evening overseeing the school dance was right up there with killing myself on my list of enjoyable things to do tonight. And as Nova had oh-so-kindly chosen me as one of the attending teachers, I simply couldn't *wait* to bound and skip my way down to The Orb to start watching a bunch of students get wasted and grind on each other.

Oh no wait, I'd rather put my cock in a blender.

The worst part of it all, was that I knew the Heirs were up to something and Darius wouldn't tell me what. And since we weren't exactly each other's besties right now, I pretty much spent all of my time alone outside of classes. Until tonight of course. Tonight, I'd get to be in the company of hundreds of people I vaguely disliked while worrying what Darius was plotting and fearing that he was going to get himself in trouble.

I glanced at the clock as I lay slumped on my couch, shirtless with a bottle of bourbon balancing on my abs. Abs which were likely going to be lost to my ever-increasing drinking habit if I wasn't careful. I'd been to the gym in the Lunar Leisure building earlier and worked out until I couldn't see straight though, so I guessed it balanced out.

A knock came at the door and I groaned, sinking lower on the couch. I wasn't drunk. I was being semi-responsible seeing as I wanted to watch out for Darius tonight, so I'd only had a few sips, but I was flirting with the idea of draining every drop, passing out and dealing with the fallout tomorrow.

The knocking came again and I cursed, placing the bottle on the floor and getting to my feet, shooting to the door with a burst of speed. I opened it, finding Gabriel standing there with a hard frown on his face and his wings folded at his back.

"Noxy," I said in surprise, mustering something of a smile, but he didn't return it.

He shook his head at me and pushed his way into the house, his wing slapping me in the face as he went.

"Uncalled for, but alright," I muttered, swinging the door shut behind him and turning to him for an explanation for the unannounced house call.

"Orio, this is…" He looked at the empty bourbon bottles on the kitchen counter then to me and I felt like he was prying open my chest and glaring directly at all my poor decisions in life.

"What?" I grunted and his brow furrowed.

"This is getting out of hand."

"I'm fine," I said dismissively.

"This isn't fine," he growled, deadly serious. He never spoke to me like that. We only ever joked around together, he was one of the few people I could actually have fun with.

"It's not as bad as it looks," I tried, but he folded his arms like a pissed off parent and I fought an eye roll.

"It's worse actually," he said, a bite to his tone. "And if you don't get a grip, things are going to spiral. You have no idea what's in the balance here."

"Then tell me," I said dryly, waving a hand. "Go on, oh mighty Seer.

Tell me what fate I'm fucking up now."

"The best one of your damn life," he snapped and my eyebrows arched at the fury in his tone.

I looked around my empty home which was as hollow as the beating muscle in my chest and shrugged. "If it's about Lionel, maybe you should be talking to Darius, because it's down to him now. I can't change his mind, he doesn't fucking listen to me."

"It's not about Lionel," he said, glancing away. "Well it is….but it's not."

"Well thanks for clearing that up," I deadpanned, glancing at the clock on the wall, realising the dance had started ten minutes ago and also realising I didn't care.

Gabriel walked over to the bourbon bottle I'd left on the floor, hooking it up and walking to the sink, pouring it down the drain while staring me right in the eye.

I ran my tongue over my teeth at his attitude. "I've got more of that."

"No you don't," he said, a challenge in his gaze. "I snuck in your back window and took it from your bedroom."

"Dammit," I cursed. I had protection spells on this place that only allowed Gabriel and Darius through them, but clearly I needed to cut down that list.

"Now listen to me, Orio," he said, slamming the empty bottle down on the kitchen counter and my spine straightened at the bossiness to his tone. "You have to start paying attention to your instincts. And I know you're the most negative asshole in the world, but I'm telling you there's hope here. There's a way out of this shit pit you call a life."

I clenched my jaw stubbornly but he didn't stop, prowling over to me like a man on a mission and pointing at my face.

"You're wasting yourself," he snarled. "You're so fucking special, Lance, if I could only show you, you wouldn't even recognise the person I know you can be."

"What do you want me to do then to be this special little person, Gabriel?" I hissed. "Put on a tutu and throw glitter around the room?"

"No, you asshole," he got up close to me and took my face in both of his hands. "I want you to see your potential and step into it. Because the path you're on leads you nowhere good, Lance. Do you get that? I'm talking about an early grave here. And I don't really give a damn if the stars think it's a bad idea to tell you that, because I'm done trying to nudge you in the right direction, I'm forcing your hand. So put some star damned clothes on, walk out that door and go do your duty tonight because if you don't, I swear to you, you'll regret it."

I stared at him in surprise, his words finally cutting through the fog of miserable bullshit in my head. He was a Seer and I took that very seriously, because I knew the power he wielded. He could *see* my fate. And as much as everything seemed pointless, I didn't actually want to die yet. And the look in his eyes said I wasn't long for this world if I didn't find a way to change. I had no idea how I was supposed to do that when the stars kept throwing shit at me, but I guessed I had to try. Because my friend looked broken for me and I didn't want this burden weighing on him.

"Okay," I agreed and the tension ran out of his shoulders, relief filling his gaze before his eyes glazed over with some vision. When he came back to me, he let me go and nodded, darkness wreaking havoc in his eyes.

"Why do you still look sad?" I asked, my chest squeezing uncomfortably.

"Because sometimes terrible things have to happen for new paths to arise, and I have to let them."

"Way to soothe me, brother," I jibed and he cracked half a smile, though it quickly faded again. He pressed a hand to my shoulder, faith shining in his eyes.

"I know you'll do the right thing in the end. I trust you."

"Wanna give me a heads up on what the right thing is?" I tried but he shook his head, a knowing smile on his lips.

He remained quiet for a moment then nodded stiffly. "At nine o'clock you need to be away from the Vegas and the Heirs for at least ten minutes," he said. "Alright?"

"And you're not going to tell me why, are you?" I sighed.

"Nope. But you'll be fine, Orio. Just keep doing what I've suggested before now too."

"Find the light, yeah?" I said with an eyeroll.

"It's closer than you think," he said with a smirk as he headed to the door. "I'm gonna hang around campus for a bit. I'll catch you later." He stepped outside, spread his wings and took off before I could answer his cryptic expression, but I was pretty used to him acting like he knew something I didn't, so I wasn't gonna overthink it.

I sighed then shot to the shower, washing in record time – which was saying something – then speeding to my room as I dried myself and throwing on a pale blue shirt and black slacks, vaguely styling my hair. Then I sprinted out of the house and raced along in the direction of The Orb, slowing as I reached the path leading to it where students were filing inside, all of them wearing fancy clothes.

My gaze cut through them all to the Vegas as they reached the entrance and my eyes dipped to Darcy's ass before I could stop myself. She wore a fitted navy dress with lacy sleeves that hugged her curves so perfectly it made a possessive growl fill my throat.

I put on another burst of speed, following them inside, my eyes on her exposed neck where loose locks of black and blue hair tickled it, falling down from the bun she'd styled it into. My fangs tingled with the desire to drink from her, but a much more off limits desire simply to have my mouth on that golden skin took hold of me too.

I followed her inside like a shadow and watched as she looked around at the decorations, the place transformed into a ballroom with the theme of fall.

Golden leaves swept across the room in an endless magical breeze and vines sprawled across the ceiling, their leaves turning green then orange, red, gold, before falling to join those dancing on the floor. She gazed up at the magic in fascination and I cocked my head as I watched her, wanting to see more of that look in her eyes again, the one where she seemed to devour the world in front of her. It made me long for the person I used to be, the one who'd once been so enthused by life, who'd thought anything was possible.

She started to move deeper into the crowd with her sister, seeming to be searching for somebody and I made the flash decision to snare her attention. Just for a second. So I could steal a little piece of her.

I moved up behind her, my fingers brushing her elbow and her head turned, her breath hitching as I moved to her side.

"Evening," I murmured in her ear, energy buzzing in my veins like a drug. The interaction only lasted two seconds and yet as I walked past her, that energy remained in me and I held onto it as hard as I could, thinking of the darkness I'd been a slave to only moments ago and not wanting it to creep in again.

Washer waved enthusiastically at me from beside Nova at the bar and I sighed internally as I walked over to join them, knowing it was going to be a long ass night. But so long as I could steal the odd glance at Darcy Vega, maybe it wouldn't be so unbearable. Though I couldn't help but think of Gabriel's words about terrible things needing to happen sometimes. And I had the awful, writhing feeling that the Heirs were going to do something they couldn't take back tonight. And something in me shifted as I realised I was going to try and protect the Vegas from their wrath.

CALEB

CHAPTER TWENTY-FIVE

I stood to the side of the room while everyone else enjoyed the dance. But tonight wasn't going to be fun for us. We all knew what was expected of us and despite my agreement to it, I was still feeling all kinds of reluctant.

Seth had peeled away to dance with Darcy already, drawing her into his trap like a spider luring an innocent little fly into his web.

I looked over at them, the happiness in her eyes as he spun her beneath his arm making my stomach knot. I didn't like this. Seth was always too easily tempted to the dark, taking pranks too far and asserting his dominance over other Fae with a flare of anger which lashed out too harshly at times.

Only I knew in my soul that the cruelty he gave into wasn't really him. And when he got like this, I couldn't help but want to shake him and remind him of the things which he really enjoyed. If he didn't watch out then sometimes I worried he'd let the hierarchy and politics we'd been born into burn out that free and innocent light he'd always exuded, and the thought of that made my heart ache with a desperate kind of pain.

I knew he wasn't the only one of us being moulded into something far harsher than we may have chosen to be. But wasn't that the point? We didn't get a choice because we were born for power. And with power came a whole lot of responsibility, the least of which being that we had to maintain our positions at the top of the pecking order at all times.

Darius hadn't shown his face yet and I knew he wasn't really happy about what we were going to do tonight either. Not that I'd been able to get him to admit that. He'd damn near bitten my head off when I'd tried one last ditch attempt to convince him to back down.

I got it. His dad wasn't like my mom. Lionel Acrux ruled with an iron fist and his word was law. Max had convinced me to play along, promising me that it was the best thing for our brother and I wanted that, so I'd agreed.

But as my gaze landed on Tory Vega where she stood alone at the bar, looking utterly devastating in a black gown which clung to her figure like a spill of oil, those doubts rose in me again.

She ordered herself a drink and I shot through the crowd before I could stop myself, coming to a halt at her side and leaning against the bar like I'd been there for hours instead of moments.

"It's not too late," I said, unable to help myself as I cast a quick glance around the room for the other Heirs. I wasn't entirely sure what they had planned for her aside from it taking place at the pool, but I knew it wouldn't be anything good.

Tory turned to look at me, offering me half a smile as she gave me a solid once over with those deep green eyes of hers which made my chest puff up and my dick start paying a whole lot more attention.

"Not too late for what?" she asked, taking a sip of her drink and drawing my focus to the blood red lipstick she wore.

"To sneak out of here and have some *real* fun," I offered, reaching out to brush my fingertips along her arm. If she'd just agree then I could get her out of here in less than a heartbeat, I could save her from this attempt to get rid of her and spend the night dedicating myself to her pleasure.

I told myself I was offering that because she was my Source and it was my duty to protect her, but it was more than that, like this feeling in my gut that what me and the other Heirs were planning was the wrong thing. The wrong move. I still believed it would make us look weak rather than strong and though I'd been forced to back down against the three of them, I got the feeling this wouldn't even work anyway. These girls might not have been raised in this kingdom, but they were Fae and I was sure they'd come back fighting no matter how hard we went at them tonight, so why do it?

Tory looked like she was actually considering my offer but then she just shook her head lightly in refusal, dashing my hopes.

"You'll have to work harder than that if you want me," she taunted and any other night I'd have been more than willing to take her up on that offer, but tonight I needed her to let me get her back to my room first.

I leaned a little closer, my mouth against her ear as I spoke seductively, trying to coax an agreement from her lips. "I promise you, I'll work *really* hard."

She looked at me with heat in her eyes and for a moment I thought I had her, but then she shrugged a little and shook her head like she'd never considered it at all.

"Tempting...but no."

I pursed my lips in disappointment, opening my mouth to say something else to convince her, but before I could figure out what that might have been, Max and Darius appeared at the other end of the bar.

The two of them shot me and Tory death glares like they knew exactly what I'd been up to and my stomach dropped as I gave in to the inevitable.

Darius beckoned me over and I straightened, suppressing a sigh. I might not have liked this but I knew where my loyalties lay and that would always be right alongside the other Heirs.

"Off you run," Tory muttered and I hesitated a moment, not liking the implication that I was being summoned like a good dog, but I also couldn't deny that my place was with them. And if I had to choose then it would be my brothers every time against every alternative.

I smiled ruefully as I took a step away. "I'm not switching allegiances, Tory," I said, resigning myself to how the night had to play out now. "No matter how good you look in that dress. We still can't let you take our throne."

I walked away but I heard the words she muttered bitterly at my back. "I don't want your damn throne."

I just wished her saying that was enough for the Councillors to accept it.

"What were you saying to her?" Darius asked in a low growl as I joined him and Max.

"Asking her to come back to my room tonight so that I could spend the evening fucking her instead of watching the shit show which will come now," I admitted because I'd made it clear enough that I wasn't really on board with this plan anyway and I wasn't going to lie to my brothers even if they wouldn't like the truth.

Darius scoffed. "So I assume she shot you down," he said cockily and I just couldn't help myself as I replied.

"She didn't the last time though."

A growl tore from Darius's throat and he slammed his drink down on the bar hard enough to shatter it.

Max stepped forward and placed a hand on both of our arms. "There's no time for this macho bullshit tonight," he said firmly, trying to calm us with his gifts and I let him do it because I was feeling too star damned jittery tonight anyway. If we had to do this shit, then I just wanted it over and done with.

I looked around for any sign of Seth but found him and Darcy missing which meant that part of their plan was probably already reaching completion and I gave up any more dumb ideas about putting this off.

Darius glared down the bar at Tory who raised her chin defiantly before flipping him off like she wasn't the least bit afraid of him. Shit. She was fucking crazy. Hot as hell, but batshit with a death wish too. She turned her back on him to make it even worse then slipped away into the crowd.

Darius looked inclined to stalk after her, but as he shoved away from the bar, his Atlas began to ring in his pocket and I caught sight of his father's name on the caller ID before he answered it.

"I take it you won't disappoint me again tonight?" Lionel said in a cold voice which made the hairs along the back of my neck stand up. I probably shouldn't have been using my gifts to listen in on the conversation, but Darius probably should have used a silencing bubble if he didn't want me to anyway.

"I'll get it done," Darius bit out.

"Good. Because your brother is here in my office with me, waiting to hear from you about your success, aren't you Xavier?"

"Darius?" Xavier's voice was pitched with fear but as I gave Darius a concerned look, he clearly realised I could hear his conversation and threw a silencing bubble around himself to hide the rest of it from me.

It didn't matter though. I could tell from the way his heart was racing and his knuckles were whitening where he gripped his Atlas that he was afraid of something.

"You see now why we have to do this?" Max growled in a low voice, his gifts clearly tuning him in to Darius's fear too and I nodded in acceptance.

"Yeah," I breathed. "I get it."

An excited squeal cut the air to shreds and I glanced around to find Geraldine Grus rushing through the room in a huge pink dress which looked like one of those old fashioned toilet roll doilies.

She threw herself at Tory in excitement and the two of them hugged each other tightly in greeting.

"Thank fuck she's okay," Max breathed beside me and I turned to him with a faint frown.

"You been worrying about Grus, big boy?" I teased and he instantly tore his gaze from her and shrugged off the concerned look in his eyes.

"Well it would have sucked if a Nymph got all of her power," he said.

"Besides, she's one of the only Fae in our class who is even semi capable of using her magic against us so..."

"So?" I pushed but at that moment Darius finished his call and dropped his silencing bubble.

"Let's get on with this," he said darkly. "Where did Roxy go?"

I picked her out among the crowd as she broke away from Geraldine and started heading for the exit, training my heightened senses on her and hearing her ask that hat kid if he knew where Darcy had gone.

"The hat kid just told her to go look for her sister outside," I said, pointing at Tory just as she slipped out the door.

Darius straightened his spine like he was marching into battle and he strode away through the crowd without waiting for us.

Max and I followed him at a bit of a distance, letting him take the lead in this as he led the way outside and turned left of the exit, trailing Tory's steps while he hid the sound of his within another silencing bubble.

She didn't even know a monster was stalking her in the dark and as I began to worry about what we were doing again, Max caught my arm.

"It has to be this way," he insisted in a low voice, forcing me to nod in acceptance.

"Doesn't mean I gotta like it," I muttered.

Shimmering orbs of light marked either side of the pathways and Tory headed down the one that led towards the Lunar Leisure building like even the stars were guiding her fate to this now. Darius stalked closer to her, closing in on her while she never once looked back.

At the very last second she whirled on him, her eyes widening in surprise as he painted on a cruel grin which I'd seen him wear plenty of times before. I trained my gifts on them to listen in while Max and I remained out of sight in the shadows, wondering if she might try and fight back Fae on Fae. With a strong enough blast of her power, she might even be able to run from him, but I seriously doubted fate would be that kind to her.

"Out for a walk?" Darius asked as Tory took a step back.

"Something like that," she replied, looking beyond him like she was hoping someone else might be out here but she didn't spot us within Max's concealment spells. "Did you want something?" she asked when Darius remained quiet and I could hear his heart racing like a war drum in his chest as he psyched himself up for this. He didn't like it any more than I did, I was certain of that. But whatever was going on with his father was enough to make him do it anyway.

"Last chance, Roxy. Take your sister and leave this academy. Go back to your little mortal lives and leave Solaria in the hands of people who are worthy of the throne," he said darkly but I could hear the hint of a plea in that request too, like he was really hoping she'd just agree and we wouldn't have to go through with this.

"I'm not going anywhere," she replied defiantly. "So you need to get over it."

"Is that your final decision?" he asked, taking a step towards her which made her heart rate spike but she still held her ground like a true Fae.

"Yes," she spat.

"Then I guess I'm going to have to change your mind," Darius sighed.

She scowled at him and made a move to turn away, but his hand snapped out and he caught her arm, tugging her close and ending this before it had even begun.

"Let go of me," Tory demanded, trying to shake him off.

"No, I don't think I will," he growled. "You're going to learn a little lesson about respect. I won't have you turning your back on me again." There was real anger in his tone as he spoke to her and I got the feeling he was mad at her for not just giving in, bowing to our will like we needed them to. Because now he was going to have to become the monster he tried so hard not to be and I guessed in his eyes that was all her fault.

Tory struggled but he caught her other arm too, dragging her so close that their breath mingled as she stared up into his eyes.

"Don't fight me. And don't scream," he said, his voice laced with Coercion.

I could practically feel her trying to fight off his command but the ring of power he'd used to Coerce her was still heavy in the air and I knew he'd made sure that she had no chance of that.

Darius smiled like he was giving way to the devil in him then turned and started marching her towards the Lunar building up ahead.

I exchanged a look with Max as he dropped the magic which had been hiding us and he looked to me.

"Let's get there first and make sure everyone else is in place to watch the show," he said firmly and I nodded because there was no other choice left now anyway.

I grabbed hold of him and tossed him over my shoulder before shooting around the side of the building and carrying him inside. There was no going back now. And I just wanted this night over.

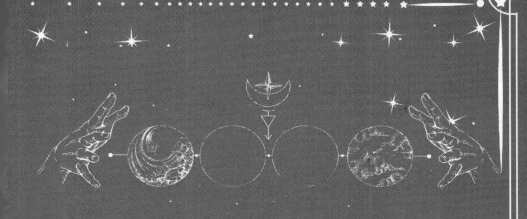

ORION

CHAPTER TWENTY-SIX

I'd watched Darcy and Seth dancing until it had felt like my eyes were going to bleed. I hadn't taken a single sip of the beer locked in my grip and I'd tuned out Washer as he'd recounted stories of his days here at Zodiac Academy and all the 'cheeky' things he'd gotten up. Most of which seemed to involve his cock. As Nova was off dancing with a couple of the female staff, I supposed he felt like it was a great opportunity to tell me his messed up stories.

When Darcy and Seth had disappeared in the direction of the exit, I'd gotten anxious. And as the minutes ticked by, the desire to hunt them down grew to a desperation.

"I need another beer," I muttered to Washer and walked straight off.

"But that one's full," he called after me and I placed it on a table, ignoring him as I headed for the door, pushing students out of my way as I went.

My jaw was pulsing as my teeth rammed hard together and my heart rioted as I made it outside. If Seth was planning something, I had to warn her.

I couldn't just stand idly by and let him hurt her. It was my duty because she was my Source. At least, that was what I was convincing myself.

There were a few students hanging around outside, but none of them were her, so I turned down the path and started my hunt, praying I wasn't going to find that asshole kissing her or worse. I cringed at the thought and my fangs sharpened as the beast in me awoke. I was in a dangerous mood, a volatile one, and I wasn't sure exactly what I was going to do if I found them together.

As I made it further around The Orb, my gaze landed on her alone, standing off the path with her back to the building and her eyes closed. A line of tension was on her brow and she looked like she didn't really want to be found, but I was still walking, full of relief that she wasn't here with Seth Capella. But that didn't mean she was out of the woods yet. The Heirs were up to something and I needed to make sure she was aware of that.

I approached her, recognising this need in her for some space because it was how I felt at every party I'd ever attended. And as I came to a halt in front of her, studying her beautiful face and revelling in the quiet in the air, I wondered what it would be like to lean in and taste her lips. To feel her pulling me closer and welcoming me into the warmth of her body.

Her eyes opened, landing on the predator before her and surprise crossed her features, but not fear.

"Oh," she breathed and dawning concern fell over her as she realised we were alone. Her eyes darted to the path like she was hoping to find more company, but we were alone.

She pushed off the wall, clearly intending to leave but I stepped straight into her path.

"Professor," she warned, clearly fearing I'd come here to bite her. But that wasn't my intention, even if I did hunger for her blood with the desperation of a starved animal.

My hand fell to her waist, pinching the material of her dress as I leaned in to the maddening urges in me to get closer to her. She was the sun embodied and I'd spent so long in the dark, all I wanted was a few moments in its heat. Was that really such a crime?

Yes, it was. But still…Gabriel's words lingered in my mind and though I knew this was every shade of wrong, it also felt every shade of right.

She sucked in a breath and goosebumps rose across her neck, making my fangs prickle and my cock jerk. Did she feel this too? Was I as tempting to her as she was to me? It didn't seem possible. And yet the look in her eyes said maybe it was.

I withdrew my hand, regaining my self-control and sharing a look with her that said she knew I'd crossed a line, but she didn't reprimand me for it. I was only indulging a little. Just enough to feed the creature in me who demanded more of her. Gabriel had told me to lean towards the light, and there wasn't any Fae that burned brighter to me than her. But I wasn't supposed to be here pushing the boundaries of my sordid fantasy of her, I was here to pass on a warning.

"Why do you keep flirting with the devil?" I asked and she frowned like she thought I was talking about myself. "Seth Capella."

She folded her arms, tilting her chin as her walls immediately went up. "You're my Liaison, sir, not my life guru. If I want to date Seth, I will," she said coolly.

Great. This is going swell already.

I glanced at my watch, cursing internally at the approaching time. Almost nine o'clock. I had to deliver this warning then follow Gabriel's orders to leave.

I could hear approaching students and knew it wasn't a good idea to be found here alone with her. It would look shady.

"Keeping you am I?" she asked bitterly.

"Yes, now give me your wrist." I reached for it, needing a cover story for why I was here if anyone showed up, but she stepped back again.

"Really? You're going to bite me tonight of all nights?" she hissed, but I was too distracted to answer, throwing a look down the path again as laughter headed this way. I stepped forward to take hold of her and suddenly she laughed. At me. And the sound was like gunfire ripping through my chest.

She narrowed her eyes, the power shifting into her grasp as she realised why I was acting this way. But I couldn't have that. She wasn't in control here. I was.

I darted forward, crushing her against the wall and baring my fangs at her, forcing her to submit. Her heart hammered against me and being this close to her was a mindfuck of mass proportions.

"Not strictly allowed this, is it sir?" she said icily, her words cutting deep as she realised she had some ammo against me. And I needed to unload her little weapon fast.

I kept my hand locked around her arm, my gaze on her neck as the urgent desire to feed from her that way ran through me. It was a more intimate way of feeding, though I knew even more intimate ways than that – not that I was thinking about those. My cock was going to give me away if I didn't move soon, but I couldn't let her go. It was too exciting having her like this. And why shouldn't I bite her? She was my Source after all.

"And where did you get that idea?" I asked dryly, hoping to throw her off the scent of my misdemeanour.

"From the shifty way you're acting. Why did you follow me out here anyway? You could have bitten me inside."

I shrugged. "Seemed like easy prey."

Warn her and leave for fuck's sake.

But I was enjoying this interaction a little too much and I still had a couple of minutes to kill.

She released a cold laugh and the acid in her eyes made my grip loosen on her. Maybe I'd imagined her desire for me after all. Maybe I really was overstepping the mark here in more ways than one. And I didn't like the thought of that.

"I don't buy it," she said.

"Why am I even tolerating this conversation?" I muttered to myself. We'd moved into dangerous territory. I had her pinned to a wall and I still wasn't biting her. And honestly, the thing my mouth wanted to do most wasn't even in the biting territory. One kiss from her would be a sin, but it might just be worth getting down on my knees in penance for.

You can't. You're her professor. Her enemy.

Fuck.

"Fine," I sighed like I was tired of this conversation, but it was the most tantalising one I'd had - possibly ever. "I shouldn't be here alone with you. It's not appropriate."

Her brows arched. "We spend time alone in your office every Monday."

"That's different," I growled, glancing up the path again. Students were going to come this way. I really had to move.

"What would happen if I told Principal Nova about this?" she asked, making my heart lurch violently.

"Would you?" I hissed. Hell, maybe I'd underestimated this girl. Maybe she'd throw me to the wolves for this. But then a shiver ran through her that was so telling, I was certain it was to do with me. Her pupils dilated and she wet her lips in a way that drew me to her so forcefully, it took all of my willpower to stop myself from kissing her.

"Try me," she whispered, but her body had given the game away. She wasn't going to tell because she felt this too, it was written into her flesh, the way her eyes dipped to my mouth and her throat bobbed. I wasn't sure she was even aware of how much those eyes were pulling me in, begging me to commit a crime with her.

I slid my fingers up her arm, temptation like a demon whispering in my ear. Just one taste. Could it really do that much harm?

My hand slid onto her throat, caressing her velvet soft skin and I leaned in, feeling like the stars were pressing against my back and forcing me closer.

Blue tilted her chin up, her lips an offering I wanted to seize. And I knew in that second I was going to do it. I was going to kiss a Savage Princess and damn the consequences. Because this girl was everything good in the world I'd been missing and I had to know what it felt like to drown in her. Even if it meant my downfall. Even if I corrupted her to her core.

Someone cleared their throat and we both jolted, my Vampire hearing picking it up tenfold. *Fuck!*

I glanced back, finding Seth there with an impatient expression on his face and I immediately looked back at Darcy.

"What's he doing?" She tried to push me back, but I didn't budge.

"He's waiting for me to bite you," I said, pulling back an inch and hating that it felt like a chasm. "So he can have you back."

She shivered, her eyes growing distant and I knew the heated moment that had passed between us was now dead and gone, never to fucking return.

"Well get on with it," she hissed. "Or are you going to continue playing with your food?"

I'd run out of time, too enraptured by her to do what I'd come here to do. But I had to try. I leaned in to speak in her ear, my voice nothing but a breath of a whisper. "Stay away from him. Go inside." We were so close and her scent was like a drug, making my thoughts hazy and hard to grasp. *Please listen to me, Blue. I don't know what will happen if you don't.*

I hoped it was enough because my time was up and I had to walk away like Gabriel had instructed. I knew better than to go against his guidance.

With a wrenching feeling in my stomach, I pulled back, leaving my teeth firmly out of her and I shot away with a burst of speed, knowing if I moved any slower I'd pause to smash my fist into Seth's face.

I just hoped I'd done enough to make her listen.

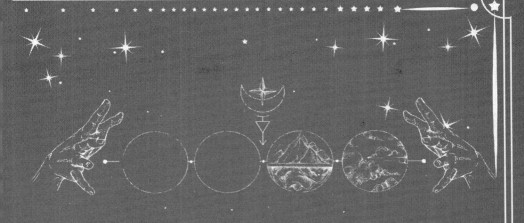

SETH

CHAPTER TWENTY-SEVEN

Now that Professor Bites-A lot was gone, I had Darcy Vega all to myself. She looked like a daydream on a whipped cream cloud and I was the big bad wolf here to eat her cloud and watch her fall to her doom. And the more I looked at her and pinned all my problems on her, the easier it became to turn into my most psycho self. Because she and her sister were the reason I was missing out on my family moon march. They were the reason I couldn't go home, the reason my mom was cutting me off. And more importantly than all of that, they were the reason I was going to potentially lose my seat on the Celestial Council if I didn't deal with this now. So yeah, I was embracing my inner demons, because they liked the taste of pain and suffering and made my smiles a little easier to wear. Especially when I cut off my weaker emotions and stuffed them deep down inside me where not even I could find them.

I jogged to her side, winding my fingers between hers and locking them tight. "All good?" I asked brightly and she nodded, though there was a faint frown on her brow left there by Orion. She clearly hated him biting her, though I didn't really get it. A Vampire's bite could be hot as fuck, and I definitely enjoyed it when Cal pinned me down and drove his fangs into me, but I supposed when it was an asshole professor it kind of *sucked* the fun out of it.

I towed her along the path with a smile on my lips, guiding her to a bench which sat before a large bush where Kylie and her friends were hiding. I'd needed someone willing and as I didn't wanna implicate my pack in this, I'd chosen Kylie and a few of her friends to help out. Dick move? Pretty much. But Alphas had to protect their own.

I dropped down onto the bench and pulled Darcy down beside me, pressing my face into her hair. My smile fell away as I breathed her in and something yanked on the inside of my chest.

I'm a ruthless Fae. A leader. And one day I'll be a lord. This is for the greater good.

"What's wrong, babe?" I asked as my mouth skimmed over her ear. She seemed tense, distracted. And I wasn't really used to girls being this aloof with me when I turned on the charm.

"Nothing," she said quickly and I leaned back, tilting my head to one side as I examined her expression.

"Liar," I teased. "Did Orion hurt you?" If he had, I'd bury him. But then again, I was about to do far worse to her than he could have, so that little vow was kind of pointless. Me and her were about to go in very opposing directions. She might run all the way back to the Mortal Realm never to be seen again, though the thought of that didn't sit quite right of me. Still…I'd get over it. I had a heart of iron. I was a heartless beast just like my mom always said I was. And tonight, I'd make her proud.

"No," she admitted, but something still didn't seem right with her.

A rustle sounded in the bushes behind us and irritation ran through me. *They have one fucking job. Stupid freshmen can't even cast a silencing bubble. Useless.*

I ran my tongue across my teeth, needing to hurry this up and becoming entirely aware I was hesitating. But there was no room for weakness now. I had to Fae up and do what I was born to do; push rivals down in the dirt and prove I was superior. It was our way. And I didn't need this girl's affection when I had the Heirs. We were all each other had ever needed and I realised now they were the only ones who would ever truly understand me. We were in this together. Brothers until the bitter end. And they'd have my back no matter what decisions I made, because we made them together. A united front. The kings of Solaria. And it was time to do these girls a kindness and destroy them thoroughly, efficiently and in a way they could never recover from.

I brushed my fingers over Darcy's cheek, drawing her attention to me and she gave me the big eyes which worked to tug on my heartstrings. But I crushed away any sympathy I felt, falling deeper into the darkness that lived in me. "If he bothers you, I can get my pack to make him back off. We don't normally take on professors but..." I smirked, leaning in closer, my fingers sliding down to cup her chin and tilt her mouth up in line with mine. "You're worth it."

At least I'd have one last taste of sweetness before I became the most bitter creature she'd ever known. My hand brushed her knee and she moved into the arc of my body, a need in her eyes that demanded answering. And as she offered me her lips, I took them, tasting them slowly at first before I grabbed hold of her, dragging her firmly against me. I drove my tongue into her mouth in the filthiest way I knew how, pulling her fully into my lap so her dress rode up her thighs and my cock swelled. It was meant to be a show for the camera, but I lost myself to Darcy for a stolen eternity, possessing her, making a Vega bow to me in the best way I knew how.

I groaned as her tongue met mine for every stroke and her fingers clenched in my shirt, almost making me forget what this kiss was intended for. Because it was a villain's kiss, a distraction designed to buy me time for the crushing blow I was about to deliver.

I slid the blade from my pocket and gripped the back of her neck, locking her in place against me as I prepared to sacrifice a piece of my soul for the throne.

"Seth," she yelped, breaking our kiss as I held on tighter, not willing to lose this chance.

I caught hold of her bun and with one clean slice, cut it off in my hand, my fist tightening around it as a ripple of cruel satisfaction pooled in my chest. There. It was done. I'd done my duty. But why was that satisfaction already starting to turn sour?

"No!" she gasped in absolute horror, shoving me back and I released her.

She fell from my lap in a heap onto the path, grazing her knees and I let the monster in me take over fully. I needed to put on a good show now. Needed to make it hurt, needed the world to see her weakness so they knew never to place their faith in a Vega again. Because the true Heirs were rising and no one could defeat us. Not even the spawn of the Savage King.

A single lock of blue hair came free from my grip, fluttering down onto the ground before her and she snatched it, her hands trembling as she stared at it, her eyes welling with tears.

I watched her break, refusing to look away as I faced what I'd done. I could take it. I wasn't going to feel guilty. I'd done what I had to. This was who I was. And now she was seeing her enemy under the stark light of the moon and she wasn't strong enough to fight back. So I'd won. And that was all that mattered. Right?

A satisfied smirk pulled at my features as I felt the lens of Kylie's camera on me. "Told you I'd get your hair," I said, my voice a cold thing that sucked all the warmth from the world. "And since Max told me the little sob story behind it, I was even more determined to get my hands on it."

Her lower lip trembled and tears washed down her cheeks, and some Wolfish part of me begged to comfort her for a moment before I forced myself to remain where I was. I was her fear embodied and I'd play the role to a T. I could practically feel my mother's pride over this when I told her. Maybe she'd let me come home now. Maybe she'd let me come to the moon march.

Giggles filled the air and Kylie burst out of the bushes alongside a bunch of her friends, her Atlas held in her hand. "I recorded the whole thing," she told me triumphantly.

I kept my gaze on Darcy as her palm opened like she was about to cast magic and I rushed forward, closing her fist in mine as I crouched before her.

"Nothing personal, Vega," I whispered, hoping she'd see that I really meant those words. She was a sweet chick, it wasn't about her. It was all politics. And politics were dirty. "It's the way of Fae. If you don't want things getting even worse for you, then take your sister and get out of our academy." I winked, getting to my feet and slinging an arm around Kylie as a final fuck you to Darcy, not focusing too much on if she'd ever trust a guy again after this.

"Let's go to Lunar Leisure, I don't wanna miss the fun," I said loudly so Darcy would hear me, keeping her hair locked in a tight fist.

One down, one to go…

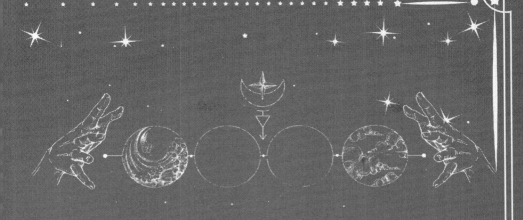

ORION

CHAPTER TWENTY-EIGHT

I stood to one side of the doorway in The Orb, remaining in the shadows as the party grew more wild and my skin itched with the urge to leave. But not to go home, to go back to where I'd left Darcy with Seth, because I had the awful feeling I'd made a mistake in following Gabriel's advice.

Tyler Corbin ran past me with Sofia Cygnus over his shoulder like he'd just kidnapped her and I watched flatly as he tripped over his own feet and they slammed down onto a table, sending a bowl of punch flying as they burst out laughing and I dragged a hand down my face, my tolerance for this night finally running out.

I slipped out the door, figuring I'd check up on Darcy one last time. It couldn't do any harm. I'd followed Gabriel's instructions, it was ten past nine, so what could really go wrong now?

I picked up my pace as I rounded The Orb, my heart beating uncomfortably, a sense of dread in the air that set me on edge.

I put on a burst of speed and made it to where I'd left them, finding Darcy on the ground in front of a bench, her hands clasped over her butchered hair and choked sobs leaving her. I froze, an icy coldness dripping down my spine as I found her shattered, knowing exactly who had done this to her without needing a single word to leave her lips. A splinter of rage seemed to lodge in my chest, never to be pulled free.

I should have wanted this. To see her on her knees with her strength dashed to pieces, but instead I felt her pain as sharply as if it were my own.

I shot forward, pressing my hand to her shoulder and she jolted at the contact, twisting around and throwing out a palm with a snarl on her lips. A huge crack tore across the path as earth magic left her and I darted aside before it knocked me over. *Holy fuck.*

Her eyes flared with the fury of hell and I saw the Fae in her for a second before she turned away and tried to hide her face from me, leaving my chest in knots.

No...Blue.

I sank down to my knees in front of her, hatred seething in me towards Seth Capella. He was callous, I'd seen it before. But this was taking things to a new level, and I could see it meant something far deeper to her than I would ever know.

"Have you come to say I told you so?" she bit at me as tears continued to stream down her cheeks and all I wanted to do was pull her close and wipe them away. This girl didn't deserve to be crying down in the dirt. This was wrong. I may have wanted the Vegas dealt with, but never like this.

"Get up," I urged, taking her arm and pulling her to her feet. She needed to use this anger, twist it into armour and wear it on her flesh when she sought revenge on Seth. It was the way of our kind and she needed to know that, but the words wouldn't pass my lips because they were the words of a traitor. I should have been glad Seth had done this, but no part of me allowed for that. This was dirty fucking tactics.

"Why'd you come back?" she choked out, tugging her hand free of my grip and wrapping her hands around her head again.

He'd made a right mess of her hair, taken away all of the blue ends and leaving a patch of scalp on show, but it could grow back. All she needed was the right potion. She searched my eyes, looking so mistrustful of me that some long lost part of my personality awoke, trying to offer her something to lighten her mood.

"My spidey senses were tingling," I said with a low laugh and she frowned at me. *Great, that went down well. Idiot.*

"Was that a joke?" she asked, her voice raw and laced with confusion.

My mouth hooked up at the corner as I attempted to coax a smile from her. I needed her light to return for selfish reasons and apparently I wasn't beyond making a fool of myself in an effort to make her smile again.

"It was," he said. "A pretty good one I think." I tugged her closer, breathing her in and continuing along this track of insanity I was on, determined to brighten her mood. "Now the blue is gone, how will I tell which twin is which?"

A laugh escaped her in the form of a hiccup and my inner beast purred. "You're right, however would you tell?" She sniffed, wiping at her damp eyes with her lace sleeve, smearing mascara across her cheeks.

She still looked beautiful with her heart shattered, her hair ruined and tear lines streaked down her face. Her destruction was a cruel work of art, but not one she couldn't recover from. She was more Fae than that. But as I opened my mouth to speak those damning words, a scream cut through the air that tore through my head.

Panic splintered through me as I recognised Tory Vega's voice and knew in my soul who was responsible for that scream. I let go of Darcy, running away towards the source of that sound but not so fast that I left her alone. I needed to hurry all the same, because Darius and the other Heirs were apparently hellbent on terrorising the Vegas tonight, and it was clear they weren't close to done.

DARIUS

CHAPTER TWENTY-NINE

I kept up a fierce pace as I tugged Roxy along, the point where I held onto her arm seeming to burn like hot coals against my skin.

The stars were bright tonight and between the constant pounding of our footfalls, I could have sworn I heard the whispers of them watching us. Watching *me*.

I swallowed a lump in my throat and kept going, not looking at her because if I looked into those big eyes of hers, I knew I'd see myself reflected in them. And I didn't want to look at the man I had to be tonight. If I found true fear in her gaze as she looked up at me then I knew I really would crack. Because tonight felt important. The kind of important that meant fate was spinning on a dime and whichever way the coin fell could determine everything.

What I was planning to do to her was the kind of monstrous thing my father would praise. The kind of cruel lesson he would have enjoyed teaching me. If I did this then I would only be creeping further into his shadow, moving nearer to the destiny he'd picked out for me which I had never wanted to fulfil.

But maybe I'd been a fool to ever believe I could be anything other than this. To defeat a monstrous man, I would have to be an even greater monster.

She wasn't struggling, still held under the sway of my Coercion and the thought of me stealing her will away like that stripped pieces from my already tattered soul.

All the things about her which I'd admired most, that fire which blazed within her and drew me closer so easily were dampened by that hold I'd stolen on her actions. I hated it. I knew what it was to be forced beneath the heel of another. To have the right to fight back stolen from you as well as to suffer their cruelty. I was embodying the one man I'd never wanted to become and yet I couldn't see any other way.

This wasn't about me or her or the throne. It was about my little brother who needed my protection. And maybe she would have understood that if I explained it, because she loved her sister as fiercely as the sun, so I was sure she would make any sacrifice for her too.

But of course I could explain no such thing to her or anyone else. So in the eyes of the world who watched me, I would simply be the villain. But perhaps for the one person I had left in this world who held some true purity about him, I could be his salvation. So that was what I had to focus on. Xavier needed me to do this. So it would be done.

"Where are you taking me?" Roxy breathed, the fear in her tone making my jaw clench. There wouldn't be any coming back from this. I knew it. Father knew my weakness now. He knew just how to strike at me. Which meant he owned me more surely than he ever had before. I was his creature, set to do his bidding. Broken the way he'd always wanted to break me so that I was little more than a puppet on a string. His Heir, his right hand, a doppelgänger of the dark creature he'd become a long, long time ago.

"We're going to see some friends," I said, my tone clipped. I couldn't say any more than that. I just had to get through this. Finish it.

I drew her into the building then tugged her along through the silent gym and on into the pool locker rooms beyond it. She couldn't fight me thanks to the Coercion I'd placed on her, but I could feel her muscles tightening like a coil in a spring.

Why couldn't she have just bowed out of this game the moment she'd been dragged into it?

I pulled her through another set of doors to the huge swimming pool and I pursed my lips at the gathered crowd, wishing we could have done this without the witnesses. But that was the whole point, we had to show the world how low the Vegas could be pushed and make sure any murmurings about them rising to power and reclaiming their throne were fully squashed. This wasn't a Fae on Fae fight against some untrained girls, it was proof that they weren't Fae enough to overcome their own fears which would show everyone just how weak they really were.

Marguerite and her friends shrieked excitedly and my irritation rose at the sight of the girl I'd once taken to my bed. She had turned out to be the kind of psycho mistake I hadn't wanted to make, and by the gleeful look in her eyes as she watched me hauling Roxy in here, I got the impression she might have been thinking this meant something so far as me and her were concerned. But that was absolutely not the case.

A group of Seth's wolves started howling with excitement, pushing and shoving each other by the edge of the pool while they drank bottles of beer. There was no sign of their Alpha yet, so I guessed he was still working on his part of this plan.

My gut knotted as I thought about that so I turned my mind away from it and focused on each step I took as I tugged Roxy along the length of the pool. I eyed the sign warning that the water was six meters deep and wondered how far her fear of water really went. Would this even be enough? Was it more to do with open water, or was it about the prospect of drowning? Though I guessed anyone would be terrified if they were trapped beneath water and unable to escape so I had to assume this was enough.

She tipped her head back to look up at the three diving boards at the far end of the pool and I felt a tremor of fear shiver through her flesh where I held her, but still, I didn't let go. I only had to think of my brother, terrified and waiting for me to finish this and I knew I wouldn't falter.

Caleb had clearly used his speed to beat us here and he and Max stood waiting by the diving boards, the two of them looking like polar opposites in their attitudes to this. Max was practically sparking energy, giving himself to the challenge of this and most likely using his gifts to bolster the emotions he wanted to give off while squashing any feelings of doubt or guilt out of existence. Caleb wasn't giving anything away as he watched us approach, but his eyes lingered on the girl I was pulling along and I knew he didn't like this even if he was going to go along with it for the sake of unity within our group.

I came to a halt beside them and decided to get this whole thing over with as quickly as possible, spinning Roxy so that she was looking across the pool to the crowd of onlookers before dropping my arm around her shoulders and offering out a cocky smirk for everyone to see.

"A lot of people have been talking about the return of the Vega Heirs like they're something special," I called, causing the crowd to fall silent as they listened to me. "But I am yet to see anything impressive about them. This one can't even fight off basic Coercion."

I shifted her against my chest, wondering if she might say something against me or try to ask the people watching this to help her. They wouldn't. But if she begged convincingly enough then maybe we wouldn't even have to go through with this. So long as she was seen on her knees and at our mercy then wouldn't that serve the purpose?

"To rise to the top, we fight against our fears and come out triumphant!" Max cried, spouting the same things our parents had drummed into us countless times. I'd faced challenges like this over and over again throughout my childhood, my father seeming to take pleasure in terrifying me in any way he could manage while forcing me to fight through my fears. "So shouldn't one of the girls who claim to be our queens have to prove that she can do the same?"

Roxy frowned at Max and he stalked closer, leaning in to speak to her with determination and malice rolling from his skin.

"Thanks for sharing your fears with me," he purred. "It made planning this so much easier."

I looked between the two of them, wondering if she'd crack, beg, plead. But of course she didn't because nothing about her was easy, and she wouldn't even do that much to save herself and us from having to do this.

Max leaned closer, brushing a finger down her arm and smirking as he tasted her emotions and I bristled as he laid his hand on her.

"Come on then," I said, taking my arm from her shoulders and giving her a little push to get her moving once more.

As we passed Caleb, he threw Roxy a reassuring smile like he was trying to tell her she'd be just fine and I gave him a scathing look, growing more than a little sick of his conscience showing its face and making me feel like even more of a bastard for what we had to do here. He knew full well that I had no fucking choice and even if he was willing to go against his mother's wishes on this, I didn't get the luxury of being able to challenge my father on anything.

I walked Roxy past the two lower diving boards and stopped by the ladder which led up to the ten meter board, wanting this done.

"Come on then, Roxy," I said, leaning in close to speak with her, like that made some difference, like it made this any better. "Up you go."

She lifted her green eyes to mine, wetting her lips and drawing my attention to her mouth before I peered back into her soul again. It felt like the weight of all the stars in the sky were pressing in on me, whispering and murmuring things which I couldn't make out, but which sounded like a distant storm in my ears. Something more important than I was able to fully understand was happening here but I didn't know if that meant I had to push on with this task or turn back from the path I was on.

"I can barely swim," Roxy breathed and it wasn't a plea for help or even anything at all like one. Just a statement of fact because she wanted to be certain that I knew that. She wanted me to understand fully what I was going to do to her if I forced her to do this. And I couldn't deny that it made me pause. I knew what this made me. *Who* it made me, but it wasn't like there were any other choices available to me either. Xavier was there with that monster now and I had no idea how far he'd go to punish me if I failed him again now. "I'll drown if I jump in there."

Never.

The word echoed through me with a finality which I knew to be true. I might be willing to do this to her, to terrorise her and make her hate me more than any other man she knew, but I wouldn't let her die here. That wasn't going to happen. But the fear in her eyes forced me to see all of the worst things in myself and for the briefest of moments my resolve cracked.

Surely if she bowed and agreed to leave I wouldn't have to do this? Father would have to be satisfied by that.

"Are you ready to bow to us then?" I asked almost desperately as I shifted so close to her that I could practically feel the racing of her heart inside her chest. "And leave this school behind?"

She looked into my eyes but instead of all the fire and fury she normally offered me, I just saw a girl looking back at me. A girl who had had her life here stolen from her when she was a baby. Who had been thrown away and cast aside and had never belonged anywhere until she found her way back to Solaria.

She wasn't the cruel creature we'd expected her to be as a daughter the Savage King. In fact, she wasn't even really a threat to us. At least not yet. She was lost and searching for something which might be the key to filling up all of the empty places in her soul. And I could understand that urge better than most.

My lips parted as my determination began to falter and the whispering of the stars almost seemed like a roar of a storm building in the distance. I didn't know what I was going to say or do but for some reason, I didn't want to do this anymore…

"Start climbing! All the way to the top!" Max yelled from behind us, his Coercion so powerful that I almost succumbed to it too as it caught me off guard.

Roxy jerked away from me while I was still reinforcing my mental shields against his power and before I could do any more than watch her go, she'd kicked off her stilettos and was climbing up the ladder.

I took a step forward as if I might have been going to stop her, but Max caught my arm, a silencing bubble sliding around the two of us as I looked to him.

"If you change your mind, what will happen with your father?" he demanded in a low voice, the look in his eyes telling me he'd figured out too much about the reality of my situation despite my efforts to keep these secrets from him.

I looked into his eyes for a long moment then dropped my gaze to my feet again. "He'll punish me," I muttered, my skin prickling at the half truth because I knew it wasn't *me* who would bear the brunt of that.

"I've felt a fraction of the fear you've been living with over this punishment and I know for a fact that I don't want you to face it. So tell me, Darius, is she worth what it will cost you to turn back now?" Max asked seriously.

My gaze moved to Roxy as she continued to climb, her long black dress tangling around her legs as she went while the crowd of assholes who had been invited to watch this all chanted, *"Jump! Jump! Jump!"* as they hungered for her destruction.

My throat thickened with the words I didn't want to have to speak but as much as I might have hated being the man I was embodying tonight, I knew that I would sacrifice that and more for my brother's safety. Even her.

As I made that decision, Max seemed to sense it and he nodded firmly as he released me.

"I won't see you suffer for a Vega," he said seriously. "Which means this is already done." He dropped the silencing bubble, saving me from having to reply and I looked up to Roxy again, watching as she made it to the top of the ladder and pushed herself to her feet on the diving board.

Max strode to the edge of the pool, twisting his fingers as he cast his magic into the water and the steam rolling off of it quickly vanished as the temperature of the liquid plummeted.

The doors banged open at the far end of the room and Seth howled excitedly as he raced inside, cupping his hands around his mouth and calling out to us as he approached. "I was worried I was going to miss the show. I've just finished destroying the other one!"

I nodded, understanding what that meant. This was half way finished already so now we just needed to do our part. Then Xavier would be safe and I could focus on him instead of letting myself be distracted by a girl who could never be mine anyway.

"Come on," Max commanded, jerking his chin to get me walking with him to the edge of the pool.

We raised our hands and took control of the water before us, making it twist and writhe like a storm was cutting through its icy depths.

"Are you ready, little Vega?" Max yelled out and the crowd of students chanted louder, their bloodlust growing. I was grateful to him for taking charge of this though I knew it made me a coward too. But there wasn't any other way and so long as I focused on Xavier, I knew I could get through it with my brothers at my side.

"*Jump!*" Max yelled, his Coercion as powerful as a battering ram.

Roxy stepped forward but then she jerked to halt and Max hissed a curse.

"She shook it off," he growled and for some insane reason I felt like fucking laughing over that. Because of course she fucking had. That girl was as stubborn as the moon.

"On it," Seth said with a dark grin and a moment later a howling wind tore through the room, racing up to the rafters and he started directing it at her back.

But Roxy wasn't the kind of girl to let herself be pushed, so before he could build up enough force to shove her over the edge, she took a running jump and launched herself off of the end of the diving board.

The seconds it took for her to plummet towards the water seemed to stretch on endlessly as I watched her fall, the black material of her dress whipping around her legs as a scream tore from her lungs which sliced right through me.

She hit the water hard, disappearing beneath the turbulent surface and I swear the seconds counted down in minutes as I stared as the writhing liquid and waited for her to appear again.

Seth was laughing and the crowd were screaming for Vega blood but I just stood there, staring at the water and trying to locate her within it.

I reached out with my power, using the connection I had already formed with the water to search for her in its depths. I released the breath I'd been holding as I felt the kick of her legs against the water and my gaze flicked to a point in the centre of the pool a second before she surfaced with a gasp. She'd taken her dress off to make it easier for her to swim and was only in her underwear as she looked around in a panic.

My relief only lasted a moment as Seth leaned in close to me and whispered in my ear. "Do it, Darius. Finish this. Let's get this fucking over with."

And despite my limbs feeling weighted with this decision, I knew it was already made so I gritted my jaw and followed his command, yanking the water out of the pool in a spout that rose up beside her and cast her in its shadow.

Roxy tried to swim away from it, but I flicked my hand and sent it crashing down on top of her, knocking her beneath the surface once more and spinning her around in a current of my creation. I refused to let myself feel anything at all aside from the concentration it took to control the magic until I released her from it again as she started swimming for the surface once more.

Max flexed his fingers beside me and the surface of the water began to freeze over, my heart pounding as I watched the liquid solidifying as he locked her in the depths of the pool.

Seconds dragged past then suddenly her hand hit the ice, my gaze locking on the sight of it smacking against the opaque slab as my pulse began to thunder and a roar sounded in my ears.

The stars were screaming inside my skull, mocking, taunting, laughing, cursing me – I wasn't even sure what, but I knew they were watching, judging, changing fate.

This was so fucked up. The worst thing I'd ever done at my father's command, and I hated to think what more he might demand from me now.

Roxy's fist started slamming against the ice and I shifted forward an inch, unsure what I even intended to do before Max caught my arm and gave me a hard look.

"It'll be over soon," he growled and I nodded, but the sick feeling in my gut wasn't lessening.

Suddenly the ice began to tremble and cracks spiderwebbed across it as Roxy unleashed the brunt of her power from beneath the surface.

She managed to punch a hole right through it, gulping down a breath of air as Max's grip on my arm tightened and his power slammed up against the barrier of my own.

"I need more power to hold it," he gritted out, his demand clear and I forced my barriers aside for him, allowing our power to merge as he drew on the well of magic inside me and reinforced the ice so that she was trapped beneath the surface once again.

More and more cracks spread over the ice which coated the top of the pool as Roxy threw her magic against ours in a brutal, potent wave and the cheers of the crowd turned to murmurings of doubt, making this whole thing so much more vital than it had been before.

If she managed to break through that ice then this would backfire spectacularly. She'd prove just how powerful she was by breaking free of us and overcoming her fear after all and I could only imagine my father's wrath if that were to happen.

I thought of my brother and nothing else as I poured more magic into my connection with Max, helping him reinforce the ice as I moved my own water magic around her from beneath, focusing on the movements of her legs, the pounding of her heart.

I was ready to pull her from the water the moment she stopped fighting. This wasn't going to end in her getting hurt in any way beyond terrorising her. And even doing that might have been enough to break something in me. Because I already knew that this line I had crossed wasn't one I could ever turn back from. I was just like him now. Just like the man I'd always sworn I would never become.

My jaw was locked with determination while my resolve began to shatter inside my chest piece by piece. Just a little bit longer. A few more seconds.

Not for me.

But for Xavier.

ORION

CHAPTER THIRTY

As I made it to the Lunar Leisure building and the raucous cheers of a crowd grew to a din in my ears, I glanced back at Darcy, saw the gleaming panic in her eyes and shot away from her with a burst of speed in search of her sister. It sounded like the danger was ahead of us anyway, and her fear over her sister sent another bolt of determination through me to stop the Heirs.

I made it inside as cruel laughter tangled with the air and a snarl rolled from my tongue as I spotted the ice and the girl trapped beneath it.

I reached the edge of the pool and dove off the side, casting a torrent of water from my palms which melted the ice before I hit it. I sank deep into the freezing pool, the raging storm of magic swirling around my body, gripping my limbs and I powered through it with the strength of my own magic, carving a path through the water all the way to Tory's unconscious body which was sinking deeper into the pool.

I hooked my arm around her and kicked hard, using my gifts to harness the water and propel us to the surface faster.

I snatched a lungful of air as I breached the surface and locked Tory tight against me as the noise of the crowd dropped to excited chatter and slightly more nervous laughter. My jaw pulsed as I swam for the edge of the pool, trying not to think about what was going to happen if she was dead. If the Heirs had fucking killed her. If Darius had.

Darcy released a desperate sob as I lifted Tory up on the side of the pool and she caught hold of her arm as I heaved myself out of the water.

My heart ticked like a bomb waiting to explode, but I had to focus, I had to fucking heal her.

"Tory," Darcy sobbed and my mind was cast back to the past to the moment when I'd watched my own sister die, her name tearing from my lips with as much grief as Tory's name had left hers.

My pulse rioted in my ears as I knelt on Tory's other side and pressed a hand to her forehead, her skin was so cold and her heartbeat wasn't reaching my ears. I wasn't sure if that was because Darcy's was beating so loudly or because it wasn't there, but either way I had to act as fast as fucking possible to try and bring her back.

Darcy took a shuddering breath, her eyes locked on Tory's still features, her blue lips.

Come on. You're a fighter, Tory Vega. Wake up.

I sought out the water in her lungs with my Element, latching onto it as I continued to pour healing magic into her veins. And with one assured tug of magic, I forced her to cough.

Her eyes flew open and she heaved as the water came up, spluttering as I lurched aside to get out of the way. She was in her underwear, her body shivering violently, but as Darcy wrapped her in her arms, I knew she'd be just fine.

The Heirs on the other hand....

My gaze snapped to them as all four of them started backing towards the exit and anger crashed through me like thunder.

"IF A SINGLE PERSON IN THIS ROOM MOVES ANOTHER INCH, YOU WILL BE FACING IMMEDIATE EXPULSION!" I bellowed so loud that not a single student in this space could miss it.

The Heirs stopped walking, falling silent.

Darius scraped a hand down the back of his neck, his jaw flexing and his eyes a sea of untold darkness.

Seth was rubbing against all of them as if trying to soothe them and the sight of Darcy's hair peaking from his pocket sharpened my anger into a deadly blade.

"Face the fucking wall," I commanded, making half the students here flinch, but not the fucking Heirs. No. They were the kings of the star damned world, and they clearly thought they could trample over anyone they liked and get away with it.

I tried to catch Darius's gaze, but he wouldn't look at me. His jaw was set, his features a mask of cold detachment and I had the horrible feeling his father had really won this time. He'd finally succeeded in moulding his son into his own image, and *fuck*, it was terrifying to see the result of that staring back at me. The four of them turned as one, obeying me as they lined up facing the wall and I paced while I decided what to do with them.

My muscles flexed as the rest of the band of onlookers grouped together like that would save them from my wrath.

"Are you alright?" Darcy choked out behind me and that was enough to set my veins alight all over again. This wasn't Fae. This was a coward's move. And it made my skin prickle with revulsion.

"I'm sorry, Darcy," Tory said in a raspy tone and my chest tightened like it was in a vice.

"You have nothing to be sorry for," Darcy whispered.

I stared at the back of the Heirs' heads, knowing there wasn't anything I could truly do in punishment for this. The Celestial Councillors would back them to their graves, even if Tory had died. They would have found a way to make it look like an accident, protected their precious little prodigies. And in the face of that power, I felt useless. Because what was the point in rules and codes and morals if they meant jack shit to the people ruling the world? And it made me realise I was standing in front of four people who would one day hold the fate of Solaria in their hands, and this one act was enough to make me doubt my desire for that. I'd never cared much for the other Heirs, but I'd thought they were better than this. I'd thought their parents were. But now I was standing in the wake of their capabilities and found they had chosen to act with underhanded tactics and it left a bitter taste in my mouth. Darius most of all. Because I knew he wasn't this man. And yet it was terrifying how easily he could become a monster.

The crowd of the Heirs' followers started muttering between themselves and some made a bid for the exit which was a fool's attempt.

"No one is leaving this room until I hear what happened," I snarled at them and the straying students backed up into their ranks like frightened sheep before a wolf.

I prowled toward the Heirs, my gaze locked on Seth before I grasped his long hair in my fist and slammed his head against the wall with a loud crack. Fuck, that felt good.

"Do you have anything to say about what happened to the Vega Twins tonight?" I demanded as Seth let out a hiss of pain between his teeth and satisfaction rolled through me.

That's for Blue, you entitled prick.

"No, sir," Seth said in a low voice.

Of course he fucking didn't.

I stepped toward Max beside him, pressing his face into the wall until he cursed me under his breath. "How about you. Rigel?"

"No, sir," he muttered and I knew exactly how this was going to go.

I moved to Caleb, leaning in to speak in his ear. "Have you been fucking with your Source, Caleb? You know that goes against the Vampire code and I might just be in the mood to get your fangs ripped out for it." It was an idle threat. Melinda Altair would move the heavens to keep her son out of trouble. But several breaches of the Vampire Code could end in such a thing, and I hoped he at least believed I might have a way to pull it off.

Caleb's broad shoulders tensed in anger and I knew he was holding back his instinct to fight me. One more infraction tonight and his mommy might just have to come and question me about why her son's head had been torn off. "I'm aware of the code, sir. I didn't do anything to her."

"Bullshit," I snapped, rage simmering in my blood.

I moved to Darius next, resting a hand on his shoulder as the bond drew me to him, begging me to make amends with him. I didn't care for its wants, but I did care that I got a real answer from him. The others could get fucked, but Darius would at least be honest with me. He shrugged my hand off but I wrapped my arm tightly around him instead, forcing him to feel the bond between us and the tension in his body doubled as he battled against it.

"Are you going to lie to my face too, Darius?" I asked.

Darius shook me off. "Can't lie to your face when I'm facing a wall, can I sir?" His tone was mocking and designed to shut me out, making the Guardian bond flare sharply inside me, demanding I fix things between us. But fuck him. He was the one who did this. I wasn't going to pander to him even if the bond destroyed me from the inside out.

I whipped him around, releasing him in the same moment and he stared at me with an icy detachment worthy of Lionel Acrux. I sought out the boy I knew and loved in his eyes, finding it so fucking hard to find him there that for a second, I was afraid of how far gone he was.

"One last chance," I said in a low voice just for him. "Explain."

Darius's eyes slid from my face to Tory, his jaw ticking and a flicker of pain in his eyes, making relief fill me as I found a man there not a monster.

"We want them out," Darius said in a low tone. "We're just trying to get them out - you know the pressure we're under. Max found out their fears and well...we brought them to life." He shrugged like it was nothing, but it was everything.

I shook my head in disappointment. I knew he was being threatened, I knew the risk he was taking by defying Lionel, I knew he was putting Xavier in the firing line but this...this was the work of a heartless tyrant. Not a Fae who deserved the throne. "I thought *you* of all the Heirs were better than your parents."

Darius's face contorted and I turned my back on him, showing how little I thought of his actions tonight. I'd worked tirelessly to help him prepare to take Lionel's seat on the Council as soon as possible, to crush him beneath his heel. But had I been blind to what he was becoming right before my eyes? Was he Lionel's puppet now?

It wasn't like I couldn't understand his need to protect Xavier, but dealing with the Vegas in this way wasn't necessary. It could have been handled far better, with far more dignity. And now the whole world would see how he and the other Heirs dealt with a threat. And it wasn't with any fucking nobility, that was for sure.

"Everyone present in this room bar the Vega girls is now in detention with me for a full week. Capella, Altair, Rigel and Acrux, you will take two weeks and you're on a warning. One more stunt like this and I don't care if you're the sons of the stars themselves, you will be expelled from Zodiac." That was about as far as I could take this. The Councillors wouldn't stand for any further punishment than that. It was fucked up, but I was beginning to think the world was fucked up. And power was at the centre of it all, corrupting the good and intensifying the bad.

"You know what, Orion? Go fuck yourself," Darius snarled, barging past me and marching straight out of the door.

I bristled at the detached way he spoke to me, glaring after him and fighting the bond with all I had as it demanded I follow. But I wasn't going to go running to him like a whipped guard dog. He'd made his choice tonight. He'd had plenty of opportunity to discuss this with me, to come up with some alternative. But no, this was the Heirs' choice. And right now I was sickened by the thought of bowing to them all one day.

"Detention?" Tory hissed. "Is that it?"

My teeth ground in my mouth as I remained silent, not having an answer that would satisfy that question. Though it tugged on some long lost piece of me as I looked at her, unable to help see anyone but Clara staring back at me.

"How can you let them get away with this?" Darcy demanded and my eyes switched to her, that yank in my chest deepening. *Because I have no fucking choice, Blue.*

I moved to crouch down before them both and reached for Tory's hand, offering the only thing I could in that moment. "You need more healing."

"Not here," she muttered, her eyes whipping to the onlooking crowd. "I just want to go."

I ignored her, pressing my hand to her shoulder and working to heal her further as a turbulent storm built in my head. I poured all of my energy into doing this, feeling like I was right where I should be as I gave my power to this girl and wondering why it felt like all the stars in the sky were watching us. I had the niggling feeling that I'd let them down somehow, but that was foolish. I wasn't on their side in this war, but that didn't mean I'd wanted this.

I stole a look at Darcy as she clutched her sister's hand and wondered if they really would leave now. Go back to the Mortal Realm. Run for their fucking lives. They had barely had time to adjust to the ways of Solaria, of the Fae, so why would they stay?

The Fae in me wanted to see a fight in their eyes, but there wasn't any. They looked defeated. And something about that didn't sit right with me.

Not like this. You don't bow out like this.

Tory curled her legs up to her chest, her teeth chattering as the cold continued to grip her body. She reached out to Darcy's hair as if noticing it for the first time and Darcy's throat bobbed in a way that made me want to drive my fist into Seth Capella's chest and tear his heart clean out of it.

It'll grow back. She just needs a hair growth potion. Someone will surely tell her about it.

"Draw on your fire magic," I muttered to Tory. "It'll help warm you up."

Her gaze slid to me for a moment and she shifted away from me a little but I didn't let her go. I knew she saw an enemy in me and maybe that was an accurate assessment. But I was still her teacher, I still had a duty to her outside of this feud and I didn't care if she knew I didn't condone what had been done her.

"I'm just making sure all of the water is out of your lungs and healing any damage it did," I explained in a flat tone, my heart sinking further and further in my chest as I stared at this girl and the result of Darius's fury. *He chose to be like Lionel tonight. He chose this path and I fear he won't come back from it now he's on it.*

"What happened to you?" Tory asked her sister, her voice still raw.

Darcy's lips parted then closed again and her gaze moved to Seth, Caleb and Max beyond me and Tory followed her line of sight. She quickly looked away again and my magic started to empty out as I healed away the last of the damage to her lungs, dropping my hand from her shoulder.

Tory stared at me uncertainty then dragged her knees closer to her body, clearly aiming to cover up the lacy underwear she was in. The crowd were still watching and this other level of humiliation was not going to continue.

"Caleb, take off your shirt and give it to Miss Vega," I snapped.

Caleb hesitated a moment before he started to unhook his buttons.

"I don't want anything from him," Tory said, her voice low, full of horrors, but her decision was clear.

Caleb paused and I let out a low growl at the situation, shedding my own jacket and handing it to her. Darcy guided Tory's arms into the sleeves and tugged her wet hair out from under the collar. I was relieved when she got to her feet and buttoned it up, sure she'd be fine. Maybe not mentally, but physically at least. Her eyes remained on her feet and I had the quiet hope that this girl would not let the Heirs douse her fire. She was stronger than this. Stronger than she could even imagine. Both of them were.

"I'll walk you back to-" I started, but a high-pitched scream filled with terror punctuated the air from somewhere outside the building. *You've got to be fucking kidding me, stars?*

"What now?" I growled as I turned and started jogging towards the exit.

Darcy and Tory caught up to me as I made it to the double doors and my instincts told me not to leave them behind as I shoved the doors open and reined in the urge to use my Vampire speed.

I marched along the path, my fangs extending as a chill rolled down my spine and I quickened my pace towards The Orb.

A crowd were gathered there as the light of a fire reflected within the golden exterior of The Orb and alarm rushed through me. *What the fuck is going on?*

"Move aside!" I commanded and the crowd parted to let me through.

The twins stayed right behind me as I went and my fingers itched for the sword concealed as a switch blade in my pocket as I made it to the front of the crowds.

"Who is it?" a boy muttered to my right.

"Do you think it was a Nymph?" a girl whispered fearfully.

The heat of a fire poured over me and the vile smell of death hit my senses just before I saw the body.

"What the hell is that?" Darcy whispered in fear.

"I've only ever seen Dragon Fire burn like that," a boy's voice came from my left, but as I stared at the roaring blaze before me, I was sure this wasn't Dragon fire. It burned with the white hot heat of an inferno, unlike the red blaze of a Dragon's. It could have been Elemental magic, and yet…they would have had to be one helluva a powerful motherfucker to make a blaze like that.

I raised my arms, dousing the fire in a wave of water, fighting with the power of it as my magic ran even lower. And as the flames finally went out under the onslaught of my gifts, my eyes locked on a charred body on the ground, a lump lodging in my throat.

The twins suddenly stepped around me to get a better look and my mind went into a spiral as I tried to work out what the fuck had happened here. Who was that? And who had fucking killed them?

"Holy shit," Tory breathed and Darcy clapped a hand to her mouth.

My mind finally snapped back into gear and I straightened. "All students will return to their Houses now!" I barked. "Any witnesses who saw these flames being cast or anything suspicious leading up to this death will come forward immediately." I spotted Washer in the crowd and pointed at him, his face pale and his eyes wide as he stared at the body on the ground. "Get Elaine!" I commanded him and he nodded, blinking back into reality and darting away into the crowd.

The students surged around me in a sea of moving bodies as I threatened them with detention and worked to maintain order. I didn't know how this had happened or who that was lying on the ground but I needed to find Darius. Because this death had been caused by someone immensely powerful and I needed to be sure he was safe. A sickening thought crossed my mind that that charred body could be his before I felt the powerful thrumming of the Guardian bond between us and immediately knew it wasn't, the tension running from my shoulders. *He's fine. I just need to find him.*

I lost my temper with all the remaining students who were still trying to see the body or even snap a photo of it.

"IN FIVE SECONDS I'M DOUSING ANYONE STILL HERE WITH ENOUGH WATER TO WASH YOU RIGHT OUT OF THE GROUNDS!" I bellowed and the lingering students hurried to comply, a few releasing squeals of fright.

"What are you two still doing here?" I barked as I spotted the twins and they spun towards me in surprise.

"We were just..." Darcy began, trailing off as she failed to come up with an end to that sentence. Panic washed through my chest and my jaw ticked as I gazed at them. They needed to go, get back to their Houses. There was a fucking murderer on the loose.

"Get the hell out of here!" I snapped and Darcy flinched, the two of them stumbling away from me and running along the path with the other students.

My breaths came heavier as I dragged my fingers through my hair and walked up to the body, gazing down at the remains and trying to spot any sign of who it could be.

The stars seemed to shine brighter above me and I looked up at them for answers, feeling like I was being watched. A shadow crossed them above and my heart swooped a beat before Gabriel landed behind me, tugging my arm to make me face him.

"Gabriel," I gasped, gripping his shoulder hard. "What's going on?"

"You need to go," he said, panic flashing in his eyes.

"Go where?" I asked in confusion.

"To Darius. Now, Lance," he said frantically. "He's about to go home to kill his father. The Guardian bond will draw you to him the moment the fight begins. And you'll die in the crossfire before Darius is brought to his knees at Lionel's feet."

"What?" I breathed, my mind not catching up as the madness of this night continued.

"Hurry," he barked as the sound of approaching teachers came from further down the path. "You only have minutes to stop this fate. He's in his room, but not for long."

I nodded and I could practically feel the dice beginning to roll on this fate.

Fuck, I was dead if I didn't move.

I shot away from Gabriel with the full speed of my Order and a thousand whispers filled my ears that I couldn't understand, like the stars were talking among themselves in the heavens above. And I felt all too close to their embrace as my death hung in the balance.

Darius, what the hell are you doing?

DARIUS

CHAPTER THIRTY-ONE

Bile burned the back of my throat as I strode up the stairs inside Ignis House, taking them two at a time and storming into my room.

I threw the door open and it hit the wall so hard that it cracked right up the centre of the solid wood before I kicked it back into place again.

My heart was racing so rampantly that I could feel my pulse everywhere within my body, my muscles shook and quaked and the Dragon in me was clawing at the confines of my flesh, roaring to be set free.

A bellow of fury escaped me and I grabbed the edge of my treasure chest, heaving the whole thing over and sending gold coins and precious gems scattering across the carpet in every direction.

I curled my fist, striding towards the gilded mirror which hung from the wall with the full intention to slam my knuckles straight into it to destroy it, but I fell still as I caught sight of myself in the mirror.

There was a darkness in my eyes which made my heart skip a beat and in the dim light of my room with only the flicker of orange from the fire in my hearth, I could have sworn the man looking back at me was my father. Fist raised ready to strike, fury burning through him hotter than Dragon fire and not a single scrap of mercy clinging to his hulking frame.

I drew in a long breath, the shaking in my muscles increasing as I fought against the truth which was staring me in the face.

I really was becoming him. My nightmare. My demon. My monster.

What I'd done tonight...the fear I'd caused that girl for no other reason than wanting to force her to bow to my superior power, that was all him. It was precisely how he would have behaved and my stomach churned as I realised that he was going to be proud of me for this.

I doubled over, clutching the edges of the dressing table which stood before the mirror and staring down at the dark wood, focusing on the grains which ran through it so that I didn't have to see my father looking back at me from my own reflection.

This was what he wanted. And all I'd ever sworn I'd never become.

I'd foolishly thought I had more time. Time to learn the dark magic Lance had been teaching me, time to master my fire and water magic, time to grow fully into my strength so that I could challenge him, beat him, destroy him.

I'd fallen asleep countless times dreaming of that monster crushed beneath my heel but instead I'd turned all of that rage and hatred on a girl who hadn't done a damn thing to me aside from standing in my way.

I closed my eyes but the moment I did, all I could see was her, the way her body shook from the cold and how her green gaze had found me while she lay at the side of that pool, clutching her sister tightly as their love burned between them.

She'd seen me then. The very worst of me. She'd looked into my eyes and I knew that she had known what I was and somehow that had been the thing that broke my resolve, that shattered my will and tore through my determination to see them broken.

But it was far too late for that by then. We'd done it. I'd embodied the man I'd always sworn to fight against. I'd become him just like he'd always wanted and the way she looked at me was the exact same way Xavier always looked at him.

Like I was the worst creature she'd ever had the misfortune to meet. Like her hatred for me was a river of blood which pumped through her body with every beat of her heart and would never run dry.

I was filled with the most sickening certainty that I'd done something I would never come back from. I'd passed through a barrier I hadn't even known was in place before me. And now that I had, I knew it would only become easier and easier to pass through it again. Each action I took from here on out would be defined by the cruelty I'd displayed tonight and I could never undo it. Never take it back. Never fix what I'd broken inside the girl who had made me burn from the very first moment I'd met her.

I shouldn't have cared. I shouldn't have given a single fuck about some lost princess with emerald eyes and fire in her soul. But I did. I did and I'd still done what I'd done. I'd still acted on the orders of the man I hated and let my soul pay the price of my actions.

I tried to cling on to my reasons for doing it. To remind myself that Xavier was safe because of me. But he wasn't. Not really. Not while that monster still ruled over us and governed our fates.

I was sorely tempted to just shift and let the beast in me be free but I was fighting the urge, focusing instead on the man who had caused all of this and the only chance of freedom I could even imagine.

My eyes snapped open as I came to a decision. One I'd already made a long time ago with Lance by my side and the stars looking down on us. I was going to challenge Lionel Acrux and destroy his hold on me while destroying him in the process.

I would take his place on the Celestial Council and if I was lucky, he would die in the fight it would take for me to steal his position from him.

But this wasn't going to be a dream for the future anymore.

No.

This was going to happen now.

Because I couldn't go on like this, a slave to his wicked desires and a pawn in his depraved games. I'd broken something tonight in myself and in a girl who didn't deserve a moment of my torture upon her flesh.

There was no fixing that.

But there was something I could fix and that was Lionel Acrux.

My head snapped up and I glared at my reflection again, drinking in the similarities between the man in the mirror and the one who had haunted my nightmares for too fucking long. He'd wanted me to become a monster? Fine. I'd be his monster.

I yanked open the top drawer of the dressing table and reached for the bag of stardust I kept there, intending to head straight to his gold clad manor and end this now. I had the rage and desperation of a broken man coursing through me and I would use it as a weapon against the man who had given me life.

But as my fingers brushed the pouch of stardust, a wind whipped around me and someone snatched it away so fast that I barely even caught the movement. The lights flicked on and I looked up, finding the image of my father in my reflection gone as my own features were thrown into focus by the light and all of the differences between us were showcased.

Behind me, standing by the window with the pouch of stardust clasped in his fist was Lance, his furious gaze boring into my back as he bared his teeth at me to reveal his fangs.

"Give that back," I demanded, whirling on him and standing up to my full height.

"No," he replied just as fiercely, holding the pouch out towards the fire as I took a step towards him and making me pause.

"What the fuck are you doing? Give me the stardust, Lance. I need to go."

"You can't challenge your father like this," he warned and my frown deepened as I tried to figure out how the fuck he knew where I'd been heading and what I'd been planning to do. "Gabriel had a vision about the way it will turn out - you won't win."

"I will," I snarled, stalking forward again but Lance threw the bag of stardust into the flames before I could even cross half of the distance between us.

An explosion of dark flames tore from the fireplace as the precious substance was consumed by the fire and a roar escaped me as I barrelled forward, slamming into my so called best friend and grabbing the front of his shirt as I pinned him against the wall.

"I can't let you lose that fight, Darius!" he bellowed, trying to shove me back as he bared his fangs at me, but I refused to let go.

"Gabriel cannot predict my future!" I roared in reply. "I barely know that half plucked turkey - there's no way he could *see* the outcome of my actions. I would have-"

"He *saw* me die," Orion hissed, cutting me off and sending panic slicing through my veins.

"Liar," I breathed, but I could see the truth in his eyes.

"You're not ready," he said in a rough voice, reaching up to clasp my face between his hands as he forced me to look him in the eye. "Not yet."

"Then when?" I demanded but he could only shake his head and I whirled away from him in a fury, my whole body vibrating as I fought the shift which was trying to take me hostage.

"I don't know," Lance admitted, shattering my hope for salvation and making me fist my hands in my hair as I turned to look at him again.

"You saw what I did tonight," I rasped. "What I became because of him and you know it won't stop there. He knows now how far he can push me all the time he uses Xavier as a bargaining chip. And every time I do something like that it will chisel away at the man I want to be piece by fucking piece until

I become the very thing he wants me to be."

Lance said nothing, his hands falling to his sides as he just looked at me and I knew full well what he was seeing. I'd seen the horror in his eyes when he discovered what I'd done to Roxy. I'd seen the disappointment and worse than that, the fear. The fear that I really would fall into the fate my father wanted for me and we would never escape it.

"You will beat him," Lance said firmly like he could see me shattering and wanted to try and hold the broken pieces together. "Just not today."

"And what about the creature I'll become in the meantime?" I breathed, self loathing filling me as Roxy's scream resounded in my mind and the press of fate weighed so heavily on my shoulders that I could barely stay standing. "What happens when I can no longer stomach the sight of my own reflection? What happens when the man you want so desperately to destroy Lionel Acrux ends up being just as bad as him in the effort it takes to stand against him?"

"You find something to hold on to," Lance said. "Something to anchor you to who you are and you don't fucking let go of it."

I scoffed at that empty fucking suggestion and turned to look out of the window I'd left open where I could see the stars twinkling in the sky beyond.

"That's the problem though, isn't it? I have nothing but sand in my pockets and sin in my heart. I can't hold on to the good in me, Lance, because thanks to that man, there isn't any of it left anymore."

He opened his mouth to say something else to me, but the beast beneath my skin was done waiting for me to give it permission to break free.

I took a running jump out of the window and the Dragon tore from my flesh with a roar that shook the glass House behind me as my clothes were shredded clean off of my body.

I turned towards the stars and flew straight for them, diving into the clouds and letting a furious stream of fire tear from my lips and billow over my body.

I flew higher and higher, searching for a break in the clouds so that I could look upon the stars and curse them for my fate and how often it was twisted against me, but I couldn't find an end to the clouds no matter how high I flew.

And the only thing I found among the mass of grey I flew through was the look in Roxanya Vega's eyes as she saw the worst in me, and I felt my entire life shatter like breaking glass around me.

Perhaps I was always destined to be her monster, but I found I hated that fate with far more passion than I'd ever be able to hate her.

AUTHOR NOTE

Well, that was a rough ride!

It's been a little over two years since we wrote The Awakening and to be honest, when we set out on this journey to tell the boys' side of the story it seemed like a bit of fun. We had always known the things the guys had been up to in the background of the twins' stories in theory, but actually living it while writing it was something else entirely.

This actually turned out to be a pretty difficult story to bring to life in its own right. I think over the course of writing the subsequent books in this series and watching these guys grow and embrace so much more for themselves than they were capable of before the girls came into their lives, we forgot just how damaged they were to begin with. But experiencing the things they've suffered through and getting into their minds while they were still so lost and broken really brought it home to us.

These guys have been through a lot and they definitely made a ton of mistakes, but hopefully this chapter of their story helps you see them a little clearer, understand them a little better and maybe even find it in your heart to forgive them a bit more for their choices – though in all fairness they definitely were assholes so a bit of anger at them is still cool too.

This series is a really special one for the two of us and we just want to thank all of you for the unbelievable amount of love we receive for the world of Solaria and to express how endlessly grateful we are to each and every one of you for your continued love and support of this series. And don't worry, we have been spending the past few months working really hard on developing the final books in the series and we will be bringing Zodiac Academy Book 7: Heartless Sky and the final one book 8 to you very sooooon.

Once again, we love you, we are sorry for the pain we cause, and we promise to continue the torment until the very last page...and maybe even beyond...

Love, Susanne & Caroline x

ALSO BY
CAROLINE PECKHAM
&
SUSANNE VALENTI

Brutal Boys of Everlake Prep

(Complete Reverse Harem Bully Romance Contemporary Series)

Kings of Quarentine

Kings of Lockdown

Kings of Anarchy

Queen of Quarentine

Dead Men Walking

(Reverse Harem Dark Romance Contemporary Series)

The Death Club

Society of Psychos

**

The Harlequin Crew

(Reverse Harem Mafia Romance Contemporary Series)

Sinners Playground

Dead Man's Isle

Carnival Hill

Paradise Lagoon

Harlequinn Crew Novellas

Devil's Pass

**

Dark Empire

(Dark Mafia Contemporary Standalones)

Beautiful Carnage

Beautiful Savage

**

The Ruthless Boys of the Zodiac

(Reverse Harem Paranormal Romance Series - Set in the world of Solaria)

Dark Fae

Savage Fae

Vicious Fae

Broken Fae

Warrior Fae

Zodiac Academy

(M/F Bully Romance Series- Set in the world of Solaria, five years after Dark Fae)

The Awakening

Ruthless Fae

The Reckoning

Shadow Princess

Cursed Fates

Fated Thrones

Heartless Sky

The Awakening - As told by the Boys

Zodiac Academy Novellas

Origins of an Academy Bully

The Big A.S.S. Party

Darkmore Penitentiary

(Reverse Harem Paranormal Romance Series - Set in the world of Solaria,
ten years after Dark Fae)

Caged Wolf

Alpha Wolf

Feral Wolf

**

The Age of Vampires

(Complete M/F Paranormal Romance/Dystopian Series)

Eternal Reign

Eternal Shade

Eternal Curse

Eternal Vow

Eternal Night

Eternal Love

Forbidden Fairytales

(Complete M/F Fantasy Series)

Kingtom of Thieves

Kingdom of Wishes

Kingsom of Shadows

**

Cage of Lies

(M/F Dystopian Series)

Rebel Rising

**

Tainted Earth
(M/F Dystopian Series)
Afflicted

Altered

Adapted

Advanced

**

The Vampire Games
(Complete M/F Paranormal Romance Trilogy)
V Games

V Games: Fresh From The Grave

V Games: Dead Before Dawn

The Vampire Games: Season Two
(Complete M/F Paranormal Romance Trilogy)
Wolf Games

Wolf Games: Island of Shade

Wolf Games: Severed Fates

The Vampire Games: Season Three
Hunter Trials

The Vampire Games Novellas
A Game of Vampires

**

The Rise of Issac

(Complete YA Fantasy Series)

Creeping Shadow

Bleeding Snow

Turning Tide

Weeping Sky

Failing Light